LADY CLEMENTINE AND THE TEARS OF HATHOR

THE EXTRAORDINARY TREASURE HUNTERS
BOOK ONE

CAMILLA TAIPALVESI

WANDERLUST BOOKS

Copyright © 2024 by Camilla Taipalvesi

All rights reserved.

No part of this book may be reproduced in any form or by any electronic or mechanical means, including information storage and retrieval systems, without written permission from the author, except for the use of brief quotations in a book review.

This book is a work of fiction. Names, characters, places and incidents either are products of the authors imagination or are used fictitiously. Any resemblances to actual events, locales or persons, living or dead, is entirely coincidental.

Cover design by Miblart

https://miblart.com/

Editing services by Jo Gatford

https://www.jogatford.com/

 Created with Vellum

CONTENT WARNING

This treasure hunting adventure contains violent situations, some foul language, and themes of racism reflective of the late Victorian era, including the protagonist's experiences with her biracial identity.

For all the girls who kept their adventurous spirit alive, even through the toughest of times.
This one is for us.

PROLOGUE

"My lady. Your aunt, the Duchess of Clearwater, is here to see you." Mary's voice came from the sideline of the training area — also known as the garden of Willow House.

"What?" Clementine instinctively glanced over to her maid at this unexpected announcement. She immediately realised her mistake when a sharp kick made contact with her ribs, sending her staggering a few steps backwards. Her heavily boned, extra padded corset absorbed some of the impact, but she was still left gasping for air.

Before she could recover, her jiu-jitsu instructor, Mrs Edith, gave no mercy, closing in swiftly to sweep Clementine's feet out from under her with a quick, low turn. In a twirl of skirts, Clementine fell on her back, as she had been trained, with no more injury other than her pride.

"Oomph," she gasped for air yet again. She tapped the grass to signal her surrender and Mrs Edith came promptly to help her student up with a frown.

"My lady, you need to work on your focus. Your maid distracted you today and you cannot allow yourself to be distracted by anyone, not even Her Grace or Her Majesty herself. When you are defending yourself, you focus on the opponent and no one else. Your life and virtue might depend on it, and you can be sure that your opponent won't be fighting fair. When your focus wanders, they will use everything they can to get the upper hand, and I expect you to do as much, or worse, to survive — even if you have to fight as dirty as they do. Understood?"

Clementine nodded and felt her cheeks turn pink from embarrassment. She knew Mrs Edith and her services were rare and costly, and hated to waste the opportunity to do her best. Mrs Edith patted Clementine's shoulder in a comforting manner, which somehow made Clementine feel even more mortified by her mistake. She did not like making mistakes. Mary hurried to help her mistress to smooth her crumpled and grass-stained skirts.

"Don't be disheartened, my lady," Mrs Edith said, with a slightly gentler expression. She was usually about as gentle as a piece of granite during her training sessions. "You are young, Clementine, but you are also a fine student, thanks to your mother, who had the brains to start your physical training early. She gave you a good head start with her own knowledge of fighting, but that alone is not enough. You learn more, re-visit your learnings, and learn from your mistakes. Then you adapt to each situation as best you can. I know you are doing your best, most of the time."

"Thank you, Mrs Edith, for the lesson. It truly is always a pleasure. Will you stay with us for some tea?" Clementine asked, as her manners demanded, and also because she did really enjoy Mrs Edith's no-nonsense company.

"Ah, thank you for the kind suggestion, my lady, but it would be best for you to go and see Her Grace. I have another class to attend to, but I will see you again in a week." Mrs Edith bowed to Lady Clementine and she answered with a bow of her own, as if they were inside a dojo and not in the back garden of Willow House, the ancestral home of Lady Clementine and her father, Earl Jonathan Whitham.

"I'll see myself out, thank you, Mary," Mrs Edith nodded, before Mary had even uttered a word, and left with a determined stride. Clementine admired the confidence in Mrs Edith's walk. There was nothing of the small steps ladies were taught, lest their stride lead them ahead of the men who accompanied them.

"Mary, how do I look?" Clementine asked her maid. They had been together ever since they were mere children, and in truth had formed a friendship of trust. Mary hid a smile; her own impeccable maid uniform was in perfect shape, with not a hair out of place. "My lady looks as good as anyone could after being tossed about in the garden."

Clementine shushed Mary with a laugh. "But Mary, what would someone think if they heard you? Tossed about in the garden? Perhaps they would suspect a wicked gentleman was involved!"

Mary giggled and helped Clementine remove the padded corset, revealing a much simpler one underneath that held her plain, grey muslin dress in shape. It was loose enough to allow Clementine some movement when she exercised, and cut just above her ankles to allow her to avoid tripping — most of the time. Mary ran her deft fingers through Clementine's black hair and formed it into a simple chignon once more.

"I think you're ready to meet Her Grace in the morning room, unless you wish to change outfits," Mary remarked, and tucked the padded corset under her arm.

Clementine shook her head and flashed a smile. "This is my home — well, my father's — so I should hope I can dress how I like in front of my aunt when we are here. I doubt she'll chase me out of my own home. Thank you, Mary, and please return that corset to my closet for next time. See if it needs some mending; I think I heard something ripping. Though it might have been my ribs, on second thought."

Mary chuckled. "Anything else, my lady?"

"Oh, have the gardener see if there is anything to be done with those hydrangeas." Clementine gestured at a sad pile of pink petals near the pear tree. "I think we might have trampled them when I threw Mrs Edith over my shoulder."

"It was a great throw, Lady Clementine," Mary smiled. "I will inform the gardener." She curtsied and left the garden.

Clementine wiped her sweaty palms against her skirts and wondered what her aunt was doing here at this time of the morning without a warning. For a moment she feared that perhaps the Duke of Clearwater had taken a turn for the worse. He had been sick for so long that everyone seemed to be waiting for the news of his passing. It was cruel of the nobility, but what could one do? The society they lived in could be cold and uncaring.

Clementine did not much care for the society she was part of, unlike her aunt. Truthfully, she and her aunt were not particularly close. Things had become even more strained after the whole fiasco of Clementine's mother leaving England after her disgraceful divorce from Clementine's father. The duchess rarely came to Willow House; more often than not, Clementine was summoned to the duchess to hear what she had done wrong at one event or another.

She came into the yellow morning room and found her aunt, the Duchess of Clearwater, sipping tea with a frown. Clementine did not wonder why the frown was there — her aunt frowned upon many things — but it was the slight shake of the duchess' hands against the saucer that worried her.

"Your Grace," Clementine called, and curtsied in front of her aunt.

"Ah, there you are. And what in heaven are you wearing?"

Aunt Theodora stared at the dirt-stained, dowdy muslin dress, accessorised by Clementine's pink cheeks and fluffed chignon.

"Apologies, Aunt Theodora, I was in the middle of an exercise lesson when I was informed of you stopping by. How lovely to see you," Clementine said politely, and poured herself a cup of tea with two sugars and milk before helping herself to a scone with raspberry jam. A workout left even a lady peckish. She ate the delicate pastry in a few bites.

Aunt Theodora stared for a moment, biting her lip, and sighed. "You really are allowed too much freedom, but your father– Oh, never mind that for now." She put down her teacup for a refill, which Clementine provided.

The duchess looked at Clementine with a bleak expression and fell silent.

"Aunt Theodora, whatever is the matter? It is hardly typical for you to stay so quiet about how I dress, or how my hair should be styled to perfection in case a suitor should call on me," Clementine said, unable to help herself.

Even though the duchess did not approve of much Clementine did, and had not approved of her mother, Clementine still spoke as frankly as she could to her aunt, without angering her too much. Clementine had been taught to voice her opinion from a young age, so that's what she did, much to Aunt Theodora's annoyance. After Clementine's mother had left amidst a scandal almost ten years ago, Aunt Theodora had done what she could to be a mother figure to young Clementine, which had resulted in Aunt Theodora trying to mould Clementine into a delicate English rose, which she simply was not, and this caused frequent clashes between them. Clementine felt more like a pineapple plant: out of place. Luckily, Clementine's papa was the one to give Clementine the freedom to do as she wished with her education and activities. Even Aunt Theodora could not go completely against Papa's wishes, even though he was often away exploring ancient wonders.

"Clementine–" Aunt Theodora began.

"Or how I should eat only a little in a company that is far higher ranking than my own? Or how I should never be seen attending a meeting by the women's suffrage movement," Clementine added, licking excess jam off her fingers. The list of things her aunt didn't approve could go on for hours. "I do not see why I shouldn't. It's such an important–"

"Child, listen to me," Aunt Theodora said, sharply enough to make Clementine startle. Aunt Theodora put down her cup and rubbed her forehead, in clear distress. Clementine grew worried and moved to sit beside her. Aunt Theodora was acting strangely and it worried Clementine much more than their usual bickering.

"Aunt Theodora, what is it? Is it about His Grace? Has the illness…?" Clementine started, but her aunt shook her head, her grey curls bouncing under the fluffy feathers of her hat. She smoothed her dark blue brocade dress, which didn't have a single wrinkle on it, so Clementine knew her aunt was taking her time to arrange her thoughts. Whatever it was, it couldn't be good.

Clementine's heart started to beat faster and the sound of it filled her ears. Her hands formed fists on her lap and her aunt gently laid a hand over Clementine's, turning to face her niece. The gesture made Clementine even more afraid. Her aunt did not show affection to her, not like this. The duchess' way of showing affection was making sure Clementine was bent to the expectations of her aunt, and thus ready for society's expectations.

"My darling Clementine," she sighed, and her blue eyes met Clementine's dark brown ones, "I take it you have not yet seen today's morning paper?"

Clementine shook her head. "No, Aunt Theodora. As I said, I was in the middle of my morning exercise routine — to help keep my constitution healthy."

Aunt Theodora smiled and brushed a strand of dark hair off Clementine's forehead with a silk-gloved finger. Clementine shivered at these odd expressions of tenderness. It was as if a cloud of doom had descended on them, just waiting to explode with thunder.

"We have had many differences, you and I, but we are family, so know that I will do everything I can to help you," the duchess said.

"Aunt Theodora, you are scaring me. What is it? If it is not the duke then–" Clementine's voice suddenly quivered, coming out in a mere whisper, "Is it... Papa?" She could feel a knot in her stomach so tight it seemed to prevent her from taking a deep breath.

"Yes, Clementine. The papers– Well, the papers stated today that your father has gone missing. Most of his expedition crew returned from Egypt and reported him missing from one of the archeological sites. Apparently there was a bad sandstorm and he disappeared in the midst of it. The locals believe there is very little chance of survival." The duchess paused and waited for the information to get through to Clementine — no matter how much she resisted, it seeped through her skin and sank deep into her young heart, making it as heavy as when her mother had left.

"Then, he is dead? But I do not understand, I received a letter from him only a few days ago." Clementine's voice was hoarse, as if she had been screaming aloud rather than just in her head. She loved her father more than anyone in the world. He promised he would take her with him the next time he travelled, now that Clementine was of age and out in society. He promised he wouldn't leave her again!

The duchess squeezed Clementine's hand gently. "That letter was likely sent before the sandstorm. We do not yet know for sure if he died, but we must be prepared for anything. We know that Mr Hunt stayed to look for any confirmation, one way or another. He was your father's assistant, and this was very kind of him, even if he is known as a, well—"

"A rake, you mean? That's what the other young ladies have been calling him. Not that he ever bothered to meet me," Clementine blurted, even though she shouldn't have lashed out at that stranger of a man. She felt the need to throw her cup across the room, but instead rose from the plush velvet sofa to pace back and forth, kicking the edges of the thick carpet.

"Clementine, do not be so harsh to judge. A man can be many things at once, and not all the qualities might be true. He is looking for your papa, my dear brother, and refused to return with the expedition crew. We should be grateful to him. When he returns, we will know more." Aunt Theodora stopped abruptly, as if she had more to say.

"What? Is there something else? Tell me, please. I am not a child anymore, but a nineteen-year-old woman, out in society, and ready to hear whatever it might be," Clementine pleaded.

Something flashed in Aunt Theodora's eyes and she sighed.

"It is only that, well, if there is no evidence of your father still being alive, or of his death…" Aunt Theodora's voice was quiet. "Goodness, I do not say these things lightly. I want my brother back safe and sound. But in the circumstance that there is no clue as to what actually happened, it unfortunately means a long wait until he can officially be assumed dead."

"What? How long?" Clementine shook her head, "And what does that have to do with anything right now?"

"My dear," Aunt Theodora stood, and her dress' heavy trail of white lace rustled gently against the carpet, "It means that you will not have your fortune, inheritance, or even a dowry until seven years have passed since his disappearance. It is, in my opinion, a fate worse than if he had been found dead already."

Clementine gasped as her desperation took yet another form. "No, no, that cannot be. Papa promised he would take me with him; that I could be an explorer like him. That I needn't marry someone I didn't love just because a woman of my age is supposed to. He promised!" Clementine stifled a loud sniff and covered her mouth.

"I know what modern ideas your father had, and it was his right to do so as your father and legal guardian, even though I disagree utterly with his plans for you," Aunt Theodora said in a firm tone. "We must be ready for all possible outcomes, Clementine. With that, I will help you. I will sponsor your season, help you find a suitable husband, and the duke and I will give you a plentiful dowry to seal the marriage. I needn't say that with your unfortunate family background it will be hard to arrange a well-made marriage above your status without your father here to vouch for you with his fortune, but at least you have me and His Grace on your side."

Clementine's misty eyes flashed with anger. "My 'unfortunate background'? You mean my mother, who proved people right in their prejudice that all Oriental women are snakes and not to be trusted? Is that how I am seen as well? A mixed-race girl with no chance of ever being as trustworthy as a full-bred English woman?" Clementine raised her chin in defiance, though her aunt was much taller than she.

The duchess sighed again and shook her head. "Child, I do not see you like that. But other families with daughters to marry off will use your family history against you to benefit their own marriage arrangements. That is the unfortunate truth, and while I wish it were not so, I will face reality and hope you will steel yourself to face it as well. I will help you get a decent marriage. No niece of mine will end up a spinster, nor a laughing stock of society. Your future is at stake here, and I will not tolerate any nonsense talk of modern women and their rights."

A fat tear rolled down Clementine's cheek, but the duchess continued without mercy. "I know this hurts, child. But take hope in the fact you have people around you who care, and who will make sure you will be well taken care of. In fact, I need to have an audience with Her Majesty. She is most worried for your papa and wishes to discuss your situation with me, in light of such stressful times."

Clementine must have looked surprised, and the duchess smiled wryly. "You might not appreciate what I do for you, but you are blessed to have connections that will help you balance your past. That is more than what many other girls have, so try to be grateful, Clementine. The late Prince Albert was an admirer and supporter of your papa's work abroad, and Her Majesty honours her husband's memory by taking an interest of his under her wing. I believe she feels he is still with her in these moments," the duchess smiled sadly.

"I see, how very kind of Her Majesty to take note of someone like me. I hope you will speak well of me, Aunt Theodora, and of my father's wishes for me," Clementine said tonelessly, and curtsied.

The duchess raised an eyebrow. "I will tell Her Majesty how eager you are to get a reliable husband to provide for your safety in your father's absence. I will send word should I hear anything from Mr Hunt, in case he brings news once he returns, and– Well, it will be good to hear it from him directly." There was a slight off note in the duchess' voice, and she turned to ring for Mary to come and take care of her mistress in this moment of distress.

"Oh, and Clementine?" The duchess turned to Clementine, who met her gaze with eyes that were not filled with tears but anger. "You will not be wearing any mourning gowns. We will proceed with your social activities as planned. You will appear as if you are full of hope and not frighten possible suitors with unnecessary crying or brooding. Is that understood?"

Clementine raised her chin and swallowed back furious

tears. "Why should I mourn? As far as I am concerned, my papa is alive, and I intend to find out what has happened to him."

"You will focus on your studies, and most of all you will focus on meeting as many young men as I can find."

With that, the duchess left, and Clementine sat down on the sofa with shaking hands. When Mary came in, Clementine simply said, "Mary, bring the brandy. I need to write some letters."

TWO MONTHS LATER

Clementine had been unsure whether she could ever feel the same pain as when her parents divorced and her mother had left. Clementine had only been eleven years old, and some of the pain had ceased to feel like an open wound, but whenever she searched her heart, the absence of her mother would always be there. A dull pain and sadness that reminded her of a broken family and a tainted past, despite her love for her mother. And now, the fresh pain of not knowing if her father was alive or not was eating away at her very being.

The first weeks had been the worst, and she had asked the butler daily if there had been letters, telegrams, or even rumors of any kind. She studied desperately each edition of the daily papers for any news that might bring her some relief, but so far there had been nothing.

The letters she had sent to officials in Egypt and other known excavators did not bring any new information. Mr Hunt had not replied to any of her letters either, though some of the others insinuated that he had left Egypt already, abandoning the search for her papa.

The days were easy enough to occupy, with the many social

callers who had come to wish her well, or out of curiosity, but the nights had been awful. Clementine either could not sleep or woke up in cold sweat from some nightly terror that evaporated from her memory as soon as she opened her eyes, leaving only the trembling and racing heartbeat as a clue of her nightmares.

On the nights she couldn't get back to sleep, she instead practised the movements her mother had taught her. Martial arts practice was not only about fighting, but of control and serenity too. The familiar routines of a movement series helped Clementine calm herself down, which then allowed some sleep afterwards.

Today, there would be a mandatory dinner at her aunt Theodora's house, the magnificent Clearwater Abbey, with someone Aunt Theodora wished Clementine to meet. No doubt it was a possible suitor whom her aunt had deemed suitable enough for Clementine. Aunt Theodora had wasted no time getting on with having her niece securely engaged and married off. As the weeks and months went by, Clementine felt she had seen all the possible men available, ranging from younger boys to men as old as her father. Clementine had refused all of them. She still lived in her father's house, which was equipped with a full staff of servants. Aunt Theodora had asked if Clementine wanted to move to Clearwater, but Clementine would not part with the freedom of how she chose to spend her days. She had told her aunt that she and the housekeeper had run the house successfully even before the terrible news, since Papa spent a great deal of time abroad.

Aunt Theodora couldn't force Clementine to move, but that wasn't to say she didn't have a close eye on her niece's daily routine. Without a man in the house, or someone old enough to chaperone, all the callings from suitors were arranged at Clearwater Abbey.

Clementine knew she had to get herself ready soon, but took

a moment to gaze outside. It was a peaceful afternoon and Clementine cherished the feeling, short as it might be.

Willow House, was in some ways a modest country home. With only fourteen rooms for guests and five acres of land, it was certainly smaller than many other neighboring estates. But it had always been plenty for Clementine.

The silver willow trees moved softly in the wind. Clementine, secretly, had always thought their long, drooping branches to be rather romantic, as they could very well hide lovers kissing in the garden. Not that she would ever let anyone know those thoughts. It was purely due to the Jane Austen novels Clementine enjoyed reading — mostly for their sarcastic wit about the silly society they all lived in, but also for the romance. As much as Clementine wished she had been born a boy — so many things would have been so much easier — she did sometimes have to admit liking certain aspects associated with the female sex. Reading romance novels was definitely one of them, and they were no less entertaining than the history books her father brought home from his travels. Books were one of her many joys, and she feared for the day when some husband might want to limit her reading. Clementine understood that her father was quite forward-thinking in allowing his daughter almost the same education (at home, anyway) as a son would have received. Perhaps Papa had not known what to do with the more feminine parts of her education after her mother Lan had so abruptly left their lives.

Clementine's thoughts lingered on her parents, not knowing how to stop, other than to distract herself with something. She sighed, pushed herself up from her comfortable seat and rang for the tea service to be taken away.

Mary soon popped in to ask if Clementine would like anything else, or if they might choose her dinner dress and jewels for the evening.

"Oh, right," Clementine said, "I think I am missing a pair of gloves for dinnerwear. The last ones were horribly stained when Mr White poured red wine on them — after pouring too much wine inside himself during the evening."

Mary snickered and smoothed her black maid uniform. "Yes, well, there is only so much that can be done for stains on white silk, my lady. I did try my best, but the fabric ended up getting thinner, not cleaner, unfortunately."

Clementine waved away Mary's apology. "That is quite alright, I know you did all you could. Heaven knows I would not know how to even begin cleaning a stain like that," she smiled, embarrassed. Running a house with servants was something ladies of society were taught — but the practical side of it? Not at all.

"Perhaps your tutor might help you learn the secrets of laundry?" Mary suggested.

Clementine rolled her eyes. "If she thought that might help me win a suitor over one of the competing ladies of the season, she might well teach me how to wash, iron and mend. To be honest, I wouldn't mind learning, but it is not for a proper lady, apparently."

"Shall we prepare for the evening, then?" Mary asked.

"Yes, I suppose it is mandatory. I will go slightly earlier anyway. I want to greet His Grace before the formalities. It seems he is still too unwell to leave his chambers, and hopefully I can take this opportunity to wish him well."

"Yes, my lady. I think he will appreciate it," Mary nodded. "Perhaps some fresh flowers from your garden as well? The sweet scent of summer flowers would surely cheer anyone in their sickbed."

Clementine looked outside once more, assessing the selection in the garden. "That is a lovely thought, thank you, Mary. Perhaps a bouquet of lilacs and something else. Let the gardener decide what looks good enough to be taken. But definitely lilacs. They are my favourites, after all," Clementine smiled. She loved the scent of lilacs in those light evenings when all of summer still lay ahead.

"I took the liberty of preparing your bath with lilac soap and oil, I hope you don't mind, my lady," Mary said as they left the drawing room, and rang for a footman to discuss the matter of the flowers with the gardener.

"I very much appreciate it, Mary," Clementine said. "You know exactly what I want."

* * *

THE BATH WAS SIMPLY DIVINE, and Clementine took her time to soak in the scented water. In these brief moments of relaxation, Clementine could almost forget that her future was looking so uncertain. Would she be allowed to stay here until her father returned? What would happen if it turned out that he would not return? And what of the seven-year wait before her father could officially be pronounced dead? Clementine could not stand the thought of seven years of not knowing, not being able to move on, and not being able to say goodbye to her father. It seemed like torture to even think about it. Surely there must be some other way. But try as she might, Clementine could not see any solution to improve her situation that did not include her being married off to some bachelor of the season. It would not do, not at all.

If Clementine had her way, she would be off with her father to explore the world, seeking more knowledge of the past to bring glory to their queen. Wouldn't that be a useful life — a remarkable one, even — instead of being stuck in a house full of social duties and babies? If only her father would come back and make things right. If only Clementine could help with the efforts of finding him.

She sighed and called for Mary to help her up from the tub.

"I was just about to warn that you would soon look like a

prune if you stayed much longer," Mary noted as she helped Clementine to step out.

"Perhaps having prune-like skin will scare off the eligible bachelors. I'm sure my aunt has me seated next to one," Clementine scoffed.

Her skin glowed from the bath, and there was unfortunately nothing prune-like about it. She had been blessed with her mother's deep dark hair, and that, combined with her father's fair skin, made the contrast quite stunning, even if Clementine said so herself. Not that her looks were appreciated by the cream of society; she was deemed too dark, too different, or too exotic to meet English beauty standards.

She did her best not to care and was joyful of her looks. Modesty was a virtue, but one had to be aware of one's qualities. Her mother's Indochinese background was most evident in Clementine's hair, the shape of her face, and her brown eyes. She also had a streak of light brown hair for some reason, and as a child she often remarked how that was the only thing of her father in her. It was a curiosity, but not a bad one. To Clementine, she contained the best qualities of both her parents. To society, she was deemed too Oriental, even though she was born here in England. It was a constant battle to prove that she belonged, and at times she was not sure why she needed to belong in company that insisted on pointing out how her heritage forever made her an outsider.

Clementine wrapped herself in a robe and sat in front of her dressing table while Mary lightly curled her hair with a hot iron and lifted the cloud of dark curls into a half-updo with the help of pearl-ornamented combs.

"So, which dress would you like to wear, my lady? " Mary gestured to Clementine's bed, where she had laid out the options.

Clementine considered the dresses in front of her. She felt like lilacs today. *Why not?* It was her favourite dress and she often wished to wear it, even though a lady must not be seen wearing the same dress too often. Clementine doubted her aunt would turn her away from her door just because she was wearing the same dress she had worn to another dinner party a few weeks ago.

"I am guessing it's the lilac one that calls to you, my lady?" Mary tucked away a stray of hair that had come out of her neat braid.

"Yes, I do love that one. And since I do not yet mourn — I refuse to mourn, in fact, before there is evidence that Father is… Well, until that day, I will wear whatever I bloody well want."

Mary pretended to gasp at her mistress' words but smiled as she took away the other two dresses. Clementine had been known to sometimes speak in an unladylike way, for which her aunt often chastised her. But in her own home she reserved the right to say anything she wanted, and if there was an issue with that, then Papa had better get home soon to reprimand her.

Mary came back with the amethyst jewellery to match the dress. "Would you like the shorter gloves then, to replace the ruined ones?" Mary asked. Clementine shook her head. "Oh no, let's not bother with that. If a suitor frowns at me for not wearing proper gloves for a dinner party, that's all the better for me." Let them frown and withhold any proposals that might be lingering on their lips.

"Right, I think I should get going. Will you tell them to get the carriage ready?"

Mary curtsied and left to give the orders. After a moment of consideration, Clementine took her favourite fan with her. It was her favourite not only because of its large size and beautiful cream silk, painted with orchids and swallows, but also because it was a weapon, and it had been her mother's.

Anyone simply looking at the fan would see its beautiful pattern and delicate lace trimming, but if someone tried to hold it, they would notice its unusual weight. It was made of metal, and her mother had used it to teach Clementine tessenjutsu, the art of fighting with a war fan. If wielded correctly, the fan could be used to ward off unwanted attention. It was not only heavy enough to land a blow that could stun an opponent, but with a flick of the wrist, the ends of the slats would reveal sharp, needle-like spikes. Clementine loved it, and saw its potential for all ladies who carried a fan, unaware that they could defend themselves with such a casual accessory. Clementine had often discussed adding tessenjutsu to Mrs Edith's selection of martial arts, but Mrs Edith preferred using only one's own hands, feet and body. Still, Clementine often carried her fan with her, just in case there was a chance to use it. Not that she wished for it, but it would be a shame to let such a beauty be used only for fanning.

And there was something comforting, even soothing, about carrying her mother's battle fan with her. It made Clementine feel as if her mother was still somehow involved in her life.

* * *

As CLEMENTINE CAME DOWN the main stairs to the front door, she saw Mary waiting with a beautiful bouquet of lilacs. The light purple flowers gave off a gentle scent and the contrast with the green leaves was simple but gorgeous.

"Oh, thank the gardener for me, will you Mary? The bouquet will surely give joy to His Grace."

Mary curtsied and Clementine bid her farewell, climbing into her carriage with the flowers. She settled herself in the cushions as the carriage jerked forward towards the main road that would take her to Clearwater Abbey.

THE APPLE ORCHID

The Duke and Duchess of Clearwater had, of course, ample amounts of land, as well as villages and tenants to look after, and were known for their fair treatment of the people who lived on their estate. Clementine watched as the forests and fields turned into orchards and gardens, and soon the magnificent Clearwater Abbey came into view, with all the dignity of a grand country house that had stood there for centuries. Round towers broke the heavy silhouette of grey stone and vines grew on the sides of the house.

* * *

The carriage pulled up in front of the house and a footman opened the carriage door, offering his hand to Clementine — not that she needed it, but it would've been rude to refuse and embarrass the poor man. So she took his hand, and if he was surprised by her ungloved fingers he did not say so.

Clementine hopped off the carriage, much like she had always done. Not as a lady should, but in a way that felt natural to her, even in her evening dress with its fringed skirts and bustle. The fabric gathered into beautiful drapes and frills on her backside, cascading into a trail that slithered behind her on the sandy path. Another footman approached her from the house, offering a hand to her in assistance for her walk to the main doors, as if she were unable to manage by herself. Perhaps next she would be carried everywhere, if young ladies were deemed too delicate to even touch the ground with their feet. Suddenly the thought of going inside the house, with all its rules and expectations, felt even more exhausting, and Clementine's hand stopped in mid-air.

"My lady?" The footman's extended hand was left hovering, as if he was unsure whether he should still be offering his assistance.

"I, um... I wish to walk in the gardens for a moment. Please let Her Grace know I will soon come and pay my respects to His Grace as well. Perhaps I shall find some more flowers to add to my bouquet," Clementine gestured at the lilacs in her arms.

"As you wish, my lady." The footman placed his hand behind his back, likely with some relief. "May I suggest the gardens by the east side of the building? The apple orchard is in full bloom."

Clementine thanked him before marching along the side path towards the eastern gardens of the estate. In the setting sun, the shadows grew long, and the golden hue was getting dimmer. She was rather glad she had decided to come earlier to give her a chance to gather her thoughts before going in for 'the show', as she liked to call these events. Soon, the real social season would start, and her days would be filled with balls, dinners, promenades and other social gatherings with various suitors and her fellow ladies, who were also thrust into the same situation of trying to find a good match as soon as possible.

* * *

CLEMENTINE STOPPED beside the apple trees and inhaled deeply. It was intoxicating. The last bumble bees were still buzzing around before retiring at sunset. The flowers were delightful, and Clementine definitely wanted some in her bouquet.

She peered at the old trees, but there were no flowers on the lower branches. She needed a ladder or a stool to be able to reach the flowering branches.

Looking around her, she was relieved to note that no one seemed to be walking around the gardens at this hour, so close to the dinner party. No one to tell her 'no', in other words. She went deeper into the apple orchard and felt like Alice in Wonderland, following an uncharted path. There must have been at least a hundred trees spread widely in front of her, and soon the house was but a distant shape behind. The gnarly trees were busy with fresh green leaves and the loveliest white and pink blossoms. Against the dark bark, it was a contrast that Clementine thought irresistible. For a moment she simply stood there, looking up at the ceiling of branches, flowers, and the sky with its sunset hues. She wished she had a blanket to lay on and simply wait until her father returned. With a sigh, she gathered her skirts and looked around for any gardening tools that might be helpful to hoist her high enough to reach the flowers.

"Aha," she exclaimed as her eyes fell on a wooden crate nearby. It was likely used for gathering garden waste, or perhaps even apples. And now it would boost Clementine to those flowers.

She fetched the box, careful not to let it touch her dress and stain it. She also avoided the muddy puddles around the trees from yesterday's rain. The trouble was that the box was much too low on its wider side, so Clementine carefully propped it on its narrow side and, gripping the bark very carefully, stepped up onto the box. The crate creaked underneath her weight, and she hoped it would not give away with a crash. Going to dinner with a ripped dress would be annoying, but Clementine was not one to give up. *Uncle will love the scent of these blossoms. And if I break my arm falling, perhaps I will be relieved of having to attend the dinner.* Clementine dismissed the thought as unlikely. A little broken bone wouldn't stop her aunt from making sure Clementine met every available suitor there was.

She straightened herself slowly, leaning against the tree. Now she was glad she was not wearing gloves, as she would have ruined the silky fabric against the bark. *Blast it.* The nearest flowers at the end of the branch were still too far for her to reach. Her fingertips could not even graze them. She loosened her grip on the tree trunk and reached out once more, stretching to her full length, and heard an ominous crack.

Clementine's reflexes were good from all her training, so she reacted before falling through the crate and onto the muddy ground. But her instinctive reaction was to leap for the branch in front of her and not to the safety of the ground. She hung from the branch and wondered if it was sturdy enough to hold her if she shuffled a little to the right, towards the flowers. She might as well get what she came for, now she was already here.

"I hesitate to ask if you are in need of assistance, or if I should fetch one of the footmen to apprehend a thief," came an amused voice behind her. The voice was not familiar to her, but it clearly belonged to a man who was quite obviously laughing at her expense.

She swore under her breath.

"What was that? Cursing, from a lady? The audacity," he chuckled.

Clementine already hated the smug voice behind her. "Thank you for your concern, sir. But as you can see, I am in the middle of something and quite capable of doing it myself, thank you."

"Oh, I can see that you are in the middle of it. It might be good for you to know that I would see a great deal more if I took a step closer, since your skirt is quite literally up in the air," he said casually, as if he were speaking of the weather.

Clementine turned her head with a startle. The man was not peering underneath her skirts but standing at a respectable distance with laughter in his eyes and a vexing eyebrow cocked as he took in the sight of her hanging there, the branch underneath her armpits.

"You have nothing to worry about from me. I am a gentleman after all, and prefer my ladies on the ground, not above it. Easier to kiss," he said in a dry, amused voice.

Clementine felt herself blushing at his words. *How dare he just stand there and... laugh?* "Yes, well, you will find no one to kiss here, and nothing to see, so you might as well go on your merry way. I only wish to pick a few apple blossoms for my bouquet, that is all, and I do not need your help with this particular task. I am quite capable."

"Oh, but I believe there is plenty to see here," the strange man said, and Clementine could hear the grin in his voice. "I wish to see how you will descend from your current position. Despite the length of your dress, I would guess you are lacking in height, hence needing the box to hoist yourself up. This means you will need to find some way back to the ground and avoid the muddy patch right underneath you, unless you wish for your lovely lavender dress to suffer the most horrible stains. I am most curious about your solution, and I am happy to observe how this scene will end. Unless you would prefer my assistance?"

Clementine could see from the corner of her eye that the man had taken a step closer. He wore eveningwear himself, and Clementine guessed he was one of the dinner party guests — a possible suitor, perhaps. His dark suit was matched with a cane and a top hat, which only made his already tall figure even taller. He could possibly even reach to pluck Clementine from her spot without issue. She did not want him to do that. In no situation would she ask him to save her; it would be too humiliating to sit beside him at the dinner table afterwards.

With a groan, she readjusted her grip, lowering herself to hang by her hands from the thin branch . She could not hold on for much longer before she ran out of strength. But she *could* test if her muscles still remembered how to do a simple swing on a gymnastic bar. She could not somersault in this dress, but she could at least swing herself down to avoid the muddy patch and the stranger's help.

"I cannot stop you if you wish to stay," she said through gritted teeth. "Perhaps as a gentleman you could pick me a few blossoms with your prominent height, since I am so lacking in mine — as you so kindly pointed out. Meanwhile, I shall make a smooth landing from here, do not concern yourself with that."

She saw the man nod with a touch of his top hat, and to her great annoyance he gently snapped off a few smaller branches right next to her; the ones containing the blossoms that she could not for the life of her reach.

"Done, as requested by my lady. Now let us see to your safe landing," he said, but did not step away. Instead, he placed his cane and the flowers on the ground and appeared to ready himself to catch her.

"Ugh. " Clementine rolled her eyes. "Just stand back, good sir. I do not wish to accidentally kick you in the head." Under her breath, she muttered something about non-accidental kicks.

She started to swing, slowly at first, because of her dress. Despite it being made of light silk, there was plenty of it, and gathering speed was a struggle. But, with effort, she made those skirts, trail, bustle, chemise and all move, swinging in a wide arc. Her hands burned against the tree bark, but she couldn't resist a squeal of delight at the momentum.

"My lady, wait–" a concerned voice came from behind her,

but she did not listen. Instead, she picked up a little more speed and finally let go. She heard him gasp as she flew forwards. The lavender fabric fluttered around her and her carefully arranged hair fell free. Clementine laughed loudly, landing softly on the ground in a half crouch, far from the mud.

She heard applause as she slowly rose up and lightly dusted bits of bark and leaves off her dress. It seemed that her dress had suffered very little injury, thank heavens, despite the silk chafing against the branch for a little while — she wouldn't hear the end of it otherwise.

Clementine swung back the dark curtain of curls that had come undone during her leap and turned to face her mocker.

"Well done, my lady. I would not have guessed you to possess the skills of a flying squirrel. Of all the skills you ladies strive to show us, I do not believe I have seen such a situation before. Most refreshing, I have to say."

The man came closer and she strained her neck to look up at him. His tall, lean body was accompanied by broad shoulders and dark sand-coloured hair, which was revealed as he took off his hat to give her a small bow. His eyes had a greenish shade and were most vexingly still full of amusement. Clementine was sure he was used to having everything and everyone with that boyish grin and flash of fine teeth. She was not immune to handsome men, oh no, but she found them annoying, as they were usually eager to use their looks and position to their advantage.

"Thank you, sir," Clementine nodded, without curtsying. They had not been introduced, so she did not know or care if he was a lord who ranked higher than her and demanded a curtsy. "Although it was not done for your entertainment, I can assure you. I merely did not want to land in the mud and ruin my dress for the rest of the evening. I do not, as you said, show my skills to random men who happen to come by when I am simply trying to pick some flowers."

"Ah, indeed. It would have been difficult to stage such a performance for seduction, hoping someone might walk by and be interested in squirrel theatre."

"Good sir, you seem to be hardly listening to what I have to say," Clementine said through gritted teeth, trying to stay polite and not snap at this idiot stranger. She resisted setting her fists on her hips and instead buried them within her skirts. "I have just explained to you that I simply desired to pick some apple blossoms for a bouquet to give to His Grace. There is no seduction on offer here or elsewhere in my company."

"A sight of your ankles, and more, as you hung on that branch, could have been seductive enough for lesser men. I, however, am a gentleman and only do to the lady as she asks." His voice had a velvet note to it suddenly, as if it had gone lower, huskier.

Clementine blinked.

"Then this lady asks for her apple blossoms, which you were *so* kind to pick for me. Please hand them over and let us part ways."

The man chuckled. "You are quite right, as I think you prefer to be. Here are the flowers. May they bring you joy." He handed her the apple blossoms.

"Thank you and good day," she said, hoping they would not sit near each other at dinner. She nodded, and with a swish of dark hair and light silk, she turned to stomp off.

"Wait," came the man's voice.

Clementine stopped, annoyed with herself — but mostly at the man.

"Yes, what is it?" she said, with strained politeness , and started to turn.

"Don't. Move," he said sharply, and she froze at the command in his voice.

Another annoying reaction, she fumed.

The man quickly took a step to stand very close behind her

and she felt something on her upper back — his fingers, tugging at her corset strings!

"You go too far," she cried, and with a quick twist she spun herself around, making him let go of her, and landed a sharp snap on his wrist with her heavy fan. Not hard enough to break bone, but enough to make it clear that she was not someone he could easily take advantage of in a shadowy garden.

"Ouch!" The man shook his wrist with a surprised look that soon turned back into that permanent amusement he wore whenever he looked at her.

She was flushed, and her breath came heavily in her tight corset, but she did not turn her gaze away from him. He would not surprise her again. His eyes briefly wandered slowly to her rapidly rising chest, very much visible with the effect of the corset, and she felt her cheeks burn. Still, she refused to move, holding her fan out in front of her, much like a sword.

"Do not think I am some helpless damsel, ready to fall for your charming smile," she hissed.

"Oh, is my smile charming to you?" He flashed said smile and she wanted to smash his face with her fan. She frowned and he laughed. "Do not worry, my lady. But do calm yourself before your loveliness bursts from that corset. I am not interested in taking your virtue."

He raised his hand in a peaceful gesture before she hurled more hisses at him. And in his hand, Clementine saw the pearl-ornamented comb that had come loose from her updo and caused her hair to cascade down.

"I only wanted to save this delicate comb from being stuck in your corset strings. It looked fragile enough to snap under such strain, which is why I asked you not to move." He cocked his head. "Luckily, my skilled hands were quick enough to snatch it before you turned on me. A battle fan, is it?"

Clementine stared at him. Not once had anyone recognised

her fan for what it was. Not that she had reason to use it on anyone yet.

"Yes, it is, in fact," she said, forgetting to be cross at him, "I am surprised you have heard of tessenjutsu. It is not a martial art commonly known here."

"I know some things, believe it or not," he said . He tucked his cane under his arm and Clementine's comb in his evening coat's pocket. "May I?" he gestured at the fan.

Clementine was so astonished that she took the silk loop off her wrist and gave the folded fan to him.

He carefully turned it around in his hands and opened it gently. "Beautiful design," he noted. "Silk, with swallows and orchids. A romantic colour, and yet…" he mused and weighed the fan on his palm. "Reinforced iron, I believe, yes?"

Clementine nodded, her eyes wide with sudden curiosity. "Yes, it is of the finest quality, or so I was told."

The man nodded and a smile played at the corner of his mouth. "I wonder now," he turned the fan slightly in his hand and gave it a sharp flick, exposing the claws with a snap. The beautiful fan looked like it had overgrown spikes on the tops of the iron ribs and ornate lace.

"Aha, my memory was correct," he said with the happiness of someone who is used to being right and has no problem being smug about it. "And how do you retract the claws?"

Clementine found herself blinking and said, "You simply flick again, but this time towards yourself."

The man did as she advised, and the fan turned into an ordinary-looking fan once more. How strange that he would know how her fan worked with such ease!

"Most fascinating," he said, giving her back the fan with a bow. "Thank you for letting me hold such a magnificent object. I would be most interested to hear more about its origin at Her Grace's dinner."

Clementine looped her wrist through the fan's silk ribbon

and realised she would be stuck with this man all evening. And the risk of him telling everyone else, most importantly her aunt, about the happenings in the apple orchard was high. She cursed in her head.

"Indeed, sir, I did not realise you would also be attending Her Grace's dinner."

"Why else would I be wandering in their garden at this hour?" He looked at Clementine as if she were a silly woman, asking such nonsense questions.

Clementine could feel her own brow twitch as she fought not to scowl. She wanted to request he to stay quiet about what had happened here, but hesitated to ask this stranger anything, since she had the feeling he would definitely use it to mock her more. The man could hardly be trusted.

"How would I know? Perhaps you were here to meet someone for a forbidden tryst." She couldn't help herself from throwing a jab at him.

The man did not flinch but glanced around as if looking for someone. "As it happens, you are the only one I met. Perchance you were here with the very same thoughts?" His crooked smile revealed a row of white teeth.

A wolf's grin, Clementine thought. Now she did not even hide her scowl.

"I most certainly am not here for that. Good day." She turned to march back to the house, not caring that it was no use bidding good day to him, since they would inevitably meet again at the dinner.

"My lady," the man called, but she kept on going, stomping her way over the roots and fallen branches.

Clementine heard a rush behind her and for a moment she felt like running and giving him a real chase — a test of his stamina versus hers. And she was a fast runner, too. But it might have ripped her dress, so she simply let him take a few jogging steps to catch up, and did not spare him a look as he fell in beside her, matching his long strides to her shorter steps.

"You really are as stubborn as a mule, aren't you," he noted .

"Hmm? I beg your pardon? Did you say something? I must have been lost in thought," Clementine said, still not looking at those green eyes she felt on her. The man was looming next to her, and she became aware of his scent. Sandalwood and soap, and something else that left her senses intrigued until she ripped her thoughts away from him. What did she care if some man had a pretty face and good personal hygiene?

"Ah, many thoughts I'm certain," he said with mock-seriousness. "The husband-hunting season is upon us, so I am sure your thoughts are occupied with what kind of traps you could lay for the poor man you have in your sights, and how to best use that fan of yours to secure the match without compromise."

Clementine stopped and glared up at him. *How dare he?*

"I'll have you know that the last thing on my mind is marriage, and the last person I would talk with about that is you. As for using my fan, I would not hesitate to use it on you again if you forced my hand." Clementine pointed the fan at him to reinforce her point.

The man smiled and took a small but defiant step closer, until the tip of her fan touched the front of his dinner jacket. Clementine's breath quickened, which annoyed her no end, and yet she did not move. He towered over her, and the scent of sandalwood felt overwhelming, even though the smell was subtle. She did not take a step back, despite her instincts, but stood her ground and lifted her eyes to meet his.

His green eyes seemed to burn into hers. "I think you forgot something, my lady," he said in a low voice that seemed almost a purr. She felt her skin turn into goosebumps. His eyes held hers as he leaned closer, and her heartbeat quickened. Would he dare to try and kiss her?

Her mind raced through different scenarios on how to

defend her honour, but at the same time her breath became quicker, and without meaning to she parted her lips. She flushed at her reaction and swallowed. "And what is that, sir?"

He leaned close to her ear. She could feel his breath on her neck and shivered. It was barely noticeable, but the man obviously heard it and gave a low chuckle.

"This," he whispered, and gently he gathered Clementine's hair on the right side of her head, carefully securing it into a half-updo with the pearl comb.

Clementine's face burned at the intimate touch, and for once she was at a loss for words. She felt his fingers lightly working in her hair, brushing a loose strand from her neck, and was unsure if she should be offended or praise him for being able to use a comb so expertly.

"There we are," he nodded with approval, "As I said, I am a gentleman, and would never do something the lady did not wish for. I thought you might need some help to make your hair look presentable for the dinner. It is not quite the same as it was before, but now it better covers the blushing on your décolletage, without looking as if you have taken a tumble in the woods." He said this in all seriousness, and yet his eyes held laughter, and the knowledge of the effect he had on women.

Clementine scowled at his daring words, and brought her fan up for another snap against his wrist — only he was quicker this time and parried her, using her surprise to bring her hand to his lips. She gasped. Her hand was ungloved, and she could feel his hot breath on her skin as he softly brushed his lips against her fingers.

"My lady, you seem to be missing gloves. A daring trend for the season, I must say," he said and straightened up with that unbearable grin on his face.

She yanked her hand back. "If I wish to be without gloves at my aunt's house, I shall do so until she throws me out," she hissed.

Before he could say anything else, Clementine was already marching away from the orchard and back to the house, pausing only to pick up the lilac bouquet on her way. This time the man did not run after her, she was glad to notice.

* * *

WHEN SHE REACHED the side entrance, she paused to look at her reflection in the windows. She touched the pearl comb softly and judged it to be well-placed. Her cheeks were still red and her eyes bright, as if she had been having an exercise lesson, which it certainly felt like she had. But overall, the man's styling of her hair left her sophisticated enough to pay His Grace a quick visit before the dinner formalities. Only a passing thought whispered to her — *was he such an expert of women's hair because he had undone so many hairdos in intimate moments?*

She quickly banished these thoughts and continued her way upstairs to her uncle's rooms, confirming with a valet that the duke was awake.

"Your Grace." Clementine curtsied as she came closer to his bed. The curtains were half drawn to let a little daylight in, but the room was dim and there was a scent of stale air. Her uncle looked small and frail in the huge bed, but he smiled at her voice.

"Clementine, my dear girl. What a joy to see you," he laughed, and Clementine went to kiss his cheek. The Duke of Clearwater was almost blind, so he made this little joke often with his guests. He had been a great athlete in his youth; a strong and powerful man. Even though his body had shrunk with age and sickness, his mind was still sharp. Though Clementine did notice he downplayed his wits from time to time, especially in the presence of his wife.

"Would you like me to open the window for you? It's a bit

stuffy in here," Clementine asked, setting down the flowers on the bedside table.

"Yes, that would be good. Poor Jones is always worried I'll catch a cold, so he keeps them closed."

Clementine opened one of the white paneled windows and let in the evening air.

"Lilacs and apple flowers," her uncle noted, turning his head towards the bouquet.

"Yes, Uncle. The lilacs are from our garden and the apple blossoms from your orchard. It is lovely this time of the year."

"Yes, it must be," the duke smiled. "And are you here only to see your old uncle, or is there another suitor lined up for you?"

"I'm afraid so," Clementine sighed. "Aunt Theodora won't tell me who — she simply summons me here to meet and greet whoever she has found. Do you know there was a boy of fifteen she introduced to me last? I couldn't believe it. She really is trying, but..." She sighed again.

"But you want to marry for love," her uncle finished.

"Well, yes, if I am lucky enough to find love. But most of all I want the possibility to see the world, to discover wonders, and enjoy the feeling of freedom instead of being passed from my father to my husband."

"That is the way it is usually done, isn't it?" the duke laughed. Clementine huffed and he laughed again. "You modern women, going after votes and all. No, don't misunderstand me. I think it is marvellous that times change. Otherwise we wouldn't get anywhere, would we? But it does sound like a tiring, uphill battle. I hope you are ready, that's all."

"If only we could hear that Papa is safe and alive," Clementine sighed. "You know he promised to take me with him the next time he went away? He wanted to make me his equal. I cannot understand why Auntie doesn't respect that, and just pushes me like a cow to the highest bidder."

She sat down on the bed and took her uncle's hand in hers. It was dry and wrinkled but still big enough to cover hers entirely.

"Clementine, did you know that your father made a will?" Her uncle sounded serious now.

"I did. It names me as his heir, as I understand. Papa told me so himself."

"Prepare yourself then for some unpleasant news, Clementine."

"What?" Clementine's heart sped up.

"You see, Theodora contacted your family solicitor once we heard your father was lost in the desert."

"And?" Clementine's throat felt dry.

"The will does name you, but with the addition that the heir could be you or the closest male relative. The solicitors are hunting for any male relatives at the moment, and that is one reason why your aunt is hurrying to marry you off. The public does not know that you won't inherit, so despite your unfortunate past—"

"You mean my mother," Clementine muttered, tired of the topic already.

"Yes, the divorce and rumours around your mother unfortunately follow you. But your inheritance can still make you a desirable match to many bachelors. Your aunt wants to see you married before any possible male heir is found and your inheritance lost."

"So she wishes me to trick some poor man to marry me in the hopes of a great dowry which might never come? That... That is no way to start a marriage, Uncle!" Clementine felt herself shaking. "Besides, there might not be a male heir at all. And, most importantly, Papa might still be alive!" Her voice had gone up a few notches.

"Calm down, dear. I meant no harm. But let this be a lesson to you. Clementine, you could have summoned the family solicitor yourself to find out where you actually stand. I like your father very much — he and I shared the joy of digging out the treasures of the past — but he is not necessarily the most organised. He might say he wants to make you his heir, but has he made the necessary changes to his will to make that happen? Apparently not."

"I– but–" Clementine started, but her uncle waved her words away.

"No buts, Clementine." He sounded very much like a teacher scolding a student. "You always say you want your freedom, but that means taking responsibility for yourself, your decisions, and actions. In this world, you have to strive to make your own choices if you want to be free. And if there is something or someone stopping you from making those decisions then you find a way to go above their jurisdiction. Remember this, Clementine. As a woman, it will be harder for you, but you can always try to use your knowledge to take control of your own life."

"I'm sorry, Uncle. I did not think I could do anything."

"Nonsense, child. You have always been one who acts, and not always to your benefit, mind you." He smiled at her. "Don't let your aunt blindly lead you in the direction she chooses, if that truly is not what you want. But to make a decision like that, you need to have all the facts for yourself, and not be afraid of what the truth might be."

"I will keep this in mind, Uncle, thank you."

"Now go and get to that dinner. I will join you later, when we will finally have more news of your father."

"What?" Clementine gasped.

The duke frowned. "Theodora did not tell you?"

"No, what should I know?" Clementine asked, with a gut-wrenching feeling.

"Mr Hunt has returned, and we will discuss his news after the dinner. Theodora really should have told you this. I can only imagine–"

"That she wanted me to go along with this suitor dinner she has arranged without being upset," Clementine cut him off. *The outrage!* She rose from the bed. "I must go, Uncle."

"Yes," he sighed. "Remember that your aunt is only thinking of your best interests, although her methods leave something to be desired. Try not to eat her alive, Clementine."

"I can't make promises, Uncle, but for you I can try to keep myself civil — at least while there are guests. I will see you later." She kissed him on the cheek and left with a flurry of skirts.

MR HUNT

Her uncle had been right; Clementine had been much too passive in waiting for news about her papa and assuming things would work out as had been promised. She was old enough to understand that if it wasn't in writing then it wasn't official, and she could be in serious trouble if there was a male heir. She picked up her lilac skirts and continued swiftly towards the hall that would lead her downstairs.

Just before the staircase, she heard a familiar voice: her aunt, behind one of the doors to the ballroom, sounding quite upset. Clementine did not mean to eavesdrop — much — but she slowed down just a little and pretended to study a striking flower arrangement on a nearby table. After all, Clementine was quite curious by nature.

The voices were muffled but she could clearly hear that it was her aunt speaking, only her voice was missing its usual regality.

"How can it be?" she said, "It has been more than a month and there is no news?"

A man answered, but Clementine could not quite hear the words.

"Well, it can't be helped. You must stay for dinner and we will discuss this with Clementine later," Aunt Theodora said.

Clementine's eyes went wide, and without further thought she swung the door open and marched into the room with a swish of lavender trailing behind her. If Aunt Theodora had news of her father, she must hear it immediately!

Clementine rushed into the ballroom holding her skirts in fists of silk and found her aunt quite startled at her sudden entry. Since they were not alone, Clementine's manners took over and she hurried to curtsy as gracefully as she could.

"Your Grace," Clementine said, slightly out of breath, "I apologise, but I happened to hear your voice. Aunt Theodora, I must know–" Clementine's words cut off as she finally focused on who her aunt had been talking to.

"You!" The word burst out before she could stop herself, and the green eyes looking at her flashed with that infuriating amusement yet again. The man inclined his head, and Clementine noticed that his hair was slightly curly and his modest sideburns were just fashionable enough. *Focus now.*

"Really, Clementine," the duchess sighed. Then she frowned at the two young people. "Do the pair of you know each other?"

"We, ah," Clementine fumbled for words, "We simply ran into each other while arriving at your house, Aunt Theodora. No formal introductions were made."

"Quite so," the man agreed. "The young lady left quite an impression, even with the short encounter we had."

Aunt Theodora raised an eyebrow but proceeded with the introductions.

"This is Lady Clementine, daughter of Earl Whitham and my niece."

"I should've guessed, my lady." The man's voice betrayed none of the amusement that was apparent in his eyes, though there was something else there too. Recognition, perhaps? His tall frame was no less impressive without the top hat, and his formal dinner suit was impeccable. Clementine nodded and gave her hand for him to kiss, despite feeling quite ready to be over with the polite introductions. He bowed deep, as if to remind her of her lack of height, and again brushed his lips to her bare knuckles.

"I am pleased to finally meet you, formally," he said with a delicate pause, and Clementine shivered as his warm breath tickled her hand. As soon as he straightened up, she yanked her hand back and looked up at him, as if daring him to say something about their previous meeting.

"And this," the duchess continued, gesturing to the man, "is Mr William Hunt. He worked with your father, as you might remember, Clementine."

Clementine's eyes widened. *So that's who this rascal was, and he wouldn't even tell her!* They had had ample time to converse in the orchard, but not once did he mention any news of her dear Papa! Clementine curtsied as a reflex, but could not help her words escaping her.

"I– I apologise, but I cannot believe you would not say something — anything — of the news regarding my father when we met briefly outside." She struggled to sound polite, and as if they had merely bumped into each other before.

"My lady seemed unwilling to pause for an exchange of words, let alone anything else."

Unbelievable. Clementine's eyes narrowed in anger and disbelief, and she was about to say something she might regret. Mr. Hunt regarded her with a challenge in his expression.

"Clementine," Aunt Theodora's tone was firm, and Clementine was forced to clamp her mouth shut. "Mr Hunt only returned to England today. We will discuss the matter of your father after dinner. This is, after all, a family matter, and we wouldn't want idle gossip to ruin your opportunities, my dear."

Clementine wanted to say something, but her aunt had one of those looks that gave room for no questions. Clementine glanced at Mr Hunt, whose observant eyes met hers, and she held them, pleading for him to say something, to release her from the torment of having to wait for hours. He was a rake and an annoying, arrogant man, but surely he would not be cruel.

Mr Hunt searched her eyes as their gazes locked. Finally, after what felt like forever, he cleared his throat.

"Perhaps it is best to at least tell Lady Clementine that I have not yet found Lord Whitham's body, meaning the evidence of his death is still lacking." He carefully addressed these words to the duchess, but his eyes didn't leave Clementine's.

The duchess nodded with approval. "Yes, thank you, Mr Hunt. That much can be said to put my niece's thoughts at rest, at least for the duration of our gathering. I do apologise for her manners."

Clementine felt she could breathe again and lowered her tense shoulders. Thank goodness there was still hope, although she did not wish to think what this meant for everything else. Could she truly wait for seven years before she could start her life? Still, the main thing was that her papa could still be alive somewhere. She mustn't lose hope.

"Now then, perhaps we can all move on to the dinner formalities, and we will continue this discussion afterwards . As for now, please kindly escort my niece downstairs and let us start the evening with merrier topics." The duchess nodded and left, her heavy crinoline heaving underneath her green and white ornamented brocade dress. Aunt Theodora did not yet believe in the more practical-sized bustles the young women favoured these days.

As her lungs remembered how to breathe, Clementine gently pressed one hand against her lilac corset, trying to even out her breaths. She felt flushed and tired all of a sudden, as if after strenuous exercise.

"Perhaps the fan would be helpful? It is quite simple to use, you know," came Mr Hunt's teasing voice, and he gestured at the very same fan she had hit him with earlier that evening.

Clementine scowled at him but flicked the fan open, without the claws. She fanned herself for a moment and it did help her feel less flushed.

"That's better, isn't it?" Mr Hunt flashed a smile and offered her his arm.

Clementine closed her fan with a snap. "Before I give you my arm, can you promise me you did not know who I was when we met earlier? That you did not purposely withhold information from me all the time we were in the garden?"

"And why is that so important to know right now?" Mr Hunt asked.

"Because if you did, I shall not find it easy to trust anything else you might say to me — to us — during the course of this evening. It would have been a wicked thing to do," she snapped.

"Ah, a question of trust," he smiled at her. "Well, my lady, I can swear I did not know for certain who you were when we met. Your looks are quite striking and different, if I may be so bold to say, so I had my suspicions about your identity. But I guessed only as you marched away, when you mentioned that your aunt is the mistress of this house. I might not be that up to date with the social circles, but I thought it unlikely that Her Grace would have several nieces, especially since your father only talked of one daughter."

Clementine nodded and looped her hand into his, finally. Their height difference made it a little straining to talk to him, but she looked up with new eagerness in her voice.

"And did my father mention me often on your travels?" she couldn't help asking.

"Rarely," Mr Hunt said as he guided her through the large oak doors to the corridor that would lead them down the grand staircase, "But he painted a very different picture in those few moments he did mention you."

"Oh, how so?" Clementine was hungry for anything her father might have said.

"Well, he mentioned a young woman who had great interest in history and culture. But the old chap failed to mention that his daughter is a tree-creature who steals flowers at any cost, and who is yet to grow into proper adult height." He demonstrated this by glancing down at her. Her head barely reached his chest.

Clementine's eyes were like pits of fire, and if she could have thrown actual daggers at him, she would have. "Excuse me?" Her voice raised just high enough for some curious glances to be directed at them as they reached the landing.

Mr Hunt laughed and shook his head as if Clementine had been telling some funny story to him. "Oh, Lady Clementine, you might get to see this bachelor blush with your bold tales."

Clementine's cheeks reddened. With her eyes wide, she forced her lips into a most unnatural smile and pretended to laugh as they descended together, continuing their fake cordial discussion. "Ah, Mr Hunt. As if I had any interest in seeing anything more of you." As they reached the last step, she took off with the smallest of curtsies, leaving him behind.

Clementine looked around and saw her cousin, Richard, the future Duke of Clearwater. She was delighted to see him and went straight over, not caring if Mr Hunt was alone or not.

"Dickie, how lovely to see you," she beamed.

Lord Richard had his father's looks but his mother's constitution, it seemed. He was robust; the picture of English health and jolliness. He had a proneness to red cheeks whenever he had even a glass of alcohol, and he was already holding a half empty glass in his hands.

Richard bowed to Clementine and kissed her cheek fondly. They had known each other since they were children and had a relationship closer to brother and sister than cousins. It was good that no one had ever suggested for them to marry, for it would have been strange and not desirable at all, Clementine thought. Her cousin had the title and a fortune, but Clementine suspected his prospects were much higher than to marry a cousin of lower title, lesser fortune, and scandalous family past. Richard certainly did not seem as if he was in a hurry to marry. He seemed quite content in helping to run the estate and spending whatever remaining time he had at White's, the most exclusive gentlemen's club. Clementine had no details of what happened at these clubs, but it must be of some importance since women were not allowed to enter, ever.

"And how are you tonight, dear cousin? Ready for another suitor, are you?"

"Oh yes," Clementine said with a sigh, "I cannot wait to see what Aunt Theodora has in store for me today. Why she isn't concentrating on you, I don't understand. You are her son and the bachelor of great fortune, yet without a wife." Clementine had never seen her cousin display any romantic intention to anyone.

Richard barked a hearty laugh. "I for one am glad you are taking the pressure away from me, dear cousin. What's the rush, anyway? One can enjoy life and freedom before being tied down, eh?"

Clementine rolled her eyes, opening and closing her fan with annoyance, signaling in delicate fan language that her cousin was being cruel.

Richard's eyes did not miss the message and he grinned sheepishly, giving the slightest bow. "Apologies, dear cousin, I spoke with the privilege of a man. It is true that we are allowed more freedom before taking on what great responsibilities our families have in store for us."

"Yes, well, if us women were also allowed by default some of these great responsibilities, then perhaps we too would be too busy for frivolous pastimes, and might actually be of more use in this world than to be mere company for tea or garden strolls."

"Did someone mention garden strolls?" came a familiar voice behind Clementine.

She did not have to turn to know that it was Mr Hunt who had decided to join them.

Richard's face cheered up. "Ah, William! Happy to see you back! I have missed your company at White's, and those stories of exotic lands and, erm, people." His eyes briefly met Clementine's with apology, but Clementine merely lifted an eyebrow and turned to greet Mr Hunt — William — with the barest of curtsies.

Mr Hunt bowed and shook hands with Richard. "My lord, very good to see you well! My lady," he bowed to Clementine, "Did you have a wish for a stroll in the garden? I hear the apple blossoms are lovely now."

Clementine's dark eyes flashed with warning but Mr Hunt's green eyes merely glinted with infuriating amusement, somehow managing to mock her without words.

"Indeed! My cousin here was aching for a garden stroll after dinner," Richard smiled, and Clementine stared at her cousin with wide eyes. She lifted her fan to rest on her left cheek to signal NO. Neither man paid her any attention, though Mr Hunt seemed to fight a smile, based on the twitch at the corner of his mouth.

"That is interesting, I was also curious to see the famous gardens here."

"This is Lady Clementine Whitham. And this is Mr William Hunt. We were in the same boarding school, along with his brother, the Baronet of Knightwood," Richard continued his introductions, apparently oblivious to Mr Hunt's familiarity with Clementine's father.

Clementine inclined her head. "Mr Hunt and I are already introduced. He is the one who worked with Papa on the excavation of the tombs in Egypt. Though we will need to wait until after dinner to hear about his time in Egypt." Clementine's voice did not lack sharpness.

Richard's face gained a few more red blotches as he finally realised the connection. "Ah, indeed. Well, I suppose you will have much to discuss, then. Perhaps on that garden stroll?" He nodded awkwardly to them both and headed off to fill his glass. Clementine wanted to throw her fan at her dear cousin for being so dense, and for abandoning her with Mr Hunt.

"Well, that was not discreet, leaving us alone like this," Mr Hunt chuckled as he turned back to Clementine.

Clementine fanned herself slowly and her eyes threw daggers at her cousin's back. "Oh, don't be a fool. There is someone else I am supposed to meet and fall in love with. He has not yet arrived, so I have no idea who he is, but you may rest assured that you are not my intended match. My cousin is a dear, but subtle he is not. You know him well?"

"It has been a long time since boarding school, but yes, I do know him. He has a good heart, but he has always been something of an bull in a china shop."

Clementine nodded and a fond smile crept onto her face, despite the company. "I did not see him much during those times, of course, since he rarely visited home and I did not spend that much time here. But we used to play together as children and I do give him credit for playing rough with me, most of the time."

"Let me guess, you beat him up with your fan. "

"How well you know me," Clementine mused. "Not with a fan, no, but I do remember beating him in a mock swordfight when we argued over who could first ride the new pony. It was his right, as he pointed out, because he was older and outranked me. It was his pony anyway, and I was just a little girl, so what was I going to do about it?" Clementine smiled at the memory. "So I challenged him to a duel for wounding my honour, and there we were with our little wooden sticks, smacking away. He did not hold back, but I won by stomping on his toes and throwing him on the ground. He thought I cheated, since no gentleman would ever step on another's toes. I said I was not a gentleman, I was a lady, and the first turn with the pony was now rightfully mine. He ran crying back to the estate and I happily took the pony for a ride around the gardens. When I came back, sniffling Richard was there, with not only my aunt but also my mother, and I was forced to apologise and promise never to act so unladylike again. At home, my mother only laughed, said she was proud of me, and praised how well I had taken to my early training of the martial arts." Her smile faded away at the thought of her mother. "Well, that was a long time ago."

"You are the most peculiar lady I have ever met, I have to say. I'm sure you resemble your mother very much in many aspects, as she has inspired you to become this... funny little creature. "

Clementine's face changed and she half turned away from Mr Hunt, pretending to observe the crowd around them. "Yes, well, as you and everyone else knows, my mother is not here."

Mr Hunt had no reply for her barely hidden sarcasm, and they stood in silence for a while as people around them chattered. A footman passed them with a tray of champagne and Mr Hunt took two glasses, offering one to Clementine. She wanted to keep a clear head but thanked him and sipped the dry drink just to have something to fill the silence.

"Since you know so much about me, and members of my family, what exactly are *you* then, other than an assistant in my father's exploration adventures?" she asked, her voice lacking warmth. She briefly wondered if her mother would ever stop being a touchy subject to her. "What kind of creature are you, Mr Hunt?"

"My lady, I could not possibly tell. It would be an unsuitable tale for such young and innocent ears," he smirked and took a sip from his glass.

"Ah, of course," Clementine said, "You are the type of creature who takes joy in being insufferable just because you can. A man with a good name, good looks, who thinks those alone means he is a godsend to the ladies in his company? I do not know if there is a name for this type of creature other than... an overconfident rake?" Clementine turned to him with a sweet smile on her rouged lips.

Mr Hunt did not betray any surprise or feeling of insult. "My lady, I assure you, that of the two of us, it is not I who suffers from overconfidence."

Clementine could feel his green eyes laughing at her. She was ready with a sharp answer, but just then the duchess came to fetch her to meet Lord Thompkins, future Baron of Kirkham.

The man looked barely old enough to be out in society. He had attempted to grow a mustache but the light, thinly growing hair made him look unkept, and the sleepy look in his eyes took no inspiration from meeting Clementine.

Clementine curtsied after the introductions and the man before her took her hand to kiss. His hand felt limp, as if he was reluctant to touch her ungloved fingers. He released her hand as soon as he bent over it.

"Lady Clementine, a pleasure to meet you. I trust you are in fine spirits tonight?"

She sighed and nodded graciously to him. "Yes, my lord, I am in fine spirits tonight. And how are you?"

"I have been better," he sniffed and stifled a yawn that was still clearly visible. "Shall we eat soon? I am quite starving."

"But of course, Lord Thompkins," Aunt Theodora cut in with the bright laughter she always reserved for these occasions. "Dinner is ready to be served."

Dickie came to stand at his mother's side and she took his offered hand. Lord Thompkins did not offer his hand to

Clementine, so she merely stood next to him as they went towards the dining room. Last in the procession was Mr Hunt, who walked behind Clementine.

* * *

A WARM GLOW welcomed them as dozens of candelabras lit the room and reflected in the crystals of the three magnificent chandeliers above the dining table. The table itself stretched long, with a full formal dining setting and elaborate floral pieces. Their scent filled the air and Clementine saw with delight that the floral arrangements held several lovely buds of a particular orange rose that greeted the diners with an intoxicating fragrance of summer. The duchess sat at the end of the table with Richard and Lord Thompkins on either side of her. Clementine took her own place, where it said Lady Clementine on a small seating card, next to Lord Thompkins and opposite Mr Hunt.

Clementine hurried to introduce Mr Hunt to Lord Thompkins.

"Mr Hunt here works with my father and has just returned from Egypt. They have digging sites around the Dendera Temple. Very fascinating," Clementine said.

"I do not really care for antiquities. Anything older than last year simply bores me to death," Lord Thompkins said with his tired-of-everything expression.

"I see. Well, I am quite my father's daughter and find the ancient times to be most interesting. There is so much we do not yet know; so much we could still learn about human civilisations and buried treasures," Clementine said.

"I quite agree, my lady," Mr Hunt said. "There is nothing like the sense of discovery. What we have excavated around the temple is simply marvellous. Items that have been preserved for thousands of years, still intact. It is truly gratifying."

Clementine found herself nodding eagerly at Mr Hunt's words.

"Sounds like you cannot wait to return," Richard chimed in. "Mind you, I'd love to join, but duty calls here."

"And where is Duke Clearwater?" Mr Thompkins asked.

The table fell silent for a moment at this question. The circle of aristocrats knew well that the duke had been ill for a long time and that it was really only a matter of time until there would be a new Duke of Clearwater.

"My husband sends his apologies. He would have loved to join this dinner, but alas he is not well enough," the duchess said.

"How unfortunate. Neither the lady's uncle nor father are here to negotiate the marriage then?" Lord Thompkins said casually, slurping his soup.

Clementine rarely lost her appetite, but she had an urge to pour her plate of mulligatawny soup in his lap. Instead, she took a deep breath.

"Yes, for now," the duchess said. Even her voice had turned slightly sharper. "But I can assure you that I speak for Clementine's father while he is, hmm, away. Our dear Clementine is very eager to find a suitable husband."

Clementine met Mr Hunt's eyes. He cocked his eyebrow, as if to say that she was ridiculous to even entertain the idea. The soup was cleared away and a dish of salmon and radish sauce was served next. Clementine poked at her dinner while the duchess asked eagerly of Lord Thompkins' interests and wishes for the future.

"I am a man of simple wishes. I want my title once my father dies, and for that I need a wife who can produce at least one heir. She has to come from a good stock and be of humble nature. I do not have interest in travel, so my wife will stay with me at home to tend to the usual social nonsense where absolutely necessary. I will be mostly at the club and will participate in the estate running as little as possible."

"And is this what your father and mother wish?" Clementine couldn't help asking. "To my understanding, the Baron of Kirkham is quite active in attending society events with the baroness. I believe I saw them at the opera not a fortnight ago."

"That is useless, and when I am the baron we will spend no money on such nonsense. Frugality and faith; these are the matters I want to be remembered by. The influence my mother has on my father is ridiculous. She asks for anything she wants and he dotes on her, can you believe it? My wife will not have the same liberty with me."

The table had grown quite silent at these remarks, which were hardly suitable for dinner conversation. Even an intimate one.

"It sounds like your parents are very much in love, and happy," Clementine blurted. "I congratulate them for finding that in a marriage. It does not seem to be a priority, would you say?"

"Nor should it be," Lord Thompkins scoffed and dug a piece of fish bone from between his teeth. He wiped it on his plate and Clementine fought the urge to flip the whole table to make this dinner stop.

"A marriage is a business deal," he said to Aunt Theodora, "You sell your niece to me, and in exchange, I will take decent care of her and make sure her basic needs are well met."

Clementine's eyes narrowed. She was very close to losing her temper.

"So your wife has to be sold to you from good stock and in exchange you will feed her, keep her warm and safe? That sounds to me as if you are purchasing a dog from a breeder." Her voice had a strain to it, and she sipped her wine to keep her hand from shaking.

"Precisely. A good bitch is a good bitch, that is a fact," he nodded.

"I do think you are crossing a line here, Thompkins," Richard said, "My cousin is not a bitch to be bought."

"All women are. Why else would we marry them? We must know their background, health and basic manners. It differs little from selecting a good dog." He crossed his arms.

"It is clear to me that you know very little of the fairer sex. Perhaps it would be better for you to spend some more time learning before considering marriage?" Mr Hunt said in a tone that did nothing to hide his distaste for Mr Thompkins.

Clementine glanced at Mr Hunt. He sneered just slightly, as if to ask how long Clementine was going to stand this man.

"Perhaps a change of subject would be appropriate," the duchess tried to intercept, "What about the gardens—"

"I really do not see what the problem is," Lord Thompkins cut her off, which was unheard of. A baron's son interrupting off a duchess? The outrage! Aunt Theodora was left quite speechless.

"My dear chap, you are treading in some deep and dangerous waters. You have insulted both Lady Clementine and our gracious hostess, and that does not speak well of you. You should apologise to them both," Mr Hunt said.

"Hear, hear," Richard said, his face flushing red with anger.

"Hardly. And I do not think the second son of a baronet has enough rank to tell me what to do. I do not think I am the problem here, but *you*, my lady," Mr Thompkins turned to Clementine.

"Indeed?" She squeezed the glass in her hand.

"Yes. Since your father and uncle are not here to vouch for you, I do not yet know if you are good enough to take the position of being my wife. You are an earl's daughter, but your mother is an issue in my eyes. I would like a full report on her actions that led to the divorce, and how much of it was due to Oriental influence."

"Excuse me?" Clementine couldn't believe her ears. "What do you mean by 'Oriental influence'?"

"Why, the differences of superior and less superior races, of course. You are half of your mother's Oriental side, and while at least half of you is of proper English stock, there may still be something of those undesirable traits inherited from your mother. It is my right to know what might affect my future heirs, should you be my wife."

Clementine could no longer listen to this. With a splash, she swung her wine into Lord Thompkins' surprised face, finally wiping off that sleepy expression of his.

"This dinner is over. Good day!" With that, she rose from the table and marched back upstairs to the one place where she could have peace to calm her rage: the library.

THE FAMILY DISCUSSION

*I*n the safety of the library, Clementine let out all the few curse words she knew, and a few she came up herself. *Horrible, disgusting man!* How could Aunt Theodora entertain the idea of a marriage with someone like that? Clementine huffed and kicked her skirts around her.

Only a few minutes passed before footsteps approached the library. Clementine turned, ready to face her aunt, but to her surprise it was the tall frame of Mr Hunt that stood in the doorway. He ran his hand through his hair and closed the door behind him.

"Oh, they sent you in, of all people?" Clementine noted. "Is this the first part of my punishment?"

Mr Hunt lips twitched and leaned against a bookshelf to keep a respectful distance. The soft light of gas lamps and candles made his face glow and his smile even more annoying.

"Actually, I escaped and followed you on my own. Your aunt is apologising to the idiot, and Dickie is trying to shove him to a carriage. One of the servants said you would likely be in the library. They also warned me to let you be after hearing you scream at your dinner guest. They said something about the lady being known for her temper," he chuckled. "I have to confess, I've never seen wine thrown in someone's face at a formal dinner. One sees that kind of thing happening at pubs, or other establishments where women are made of fire."

"Oh," Clementine said, her face flushing. She could imagine the establishments he was referring to.

"And since I am not the utter bastard you seem to think of me, I also wanted to see if you are alright. That man was a nasty individual." His tone was still amused but his green eyes had softened just a bit. Or perhaps it was just the play of light and shadows.

Clementine looked at him with some surprise. Her hand touched her chest lightly, as if to see if her breathing had evened out. "I... Well, I am alright, I suppose. He was rude and horrible, and no one did anything about it, so I did," she said in a defiant tone.

"You certainly did. Based on this evening alone I feel confident in saying that you are a woman of action and surprises, it seems. And a flush of excitement brings out a lovely colour on your cheeks, I must say."

Clementine stared at him and dropped her gaze to her décolletage, which was unfortunately again flushed with red. "Are you trying to insult me?" she blurted.

"I tried to give a compliment, my lady," Mr Hunt said. "Most ladies are more receptive to compliments than you seem to be."

"Well, you would know," Clementine muttered.

Mr Hunt's eyebrow rose. "Oh? And how would you know what I know? You've looked into my reputation, haven't you?"

"N-no, I have not. It is well-known among the other ladies," Clementine stammered slightly.

"Indeed?" He approached her, ignoring the rules for proper distances, and Clementine felt like a mouse that had caught a cat's attention. He leaned nearer. "And what else have they said of me that has caught your interest?" he whispered close to her ear. Clementine's heart beat faster and she cursed her feminine reactions to a handsome face.

"Absolutely nothing of interest, I can assure you. Now, if you don't mind, we really should talk about my father."

"I was about to suggest the same, but the two of you have kept me well entertained," came the Duke of Clearwater's dry voice.

Clementine jumped and looked behind her. Her uncle was sitting in an armchair near to the fireplace; its long back completely concealed his frail body from view.

"Uncle, I didn't realise you were here. This is Mr Hunt, who has returned from Egypt today to share his account of father's disappearance, finally." Clementine felt out of breath. *How embarrassing!*

Mr Hunt cleared his voice and went to greet the duke. "How do you do, Your Grace?"

The duke offered his hand for a shake. "It is good to see you, Mr Hunt, in a manner of speaking…"

"I had the chance to meet your enchanting niece," Mr Hunt said.

Clementine hurried to kiss her uncle's cheek. "Are you comfortable, Uncle? Shall I ring for a drink for you?"

"Based on what I overheard about the dinner, I think we could all use a drink. You too, Clementine. If even a library cannot calm you, you must be in great distress, dear child. Poured wine on some poor bugger, my, my…" the duke said with a smile. His pale face was hollow-looking, and only the dancing flames brought some colour to his cheeks. His once formidable frame had shrunk, as if the life force was bleeding out of him. Clementine did not wish for her uncle to die, but it saddened her greatly to see this once active and robust man just wither away. The smallpox had left him blind, and he had learned to live with it, but surviving tuberculosis was evidently too much for his old body.

"I apologise, Uncle, but surely it is clear that I'm eager — no, restless — to talk about what happened to my papa and not entertain a suitor who only wishes to insult me and my mother. It is torture to wait, especially since we have been waiting for so long already!" Clementine wrung her heavy fan in her hands and sighed. She then rang for a servant and asked for a selection of sherry and brandy to be brought.

"Please have a seat, Mr Hunt. Perhaps that will encourage my niece to take one also, and calm down. Let us wait for Theodora and Dickie to join us and then we can hear all about it."

Mr Hunt took a chair next to the duke, and after a moment, Clementine dropped herself heavily into another chair opposite, slouching in a most unladylike way.

"I just want to know what will be done next and how I can help. That's all I want: to help find my father and know for certain if he is alive or dead. Not knowing, and waiting without doing anything — I think it would eat me alive." She couldn't help saying these things out loud. The silence felt too much otherwise.

Clementine fanned herself, feeling hot from the fireplace and the frustration. "Uncle, can you not help me? Persuade Aunt Theodora , stall her?" She ignored Mr Hunt and pleaded openly to her uncle. If Mr Hunt found the situation awkward, it wasn't her problem.

The duke chuckled at this and coughed a long, dry cough. Mr Hunt swiftly rose, before Clementine could, and poured some water from the nearby pitcher into a glass, which he gently pressed into the duke's hands. "Sip slowly, Your Grace," he said, and Clementine felt a pang of guilt.

"I'm sorry, Uncle," Clementine said in a quiet voice. "I mustn't upset you and make you more tired."

"Dear child," he smiled, "You have done nothing to upset me. It is your father who has made us all upset by being away for too long and then disappearing. But my time for having any true impact on your aunt is in the past. After all, I would tire myself arguing with her and she knows this." This was said with both affection and certainty.

Clementine nodded and sighed. "I understand, Uncle."

"You might want to appeal to the higher powers," the duke said.

"I somehow do not see you praying for miracles from God," Mr Hunt noted to Clementine. "I think you would rather fetch the longest ladder there is and climb up there to demand answers from the old boy yourself."

Clementine raised her chin. "I might just do that. I am an excellent climber, you know."

The duke barked a laugh at this. "You know her so well already, Mr Hunt. You might just be a worthy enough opponent for her wit and spirit."

Clementine blushed and hoped Mr Hunt wouldn't take it the wrong way. His crooked smile suggested exactly that.

Before anyone could say anything else, the doors opened and Cousin Dickie came in behind his mother. Her face was like a storm itself.

"You insolent girl, have you any idea— Oh, darling." The duchess stopped her raging and looked surprised to see her husband here already. "I had not expected to see you up at this time. Clementine has caused something of a scene, I'm afraid."

"Let her be, Theodora. She is anxious to hear about her father. Is it any wonder a dinner might not have been the best idea today?"

"I— Well, we shall discuss your behavior later, Clementine." Her eyes shifted between Clementine and her husband. "In private."

"Sorry to keep you waiting, Father, Cousin, William," Dickie said, "We had to make sure our guest was well on his way, and it took some time to see that happen. Ah, the brandy is here." He took a glass from a servant who came in with a tray and they all followed suit.

"Oh, where are my manners? My dear, this is Mr Hunt, who has now returned from Egypt and was with Jonathan when he..." The duchess' words faded away at the wave of the duke's hand.

"Quite so, we were already introduced," he said. "I meant to ask you, Mr Hunt, are you one of Baronet Knightwood's boys? How is Edward these days?"

Mr Hunt swirled his drink in his glass. "Yes, I am the second son. My father Edward unfortunately passed away two years ago, and the current Baronet Knighthood is my brother, Edmund."

"Ah, my memory is not as it used to be, like my eyesight," the duke smiled a sad smile. "I hope he died in peace, and that he left the estate in good hands with your brother."

Something shifted in Mr Hunt's face before he nodded and spoke for a moment about how his brother was catching up on the duties as a baronet. Clementine couldn't quite catch what it was. That man was quick to hide his reactions and emotions, she mused. Still, she was sorry to hear that he had lost his father, even if he did vex her.

"So, I think I should start by telling you how sorry I am. For not being able to come here sooner, and for the whole situation of uncertainty," Mr Hunt said, as Dickie found a seat next to his parents. Clementine felt her shoulders tense and her jaw clench as she waited to hear more about the circumstances that led to her father's disappearance. Mr Hunt remained standing, and for once that amused face looked sombre. Clementine watched the grim line of his mouth and feared for what he was about to say.

"Please continue, Mr Hunt," the duke said. "I'm sure it is not pleasant to tell, but I am equally sure that my wife is eager to hear any news of her brother, not to mention my niece, who has been in much distress ever since we heard her father had gone missing."

Mr Hunt nodded and glanced at Clementine. Their eyes met, and it was all she could do to not bounce up and shake him to get the words out faster.

"As you know, Lord Whitham had been tasked by Her Majesty to search and obtain a certain item. I often accompanied such searches and that was the case when we found ourselves in Egypt."

"And what became of it?" Clementine asked. She couldn't help her curiosity, even in this situation.

"Hush, Clementine," her aunt said. "If we want to learn what has happened, we must let Mr Hunt speak without unnecessary questions!"

"Apologies, Auntie."

"In any case, I am not at liberty to speak about the item. These assignments from Her Majesty, and previously from late Prince Albert, are not public information," Mr Hunt said.

"We tracked the item to a location in the excavation area and proceeded with the search. So far, everything had gone as planned, and there were very few problems once we found the actual location. We had a good team of locals to help us through the more laborious phases. One night, we received much-awaited news: the entrance to a particular tomb had been found, and chances were high that it was exactly what we were looking for. It was getting late, and Lord Whitham, myself, and his valet made a plan to enter the tomb at dawn. So I went to sleep."

Mr Hunt paused to sigh and take another sip from his glass before glancing at Clementine again. She pursed her lips together, waiting for what came next.

"The next morning, before sunrise, I was woken up hastily by some of the team members saying they couldn't find Lord

Whitham, nor his valet, and that the tracks led towards the dig site."

"And did you follow the tracks?" Clementine burst out before she could stop herself, earning a sharp glance from the duchess.

"No," Mr Hunt said.

"What?" Clementine could not believe what she was hearing.

Mr Hunt raised his hand to stop any other outbursts. "I could not follow. The reason why I was so hastily woken was that an enormous sandstorm was approaching, and the camps near the dig sites had been ordered to evacuate back to the nearest village. Despite my objections, we had to flee with what little equipment we could gather from our tents and leave most of it behind. Some of the campsites were too slow and, well, not all made it out alive."

He looked around the room to make sure the graveness of his words was heard. The duchess looked pale, the duke was frowning, and Dickie shook his head, muttering something about poor sods. Clementine felt and looked furious.

"You left my father behind? That's what you came here to tell? What bloody good does this information give us?"

"Enough, Clementine. If you cannot control your emotions, we will be forced to have this meeting without you." The duchess' voice snapped like a whip, but Clementine could hear there was fear in it, and anger too.

"Mama, please, it's her father we are talking about. If anyone should hear this, it's her." Dickie's calm tone came as a surprise. Clementine gave him a small smile of thanks. The duchess sniffed and gestured for Mr Hunt to continue. His green eyes were cold as they looked back at Clementine.

"Make no mistake, Lady Whitham, I wanted to go to the dig site right away, but was dragged away by other members of our team. They made sure I didn't die like the others who stayed too long, at the mercy of the sandstorm. Have you ever experienced a sandstorm?"

Clementine bit her lip and shook her head. She hadn't been anywhere, and in this moment a blush of shame creeped up her cheeks for having to acknowledge that.

"A sandstorm is like a vicious beast. It will choke you, make you lose your way, and leave you to die in the desert, covered by endless sand. Trust me when I say that we would have been in mortal danger had we stayed there any longer."

His eyes held Clementine's until she gave the barest of nods.

"As you know," Mr Hunt continued, "I stayed on for a time, to go back and see if your father and his valet had been able to find shelter and survive in the tomb until the storm passed. We waited until it was safe to venture back and then had to start again to dig out tonnes of sand and rock. It took time to get it cleared, and once we did, I was the first one to enter the tombs to search for any signs of them."

He paused and cleared his throat. Clementine felt herself holding her breath.

"And I found no one there. No bodies, nothing."

"How is that possible?" the duke asked, "Did they not make it to the tombs in the early moments of the storm?"

Mr Hunt shook his head. "That is what I also thought, so I stayed and looked through the different collapsed dig sites nearby. But none of them contained any more evidence or information. You have to understand that the place in question contains hundreds of tombs, and some of their entrances had collapsed due to the storm. I am very sorry to have to tell you this, but I found nothing that could confirm one way or the other that Lord Whitham and his valet were alive or dead. Eventually, I had to gather what notes we had and come back here to report to Her Majesty before going back. I have an audience with her tomorrow at noon."

Clementine perked up. "You're going back?"

Mr Hunt looked surprised at this particular question. "Well, yes, I assume Her Majesty will still want to search for the item, and since I was there with Lord Whitham and know the area , I am assuming that I will be taking over Lord Whitham's work. And while I am there, I can look around for any clues that we might have missed."

Clementine narrowed her eyes. "So you think there might be something you overlooked?"

Mr Hunt gave half a smile. "I might be very good at what I do, but even I am not perfect."

Clementine took a gulp of her drink. It burned in her mouth and nose but it helped her not to roll her eyes at him.

"I think I know what you're talking about," she said, "Father often told me of the trap doors, secret rooms and hidden passages in his earlier excavations, and he often made me guess how the different locks and puzzles were opened. He always did say how good I was." Her voice shook a little. *Not the time to cry now.*

Mr Hunt cocked his head curiously. "Did he now? I will go back to search thoroughly for the item in any hidden parts of the tomb. And if I see evidence that someone else has been there, it might bring us closer to knowing where exactly your father ended up."

Clementine looked at Mr Hunt's face. He was serious about going back. He had been with her father in what were possibly his last moments and he knew how to get there. This was the only real chance for Clementine to find out what happened to her father, once and for all. Mr Hunt might be so focused on the item that she could search for her father. Could she do it? She was sure she could. Father himself had said how clever she was and how good a treasure hunter she would one day become. This could be that day.

She finished her drink with a cough. "I'm coming with you."

A stunned silence filled the room, and for a few moments, only the crackle of the fireplace could be heard.

"Are you out of your mind, Clementine?" The duchess turned her wide eyes to her niece. "Absolutely not, that is no place for a young woman!"

"It's about my father. Any son would be allowed to go to try and find out if their father was alive, and they would also be allowed to try and find evidence to secure their fortune instead of a haunting seven-year wait," Clementine said. "Why should I not get the same opportunity to find my father? Surely it cannot be so that only the men in the family are allowed to find their loved ones? We women care, love and are affected equally, so why should we be limited in different ways?" Her voice held anger, despite her best efforts to stop it seeping through.

"She has a point, Mother," Dickie said, and Clementine beamed at her cousin. Ever since they had learned to play on equal terms as children, he had treated her as a peer, despite her sex. "And I can vouch for William here," he nodded towards Mr Hunt, who was staring at his friend as if he was speaking in a different language. "He is a good chap and would not let Clemmie here come to any harm."

Mr Hunt tried to say something to interrupt this course of action, which was quickly getting out of hand, "I'm not sure if I am the best possible guardian–"

"While I am sure my son speaks highly of you, Mr Hunt, Lady Clementine is in the middle of a marriage search. She is already out in society and has yet to find a match. That is her priority, and the sooner she can find a husband, the sooner said husband can then allow her to accompany him in these travels."

Clementine breathed sharply. "I should not need a husband to find out if Papa is dead or alive! Have you no pity for me, Aunt?"

The duchess flinched slightly but did not back down. So

Clementine pleaded with the only thing that mattered to her aunt.

"Aunt Theodora, the prospects of me finding a good match will improve once my fortune and dowry are clear. Please let me help make my situation better instead of waiting and doing nothing!"

Her aunt's steely gaze told Clementine the answer before she said a word.

"Absolutely not, I forbid it, and my word will not be overruled." She glanced icily at her husband, who seemed to have dozed off for the moment.

"I will not forgive you for this, Aunt Theodora. There will be no suitor whom I will accept," Clementine seethed, unable to control herself in the company of a stranger. At that moment, she couldn't care less about what he thought of her manners. She rose swiftly and smoothed the layers of her lilac dress. "I will take matters into my own hands."

"Do not think for a moment that I will allow you to travel to Egypt. You will thank me once you have the security of a respectable and beneficial marriage," the duchess snapped back.

But Clementine was already curtsying and making her way out of the room.

As she left, she could hear her aunt apologising to Mr Hunt.

"She is a stubborn girl. Clever but stubborn, which must come from her mother's side. I do regret you had to witness this. She will learn her place and duty with time, as we all must."

AN AUDIENCE WITH THE QUEEN

The morning after shone brightly through the curtains as Mary pulled them aside. It was still very early, and Clementine woke with a headache. Not from that glass of brandy, but from being too upset and anxious to sleep. She felt as if someone had piled a stack of potato sacks on her neck and sat on it for good measure.

Lolling her head carefully from side to side, Clementine gratefully accepted her usual cup of morning tea from Mary, which was a fragrant cup of oolong. It was quite amusing to think that not so long ago, people in England were actually afraid to drink green tea for fear of hallucinations, but were perfectly happy to drink black tea, even though they were the same plant. Clementine's mother had laughed at this nonsense many times when they'd had tea together. She rarely spoke of her past before she came to England, but when it came to tea, Clementine would often hear her mother yearning for countless flavors of tea which were not available here.

Sipping her tea, she slowly came to realise that this was indeed an important day; she was about to infiltrate Buckingham Palace. Well, perhaps infiltrate was too strong a word —

heaven knew she wasn't usurping or overthrowing royalty. She would simply attach herself to Mr Hunt when he had his audience with Queen Victoria. It was the perfect plan, or as close as she could get!

Mr Hunt and Her Majesty were going to discuss Clementine's father, so it would be more than appropriate for Clementine to be there to join the discussion as a representative of her family. If there were doubts, Clementine pushed them aside. She was quite sure she could plead her case to Her Majesty, woman to woman. After all, Her Majesty had taken over being patron to Clementine's father and his explorations. Clementine was less sure about how Mr Hunt would react, but she would simply persuade the man to let her go to the audience as his guest. He was a gentleman, so he said. Surely he wouldn't turn her away from Her Majesty's door? No, she thought. It was the perfect plan, it had to be. And, as always, once she had made her mind, Clementine did not falter from her decision.

Rising from her bed, Clementine set aside her empty teacup. Her brain was overworking from excitement and nerves, and she had a feeling this headache would need more than one cup of tea. But she had no time to waste. Buckingham palace was at least three hours away by carriage, assuming the roads were in decent condition.

"Mary," Clementine said, "Bring out the cream dress. You know, with the red dots and lace, and the matching corset. Oh, and the red silk shawl. I believe Her Majesty still prefers ladies to wear shawls, even if they are not as fashionable as they were in her youth."

Clementine made her way to the bathtub and quickly washed herself with her favourite lilac soap.

"Excuse me, my lady, but did you say Her Majesty?" Mary asked, her eyes wide as she hurried to pass her mistress a towel.

"Yes, the queen. I will have a very quick breakfast and make haste to Buckingham Palace. I must not be there later than half past eleven today. Make sure the carriage is ready in an hour."

"An hour?" Mary gasped, but after one look from Clementine she went running.

Shortly after, she returned with the red spotted dress and helped Clementine into it. Mary was deft in securing the corset over Clementine's chemise and knew not to tighten it to ridiculous measures. Some ladies insisted on a tight corset, but Clementine preferred to be able to breathe, not faint.

Mary fastened the last drapings over the bustle and straightened the silk shawl on Clementine's shoulders. While dressing, Clementine had added the tiniest amount of rouge to her lips and cheeks. Her dark eyes needed nothing extra during the daytime, and the rouge was enough to compliment her fair skin. Her red lips went especially well with the accents of her dress and shawl.

A knock came at the door and Mary hurried to open it. A delicious scent wafted to Clementine's nose. Mary had remembered to ask for a small bite of breakfast to be brought in.

"Thank you, Mary," Clementine smiled, and dug into toast and bacon and another cup of tea, remembering only then that she would have to re-apply the rouge. Mary, meanwhile, did her best to arrange Clementine's dark hair into a braided bun beneath a red directoire hat. Clementine loved the effect of red on her near-black hair, and she had to say that despite all the silly fashion trends, she thought the narrow, slanted rim of the hat was rather becoming. It looked like a small-scale, ornamented top hat. Clementine shook her head twice to check the hat was well fastened with pins. Mary beamed when only the red and white feathers moved.

"You are a savior, Mary," Clementine said, and gulped the last of her tea, "I think I look perfectly presentable for Her Majesty."

She slipped her feet into red walking shoes as Mary handed Clementine her special fan, as well as a red parasol.

"Now you are, my lady."

Clementine nodded. "Right, that should be everything. Let's get on with it before I am late," she said. "Oh, and if my aunt happens to come by, tell her I've gone to London for some shopping. Do not mention Buckingham Palace," Clementine cautioned, "She would only worry that I shall make a fool of myself, and I dearly hope that I will not."

Mary curtsied. "Yes, my lady. May I ask why you are meeting Her Majesty?"

Clementine squared her shoulders and took a deep breath. "I will plead for her permission to go to Egypt with Mr Hunt and find my dear Papa."

Mary's eyes widened but she simply nodded in understanding. Clementine hurried away to the waiting carriage, leaving behind Mary, who seemed to be muttering a prayer for her mistress.

* * *

THE HORSES HUFFED as the carriage made its way through the countryside towards London.

Clementine found she had much too much time to think and become less sure of her plan to intercept an audience with Her Majesty. The audacity of her fast decision tried to creep its way into Clementine's thoughts, and she came close to asking the driver to take the carriage back home before her aunt found out what she was really up to.

Clementine let her gaze rest on the old trees that had formed a lovely canopy above the road. The greenery stretched until it met old stone walls that crumbled here and there, with farmlands and pastures beyond. The smell of sheep wafted by every now and then, but otherwise the open carriage allowed Clementine to breathe the sweet scent of summer around her and feel the sunshine on her skin. She knew she should protect herself from the sun, but it seemed such a waste to cover herself with a parasol when she was already wearing a hat.

The scenery was unfortunately only a momentary distraction from her whirling thoughts. She resisted the urge to bite her nails. Her hands already looked rough enough from her exercises, and for this occasion Clementine was glad of her short red gloves. The queen did not need to see her hands covered in scrapes, dry skin and bruises.

It was said that the queen knew everything about everyone, and Clementine wondered if it were true. She had met Her Majesty, of course, as a debutante, and on a few occasions in the presence of her aunt. The old queen had seemed stern and had little joy in her eyes, but her words often had a sense of cleverness and dry wit that you would not expect to look at the still-mourning queen.

Clementine had heard of the queen's love for her Prince Albert, and how everything had changed when he had suddenly passed away. Clementine wished she could have witnessed the court as it had been: a place of fun, joy and true love. Now, it seemed as if something was missing. And perhaps it was indeed Prince Albert's absence that left the queen, and her court, helplessly hollow and wanting.

Her Majesty would no doubt be surprised by Clementine's presence, so all that needed to be done was to convince Mr Hunt that he owed Clementine this opportunity to appeal to the queen herself. After all, he had failed to bring news of her father, failed to find him, failed to keep him safe. He owed Clementine — she just needed to make him see that. And once she was in front of the queen, she needed to be clear and firm about what she wanted and why. The queen had once been a young woman in difficult circumstances; perhaps that young woman was still underneath all that sorrow and could sympathise. Yes, Clementine thought, she surely would sympathise.

The carriage arrived at London and gone was the sweet summer air of flowers, forests, and fields. Clementine watched the buildings grow in numbers, covering the greenery until the colours changed to stone and grey, with the occasional gold and bronze.

* * *

SHE ARRIVED at Buckingham Palace just as the clocks struck eleven. The palace gates were open, and people were strolling leisurely on the manicured palace grounds. A fountain glittered in the sun, and the grand, majestic palace spread behind it. The queen and Prince Albert had made many changes in their time at Buckingham Palace, and it could now rival any royal residence in Europe.

Clementine reached the main entrance of the palace and silently thanked herself for rising so early and being here on time. There were many nobles and members of parliament gathered at the palace, all waiting for their meetings with the queen or one of her secretaries. Clementine was not the only noble-born woman here, so with any luck she could blend in until she found where Mr Hunt was. She strode through the doors and immediately almost collided with someone .

"Oh, excuse me," she said.

"No harm done," the bright voice of a young woman replied, "It can get quite stuffy in here. Thank goodness we do not wear those huge crinolines anymore, or we would take the space of two, easily."

Clementine chuckled. "My thoughts exactly." She looked at the woman, dressed in a dark dress and a cape. The cape was an odd choice on a warm summer day, but Clementine knew some women preferred a thin cape over carrying a parasol to shield from the sun. With some effort, Clementine remembered the woman's name from a dinner or a ball where they had been briefly introduced. "Lady Josephine. How good to meet you again, but I must run, I'm afraid."

"Of course. I too must hurry," Lady Josephine said, turning with a nod. Clementine glimpsed a curious smile playing on her lips, as if they had shared a private joke. She shrugged it off as a play of her nerves.

Clementine continued on her way through the crowd when she heard a familiar voice, "Clemmie?"

Clementine felt her body stiffen as if she'd been caught stealing an extra piece of dessert. *Oh, bollocks.* She turned to face her cousin who looked very smart, if a little sweaty, in his day jacket.

"Hello, Dickie. What brings you here?" Clementine asked casually, as if they had a habit of meeting at Buckingham Palace.

"One might ask you the same," Dickie said with a raised brow.

"Oh, I simply felt like a bit of a break from the country air. You know, the hustle of the city, some shopping, perhaps. I hear they have a wonderful new selection of gloves at Harrods."

"Indeed. And you do know that Harrods is not actually inside the palace? The gloves here are for the queen only."

"Very funny," Clementine said, smoothing a nonexistent wrinkle on her skirt.

"You look nice, Cousin," Dickie noted.

"Why thank you, I do try my best," Clementine beamed, and shifted slightly as if to move past him. He did not budge.

"Yes, you look as if you're trying to impress someone," Dickie eyed Clementine. She held his gaze and he held hers, as they had done when debating who could get the last piece of seed cake, or who would confess to a broken window after they had played war with apples. Clementine knew this could take some time, which she simply did not have. She had to give her cousin some explanation for her sudden day trip to Buckingham Palace alone.

"Fine," she huffed, and glared at him. He smirked, knowing he had won, as he often did when comparing with his supreme powers of patience to Clementine's lack thereof.

"Out with it," Dickie encouraged.

"Walk with me and I'll explain." She gestured to him to follow her through the main hall, towards the stately rooms where the queen often held her scheduled audiences. Dickie fell in beside her and they made their way through the crowds of nobles, members of parliament, guards, soldiers, and many members of the Queen's personal service.

"I am going to meet the queen," she whispered, "Uninvited."

Dickie stopped, forcing Clementine to pause as well. They pretended to eye a particularly interesting bust of King Henry VIII when a pair of the royal guard passed them.

"I knew you would try something outrageous," Dickie said with a glint in his eye, but without judgement. He had always encouraged her to be the adventurous one, since it meant less effort from him when they were up to no good.

"Which is why we need to keep moving. I can't be late for the appointment Her Majesty has at noon."

Dickie half-laughed and half-shook his head, but agreed to continue walking towards the huge French doors ahead.

"Ah, so you will try to convince Will — that's Mr Hunt — to let you ride along on his audience with the queen? That is a wonderful show of confidence, even for you," he snickered, "I truly wish I could witness this exchange, but alas I am needed elsewhere. You will tell me how it went?"

"Only if you promise not to breathe a word of this to your parents," Clementine said. "I need to appeal to Her Majesty to let me do something, anything, to help find the truth about my father, instead of waiting seven years at worst before he is presumed dead. By which time, your mother will have me married off to some horribly boring man I will never love. You understand why I'm doing this? Please, Dickie," she pleaded.

Dickie appeared mortified. "You know I would never tell on you. Well, anymore, that is," he winked. "As far as I know you were shopping for the most outrageous pair of gloves they have at Harrods."

Clementine laughed. "Thank you, Dickie. And wish me luck." She gestured with her eyes at the man guarding the door. "I still need to get to Mr Hunt to make my case."

They made their way towards the next pair of large, ornamental wooden doors, where a guard gestured for them to stop. "What business do you have here?" he asked gruffly.

"I have an appointment with the queen at noon," Clementine said. "Lady Clementine Whitham, daughter of the Earl of Whitham."

"I was informed only of one person for the audience at noon," the guard said, unimpressed.

"Oh, for heaven's sake, man," Dickie interrupted, before Clementine could think of a way to persuade the stone-faced guard. "I am the son of Duke Clearwater. This is my cousin, and she is to accompany Mr Hunt to the audience with Her Majesty. I take it that Mr Hunt is already in the waiting area?"

The guard's face shifted only slightly at Dickie's authoritative voice, which sounded surprisingly like his mother's. Clementine hid her smile with her fan, as if she were anxious of the situation.

"You would not wish to make Lady Whitham late. And," Dickie paused for dramatic effect, "have the queen wait?"

That seemed to settle it, and the guard grudgingly opened the door to the waiting area.

"Good luck," Dickie mouthed, just as Clementine slipped through the door. She beamed at him behind her fan. She still had a good twenty minutes or so to convince Mr Hunt of her plan before they would be summoned to the audience. Clementine certainly hoped it would be a summoning for them both, and not just Mr Hunt. She could barely think of the humiliation if he denied her request.

CLEMENTINE'S SKIRTS swished as she walked into the quiet waiting area. The thick carpets muted the clicking of her heels and the windows let in filtered sunlight. It was a calm room, and she wished she were allowed to just throw herself on one of the plush velvet-covered sofas and enjoy a book. No such luxury today, unfortunately. Today, she would interject herself into an audience with Queen Victoria, and Mr Hunt would help her.

Just act naturally. She forced her shoulders to relax. Two guards and one particular gentleman occupied the room, and he stared at her in disbelief as she approached him.

Armed with her most radiant smile and her iron fan, Clementine squared her shoulders and marched right up to Mr Hunt.

"Ah, Mr Hunt. I'm so glad to see that I'm not late for our appointment with Her Majesty," she exclaimed, loud enough for the guards to hear. With her eyes, she hoped she conveyed a look of: *I will explain, play along!* She held out her hand for him to kiss and he obliged with built-in good manners, rising from a sofa to greet her with a light touch of his lips to her knuckles.

"Lady Clementine. With gloves, this time." He dropped her hand as if unimpressed. She confronted his green and narrowed eyes without flinching and proceeded to put aside her parasol before making sure her slanted hat was still in place.

"Yes, well. We do not have much time." She smiled a rather toothy smile at him and lowered her voice, "I know you have an audience with Her Majesty about the disappearance of my father. I want to be there. No — I have a right to be there. It is as simple as that. Please agree to take me along so I can plead to Her Majesty to–"

"To what, exactly?" Mr Hunt interrupted, "What on earth do you hope to gain by imposing on my audience with the queen?" He did not sound approving at all.

"Why, my freedom, obviously. Eventually." Clementine couldn't believe he did not understand why she was here. Had he not paid attention to her grave position, which was so openly discussed yesterday?

His green eyes were like cold emeralds at this point, and a grim expression had replaced his usual amused look. Clementine hoped she could still turn this discussion around, but with time running out she had to decide if she should plead for his conscience to help her or threaten to cause a scene if he didn't. The latter would risk being denied entry to meet the queen. The guards would likely throw both of them out of Buckingham Palace before a word of protest could be uttered.

Clementine did not like to be a damsel in distress, unless absolutely necessary, so she sighed and sat down calmly, inviting Mr Hunt to sit beside her, which he did not.

"Mr Hunt, I am a woman of determination, and I do not back down once I have made up my mind. I know we share at least one of these qualities. So allow me to make it perfectly clear: I will not sit by and be married off while waiting for others to find out what happened to *my* father and *my* inheritance and *my* prospects. I simply cannot allow that. If you were in my position, you would not sit idly by or let yourself be married off to some old bore." Clementine paused as she noticed a slightest twitch at the corner of his lips. She cleared her throat and tore her eyes from his smile. "I suggest you take me with you to the audience so I can plead my case. You need not do anything else, and I promise to behave immaculately. You will not regret this."

He crossed his hands and looked down at her, which made it seem as if he were towering above her, given their height difference. She really wished he had taken her invitation to sit. It was hurting her neck to be constantly looking up at him.

"I sense there is something else coming up after this little speech," Mr Hunt mused. "Let's say I refuse, because who in their right mind would bring an unannounced, additional guest to Her Majesty? Especially a guest who might decide to jump off the windowsill, scale the walls, or whack the guards with her fan — or perhaps the parasol?"

Clementine blinked, or tried to bat her eyelashes, as if she did not know what he was talking about. It was true she could do all those things, in theory.

He leaned close to her and whispered, "Tell me, how exactly is any of this beneficial to me?"

She smiled sweetly, trying not to be distracted by how close he was and the scent of fresh soap that seemed to radiate from him and fill her senses most peculiarly.

"Ah, Mr Hunt, are you asking if I will make it worth your while?" she whispered back with a curved smile, which she dropped a second later. "The answer is no, Mr Hunt. I will not pay you with whatever indecent proposition you might have in your mind, but I will make it more difficult for you to walk away from this situation without causing a scene. We wouldn't want that now, would we? Only a few minutes left before the audience, so either we see the queen together, or neither of us see her. I apparently have a questionable reputation in the marriage market already, and I really don't mind making myself even more undesirable, if that's what it comes to, but how about you? Do you want to be in the middle of a scene with someone like me? Here's what I suggest: how about you give us that charming smile of yours and tuck away that frown, so we can get on with this and rid ourselves of one another's company?" She let her smile curve back onto her lips and flicked her fan open to finish her point.

His eyebrows had gone up as she spoke, and he finally

barked a laugh that echoed in the waiting room. Clementine couldn't help but glance at the guards, but they seemed unimpressed for now. Mr Hunt shook his head and rubbed his forehead.

"That was quite the speech, Lady Clementine. I cannot imagine I have ever heard a lady speak in this manner to an acquaintance she met yesterday. I admit you are brave for a member of your gender, but there is just one problem."

He turned on that radiant smirk and his eyes seemed to burn into Clementine. She felt her heart flutter and cursed herself. *Do not let him distract you!*

"And what's that?" she half whispered, half hissed.

"You assume that I have a reputation to care about." He smiled and leaned even closer, until his mouth was scandalously close to her ear. When the air from his mouth tickled her neck, she felt shivers in places she blushed to even think about.

"But if it is a scandal you wish to cause," he murmured, his voice almost a purr, "I might know one or two ways to get us kicked out of here that you would not know of." He chuckled. "Yet."

Clementine gave a soft, almost silent gasp, but knew he had heard her from the glint in his eyes. She could feel herself blushing, and hastily covered her chest with her fan, knowing somehow that it was too late to hide her reaction.

"You are exactly the outrageous rake they say you are," she whispered , trying to keep her quickened breath from creeping into her voice. "I am this close to slapping you again with my fan, Mr Hunt."

He smirked and straightened himself. "That might well be true, but it won't change the outcome of this little tête-à-tête. I win this argument. There is no such scenario on this earth in which I would take you with me, other than to bed, and that too only if you begged me."

Clementine's jaw dropped at his words and her eyes filled

with fire at the audacity of him daring to make her feel like some desperate girl! She rose slowly, grabbing her parasol in one hand while holding her iron fan in the other. She stood there, as if handling dual wielding weapons — which, technically, they were. A parasol made a good enough substitute sword, after all.

"You are the most vexing man I have ever met," she hissed at his handsome face, and that amused smirk which seemed so sure everything would always go his way.

But before Clementine could utter one more word of outrage, a pair of tall doors opened, demanding both Clementine and Mr Hunt's attention.

A man came out, and Clementine corrected her posture at once. She hastily lowered her parasol and fan and tried to make herself look like she belonged here. Confidence until proven otherwise. The smartly dressed, older man was none other than Sir Henry Postonby, private secretary of the queen. He glanced at his papers, nodding to himself.

"Her Majesty is ready to receive Mr William Hunt," he announced in a dry and raspy voice that betrayed no emotion or interest towards the guests.

Mr Hunt looked at Clementine and mouthed 'goodbye' with a grin, proceeding towards the doors. Clementine was about to either scream, faint, or throw her fan at him. Anything to stop him from going inside without her. Then Sir Henry glanced at her, and again at his paper. His stern glance put pause to Clementine's plans of mayhem for just a moment.

"And Lady Clementine Whitham," Sir Henry continued, earning an astonished look from Mr Hunt. "Please come this way."

Sir Henry went ahead and Clementine followed, past the stunned Mr Hunt. She gave him a sweet smile as she strutted into the next room with a sway of draped skirts that trailed behind her. Inside her mind, she wanted to scream with joy and rub it in Mr Hunt's face until that smirk was gone. But as a lady, she obviously could do nothing of the kind. Well, not right now, anyway.

Sir Henry led them further into the depths of the palace and past the first stately room. Clementine looked around her with open curiosity and ignored the glare of Mr Hunt as he fell in beside her. She'd never been in these rooms, so she might as well have a look while she had the chance. The heavily carpeted corridor was lit by newly installed electric lamps, and she would have loved to stop and have a closer look at this modern technology, which was seen as magic by some. Alas, she got no chance to gawk. They passed massive portraits covering the walls and Clementine's imagination began to paint secret doors behind the man-sized frames, along with secret staircases that would lead them all the way to bursting treasure rooms and other mysteries that must lie beneath the palace. She couldn't help herself from feeling a little excitement.

"Do you think there are many secret passages in the palace?"

Mr Hunt's frown softened a little and an amused look lit those green eyes.

"I dare not guess, but with the history of this place, one would think there are secret passages for many reasons." His eyes seemed to take in Clementine and her cheeks felt warm. He did not say anything inappropriate, but Clementine felt his gaze on her every feature, as if no detail could escape it.

"Yes, well." She cleared her throat and adjusted her parasol in her left hand. "For evacuation reasons, assuredly, there would be secret passages. I was wondering more in terms of secrets, perhaps forgotten treasure rooms of old, or some such," she whispered back dreamily.

"And passageways for lovers to meet and fulfill their needs," Mr Hunt said, as if he were simply commenting on the weather, but his lowered voice sent shivers up Clementine's spine.

She would not be intimidated by such talk, like some fifteen-year-old maiden still waiting for her first season in society. She had seen things, heard things, and despite her cheeks burning, her voice did not betray any surprise.

"That might well be true," she said, sounding very academic, "I of course do not refer to our current royal couple, but in the past there have been many with more interesting appetites in the matters of romance. Secret passageways likely were very convenient for the purposes of secret meetings and, um, acts of," she stumbled slightly with her words, "love," she concluded.

Mr Hunt chuckled. "Well played, Lady Clementine, up until the word 'love', you could almost have convinced me of your practical knowledge of secret trysts." He shook his head with a smirk.

She frowned. "And what of it? Is that word not something you are accustomed to, Mr Hunt?"

"Such a frosty tone, and yet your cheeks burn brightly, Lady Clementine," he leaned in to whisper as they turned yet another corner in this maze of corridors, "I rather believe it is you who has very little knowledge of love." He lowered his voice even more, until it was almost a murmur, "Or the joy of casual passion." He smiled as she gave the faintest gasp at his use of the word. "And your reaction tells me that, in fact, you know very little of life, Lady Clementine."

"Perhaps," she said, and cast an annoyed look at him. "But it is hardly my choice that my sex is treated in such a way that we are given very little opportunity, or encouragement, to seek experiences in life."

Before Mr Hunt could retort, Sir Henry finally stopped in front of an average looking door and glared at them, as if urging them to say no more. Clementine was slightly disappointed that the door was not behind a painting.

"The queen will receive you in her private rooms due to the confidentiality of this meeting."

She could hardly believe what she was hearing. Her Majesty's private rooms?

Sir Henry turned to Clementine and Mr Hunt. "Please refrain from commenting on the passageways, and the reasons for them. It is hardly a suitable topic." He cast a reprimanding glance at Clementine especially. Her jaw dropped, wanting to explain her curiosity, but Sir Henry simply raised his hand.

"Her Majesty awaits," he said formally, and opened the door for them. "After you, Lady Clementine. Mr Hunt."

* * *

THE TWO OF them stepped into a rather cozy looking sitting room. The tall windows provided plenty of light, with a fireplace dominating one wall and a bookshelf covering the other wall entirely. Persian rugs covered the floors in different patterns of blues, reds and gold, and a portrait of the queen's parents hung above the massive fireplace. In front of the windows and their heavy golden drapes was a large desk made of one solid piece of wood. The desk was piled with papers and books and pens, as well as a red briefcase. And behind the table, Queen Victoria sat writing, her figure old but regal, as was her wide mourning dress.

"Lady Clementine Whitham and Mr Hunt, ma'am," Sir Henry announced, and closed the door behind him before going to stand beside the queen's table. Clementine dropped to a formal curtsy, her skirts spreading elegantly around her, and saw from the corner of her eye that Mr Hunt bowed with equal elegance.

Queen Victoria finished her sentence without hurry, lay down her pen, and only then did she rise and approach her guests.

"Good of you to come."

"Your Majesty," they both said.

The queen was a short woman, and Clementine stood eye to eye with Her Majesty while Mr Hunt towered above them both. The queen's black dress, with plenty of detailed lace, did not compliment her in any way, and Clementine felt a pang of sadness over this once beautiful and joyful woman who had lost her love so soon, choosing to forever dress in mourning clothes. Stern and sorrowful, but still the most powerful woman in the world. Clementine was careful to keep her face neutral and pleasant as she felt the queen study her. In Her Majesty's eyes, which Clementine met calmly, there was something beneath the cold and serious exterior. A glint of curiosity, perhaps?

"Lady Clementine, Mr Hunt," Her Majesty said, gesturing to the small sitting area near the fireplace, "Please have a seat."

"Thank you, ma'am," Mr Hunt nodded, and Clementine followed him to a sofa that seated both of them, since it was quite clear that the individual, plush chair was reserved for Her Majesty only. Clementine set her parasol next to her and kept her fan on her lap, willing it to help her focus and soothe her nerves as it usually did.

"You must be wondering what Lady Clementine is doing here," the queen said to Mr Hunt. She carefully lowered herself to the edge of the chair, as if her stiff dress would not allow her to sit more comfortably. Or perhaps that too was a choice she made.

"Yes, ma'am. I admit I was surprised." He glanced at Clementine, who in turn cocked her eyebrow at him.

"Well, my dear Lady Clementine. Would you like to explain to Mr Hunt why exactly you are here?" There was a definite note of amusement in Her Majesty's voice, which Clementine liked, and she nodded eagerly, but not too eagerly. One mustn't show too much emotion in front of Her Majesty.

"Thank you, ma'am. I must admit I was surprised to hear that you were expecting me. I am here because I am my father's daughter. He would not let anything get in his way, and he taught me that same determination to make sure I do whatever I can to change my circumstances, as much as I am able. So I am here to plead my case, ma'am. Mr Hunt is going back to seek the item my father had been assigned to find before he disappeared, and I wish to accompany him to find my father at all costs." She drew a deep breath.

Mr Hunt looked like he wanted to say something, but the queen spoke first.

"And why is this so important to you? Why not let Mr Hunt go, and send you any information he might find? Why would you wish to leave your home and your suitors? I understand you have yet to secure yourself a proposal, Lady Clementine." Her small but sharp eyes demanded honesty and Clementine felt as if she were a child giving her grandmother an explanation for some kind of foolishness.

The queen's presence made Clementine feel small. She steeled herself with a quick reminder that if she could not convince the queen, this would all be for nothing. And if she couldn't find the courage to give the queen an honest answer, how on earth would she go on an adventure that required travelling to strange new places on her own, or with the insufferable Mr Hunt? *Deep breaths*, Clementine thought, and tried to relax her shoulders. She met the queen's eyes and tried to imagine herself pleading to her long-gone mother instead of her sovereign.

"Ma'am, if I may speak without decorum?" Clementine hesitated, but continued after the slightest nods from Her Majesty.

"As you well know, our sex is limited by many rules and restrictions of society. And to be honest, I find the rules sometimes very silly and unworthy of the intelligence of the many bright, talented women I know. Their abilities and curiosity for knowledge are wasted on seeking only for the best match they can get in marriage."

Clementine was exaggerating a little, as many of her female

acquaintances did not display much interest in anything else but the latest gossip over which bachelor was the most eligible, and which of the competing ladies had embarrassed themselves with a wrong word, gesture, or outfit.

"You find the rules of my society silly, Lady Clementine?" the queen interrupted, and Clementine fought hard not to show herself flinching. She cast a quick sideways glance to Mr Hunt, who looked at her with raised eyebrows, a slight smile playing on his lips. He clearly found this amusing and was waiting for Clementine to make a fool of herself.

Clementine hurried to correct herself, "Apologies, ma'am. The last thing I want to do is to cause offense. I find certain rules silly when they limit the potential of half the population." She paused for a moment to see if the queen would interrupt her, or call the guards to toss her out on the streets for such insolence. Clementine trusted her instincts, and her intuition was that the most powerful woman in the world knew something about said silly limitations on the female gender. Likely Her Majesty had herself fought to break many of those rules in her many years as the sovereign of her empire. The queen nodded and Clementine let out a breath before continuing.

"You are the queen of half the world, so I plead to Your Majesty's sympathy in what it means to be a woman without such power, while having the urgent — no, *basic* need of deciding one's fate and fortune, instead of always letting others decide for you. The only person who ever listened to my wishes on what I want to do with my life was my father. He is everything to me and he is missing. It tears me to pieces not to know what has happened to him. Even more so, it pains me to stay behind and not go looking for him. I am his daughter, his only child, and his heir apparent, as was his wish, so it should be me going to Egypt to find out if he is truly dead or not. It is not only my love for my father that drives me forward but also my own future." Clementine paused for a quick breath and to see if the queen would have her shut her mouth.

"If I were his son, his only male heir, I would be allowed and expected to go and find whatever evidence I could to have him officially declared dead. I would have the sympathy of everyone for having to wait for my inheritance for seven long years. No one would question a son going alone to Egypt, or even into the depths of the earth to either find his father or secure the family fortune. But as a woman I am to wait for people like Mr Hunt here to go and forward me their information, if and when any arises," she gestured passionately at him.

"Careful now, Lady Clementine," he said in a low voice. "I assure you, I did all I could to find your father before I returned, and will do so again when I return to Egypt."

Clementine glared at him, and the queen observed the two of them with a keen interest that Clementine took as encouragement to continue her plea.

"Yes, Mr Hunt, and I am very grateful to you, truly," she said, trying to sound sincere. He frowned slightly, clearly not fooled. "But you have no personal stake here," Clementine said firmly. "You do not have anything to lose, one way or the other. I, on the other hand, have everything to lose: my father, my fortune and eventually my freedom when my aunt decides to marry me off as soon as anyone suitable enough asks. I do not wish to marry someone I do not want to be married to."

Clementine turned her eyes to the queen and pleaded on the one thing she could be certain of: a chance for a love match.

"Ma'am, the world knows of your great true love for Prince Albert, may he rest in peace. I ask that I am given the best chance to have what you had together: a happy marriage based on true love and mutual respect. If I am married off to the first or only person who offers to take me, it will not be by my choice or consent, and thus I will lose my chance to have what you had in your marriage. I wish to have that chance."

Clementine left out the fact that she did not necessarily want to be married, ever. The queen would likely not want to hear that.

"Without my father's situation cleared, and my fortune locked away from me for seven years, I will be an even more unattractive option for marriage, and the selection of suitable matches will be limited. I am sure, ma'am, that you are familiar with my unfortunate family history, with the marriage of my father and mother ending in disgrace..."

Clementine felt a sour taste for saying anything bad about her parents. They had been so happy, once, but she would use all she could to stir feelings of sympathy, kindness or even pity in the queen.

"So please, ma'am, this is what I have come to plead from you: let me go to Egypt. I know that as an unmarried woman it is not proper to travel there alone, but allow me to at least accompany Mr Hunt so we may search for my father together. I admit I have not seen much of the world, but I am well-studied, speak several languages, and am more than able to defend my honour if needed. I will not be a burden. Instead, I might even be helpful to the search for the treasure my father was investigating, the Tears of Hathor."

Mr Hunt turned sharply at Clementine's words, and even the queen shifted slightly in her chair. Clementine felt something change in the atmosphere of the room. Had she gone too far? She cared little of what Mr Hunt thought of her travelling with him — after all, it was only a compromise she suggested, since she would never be allowed to travel alone as a young, unmarried lady.

"We will get back to your request for the journey in a moment," the queen said, "How do you know of the Tears of Hathor?"

"Oh," Clementine said, "My father often sent me letters where he told me about his travels in as much detail as he could.

In his final letter, he said he was coming closer to finding the tomb of the high priestess of Hathor."

"Indeed, how remarkable," the queen said. "And did he tell you anything else?" she asked, and Clementine felt the question hang heavily in the air.

"Well, he did send me copies of some of the hieroglyphs he had discovered. He was very good at sketching, much better than me," she smiled, even though a feeling of sadness threatened to overcome her. "I have been studying history all my life and have the knowledge of reading hieroglyphs."

"Really?" Mr Hunt could not help interrupting with disbelief.

Clementine cast an irritated look at him. "Yes, really. Believe or not, I have other interests than attending every ball and dinner and picnic of the season. Not that there's anything wrong with social events," she quickly added to Her Majesty, "I only meant that I have accumulated a knowledge of history through my own interest and my father's support. He saw it as a useful exercise to send me hieroglyphs to translate, and other oddities to try and solve from his travels."

"He shouldn't have–" Mr Hunt started, but the queen interrupted him with a look.

"Sir Henry," she called over her shoulder. Clementine had already forgotten the queen's private secretary, who had almost become part of the room's decor with his silent and still demeanor.

"I think we could benefit from some tea," the queen said. "This will take a while longer."

THE EXTRAORDINARY TREASURE HUNTERS

*I*t took a very short time for a maid to bring in a tray of tea and fine little cakes. Clementine did not feel like having tea at all, but one did not decline an offer of refreshments with the queen — even Clementine had enough manners to realise that. So she accepted a cup from the maid, noticing how a single red hair had fallen on her cup of steaming darjeeling. She decided to pay no attention to it, not wanting to cause the maid to lose her position due to such a small mistake as that. Clementine could hardly imagine her maid Mary ever bringing her a cup with hair in it, but she sympathised with accidents. So she tried to discreetly take the hair out while adding milk into her cup. In doing so, she almost spilled it all on her dress, and tried to play it off as a natural clumsiness. Mr Hunt, meanwhile, took his cup with plenty of sugar and milk. Clementine glanced at him, surprised.

"I did not think that you had a sweet tooth, Mr Hunt," she commented, as the queen helped herself to the little lavender and strawberry macaroons. One did not eat or drink anything other than what Her Majesty did, and when Her Majesty was finished, one did not continue to eat and drink. Mr Hunt took two macaroons and Clementine followed suit.

"I was brought up with the firm belief that tea is good for you only with plenty of sugar and cream. That's how my nanny used to teach me anyway. I do believe she secretly disliked tea and tried to cover the taste as much as she could," he smiled, and to Clementine's surprise the queen smiled as well.

"Ah, Mr Hunt, in that, you and I share a memory. My governess was much the same. Coming from Germany, she did not take to tea culture, and preferred to make it as sweet as possible to compensate for the bitterness. I did try to explain that there were other types of tea, or other ways of brewing it, but she was set in her ways."

Her Majesty sighed and bit into the first little macaroon. Clementine hurried to eat hers and found the fluffy almond pastry quite dreamy with its creamy filling. She licked the excess cream from her lip and it did not escape her attention that Mr Hunt's eyes stayed on her. His gaze glinted with a different kind of hunger, which again made her feel as if she was being hunted. She hoped not to blush in front of the queen and fought a scowl. Clearly Mr Hunt would do anything to distract her!

"I see you enjoy macaroons, Lady Clementine," Her Majesty commented.

"Yes, ma'am. I have never tasted them quite so delicately made," Clementine admitted, and sipped her tea.

"Good, you like food that is not English, it will help you in your future journeys," the queen nodded.

Clementine's heart jumped to her throat.

"Ma'am?" Mr Hunt's eyes turned away from Clementine. The queen raised her hand and he clamped his mouth shut.

"It may surprise you, but your plea has touched me, as I am sure you intended it to, Lady Clementine. I give you points for trying to convince me both with emotional and logical persuasion instead of falling on your knees and crying over your desperate situation. I like that very much in a young lady and I have no patience for hysterics. Women like us, who wish to do extraordinary things, must walk a fine balance that often involves judging the correct ratio of emotion and logic. Add into that courage, even if you are unsure of yourself, and you will get far in life, Lady Clementine."

Clementine didn't know what to say. She felt as if she had just received the greatest honour of her life.

"I will give you what you want, and we shall see if it truly is what you wished for," Her Majesty said, and ate the last macaroon in one bite,

"Ma'am, I must protest," Mr Hunt exclaimed, perhaps too sharply, for the queen merely glanced at him.

"We shall speak later, Mr Hunt." The queen waved her hand and sipped her tea. Clementine and Mr Hunt waited and finished their cups as well.

"Now then," the queen said, "What will be discussed now shall not leave this room, Lady Clementine. There are precious few one can trust these days, and your history — with your mother and her unfortunate actions — does not make this an easy decision." The queen paused, and Clementine realised that an acknowledgement was expected of her.

"Yes, ma'am, I understand. I am my mother's daughter in every good quality, but I am no traitor." The mere uttering of that word felt like ash in her mouth. She still did not accept her mother as a traitor, no matter what people said. There must have been a mistake, a grave misunderstanding. But to a British person, a foreigner was first and foremost an oddity, suspicious by default, and thus judged more harshly.

"Indeed, if memory serves, your mother did possess some very good qualities for navigating society in her, well, position. It is unfortunate how those same good qualities led to her ultimate betrayal." The queen shook her head. "Let us not dwell in the past. You, my dear, have motivation, and I believe personal risk or benefit is the best kind of motivation. All of your reasons to go and find your father are important ones. That is why I trust you will do exactly what is needed."

"What is that, ma'am?"

The queen smiled at Clementine. "Did your father ever tell you what the Tears of Hathor are?"

"Yes and no, ma'am. I was able to read some of the descriptions and legend from the hieroglyphs, and my father told me what he knew of them, but," she hesitated, "I do not know if the Tears of Hathor are real or a myth. They are not confirmed in any known history. Only bits and pieces are left, like a rumor."

The queen nodded. "Yes, that is accurate. The Tears of Hathor are said to contain either the tears of the ancient goddess herself, or an elixir of some kind, made by the last high priestess of Hathor, and the legend tells of the power the tears contain. Now, I realise that in the age of technical and scientific advancement, there is very little room for anything unnatural or extraordinary." The queen's thin lips turned to a smile, "Still, even in this era, people look to mystics, host seances, and experience the impossible. So could it be that some of the old legends are true, to some extent? Perhaps. It would not be the first time a legend had a piece of truth buried in it. I commissioned your father, together with Mr Hunt, to find and retrieve the Tears of Hathor for me, for the crown, by all means necessary, and in secret."

"Oh," Clementine exclaimed, looking at Mr Hunt, "I did not know they held such importance to you, ma'am. I knew my father had the favour of the late Prince Albert, but I thought Papa was an adventurer, and a public one too."

"If I may," Mr Hunt said, and the queen nodded. "Your father's public role as an adventurer, explorer and historian made the perfect facade for performing secret missions for the crown without raising unnecessary attention or suspicion from other interested parties."

Clementine looked at him as if he were speaking a language she did not understand. She blinked, trying to comprehend what was being insinuated.

"Other interested parties?" She looked between Her Majesty and Mr Hunt.

"Yes, always assume there are other interested parties. There is suspicion that someone might have intercepted the Tears of Hathor and either killed your father or kidnapped him," Mr Hunt said with a sigh.

"Why did you not tell this before, when you told our entire family that Father had simply gone missing in a sandstorm?!" Clementine's voice raised an octave before she remembered again in whose company they were. "Apologies, ma'am," she bowed her head to the queen, who waved the apology away.

"Pish, if you are to be one of my Extraordinary Treasure Hunters, you will need to learn to apologise less. Now then, I am delighted to see you two get along so well, it will make your travels much easier, I am sure. It is good that a man and a woman work together on equal terms. If you, Lady Clementine, can actually match this young rascal's mind and words halfway, then I think this will be a good start to your adventure."

"I must protest, ma'am, surely someone more experienced–" Mr Hunt started, his face grim, even if his voice strived to stay pleasant.

"You have protested, I have considered it and overruled it, Mr Hunt," the queen said with a finality that reminded everyone that this old grandmother was their sovereign, and her word was law.

"Yes, ma'am," Mr Hunt said, but made no secret of being unhappy about the decision as he glanced at Clementine. She merely raised an eyebrow, taunting him to say more in the presence of Her Majesty. Then she turned back to the queen.

"If I may, I have many questions," she said slowly, trying to organise her thoughts. "Most importantly: what are the Extraordinary Treasure Hunters? Secondly: why are the Tears of Hathor so valuable to the crown that a secret mission is needed to search for them? And thirdly: how am I to travel with Mr Hunt without a chaperone? Wouldn't that be the end of us — well, the end of me — in society? I do not care for my reputation, but I think of my aunt, uncle and cousin," she said with a pang of fear. She did not want the queen to withdraw her generous suggestion, but she hesitated to cause shame that might negatively impact them in such a way.

"Mr Hunt, why don't you answer Lady Clementine's first two questions and leave the last one to me?" the queen smiled.

"Yes, ma'am. I am a member of The Extraordinary Treasure Hunters. I do not know how many there are of us in the direct service of Her Majesty, guided by Sir Henry."

The older man at the desk nodded, his pen scratching endless notes of the meeting.

"We are pledged to give our best skills to the crown in order to retrieve important, strategically critical items from around the world. We have Her Majesty's personal guarantee of all costs covered, and permission to use all means necessary to obtain the items and eliminate possible competition."

Mr Hunt watched the words sink into Clementine's understanding. Her eyes widened slightly but she only nodded for him to continue.

"We are experts in many different fields, and our expertise is used to find objects that are often things of legend, with barely any evidence of them being real. They are sometimes items of mysterious powers, or so the myths say, and we cannot know exactly if they exist, but we will seek until we can either confirm their existence and bring them back, or make sure our competition does not retrieve them."

"So, by competition, you mean other countries? Spies?"

The queen nodded. "Yes, Lady Clementine. Either domestic or international spies with similar missions. Our network is vast, but so is theirs, and we need to do whatever we can to make sure this dynasty has the upper hand." For the first time, Clementine heard passion behind the queen's morbid looks and dry voice.

"I see," Clementine said, "And the Tears of Hathor, what power is it that you seek in them?"

Mr Hunt continued, "They are said to have the gift of fertility, as well as other healing powers. Imagine if we could analyse the elixir and make more of it. How many lives could be saved in our nation with the healing aspects of the elixir? Soldiers who might survive wars? Sovereigns who could rule forever?"

"And how many critical heirs my children and their children could produce, should the fertility powers of the Tears be true. It would mean world peace, if our family's royal lineage could continue endlessly," the queen said, her eyes bright with hope for once. Clementine imagined it was a look more witnessed in the queen's days of youth.

"Alright, I think I understand, though it is difficult to accept that this form of magic is real," Clementine could not help saying. Her head was spinning from all this information. It would take some time and evidence to believe that magic could exist in the form of these mysterious artefacts, but she suspected this was not the place for that discussion. Hazy memories of her own strange encounters threatened to emerge, but Clementine pushed those thoughts away. She needed to focus on sealing this deal. "Am I now then recruited to this group ? How will this work?" Clementine bit her lip. "And then there was my third question."

The queen smiled with a little too much delight, and Clementine felt a bad omen in the look she gave her and Mr Hunt.

"I am taking you on as a replacement candidate for your

father. Do this mission well, and you might have a *job*, as the people say," the queen chuckled. "A job for a lifetime, serving the crown. I do not care about your family background, nor of your ethnicity. The Extraordinary Treasure Hunters rarely meet one another — it is not advised, in fact — but they come from all classes and areas of the world. Here are my terms, Lady Clementine: First, you will seek evidence of what caused your father's disappearance, who was behind it, if anyone, and what was his fate."

The queen and Mr Hunt exchanged a glance that Clementine could not interpret, so she merely nodded.

"Secondly, you will follow Mr Hunt's lead, as he is the more senior of the two of you, both in age and in experience. However, I expect you to challenge him, Lady Clementine, and keep his self-assuredness in check. Is that understood?" Her Majesty aimed this question mostly at Mr Hunt, who nodded with a frown.

"And thirdly, you will report only to me or Sir Henry. The Extraordinary Treasure Hunters, their purpose, and your mission will stay an absolute secret. The crown will cover your expenses and give you a plentiful fee for your work, but understand this: should anything go wrong in… let us say, in a diplomatic context, the crown will not have any knowledge of you having worked for us. In such a situation, you will be on your own without any hope for any official cavalry. Lastly: you will leave as soon as possible, once the necessary arrangements have been handled and your passage secured for the soonest steamer. Do you accept the terms?" the queen asked.

Clementine was hit by one of those feelings her mother had described just before she had been sent into exile. She had said that sometimes you could feel clearly when you reached a crossroads of sorts in your life, and a decision needed to be made that would change everything.

Clementine was never one to hesitate out of fear, nor did she do so now. Her head was swimming, but she needed just one more answer. Everything else could come later, once she had time to think and compartmentalise her whirling thoughts.

"Yes, ma'am, I accept, as I am sure you knew I would," Clementine said, and earned a tiny smile from Her Majesty for her frankness. "But I believe my third question is still unanswered for now. How will Mr Hunt and I travel together without causing a scandal that will affect the reputations of our families? As said, I do not care for my reputation, but I worry for my family and would not wish for them to suffer because of something I did. I understand I am to have no maid with me to chaperone, which is not a problem for me. If we are to keep this a secret, it is better that fewer people are involved and I am perfectly capable of maintaining my clothes and looks, tying my own corsets–" Clementine interrupted herself when Mr Hunt started to laugh silently at her babbling of corset strings. *Of all things*, she thought, mortified at her words to Her Majesty.

The queen actually chuckled, and fanned herself with a dark fan that matched her mourning dress, right down to the embroidery and beading details. "That is very good to hear, Lady Clementine. A woman who cannot even dress herself when needed is not a useful one, now, is she?"

The queen leaned closer, and her fan resembled a cat's tail just before it pounced.

"How indeed could the two of you travel together without causing shame to your respectable families? I believe there is one thing we can arrange to make it possible, and here I will again measure if you have the motivation to follow this through, Lady Clementine."

She glanced at Mr Hunt, who had suddenly paled and was staring at Clementine.

"Mr Hunt is already a fully pledged member, and he knows to accept whatever terms I state," the queen mused.

Clementine's heartbeat sped up, and she felt as if the whole room were heaving. One part of her mind knew what the queen was about to suggest, but the other side refused to accept or acknowledge what she also had deduced to be the only possible way. She glanced at Mr Hunt. The intensity of his gaze scared her — or, perhaps not — she wasn't sure if she was afraid or if the hum in her head was merely her own disbelief. One look into his green eyes had her breathing quickening, and she actually feared she might faint right there before the queen. She took deep breaths to try to make the room stop spinning and turned back to Her Majesty, who looked even more amused.

"Yes, my dears, you will need to get engaged and pretend to be freshly in love with each other. We will explain it as one of those love-at-first-sight moments. Just as I had with dear Albert," the queen's voice took on a dreamy tone, even after all these decades. Clementine unfortunately had very little sympathy now. She looked at Mr Hunt, who had recovered his composure somewhat, and appeared to observe the situation as if he were an outsider.

Infuriating man, Clementine thought, not for the first or last time.

"So, do you accept? We will draft a letter to your families, telling them of your happy decision and how it is very much blessed by the crown. A formal, royal dowry will be promised as well, due to the unfortunate situation of Lady Clementine's assets. That should make your families happy enough."

"I–" Clementine cleared her throat, "I accept, but this is for pretense only?" She hastily glanced at Mr Hunt, who annoyingly did not appear fussed.

"Oh no, my dear. You will have to make it believable , as it is all part of your role as a potential member of the Extraordinary Treasure Hunters . Whatever your disguise, you must always try to play it to perfection, Otherwise people will wonder, and that will lead to nothing good when trying your hand at international affairs. We do not often have women in this group, but those who have given their gifts to us are paired to another male member, engaged, and eventually married to keep up their roles while they travel. Should this arrangement not work for the two of you, calling off the engagement publicly is, of course, an option." The queen paused and wrinkled her nose as if with distaste. "And divorce as a final, most radical option, as you well know, due to your mother's actions."

"I understand," Clementine said in a husky voice. Her world had stopped swimming and she felt simply felt exhausted, as if she hadn't had a good night's sleep. "Thank you, ma'am, for the trust you are placing in me. You will not regret it," she managed to say in a confident, if tired, voice.

The queen rose. Clementine hurried to curtsy and kiss Her Majesty's ring.

"Actually, my dear, you want to thank your uncle. The duke wrote to me very late last night and warned me," the queen said , "that his headstrong niece would likely arrive here with Mr Hunt, and he personally vouched for your skills and character. Dear man, he has served us well." The queen smiled the sad smile of one who has lived long enough to see many people die around her.

Clementine again did not know what to say. "I am utterly surprised, ma'am, but I will be sure to thank him for the unexpected help."

The queen nodded. "Now then, I wish you all the success, my dear, but prepare yourself for surprises and uncomfortable situations. Now go and wait outside for just a few minutes while I talk over some of the details with your groom. Sir Henry?" She nodded to her private secretary, who guided Clementine out of the room.

Clementine almost collided with the maid, who had apparently just come to carry the tray of tea away.

"Apologies, my lady," she said with a bob, her head bowed with embarrassment at such an accident.

"No harm done," Clementine muttered in a stupor. She barely heard Sir Henry give the maid an earful for coming too soon to collect the china. Clementine sat slowly on one of the narrow benches by the wall, right next to the door. The maid left hurriedly and disappeared into a servant door. Clementine could still hear the low murmurs of conversation within the room and resisted the urge to press her ear against the wooden door to hear what Her Majesty wanted to keep between Mr Hunt and herself. But it was too risky, and besides, in all honesty, Clementine was quite done with shocks and scandals for one day. She was glad her corset was firmly supporting her posture, otherwise she feared she might just melt to the floor. In fact, she wished she could take a long, long nap, and wake up to find all of this was a dream and her father had returned home.

THE HAPPY COUPLE

"Right then," Mr Hunt said as he stepped out of his private audience with the queen. Nothing in his face betrayed anything he might have discussed with Her Majesty, but Clementine sensed a tension in his shoulders, in the set of his jaw, perhaps. Those green eyes had a sharp glint in them. His face changed when his eyes met hers, and almost like magic he became the amused young gentleman without a care in the world.

"You look quite famished, Lady Clementine. Is it possible that I have neglected my fiancée's wellbeing and left her here all alone and without food?" He offered his hand to her. She glared at him, wanting to scream something about acting like everything was normal, but instead she simply accepted his hand and he led her away through the corridors until they found themselves outside of the palace into a sunny garden. Clementine blinked. A summer's day, just like the rest of them, without a care that her life had just turned upside down.

"There is a rather nice tearoom not far from here. Do you think you can manage without a carriage? A stroll seems to be something you young ladies prefer when courting, or when agitated, so we might as well start with our roles right away." There was no little amount of sarcasm in his voice.

"I– yes, Mr Hunt. Though how you can be so... so normal about it is beyond my comprehension," she muttered, but matched his pace as they slowly made their way through the palace courtyard.

"All part of the job, I assure you," he smirked at her. "You'll just need to get used to it. Call me William, by the way. We should be on a first name basis, at least when in public, if we are to be madly in love."

"You do take this very seriously, Mr– ah, William," Clementine corrected herself. "Is it Will to your friends?"

He shook his head, his lips curving. "Only if I may call you Clemmie," he said.

Now it was her turn to shake her head.

"Clementine and William it is then," he nodded, tipping his hat to a passing couple. Clementine too remembered to smile at the people that walked past them, some of whom she knew. They all seemed to be staring for just a second too long. It was already starting, indeed, this game of pretense.

"I say, William!" someone called to them.

William turned, and Clementine turned with him, since he had locked her hand in the crook of his arm. A man approached, wearing a smart daytime suit. He tipped his top hat to them.

"I hope you've had a pleasant afternoon. I was just looking for you, William, to continue our conversation." The man smiled pleasantly, but Clementine could see his deep brown eyes glancing at her with curiosity. The man's face had a sharpness, emphasised by a thin handlebar mustache, which was as dark as his hair.

"Ah, Asem. Well met," William said without a worry in his voice.

Clementine discreetly tugged at his arm for introductions. He glanced down at her.

"This is Asem Smith, a friend of mine and a fellow travelling soul. This is Lady Clementine, the daughter of the Earl of Whitham." William raised her hand to his lips suddenly, "And my lovely bride."

Clementine's jaw dropped slightly at the sudden announcement. William's eyes challenged her to react, to make a scene, so she smiled a smile she hoped was seen as charming, and pulled her hand free to greet Asem. His eyebrows rose only a little, but otherwise his pleasant expression stayed on.

"Lovely to meet a friend of Mr– I mean, my fiancé's," Clementine said in a slightly shaky voice. She extended her hand for Mr Smith to lightly kiss.

"What a surprise," Asem smiled. "William, you had not told me you harboured such a beautiful secret. My congratulations to you both. The engagement must have been quite sudden, considering recent, hmm, events," he said, and tucked his walking cane beneath his arm.

"Yes, well ," William grinned, "You know me, always ready to make the most of each day. After hearing so many tales of Clementine from her father, I fell in love with her before even gazing upon her beautiful face. It was love before first sight."

"Ah, I see," Mr Smith said, "And has there been any news of your father, Lady Clementine?"

"Only what little William here has told me. I've received only one letter from my papa, which must have been sent just before he disappeared, and that's all," she sighed.

"A letter," Mr Smith mused, "That is lucky, to have received some words, even if they were not the most meaningful, to remember him by, in case."

"Oh yes," Clementine said, encouraged by this stranger's kind words, "It was a meaningful letter. He told me details about the excavation and sent me some rubbings of some of the hieroglyphs he'd discovered around the different tombs. He often remembered me when he was away and sent these little gifts of knowledge. Dear Papa."

"You hadn't mentioned the letter was sent so recently. I thought it had been sent much earlier during our journey to Dendera," William said.

Clementine gazed up at his frowning face with surprise. "What does it matter?"

"Everything matters, my dear, now that we are to be married. I want to know everything there is to know, so that I may love all of you."

Clementine didn't know if she should roll her eyes or shy away from such words in front of another, so she flicked open her fan to cool herself.

"And what is it you do, Mr Smith?" she asked, to change the subject.

"I travel here and there, much like William. I go where I can be of use when it comes to historical relics. I have been to many corners of the world, all the way from the Caribbean to the Middle East, India and beyond."

"And were you also part of my father's crew, like William?" Clementine was curious about this well-travelled man. *Such experiences!* The exact kind of experiences Clementine herself was hoping to have.

"Not directly, no," Asem said with some deliberation. "I knew him and his crew, of course. In Egypt, fellow adventurers are bound to run into each other while travelling. William and myself occasionally exchange advice and information. You see, I am half-Egyptian and speak Arabic fluently."

Clementine smiled. "Indeed, that must be very useful." She had of course observed at once that he had darker features than an average British person, but it was not her place to point it out.

"Aren't you going to comment on my excellent English skills?" he asked with dry humor.

Clementine laughed. "No more than I would ask where you are really from, as I am certain you would not ask from me either."

"True, my lady. I see we have something in common." Mr Smith smiled widely and glanced at William. "I think, my friend, that you have chosen well."

"I hope *I* have chosen well," Clementine chimed in, and William's green eyes turned to her with a glint. She hid her smile behind her fan.

"Well, I must not keep you longer. William, may I talk to you before you depart?"

The men agreed to meet later, after Asem had concluded his meetings, and after William and Clementine had had their tea.

After bidding each other goodbye, Clementine and William were left alone, hand in hand, and all smiles on the surface.

"Before we continue, I want to be very clear, Clementine," William said abruptly, squeezing her hand to make his point, "We are not friends. We are not in love. Is that understood? We are barely colleagues at this point. Trust me, I did everything in my power to persuade the queen from her decision of making you my new partner. I do not wish to be married any more than you do. It is foolish."

"Ah, and did you tell Her Majesty that her decision is foolish?" Clementine asked wryly.

"Yes and no," William said.

He greeted some acquaintances again and Clementine beamed next to him. In her mind, she was thinking of kicking some gravel at him but restrained herself. *Must act like a smitten fiancée.*

"I told her I did not approve and did not want a young, inexperienced girl by my side to cause unnecessary trouble and worry," William continued, "I believe her willingness to give you a chance was a mistake, which I told her. You are a fool for accepting the queen's offer, so now I have told you as well. You really will be trouble for me and my mission." His hard green eyes were relentlessly accusing.

"What great challenges there must be for a young man. I can hardly imagine how difficult this must be for you, dearest William," Clementine hissed at him, hoping her smile still translated to being brainlessly in love with the insufferable man to passers-by.

"Let me make something clear as well, William," she said with a cold smile, stopping to pluck a single, blood-red poppy from the flowerbed near the palace gates. She gently turned to insert the flower into William's coat pocket, almost shyly, as if she were overcome with affection. "The last thing I want is to be stuck with you. If there were any other way — and trust me, I will keep my eyes and ears open — I would gladly be doing this without you. So no, I will not fall in love with you, nor do you have to call me a friend, either. Your reputation precedes you, so do not think you can take advantage of me, Mr Hunt, whatever we might call each other." She turned the flower gently to better face the sun, keeping her touch light on his chest. "I am not one of your conquests, desperately yearning for attention. I am here for my father and for my future, that is all. You have a very small role in all of this."

She turned to walk out of the palace gates with a sway of her white and red skirts. William soon caught up with her with a chuckle.

"You really are different from your peers, and it's quite refreshing. I find it almost too difficult to stay serious in your company," he said, amused. "I say this again, I don't think I have ever met any young lady quite like you, and I have known a few ladies, I can admit." He winked and Clementine shivered. "I see that we will not have a problem when it comes to matters of the heart , but you must promise to tell me when yearning for my touch becomes too much. I may consider adding you to the list of desperate conquests." He flashed her a dashing grin that Clementine was sure was to blame for his reputation.

Clementine did her best not to react, even though it might have made her knees just slightly weak. She rolled her eyes. "In your dreams, William, if even there."

"Oh, I shall wait for those dreams eagerly," he said. He stopped and Clementine turned to face him with a retort ready on her lips, but paused when she saw that in his hands he held another poppy, which he slowly inserted into her hair. He then leaned in, closing the distance of their height difference, and tucked a wisp of hair behind her ear in such a way that his hand softly caressed her cheek, as if by accident. She felt her cheeks burn and her lips part unwillingly in a silent sigh.

"You know, I do think I left something out of the list of things we are not. Indeed, we are not in love, nor friends, barely colleagues, but I omitted to mention anything about being lovers," he almost purred, and her eyes burned with anger at his audacity, and for the helpless reactions he so easily drew out of her.

Fine, she knew which skills to focus on then: she would need to get used to him until he had no effect on her with his words or gestures. Annoyed, she flicked her fan in warning and he pulled away with a laugh.

"Do you always have that fan with you?"

"Yes, always," she snapped, feeling out of breath. "Do try to keep that in mind when having idiotic ideas. I may not have seen as much of the world as you, but that will soon be amended."

"Understood," William said, feigning a seriousness he obviously did not give her.

He did not take her seriously in any matter. She would change that; she would make him and the rest of the world take her seriously, even if she had to bloody pretend to be in love with this oaf!

LADY CLEMENTINE AND THE TEARS OF HATHOR

* * *

Verrey's on Regent Street had a decent amount of customers. Mostly men of the finer classes, but Clementine also noticed several groups of women enjoying a break from shopping, or even hiding from tiresome suitors. This time of year, one could hardly go for a peaceful walk without a gentleman and/or his mother trying to accompany you. Clementine did not rank nearly high enough on her own, especially with her family history, but she was the niece of the Duke and Duchess of Clearwater, and thus a decent catch for some.

As they walked in, Clementine carefully cast her eyes around the various tables and saw no one of great acquaintance. Some ladies she had seen at dances and dinners, like the red-haired girl, Lady Josephine, at the corner table with her newlywed husband. Clementine tried not to stare at the young woman's face, which seemed red and half hidden behind a handkerchief. She hoped Lady Josephine was merely dabbing her face because of the warm day and not because of tears. Crying in public was not recommended, unless in great distress, and Clementine certainly hoped she wouldn't burst out crying from all the emotions of the day. She made a mental note to not wipe her face quite as hard as Lady Josephine had been.

"Mr Hunt," the maître d' greeted them eagerly as they passed through the wooden doors, decorated with gilded vines, "How excellent to have you here again to enjoy our hospitality! Will you have your usual table?" The man's mustache quivered with excitement and Clementine wondered if William came here often with different lady friends.

Even if he did, Clementine chastised her mind, *it wouldn't matter.*

"Yes, Mr Mason, the usual table will do wonderfully. What's the lunch speciality today?"

"Cold cutlets of duck breast, and a soup of summer potatoes

and leeks — a fragrant combination I am sure the young lady will enjoy as well." He bowed slightly towards Clementine. Clementine nodded and smiled, trying to portray happiness with her face.

"Ah, yes, this is my very special friend, Lady Clementine Whitham. We will enjoy a moment to feast on your delicacies," Mr Hunt nodded.

"Splendid, this way please."

The maître d' took them across the large room, past tables, waiters, and diners, to the farthest corner table, which had a view of the busy street. Clementine was guided to sit on a soft chair, and a linen napkin was placed on her lap. The silver cutlery was neatly arranged on the white tablecloth and there was even a vase of fresh roses that she could just about smell amidst the delicious scents of different dishes.

It would have been a lovely experience, since Clementine had never been here before, but the shock of the day's events weighed too much on her shoulders. She sighed and set down her parasol next to the table, sipping water from a crystal glass while William ordered for them. When the waiter left, William took off his hat and leaned back on his chair, running a hand through his short, dark, sandy curls.

"So, my dear, was this what you wanted when you barged into my audience with the queen?"

Clementine fixed her gaze firmly on his. "No, it was not. But..." she hesitated.

"But what? What did you expect?" William cocked his eyebrow.

"Honestly, I don't know," she sighed, "I only knew that I had to try and plead my case, to be allowed to do something instead of waiting until I was whisked off by some random husband and becoming one less problem for my aunt and uncle."

"Well, you played your cards nicely," he said, his eyes glinting darkly. "You got yourself a random husband-to-be and are now very much doing something to help find out what the hell happened to your father."

He did not seem to notice that he had used such coarse language in front of a lady. Keeping his tone low and somehow menacing, he did not hide the fact that he was not here for any voluntary reason.

"That trick of pulling your uncle into this scheme of yours was neat. Who would've thought that he and the queen still had such a warm relationship?"

Clementine startled. "My uncle? I did not pull my uncle into anything. How would I have known he had decided to reach out to the queen to help me?"

"Oh please, you just said you would do anything. Pulling strings to get yourself in front of the queen with His Grace's help was certainly you living up to that promise!"

Clementine set her glass back to the table with a little more force than she meant, but this was getting very tiresome.

She tried to keep her voice low. "Look, if we are to do this, we need to be honest and trust each other, to some extent at least. Otherwise we won't get very far in our investigation. So trust me when I say I do not know what you are talking about."

William held her gaze. "So you didn't know that your uncle had somehow managed to send a message to the queen to recommend your audience? You actually came to see me without that knowledge, hoping I would be persuaded to help you?"

Clementine felt herself blush at her brash decisions. But it had worked in the end! "Why is that so hard to believe? I did as my instincts told me," she said, keeping her head high, despite the heat on her cheeks.

William studied her face for signs of deception. "Perhaps you are telling the truth, in which case we need to work on you hiding your emotions better. The queen certainly said she was impressed by your determined personality."

"And what else did she say when I was forced to leave the room?"

"Little else, only some practicalities for our travel arrangements," he waved the question away. "But one of the interesting parts of it was realising something. The queen would never tell who else is in her service as a member of the Extraordinary Treasure Hunters , but I now suspect your uncle might have been a treasure hunter in his earlier life."

"That's incredible." Clementine digested the idea. "He always was quite silent about his youth, mostly talking about his many military positions, but a treasure hunter? Well, I suppose you will have to ask him yourself later today when we go back to Clearwater Abbey."

William raised his eyebrows in question and Clementine rolled her eyes, even though it was rude. "When you ask for my hand in marriage, remember? We are supposed to get engaged and my uncle is the closest male relative after my father."

William cleared his throat. "As if one could forget that unfortunate turn of events. Yes, I shall certainly ask him for your hand, and if he was one of us, he will guess why, even if he won't confirm his involvement. It may help your family to be more accepting of having me as their future in-law, in case my charm is not enough." William grinned and Clementine was again reminded that his charm might certainly be enough for her to make some very bad decisions if she was not careful.

"If only it were that easy with my aunt. She will have many questions. Well, objections," Clementine said, and hoped the lies would roll out of her mouth easily enough.

The food was brought to their table, along with a light white wine. The crisp tanginess of the wine was perfectly balanced with the creamy soup. They waited until the waiter had left to continue their discussion — or rather, the exchange of minimal information.

"So, I gather we should have some predetermined answers

that don't vary too much when different people ask us the same questions," Clementine said. The soup was divine, and she took her time savoring the summer flavors, along with a fluffy bread roll. "This is delicious," she said, "And I haven't gotten to the duck yet."

"Yes, this place has a knack for excellent food, no matter when you come here," William nodded. He too seemed to enjoy the food, and had a good appetite. Clementine had not thought she would even be hungry, but she found the excellent dishes brought some life back to her tired mind and body.

"What kind of objections do you expect?" William asked as they both reached for the last bread roll. When Clementine didn't pull her hand away, William sighed and halved it, which was rather gallant in her opinion. She wouldn't have shared — or not with him, at least.

"Well, for starters I would guess they will be baffled by why you would want to marry me after knowing me only for a day. I would also guess that there will be questions over whether something happened to force you into this, to prevent my reputation from being ruined." Clementine paused only to take a bite of the tender duck. "And if they believe we fell in love at first sight yesterday, which I don't think is likely, they will ask how we are planning to live without my fortune, on your earnings alone. Excuse me, but my aunt will certainly think your earnings won't be enough. She always wanted me to marry someone better, or at least of equal status and wealth."

"Hmm," William nodded, deep in thought. "The usual questions and doubts, indeed."

"Am I right to assume you have never done this before? How old are you anyway?" Clementine asked, then snapped her mouth shut when the waiter came to clear their plates away. She had to be careful not to yell out how very little they knew of each other if this plan was to work.

Once they had placed their order for coffee, William turned back to her question.

"I am twenty-five, the second son in the family, and my preferred pastimes — aside from treasure hunting — are riding, fencing and spending enjoyable evenings in beautiful company. Parents died years ago. I like my brother, but we are not close. My lodgings are at Knightwood House when I am not travelling. I prefer dogs to cats and have an excellent sense of humor. Your turn," he gestured with a drily amused tone.

Clementine's lips quivered at his smile. This really was the most ridiculous conversation — only the one with the queen was more baffling.

"I am nineteen, my mother is — or was — from Indochina, and you know my father. I was raised English but enjoy many non-English things such as spicy food, speaking in different languages, and not feeling superior about my own nationality. My parents divorced when I was eleven, and I have not seen nor heard from my mother since. No siblings to my knowledge, and I don't know if I am fully or half-orphan. My favourite colours are all the many shades of pink and purple, and I enjoy kicking and punching. I don't mind fencing, but Mama preferred me to use my own feet and hands to fight, so I try to use what I have. I train with Mrs Edith these days, and she too prefers fighting without weapons. I love my father and he taught me much of my knowledge in history, culture and languages. I also love scones and both dogs and cats."

William nodded as if impressed. "To be honest, I am not sure which one of us is the winner in our arrangement. You have a potential for a great fortune, despite your unfortunate family history, and I am only a second son with a dangerous job to provide for me and my wife."

Clementine felt herself blush at the mention of being his wife. His green eyes met hers and she felt again very aware of that gaze. Like the deepest forest green, its hues changing with the morning dew. The waiter returned with their coffee and poured it into porcelain cups with adequate amounts of cream and sugar.

"You really need to get used to being called fiancée, wife-to-be, beloved and so on," he said, amused.

"Yes, well, this did come rather suddenly, so excuse me if I cannot yet wrap my head around those words. I cannot fully control my reactions, you know."

"You should learn fast," he said, sipping his coffee, "Adapting is vital in this job if you are to succeed."

"I will succeed, don't you worry," she said, and almost burned her tongue on the hot coffee.

"Yes, well, I do worry on both occasions. Either you fail horribly when you realise this is no fairytale adventure, and it is then my problem. Or, against all odds, you become a decent treasure hunter, in which case I will be stuck with you as my fake wife and work partner. So allow me to worry a little," he said with no little sarcasm and that lopsided grin.

Clementine sighed and closed her eyes. "One thing at a time. Now, let's get our story straight. You were mesmerised by my dazzling character, my incredible wit and independent spirit. So much so that you insisted we spend the day together, when in fact I was only hoping to do some shopping. Then you swept me off my feet and, combined with our mutual desire to find my father, we noticed how much we are alike. And behold: a spark was lit between us." Clementine paused to sip her coffee. "You spoke to the queen of me, and she gave you her blessing for us to marry and go to Egypt together. So now we wish to announce our engagement and embark on a journey to find my father, not only for my fortune and future, but to also have his blessing for this union between his loyal assistant and most beloved daughter." She crossed her arms and wordlessly dared him to find fault in her story.

William gave her a small, silent round of applause. "I think we can work with that," he said. "I can believe you were swept off your feet by my impeccable charm, but we need to work on your dazzling character, incredible wit, and what was the last one? Oh yes, independent spirit. We might need a tiny bit of work from your side to make those as believable." His tone was wry and amused, and before Clementine could say another word, he waved the waiter over to pay their bill.

She was seething, but allowed him to escort her out, and a boy was sent to fetch a carriage. Clementine said nothing, and with much irritation she took his offered hand and hooked her arm around his.

"You know, there is just one crucial detail missing in that grand tale of yours," he said, laying his hand on hers. She drew a breath at such an intimate gesture. He kept his hand lightly on hers, not forcing, not squeezing, just a tender, soft touch that seemed to melt through her gloves. He leaned closer, his top hat blocking out the sun and giving her only his gaze to focus on.

Those eyes, she thought. She could well believe many women to have fallen under their emerald spell. She felt completely naked beneath his steady, intense stare, which seemed to strip her of her very last piece of little clothing and lace. The mere idea of him seeing her nude sent heat up her cheeks. She gulped and did her best to steady herself.

"And what is that?" she asked, with a slightly shaky voice. It was wicked, oh so wicked, the laughter and fire in those eyes.

He raised her hand to his lips and she felt her breathing quicken. He kissed her hand slowly, bending over her knuckles but keeping those wicked eyes on hers.

"The proposal, my dear," he said, and she swore at her reaction when she heard herself gasp at his endearing words. This time she yanked her hand back and firmly tucked it in the folds of her skirts, as if that might stop him from knowing her hand was still tingling from his lips.

He chuckled and the low noise sent shivers up her spine. She felt like a mouse that a cat toyed with before the final killing blow.

"Clementine," he said, trying his best to be serious, but the laughter and intensity never quite died from his eyes. "How are people to believe we are to be married if you gasp and blush every time I touch or speak to you? You need to be more serious about controlling your reactions, though I do find it refreshing to be with someone so very inexperienced in these matters."

Clementine cleared her throat and found her usual distasteful tone for his experiences in romantic affairs. "Well, that tells me more about you, Mr Hunt, for I am behaving exactly as a well-mannered young lady of my status should behave. Fainting and fanning at every little piece of attention you might shine upon me, yearning for more whenever you dare to move your attention elsewhere. I am simply in character already, Mr Hunt. Oh, I'm sorry, *darling William*, that is." She hissed the last words. In truth, she was quite surprised at herself. Never did she think she would be uttering those words to a man, let alone to a stranger she was pretending to marry.

William studied her for what seemed like forever, which did not bode well for her. She somehow knew this was not yet over, even if she had managed to turn it around a little.

"Well said, darling Clementine." His smile deepened when he noticed her lack of reaction to those words, even though inside her heart was thumping up her throat. "And I might believe you, perhaps, if not for the red blotches on your décolletage." His eyes pointedly went lower, where the dress showed just a fraction of her collar bones.

She yanked her shawl tighter around her.

"It is simply a reaction to being very vexed," she said.

The carriage arrived and she explained to the driver that they were to return to Paddington Station at once, ignoring William's hand for help as she climbed into her seat.

He rolled his eyes, taking the seat opposite to her and the carriage took them towards the train station.

"You really are an independent spirit. Or at least very much showing yourself as such," he smiled. "You might actually give me a bone to crack, I'll give you that much, but we shall see."

She huffed and looked out the window, her slanting hat partly shielding her face from those penetrating eyes. *Vexing man*, she sighed to herself.

"As for the proposal," she said, "I will leave the details to you on how exactly you swept me off my feet. Just make it believable. Anyone who knows me knows that it takes a lot to sweep me off my feet. Literally." She narrowed her eyes at him.

"Ah yes, the fierce fighter. Do not worry, Lady Clementine, as I said in the orchard, I would never compromise a lady without her asking me to." Another flash of a devilish, mischievous grin.

Clementine rolled her eyes. "Perhaps it would be easier to say I allowed you to kiss me, and we were witnessed in a delicate situation, so you gallantly chose, for once, to do the right thing and not be a horrible rake, with the tears of young ladies flooding behind you."

"Have you ever considered becoming a writer?" William snorted, "You might make an easier living compared to a treasure hunter."

Clementine couldn't help but smile at the compliment of sorts. In the end, they agreed to tell a story of a spontaneous proposal, prompted by Clementine's father. Due to the circumstances, William's conscience demanded him to offer to take care of her in her hour of need, and help find her father. It seemed plausible enough, Clementine agreed, and so that was the plan.

THE ENGAGEMENT

*I*t was early evening when they arrived at Clearwater House. Clementine felt nervous but also determined. She had the backing of Her Majesty, for now at least. And even though she did not like being stuck with Mr Hunt, she was still a bit relieved at not having to face her aunt alone.

They were taken to the drawing room to meet the duchess.

"Clementine, and Mr Hunt, what a surprise." Her Grace had a stern look on her face and Clementine had to fight not to flinch when she curtsied and kissed her aunt's cheek. William bowed deeply with immaculate flamboyance, as if he were a seasoned courtier.

"Your Grace, I apologise for coming here so unannounced from London, but I must speak to His Grace most urgently of a matter of great importance." His glance at Clementine seemed to be dripping with honey, and once again Clementine had to avoid flinching when she saw her aunt's expression.

"Indeed," the duchess said with a raised eyebrow, her fan fluttering rather like an annoyed cat's tail. She turned in her heavy velvet dress and called for a servant to take Mr Hunt to the duke's rooms. William bowed again deeply to both of them before going upstairs.

"In the morning room, now," the duchess said in a tone that gave room for no other option. Clementine bent her head and followed her aunt to the morning room with swallows and birch trees on the yellow tapestries.

"Were you behaving inappropriately with that man, Clementine?"

Her aunt certainly did not waste any time. Clementine swallowed; her throat felt very dry suddenly. "No, Aunt, you know I would never."

The duchess sat stiffly on a sofa, her amber dress spreading around her like a flame that would soon burn right through Clementine's lies. She sat across from her aunt, careful not to show any other emotion but guarded excitement and a hint of being foolishly in love. She had no idea if her face betrayed any of the emotions she was trying to hide.

"What is the meaning of you arriving here together so suddenly? I thought you had gone shopping in London," the duchess demanded, snapping her fan shut. "Why does Mr Hunt rush to His Grace as if he is a suitor asking for your hand?"

Clementine couldn't help blanching just a little. Her aunt, as usual, was exactly right and to the point. It would serve Clementine better to just be out with it.

"It's because," she cleared her throat, which suddenly seemed to house the sands of the Sahara, "he is doing just that. Asking for my hand, for us to be engaged."

"What?" the duchess' eyes widened and she sprang up from the sofa so fast Clementine feared her carefully curled hair might come undone from its knots. Aunt Theodora moved surprisingly quickly in her heavy dress.

Her Grace stood in front of Clementine with her hands on her hips, fists curled, oozing shock and anger.

"Did he do something to you? Were you seen?"

"No," Clementine tried to look scandalised, "He would never. He has been every bit a gentleman."

"You know you can tell me if you are in trouble of any kind," Clementine's aunt sighed and closed her eyes. "Even if you were found in a compromising situation. We will find a way out of it."

"No, Aunt Theodora, believe me, it is nothing bad!"

"Then tell me what it is. You met this man yesterday and now you wish to marry him, is that so?"

Clementine kept her posture upright and even managed to smile. "Yes, Aunt. I wish to confirm our engagement." She deliberately left out mentioning anything about a wedding. "William — that is, Mr Hunt — tells me Papa had planned for this all along, wanting to make it official once he returned. But now, well…" Clementine did not have to feign the emotion in her voice when she spoke of her father. "Now things are different and Will– I mean, Mr Hunt, wanted to take pity on me and secure our engagement first, to help me find out what happened to Papa."

The duchess relaxed, but only a little. "Ah, so it was my brother's idea, then? Be that as it may, I cannot let you do such a rash thing with a man you hardly know."

"I trust my papa. He did what he thought best for me," Clementine said, adding in her mind that actually Papa had promised her she would not have to marry.

"Still, Clementine, this is not how things are done."

"Why?" Clementine interrupted, meeting her aunt's eyes with what she hoped was sincerity. "I believe we can fall in love at first sight, why couldn't it happen to me and Mr Hunt? I place my fate in his hands — surely that is the greatest act of trust and love?"

The duchess sighed. "Sometimes fairytales like that happen. And sometimes they are not what they seem at all. I do wish you would get to know your future husband a little better than what you know of Mr Hunt. It seemed you did not like him very much yesterday."

Clementine gave a small laugh. "Oh, that. I was impulsive, as you know I am. When he wanted to meet with me today, he explained himself and his feelings perfectly. He is an honourable man, despite his, er, lively reputation." Clementine stumbled slightly over her words. "He will do as he promised my father. According to him, nothing will overrule his devotion to his promise. And honestly, Aunt Theodora, he is not a bad catch with my current prospects. He is a second son of a baronet. I could do far worse, especially if the death of my papa is never proven. The suitors will become increasingly fewer, and the majority will be below my rank. You know this, Aunt Theodora."

"I see you have practised well on how to persuade me. But while your father is assumed to be gone, it is I who decides your marriage, with the approval of His Grace."

"Why would you decide, when William tells me this match is a wish from my father?" Clementine asked, baffled.

Aunt Theodora smiled and Clementine felt nervous. "Because I have received a letter from the solicitors. Your father's will had an interesting addendum . It states that in the event of him dying, and you being unmarried, he will grant me the power to decide what is best for you, my dear. That is clearly stated in your own father's will. I do not know what he has said to Mr Hunt, or if Mr Hunt is simply lying to marry above his station, but he need not worry himself with you. You are my concern and I intend to do my best to get you married to a more suitable man, so help me God."

Clementine's heart was beating rapidly. She again cursed herself for not having contacted the solicitor to see a copy of Papa's will. Not only was there a mention of a male heir being preferable, if one existed, but now this? How could Papa have written these things in his will and never mentioned them to

Clementine when he promised her she wouldn't have to marry; that she could be a free adventuress? Clementine drew a deep, shaky breath. *Fine, if Aunt Theodora was determined to use her authority to her last breath, it was time to counter that authority...*

"Do not worry, Aunt Theodora. I'm sure you and Uncle will be happy to give us your blessing, especially since the queen herself has already approved of our match," Clementine beamed, as if it was the happiest day of her life. She opened her fan to cool herself, as it was getting rather hot with all this excitement and nervousness. Luckily, being excited and nervous were exactly as the responses of a real bride-to-be.

"Her Majesty has agreed to this? Since when, and why?" The duchess' eyes flamed with irritation at being surprised like this, and knowing she could not deny something that the queen herself had approved. "Ah, the audience with the queen. He must have used that to seal the deal and get you into this scheme. The rascal." Aunt Theodora squeezed her fan so hard, Clementine feared it would snap.

"Scheme? Whatever do you mean, Aunt Theodora?" she laughed, but even to her ears it sounded slightly too high-pitched. Her aunt did not seem to notice.

"The scheme of your father, my dear brother, not even telling me that he had plans for your marriage already. And to his assistant, of all people!" She tutted with disapproval. "If this is what Her Majesty has approved, I cannot deny it. I can only pray that you will come to your senses and cancel this engagement before it is too late." The duchess' voice was tense with anger. Clementine knew Aunt Theodora was not used to being outranked.

"I will not cancel anything, Aunt Theodora. The queen wished us well, and she wished us to leave as soon as possible for Egypt," Clementine added. "Her Majesty is most anxious for us to find out more about what happened to Papa, and to finish his work."

"Did she indeed?" Clementine saw her aunt's eyes narrow. "How very curious."

"Yes, well, I would not dream of questioning Her Majesty's intentions," Clementine said, knowing that her aunt could not either.

The doors to the morning room opened and in came William, helping His Grace slowly forward.

"Uncle." Clementine rose to curtsy and then hurried to kiss his cheek. "You look well, as if you received some good news," she said.

Her uncle turned towards her voice and sought her hand to kiss with a tender smile. "Indeed, indeed. Young Mr Hunt here is taking you on an adventure — quite literally — though I would argue that marriage itself is an adventure too. But there is still so much to experience before the nuptials, and I think you will be in very good company when you embark on this journey together." He gently placed Clementine's hand on Mr Hunt's hand. "You two have my permission , not that I would ever contradict the blessing of Her Majesty, but you have mine too because I believe you are well-matched and will eventually learn to work together." He paused, and Clementine's eyes darted to Mr Hunt's, who kept his expression quite neutral.

"Ah yes, marriage: equal parts work as it is adventure," William laughed heartily, "I thank you from the bottom of my heart for the approval, Your Grace." He then turned to the duchess. "And I hope, Your Grace, that I will prove an adequate husband to your niece and a valuable addition to this household."

Clementine's aunt nodded stiffly. The way her lips pursed left no doubt of her disapproval. "Time will tell, Mr Hunt."

TIME TO LEAVE

A week later, Mr Hunt's carriage came into view in the early morning. Clementine had gone home to pack her travel trunk, say goodbye to her surprised household (Mary had cried), and then stayed at Clearwater Abbey, since it was closer to Reading train station.

Clementine's aunt was still not happy about the journey, about the engagement, about anything Clementine had decided, really. Aunt Theodora especially disapproved of Clementine not taking a maid with her, but the world was changing, and people did travel without servants. Especially if they were on a secret mission.

"For the tenth time, Aunt Theodora, and that is counting only today, I will be fine. I have my own wits about me, in addition to Mr Hunt to protect me." Clementine disliked saying that William was there to take care of her, but she did recognise that in some instances it was better to have someone experienced in dealing with strange cultures.

Clementine checked her reflection in her bedroom mirror. Her slanted hat was the colour of dark crimson, as was her travel dress. Her trusted iron fan hung on her wrist, as well as a small reticule. In the reticule was some travel money and the final letter from her papa. At the last moment, Clementine had also taken a book with her to read: *Around the World in Eighty Days* by Jules Verne. It had been her favourite book growing up, and she and her father shared similar copies. He, too, always travelled with it, as far as Clementine knew.

"Fine, fine." The Duchess of Clearwater thrust a small bundle into Clementine's hands.

"What's this?" Clementine asked.

"Just something I wanted to give you, since it seems I cannot persuade you to change your mind about the travel, nor the engagement."

"Thank you, Aunt Theodora. I know it worries you to see me go, but I have to do this. For Papa and my own future."

Clementine took off her kid-leather gloves and carefully opened the bundle, which contained a pair of delicate embroidered handkerchiefs. Her aunt was excellent at embroidery and had embellished them with Clementine's initials and beautiful flowers of apples and peas.

"They are lovely, Aunt Theodora. And practical, too!"

"Yes, well. I have no doubts that there will be tears in this adventure, hence the handkerchiefs. One can never have too many handkerchiefs when travelling. I myself had many taxing journeys in the past but I never complained, since those ancient rubble piles seemed to make His Grace so happy." She smiled a small smile.

"I will go and say goodbye to Uncle then," Clementine said, tucking the handkerchiefs into her reticule.

She curtsied, and then, on a whim, hugged her aunt, breathing in the scent of roses. Aunt Theodora seemed surprised but returned the embrace.

"I will come back with news of Papa, Aunt Theodora, I promise," Clementine said.

"Don't make promises you cannot keep," the duchess sighed

and squeezed Clementine against her. They did not always see eye to eye, but they were family.

* * *

CLEMENTINE WENT to her uncle's rooms, knocked, and with permission, let herself in. She found him in the sitting area, immersed in music coming from a gramophone. It had been a great invention overall, but to her uncle, who could not read as he used to, the music brought great pleasure, and he had insisted on buying one as soon as they became available.

"Dear Clementine, is it time yet?" he asked, after she had kissed his cheek.

Clementine arranged her skirts, sat next to him, and took his hand.

"I am leaving shortly." She hesitated for a moment before continuing. "You know why I do this, and I suspect you might know what I have signed up for," she said. "I know you cannot say more — nor can I — but if there is any advice you can give me, please do."

Her uncle laughed. "Never one to skirt around the subject. You are certainly your mother's daughter," he smiled, "And your father's too, for you are to continue his work. It has been a long time since I was young. All I can say is that unless things have very much changed, I urge you to be careful." He squeezed her hand.

"I know there are dangers, Uncle," Clementine said soothingly. Her uncle's hand felt like thin paper; dry and fragile with a luminescence to it. She did not want to think of the possibility that this might be the last time they saw each other.

"Yes, the obvious ones," he waved his hand at those. "I don't think you would be careless with the obvious dangers: thieves, diseases, violence, traps and so on. But I want you to be careful of others of our kind. Well, if there is such thing as our kind," he winked.

"Other treasure hunters?" Clementine was surprised by this. "Why?"

Her uncle gave her hand a gentle pat and laughed quietly. "Clementine, this is precisely why it is good that you have Mr Hunt to guide you. You do not yet know of the many dangers, and while you can stand your ground, you might still benefit from Mr Hunt's practical experiences. Watch out for other treasure hunters — they are as likely to help you as to stab you in the back to claim your findings. There are treasure hunters outside of the queen's service as well. It is a very international business. And really, in the end, Her Majesty does not care who brings her the bounty; she will reward anyone who pulls through. Remember that. Don't trust anyone. Even with Mr Hunt, keep your guard up, and for heaven's sake don't marry him if you have any doubts about him or this line of work."

Clementine sighed. "But how am I to even recognise a fellow treasure hunter? We are not supposed to know the network, at least not on purpose."

"Ah, if it has not changed, you will recognise them once they try to steal from you. Or they may simply try to shoot you first and then take your items. Our guns had marvellous silver bullets, in case we ever came face to face with monsters, but the real monster tends to be a fellow human. " His chuckle made Clementine shake her head, but she found it difficult to not join his laugh. To joke of such a thing as killing and stealing! Who would have thought?

" I wanted to give you something to help," he added. "On the table there is some additional money. Her Majesty does see to the costs being covered most of the time, but you never know when you need to bribe someone's silence quickly," he said casually .

Clementine ignored the absurdity of this conversation, while feeling immensely grateful for her uncle's support.

"Thank you," she said, and gathered up the money, "I will use it wisely." She paused before asking the next question. She was not sure if her uncle would answer truthfully, or at all, but she couldn't keep ignoring the subject. "When you were a traveller," she chose her words carefully, "did you ever see something you found hard to believe? With your own eyes?"

Clementine's uncle was silent for a moment. "I lost the trust in my eyes years ago," he said quietly, "But all I can say is that there are things I cannot explain. The things I saw were real in that moment, and I hope you will not turn your eyes too quickly from those situations if they happen on your journey. We live in an age of science, but it's certainly not the only power in the world. Some might call it magic." His voice was barely a whisper now. A tear rolled down his cheek and he hastily wiped a hand across his face.

Clementine swallowed. She did not want to doubt the queen's words, or William's, but hearing her uncle utter those words, and seeing his reaction to the topic, was enough to make her hold any remaining questions about the credibility of magic in the world. She would keep an open mind — that much she could commit to, at least. No more needed to be said now, and she had to hurry. She could deal with the possibility of magic later, along with all the other bits of new information she had received ever since her papa had gone missing. Surely her brain could deal with one more little addition with the potential to change everything she thought she knew about the world, science, faith and well, anything, really. Not for the first time, her brain felt like it was overflowing.

"I promise to write vague updates from our travels," she said, and squeezed his hand before she rose and curtsied, her skirts spreading around her. "And Uncle," she hesitated, not wanting to say a final goodbye — too afraid of the finality of it.

Sensing Clementine's hesitation, His Grace smiled and turned his milky eyes towards her. "Until we meet again, darling Clementine. I hope you discover the fate of your papa."

With that, Clementine left and went back downstairs, and just in time — William had just stepped through the main doors.

William flashed a smile as he saw her, looking like a happy groom meeting his fiancée after a long while apart. However, the way his eyes judged her descent of the staircase did not radiate warmth, and Clementine responded with the same flashy smile that did not quite reach her eyes either.

Next to him was Dickie, who had not taken too well to the engagement news that had spread like a wildfire through society. Her Majesty had done her part by commenting to her ladies at luncheons, teas and dinners of a match that pleased her very much. It certainly gave food for thought to those who thought Clementine had done too well, given her background and current circumstances, or that William had secured a nice catch as a second son, especially if the fortune of Clementine's father would one day be hers.

"Hello, William," Clementine greeted him without formality. Dickie flinched, and William swiftly kissed her hand. "I hope you slept well."

"Excellently, my dear," William smiled with just a bit too much teeth. "I hope you did as well."

"A word, Clementine." Dickie led her away before she or William could say anything more.

"I'll just make sure your trunk is packed, then. Don't linger too long, dear," William called after them.

Clementine was aware of their tight schedule. They needed to make it to Reading station, catch a train to London and then to Charing Cross where their train to Dover would depart in the afternoon. From Dover, they would swiftly cross the channel by ferry and continue again by train.

"What is it, Dickie?" she asked, as he more or less hauled her by her arm to a small sitting room near the front entrance.

"Last time, Clemmie. Are you sure you want to go?" He held her shoulders and stooped down to look her in the eye. He looked so grave that Clementine felt sorry for him. "You know I would go on your behalf in an instant if you asked," he said sincerely.

She smiled, and this time it was a genuine smile of fondness. Dickie was as close to a brother as she ever had and she nearly wished he would join them, but she knew the realities.

"I know, Dickie," she said, and felt her eyes start to water, "I know you would, but you know I would never ask you to travel so far. Not now, when…" her eyes shifted up and the silent understanding hung heavily and clearly between them. There would be a new Duke of Clearwater all too soon.

She gently brushed lint from his jacket and dabbed tears from her eyes. "You're needed here, to see to the arrangements, to your title, all the responsibilities of a duke. Oh, look at me, getting all teary eyed when I will be fine. I'll just miss you so much."

Dickie frowned, wanting to disagree, but he couldn't, and they both knew it. "Send word if you need anything, or if he does something to upset you," he said, and hugged her tight. In some families, cousins certainly would not hug, but they had always been close, and Clementine did not hesitate for a moment to hug him back.

"And what, you'll come with a few week's delay to rescue me? I thank you for the thought anyway," she laughed and cried at the same time. "You know I'll hold my own."

"It's not your physical health I'm worried about when it comes to Will," Dickie said as he let her go, passing her a handkerchief from his pocket to dry her eyes and nose. "It's your heart I'm worried about. Will's a good chap but his way with women, Clemmie, I don't know if this is a good match for you.

You're not, you know...?" He lowered his voice in a questioning manner and looked at her belly.

She smacked his thigh with her fan.

"Ouch!"

"Serves you right for insinuating that! And no, nothing like that has happened. He is the perfect gentleman, if very annoying at times."

"Spoken like a true bride."

"Seriously, Dickie, I know what I'm doing," Clementine said in a kinder tone. "I have to do this, both for myself and for Papa. We need to know what happened, and William will be a tremendous help. I cannot think of a better bridal gift, truly, than him volunteering to help me in my quest to find out what happened to Papa."

"Then I shall have to let you go to bring mayhem to the world. I don't know if they're ready for you, Clemmie," he smiled and kissed her hand in a most flamboyant manner. She mock-curtsied as they had often done, ever since they had been small and had to practise these moves together.

"Darling, it is time we take our leave," William called, staying by the door. "Sorry Dickie, but we have a train to catch."

Clementine took his offered hand and he put on his top hat as he led her to the carriage. She settled into the plush seat, feeling the soft, dark blue velvet under her hands as if trying to anchor herself to the moment. She was leaving, and had no idea know what lay ahead or when she'd see her home and family again. It would not do to cry all the way to Egypt, so instead she smiled and waved at Dickie who had come to see them off.

"Remember what I told you," she could barely hear Dickie say to William, who grinned and squeezed his friend's hand before climbing into the carriage to sit opposite Clementine. His top hat grazed the roof of the carriage, Clementine noted, of all things. She felt herself somehow observing their departure as an outsider, as if a part of her was attempting to linger in the courtyard, to remember all the details, even as their carriage nudged away from Clearwater Abbey.

William took out his pocket watch and nodded. "With five minutes to spare. Not too bad, Clementine, but perhaps a little more haste for the rest of our journey? We wouldn't want to miss any of the connections we have booked."

"Yes, well, it is the first time I have said goodbye to the only family I have left, so apologies if I don't beg forgiveness for being slightly slow to leave. It won't happen later. I'll do my best to run beside you, or better yet, ahead of you."

William cocked his head. "I did not realise you were so close with them."

"If Papa is… Well, if he is dead," Clementine swallowed hard, "they are all I have left. I might not always see eye to eye with my aunt, but I love my uncle. And I practically grew up with Dickie. He truly is like a brother to me."

"Ah, that explains why he is so unhappy with our arrangement," William nodded.

"What did he say to you?"

William smiled and shook his head. "Something about skinning me alive and boiling me before feeding me to his dogs if I hurt you in any way. Funny thing is, I don't think he was worried about you getting hurt by anything that could happen when travelling and exploring. "

"Dear Dickie, he shouldn't worry," Clementine sighed.

"No indeed, but I could not explain to him how your heart will be perfectly safe with me, since we are not really in love; that this is a work arrangement only. So if you have been saying to him that you worry about your feelings, please don't."

"I have not said anything," Clementine snapped, "He was simply worried because he actually cares. Do you know the concept? Caring for someone genuinely? It's called love."

William's green eyes turned a shade colder. "I might have

heard the concept. A long time ago." He turned to look out the window.

Clementine wanted to ask more but sensed this was not the time nor place.

"Do you have the ring?" she asked instead.

"Ah, the important part. The trinkets and jewellery a man should offer in ample amounts," he said in a dry, amused voice.

Clementine cocked her head. "It could be just a simple band, but it is an important part of this charade. People will need to see we are an official couple, and with an engagement ring on my finger I will blend in easier as opposed to travelling without one."

"Indeed," William said and took a small jewellery box from his pocket. He unceremoniously handed it over to Clementine.

She took it with curiosity. The velvet on the box was worn, as if it had been used for generations. Clementine removed her gloves and placed them in her lap. She then carefully opened the stiff box and sighed with delight. In the box there was a small and simple band of gold, set with a solitary jewel. It was the deepest pink and very lovely.

"It is beautiful," Clementine breathed. "An amethyst?"

"An emerald," William corrected, "A rare pink emerald."

Clementine carefully slipped the ring onto her ring finger and looked at her hand appreciatively. "It fits perfectly. Thank you, William," she added, and he nodded. "So, whose ring was this?"

William did not look as if he wanted to answer at first, and Clementine was prepared to give a speech, explaining her need to know the backstory in case someone asked. It was all part of their ruse.

"It was my mother's ring. My brother did not allow me, as the second son, to take any of the official engagement or wedding rings we have in the family, but I was able to take one of the so-called lesser jewels," he gestured vaguely to her hand.

"Oh, I see. And what made you choose this one? I'm sure Lady Knightwood had many to choose from."

"It was one of my mother's favourite rings. And the colour made me think of you, nothing more, nothing less," William said, without feeling.

Clementine did not push the matter. "Well, I am honoured to wear your mother's ring, William, even if it's not a real engagement ring." She stared at the beautiful deep colour of the emerald. "I will cherish it."

William inclined his head with a distant look in his eyes. Clementine made a note in her head to return to the topic of William's mother. She knew that Lady Knightwood had died when her sons were quite young, but no one had told her what she had died of, exactly. Now was clearly not the time for such questions, so she instead settled in to admire the ring on her finger. And the rest of the carriage journey went quietly, with both of them in their own thoughts for the upcoming adventure.

THE MÉDITERRANNÉE EXPRESS

As they waited to embark on the ferry that would carry them over the channel to Calais, Clementine looked back at Dover and its white cliffs. William was addressing one of the luggage carriers, so Clementine decided to go and buy something to eat from the coffee kiosk on the pier. She settled for sausage rolls and coffee for them both. William seemed surprised to see her carrying the steaming mugs over, with the rolls balancing on top.

"Well, I never thought you would know how to actually buy anything," William said.

Clementine rolled her eyes. "Don't be silly, of course I have. You think I have a maid with me to handle everything I do? No, my mother taught me to do things on my own. She used to say that one could never know when there might be a situation when we don't have servants to help us."

She handed him his mug and sausage roll and greedily ate hers. William looked at her with a raised eyebrow.

"That was quick," he said, taking a tiny bite of his roll.

"Trust me, it's better to keep me well fed," Clementine shrugged and sipped the hot coffee. She looked again at the white cliffs and heard the seagulls cry above them. "It is beautiful," she noted.

William glanced at the cliffs. "Yes, I suppose. I have seen them so often that I forget they are quite striking on a sunny day like this." He drank his coffee and looked at the cliffs. "It's a great view from up there," he nodded to a viewing platform on top of the cliffs. "Perhaps next time we will have time to go."

"I would love that. I confess I have never been to Dover." She looked at her empty cup. "And this is the first time I'm stepping outside of England."

William smiled. "I keep forgetting how new this is to you. Perhaps I simply do not wish to acknowledge that I am travelling with a young girl with very little knowledge of the world." He sighed at Clementine's frown. "Just try to adjust as fast as you can, it'll be easier for us if I do not need to hold your hand, literally and figuratively, every step of the way." He finished his roll and coffee with some more muttering.

Clementine rolled her eyes. "I got food for us, didn't I? I will learn, and I will manage. I always have."

William gave her his mug to be returned. "And did you remember to haggle for the price for these treats?"

Clementine looked at him. "No, I mean, this isn't the marketplace, so I did not think—"

William corrected his top hat in the windy weather. "Point proven, Clemmie. You need to learn the attitude that everyone is trying to cheat and take advantage of you. Always play for your side to win; for yourself to win."

Clementine snatched his mug and turned away, saying over her shoulder, "You have not earned the right to call me Clemmie. It's Clementine to you."

She did not stop to listen to his answer and went briskly to return the mugs.

* * *

A SHORT WHILE LATER, they were making good speed on the ferry across to Calais. The weather was pleasant, and they chose to stay on the deck to admire the views.

"Goodbye England," Clementine said, holding tightly onto her parasol. It was a strange feeling: leaving so much behind, and in exchange, getting to experience so much that was new. A mix of sorrow and excitement. And disappointment that she would experience these new things with a stranger. William didn't even like her. Nor she him. He was nice to look at, she admitted that much, but he did not appreciate her one bit. He thought of her as a nuisance, just because she lacked the life experience he was so used to.

"Well, how does it feel?" William asked as he came to stand next to her, leaning casually against the railing.

"I feel fine," Clementine said, not caring to open up her feelings to him.

"Clearly, that's why you are squeezing your parasol as if it was your only safety."

Clementine ignored her urge to hit him on the head with the parasol. "It is the wind that makes me squeeze it. I wouldn't want to ask you to jump into the sea to fetch it back to me if it slips from my hands."

"As your devoted fiancé, I would obviously do anything for you. Being madly in love makes us do bravest things, Clemmie." He winked at her.

"Do not call me Clemmie," Clementine snapped, "It somehow sounds like clammy when you say it."

William laughed. "Well, I wouldn't know if you are." Before Clementine could protest, he added, "I think it would make it more believable if we used some endearing names for each other."

Clementine glared at him. "Only my closest family calls me Clemmie. You are not it." Her voice held more steel than she meant, but she wanted to keep some boundaries with this stranger she was somehow engaged to.

He stepped closer and she felt his full height loom over her, top hat and all. She raised her chin to attempt to match his height, even though it only reached his chest.

"Clementine," he said with surprising seriousness, "As your husband-to-be, I will be closer to you than any family member you've ever had. If you wish to continue this line of work, it will be an inevitable reality, and we will be as close as any wife and husband. If you cannot play this game, it will be better for you to return with this same ferry, safely back to England. I'll send you a postcard from Egypt."

Clementine turned away from him. "Wouldn't you be happy if I decide to do exactly that?" she muttered.

"Oh yes, I would," William said, "Trust me when I say that this would be much easier if you were to wait at home for news from me about your father. You wouldn't need to feel the discomfort of travelling to strange places with a stranger, nor have to endure the strange foods and hot temperatures of Egypt. You could be at home, Clemmie, with all the familiar comforts for a lady of your class. Dinners, gossip, suitors with horrible poems and mothers-in-law."

Clementine let out a small laugh. "Here is where you mistake me, William. I am here because I have to be, yes, but also because this is what I have always wanted to do. My father promised me I would become an explorer; an adventurer like him." She turned to look at William with dark and passionate eyes. "He might not be here to guide me, but this is still a chance to do what I always wanted. How many of those ladies of my class can say the same? Is this an ideal situation to start? No, it is not. I do not like you, William, but I am stuck with you, and I will prove to everyone I can do this, and any other job Her Majesty gives to me. So there will be no going back to familiar comforts, for I never enjoyed those comforts in the first place."

William raised an eyebrow at her passionate speech. "Well, I give you points for being overly confident of your skills. You might change your mind when you're hit with the desert heat and are running out of water. Don't say I didn't warn you."

Clementine shrugged. "We will just have to see as we go, won't we? You will see that I am not only a burden. I won't promise not to complain when things get tough, but I will promise to do my damned best to make this mission successful and find my papa."

"Oh, a lady who cusses," William grinned, "Watch it, Clemmie, or I might start to take a liking to you, despite you being a burden to me."

"I promise to be very careful of making myself accidentally likable to you. Believe me, there is no part in me that wishes to be desired by you," Clementine said, and snapped her parasol shut with more force than was necessary.

William leaned closer. "Why Clementine, I might not like you, but no one said anything about desire. I certainly have not denied you being a very desirable woman." His purring voice made Clementine shiver and she let out a sputter of outrage, stifling a slight giggle from the tickle in her ear.

He laughed. *The devil*, Clementine thought, flushing with anger.

"I seem to be shivering and will go inside," Clementine said stiffly. "Alone," she added, before leaving William on the deck, chuckling at his own stupidity.

* * *

IT WAS LATE when Clementine and William finally reached the train station of Calais-Ville, Clementine was ready for her bed in the sleeper carriage, but not before a proper dinner. She was tired and hungry, and Clementine disliked being hungry the most. She could withstand many things, but hunger was one of her personal nemeses.

William went ahead, his jacket flowing in the windy summer evening, steam from the train obscuring him occasionally, like a ghost. He barked orders for their luggage to be carried in an orderly way, and Clementine was left next to their carriage to wait with their smaller luggage, which contained nothing more than toiletries and a change of clothing. She waited for a moment for William to return but eventually grew too bored, and began checking for their sleeping cabins. *Carriage two, cabins three and four.* She sighed a small sigh of relief. At least they would not have to share a sleeping cabin yet. She wouldn't put it past William to try and test her right away with something like sharing sleeping quarters. She would do it, if necessary, but preferred to have her privacy if still possible. Plenty of married couples travelled separately, and they were only engaged, so it would bring no odd questions.

Clementine did not see any of the train attendants to help her lift the bags. She shrugged and decided to go ahead and hoist the luggage up to the train herself instead of waiting for William to handle everything. She lifted her own luggage without trouble, but her skirt got tangled in one of the leather buckles, and soon she was making a fuss of herself by blocking the way of other passengers. She flushed and fumbled to free the intricate lace of her train, trying to be both quick and careful while apologising to those waiting to board the train. She could feel her cheeks blush as the lace refused to come free of the buckle. *Where was William?*

"You're in a bit of a pickle, aren't you? Careful with that gorgeous lace! Here, let me help you."

Clementine lifted her flushed face to see a woman standing in front of her. She had beautiful red hair and blue eyes that seemed to sparkle with her dazzling smile. The woman peered at the lace and soon freed Clementine with a few careful movements of her tan-gloved hands. She straightened up and smoothed her deep blue travel dress, which complimented her very well. Clementine frowned for a moment, because the English woman certainly seemed familiar.

"Thank you, I was only trying to get the luggage in, while my fiancé dealt with our travel trunks. And then I got stuck." Clementine lifted William's bag up to the train where an attendant finally hurried to help.

"You should be stuck to your fiancé," the woman laughed. "Shame on him for leaving you here on your own to hoist bags, as if you worked for the train company. Although, now that you say it, my husband Bobby has also disappeared into the steam. Vanished, just like that, can you believe?" She rolled her eyes, then fixed them on Clementine, recognition suddenly apparent.

"Well, I say. It's Lady Clementine Whitham, isn't it? Fancy meeting you here! Last of the gossip was that you were– Oh! You are here with Mr Hunt, aren't you? So the rumors were true!" Her voice was all delight, and she seemed genuinely happy to have caught the couple here, of all places. They moved slightly to let another passenger pass them.

Clementine plastered a smile on her face, finally remembering who this woman was. "And what brings you here, Lady Josephine?" They had met at some recent dances, but Lady Josephine was a few years older than Clementine, so had been out in society earlier, and they had not been very well acquainted in the London circles. Lady Josephine had also been at the Buckingham palace courtyard; Clementine remembered greeting her as they passed each other before the audience with the queen.

" Please call me JoJo, everyone does. We are on our honeymoon, going to Egypt! Very exciting. Oh, here is Bob, and is that your Mr Hunt?"

Clementine flinched, hopefully inwardly only, when JoJo

called him *her* Mr Hunt. Outwardly, Clementine smiled like a fool in love upon seeing her man. "Yes, that's him."

"Bob, darling," JoJo waved. "And Mr Hunt! How lovely to see you again. How is your dear brother? He used to dance with me at every ball before Bob here made me his bride and took me off the market, so to say," she winked at her husband.

Clementine curtsied and Lord Robert Blake kissed her hand. "Lady Clementine, fancy meeting you here. I already bumped into your chap. Good old William, always running around the world, and now he has you running with him." He patted William on the shoulder.

"I was just telling her about our very romantic honeymoon to Egypt," JoJo said, and corrected her straw hat slightly, even though it looked perfect on her. "But I never heard what these two love birds are doing here?"

"We are on an engagement vacation, of sorts ," William smiled and offered his hand to Clementine. She hooked hers meekly into his, and he patted her hand. "Clementine's father's fate is still a mystery, so while we travel and enjoy ourselves, we will of course try to find anything we can about Lord Whitham before the actual wedding."

JoJo's face was sympathetic, and, if possible, her empathy made her even lovelier. "Oh yes, of course, poor dear," she said to Clementine. "It must have been such a distressing time. But does it mean then that we share a journey — you are on your way to Egypt, too?"

"Yes," Clementine nodded. "My father was last seen in Egypt, at the dig site, so we are following his footsteps as best as William can remember. He was with Father when he disappeared and brought to us the news, as well as the wish from my father for the two of us to marry. Dear Papa," Clementine sighed, her voice breaking slightly. She was acting, but only a little.

"Quite so," William said gravely, "I could not possibly let

anything stress my wife on the happiest day of our lives, so it is better to get clarity if we can, and then focus on the wedding."

"Well then, I am glad we ran into each other. We will keep you company and help lift your spirits, if you will have us," JoJo said with her natural glee.

Clementine smiled. JoJo's smile was very contagious. She was an energetic individual, and Clementine remembered that many gossiped about JoJo being too much for any man to handle when she came out into society. But it seemed that Bob was just the right amount of calm for her.

"That would be lovely," Clementine said.

"Then we will see you for cocktails in the restaurant carriage, shall we say in an hour?" JoJo said. "Should give you time to get settled in." With a swish of skirts, she and Bob climbed onto the train.

"Where is our luggage?" William asked.

"Oh, I hoisted them up and someone from the train took them to our cabins."

"Oh Clemmie," William sighed, "Always, always keep your eyes on the essential luggage. What if I had something valuable in mine?"

"Well, how would I have known that? Do you?"

"No, I have all that matters with me," he patted his coat pocket.

"Well, no harm done then, unless they wanted to steal my chemise."

"It's a lesson to learn, Clemmie," he said, and offered his hand to help Clementine up from the platform.

"Stop calling me that," she said, ignoring his hand as she gathered her skirts and climbed onto the train.

EVENING ON BOARD

The Méditerrannée Express was every bit as luxurious as Clementine had heard. It was a convenient way to reach Southern France and continue their way on a steamer boat towards Egypt. Overnight, the Méditerrannée Express would stop and collect more carriages along the way, until they finally reached Marseille the next afternoon.

Clementine stepped into the corridor and received the greeting of a conductor in a neat blue and gold uniform. William had already disappeared into their cabins to inspect that the luggage was there. It was, and Clementine did feel like pointing out that he was overreacting, but she bit her tongue.

The blue carpets of the corridor muted the sounds of heels as people walked into their cabins. William emerged from the cabins and leaned against the lacquered wood panel of the wall, eyeing Clementine.

"So, which one does Lady Clementine prefer?"

"Oh, I don't mind. Whichever has my luggage," she said, peering into the sleeping cabins. The same dark blue carpet covered the floor . A bunkbed on one side, a small desk in the middle, and a sofa opposite the beds, as well as a small wash basin. Heavy velvet curtains framed the cabin's window. It certainly looked comfortable enough.

"The shared bathrooms for men and women are at the end of this carriage," William inclined his head.

Clementine nodded casually.

"Have you ever actually been on a train? Aside from travelling to London, I mean?" William asked.

"Yes, of course I have," Clementine exclaimed.

"When?"

"It has been some time."

"Were you more than five years of age?" William asked drily.

"Yes, as a matter of fact, I was nine. My mother took me for a local adventure," she said, her voice quieting at the mention of her mother.

William ignored her answer and leaned in to whisper, "Listen, I meant what I said. Always carry your essentials on your body. Never trust that no one might have access to your train cabin, hotel room or other lodging. People can and will be bribed. Here," he gave her the key to her cabin, "Stuff it in your corset if you don't have pockets, and keep your wits with you."

"I have pockets, thank you very much," she said with a flush as his eyes trailed the edge of her corset.

"Good. Make good use of them then," he said, "See you in thirty minutes."

With that, he turned to go into his cabin and slammed the door almost in her face. Luckily there were no others in the corridor just then, otherwise it might have looked like slightly odd behavior from a fiancé. Clementine would remember to bring that up next time he started to lecture her about making their ruse feel real.

She stepped into her cabin, closed the wooden door, and leaned against it for a moment. After all the noise of the train station, the silence was welcome. The day had been taxing, not only because of the travelling, but also because she felt many things. Sad, hopeful, excited, curious, and on top of those she also felt irritated by Mr Hunt, and the fact that she was stuck with him. She'd never been so far from home, and now she was travelling to Egypt with a man who was still practically a stranger. Not for the first time, Clementine wondered if this had been a mistake. But then she shook her head and reminded herself of her options. Never finding out what happened to Papa, not getting her inheritance for seven years in the worst case scenario, and getting married off to someone her aunt deemed acceptable. No, she shook her head again. It wasn't an option.

She did not have much time before their cocktails with the Blakes. Clementine hoped there would be food as well, or she might faint. No, that would be uncharacteristic. She would get angry and likely bite William's head off — figuratively of course.

She decided to change from her travel dress to a simple evening dress she had packed with her in the smaller trunk.

Even though Clementine had grown up with servants, her mother had insisted she knew how to live without them if needed. Her mother came from a humbler background, and had only later in life become accustomed to servants, which meant she was a very practical woman. Mother had left when Clementine was only eleven years old, but by then she knew how to make a fire to keep the rooms warm, how fry an egg and boil tea. And, perhaps most importantly, she knew how to wiggle herself free from her layers of dresses and how to dress herself, all the way up to fixing her own hair. So even though it took more time, Clementine managed to change out of her red travel dress and into a black and gold silk dress with a heavily embroidered corset.

She could feel the train moving and glanced through the windows. The summer night had dimmed to darkness, but she could just make out that the French city was slowly changing into rolling hills and villages. She was sorry that they would not stop at any of the cities or picturesque villages. She would like to explore France one day if she could. To visit The Louvre, that would be wonderful.

Since she was already ready, she went to the corridor and slipped the key to a hidden pocket. She stopped by William's room, but after a moment of listening she couldn't hear anything and thought that he was perhaps taking a quick nap. So she continued on her own to the restaurant carriage.

The carriage was full but a table was reserved for each cabin so she would have a chance for a late-night meal, thank goodness. Clementine stayed by the bar, waiting for the Blake couple to appear, and asked for a cocktail that was popular.

"Cabin number, please," the bartender asked.

"Number three, Lady Clementine Whitham."

The bartender nodded and started to mix her drink. She had not had many cocktails, but it looked lovely, with a light hue and a few blue berries, served in a beautiful wide glass. When the waiter presented it to her, she sipped it and almost coughed. "Oh," she managed, "It is strong, isn't it?"

The waiter nodded. "Gin, lemonade and sloe berries. Mostly gin," he said with a grin.

Clementine hesitated, then she pushed the cocktail away. The strong alcohol burned in her mouth. "I'm afraid I cannot drink it. May I have a glass of champagne instead?"

The waiter obliged her, of course. Why did she feel like she shouldn't even ask? Clementine reminded herself to act like a woman of her class, to act as confident as she usually felt. Act like a woman who was about to marry the man she loved. Like a woman who had travelled the world and seen much of it.

"Ah, there you are darling," William greeted her as if he had been looking forward to it. He had changed into dinner attire as well and played the part of a groom who missed his bride.

He kissed her gently — first on her hand, and then on her cheek, as if to make it clear to the rest of the carriage that they were together. Clementine blushed when she felt his breath on her cheek. His lips did not actually touch her skin, but they were so close she could almost feel them.

"Darling," she said and beamed at him, "What took you so long?"

"Oh, you know," he waved her off, "Is this yours?" He pointed at the cocktail she had sipped.

"Yes, but I did not enjoy it. Hence the champagne."

He took her discarded drink and raised it to her. "Cheers, old girl, to this journey and to us."

Clementine clinked her glass against his. "To us," she said with a raised eyebrow and sipped her champagne.

William tossed his drink down in one gulp and grimaced. "You're right, it is quite ghastly." He waved the bartender over and asked for a whisky.

"Ah, at it already, Hunt?" Lord Robert — Bob — came into view, and behind him, the ever-fashionable JoJo. She had changed her blue dress for a cream one with blue embroidery. She looked like a delicate cornflower with the sharpness of the first frost of winter.

"Clementine." She kissed her cheek as if they were old friends. "Oh, champagne. Excellent choice! I'll have one too," she said to the bartender. She glanced at Bob and William, who were deep in discussion about the latest gun models. Clementine raised her eyebrow and JoJo laughed. "Oh, let's leave them be. Who wants to talk about guns anyway?" she exclaimed, and took the glass that was brought to her.

"Here's to femininity," JoJo declared, "And for letting them have their moment before they have to be cordial with us again." She laughed and clinked her glass to Clementine's. Clementine smiled and took a mouthful from the glass, letting the bubbles tickle her tongue. "So, how are you settling into, well, almost married life? Life as a bride! I understand it came quite as a surprise to everyone."

"Oh yes," Clementine agreed, feeling the warmth of the drink spread across her cheeks, "I dare say no one but William knew. Well, apart from my father of course. My aunt was in quite a shock."

"Ah yes, the Duchess of Clearwater, am I right? A very formidable lady, isn't she?" JoJo said.

"Yes, she is. She supports me in all of this, but I do think she is still adjusting to the happy news."

"Dear me, I should expect so. Still, if you don't mind me saying, Mr Hunt is not the worst of them." JoJo took another long sip from her glass. "If you can look past his, well, past."

Clementine wasn't sure if she should ask more, since the comment clearly demanded clarification. But that surely would make it seem as if she did not know her fiancé.

"Indeed, I could have done worse and so could he," she merely said.

"I applaud you, my dear," JoJo said. "You don't seem to be bothered by the many weeping women he has left behind him. Quite the conqueror, as well as an adventurer. I'll admit that once upon a time I had my eyes on him as well," she chuckled.

Clementine felt her cheeks burn, not only from the champagne.

"Oh, my dear, I didn't mean to embarrass you. But he is very fine to look at, and men with that kind of a reputation tend to be great lovers," JoJo whispered.

Clementine was glad she did not have time to come up with a response before JoJo swiftly changed the subject.

"Do tell what plans you have for the wedding." JoJo finished her glass and gestured for the waiter to bring them two more.

"Well, we have hardly made any plans aside from this journey," Clementine said. The waiter brought the champagne and Clementine took hers, even though she still had some in her former glass.

Just then, William and Bob turned towards them.

"I'm sure you ladies have lots more to gossip about, but I believe it is time for my bride to have her supper and then we are off to bed. It has been a long day," William said apologetically.

"Oh, we quite understand," JoJo grinned and glanced at Bob. "We can't wait to go and lie down as well."

Clementine tried to ignore the remark, but a wicked grin from William made her heart race. It was most annoying, and Clementine cursed her inexperience, for there could be no other reason for her reactions to him. She hated to admit it, but William was right: she needed to get used to him, and to them as a couple, so she would not be so obviously — well, virginous, she supposed. Ignoring her initial reaction, she glared at him.

"Why William, what have you done to make your bride so cool? Look at how she looks at you," JoJo said.

Bob barked a laugh. "It's always something we do, isn't it?" he said, and JoJo chuckled.

"Oh, it is nothing," William improvised, "Earlier I merely disagreed with some of Clementine's wishes for the wedding flowers. She wants roses but I warned that the thorns might prick her, and blood could smear our happy day," William said, raising his glass to Clementine.

"Yes, well, as I said to William, thorns are a part of married life, so he should get used to them," Clementine said, smiling sweetly, but her dark eyes made no one doubt the insincerity of her smile.

"My, Clementine, you have more spirit than I gave you credit for," JoJo laughed, "Come now, a little drink will surely make your anger for your fiancé's shortcomings lessen. Clementine was irritated enough to toss back her glass of champagne in a few gulps.

"A thirsty evening, I see." JoJo gestured for a refill and Clementine gladly accepted another glass, her eyes still set on William with all the annoyance in the world.

"Women always get annoyed by the smallest things," huffed Bob behind his cigar. "If you don't remember their favourite flowers, it's the end of the world. How am I supposed to know which flower it is? Isn't it enough that I bring some flowers?" He took a deep gulp from his glass. "Ridiculous, eh, Hunt?"

"Just because you don't remember my favourite flowers, you can't assume that William doesn't," JoJo cut in, and rolled her blue eyes. "Care to guess, William? What are Clementine's favourite flowers?"

William circled around Clementine, her eyes not leaving his face. The candlelight and her gold embellished dress reflected in his eyes like flames.

He placed his hand gently on her lower back. She stiffened but did not want to cause a scene. William smiled and smelled the air. "I do not need to guess. My lovely bride-to-be reminds me of her favourite flowers every day with her scent. She loves lilacs, and is every bit as lovely as the first lilacs of the summer season."

Bob grunted, but JoJo's laughter was like silver bells at William's romantic words. Clementine flushed pink and hid her face in a sip from her refilled glass.

"See, Bob, it is not impossible! Do try to remember mine, dear," JoJo cooed.

"Excuse us," William said, leading Clementine away.

* * *

THE RESTAURANT CARRIAGE was luxuriously lit with chandeliers that glistened and threw a soft light around the dining car. Their table for two had plush seats either side of a beautiful table with a white starched tablecloth, fresh flowers and a small candelabra. The train hummed and swayed softly as the evening darkened. William helped Clementine into her seat and took his opposite her.

"You look... appropriate," he said, even though his eyes were on his menu. Clementine noticed his hair was slightly damp, darker, with the curls combed back.

"Likewise," she said, not knowing what else to say to such an odd compliment. He huffed in response.

"What looks good?" she asked, glancing at the menu, "I am quite famished, even if it is late. I am well equipped for many situations, William, but being hungry is something I hate."

"Spoken like a true upper-class lady," William said without looking at her.

"Regardless of class, people get hungry."

He put away the menu. "Yes, but the difference is realising that some won't get the food, even when their life depends on it."

Clementine also put down her menu with a snap. "I know there are plenty of people in our country and around the world who are suffering from hunger. But do not put on my head the misery that people like your ancestors failed to change," she hissed, and her stomach growled in response.

"I would guess your ancestors are also to blame for not using their wealth to feed their people," William said. .

"I am only half English, so your ancestors are more to blame," she said. It made no sense, but she was tired and cranky with hunger.

"I only point this out because we will be travelling in places where food and eating might not be a given thing. Do not forget your privilege, Clementine. I certainly don't."

"Oh, I do believe you know about privilege," Clementine said, keeping her voice low. "An English gentleman, with the power and money of the empire and good looks to compensate for what you might be missing in manners."

"I am pleased again to hear you think so well of my looks." His smile reminded her of a tiger baring its teeth before it pounced .

"That's all you heard me say?"

"Yes, if I'm honest," he said and gestured for the waiter.

"Yes, my lord and lady, may I take your order?" A waiter in white came and stood before them.

William ordered without asking Clementine anything about her preferences, but she did not want to delay getting the food by bickering about him making decisions for her.

"I trust you don't mind me ordering for both of us," William said as he raised his glass to her.

"Now you ask? After you order? But your selection was actually good, so this time I do not mind." She raised her glass to him and took a tiny sip. "I really shouldn't have more champagne. It is good, but I feel the effects too easily."

"Good to know." William took her glass and filled it with water from a carafe. "You should have told me that before."

"You did not stop to ask, just like with the food. I don't know how you and my father travelled together, but I think you would have asked his counsel more than you have mine."

"I believe we grew to know each other well enough that I was able to handle most of the everyday matters on his behalf," William said, "Including ordering his food, and knowing that I could not order anything too fatty this late or he would have gastric problems in the night."

Clementine's eyes suddenly glimmered and she blinked the threatening tears away.

William looked at her with some surprise. "I never knew gastric problems would make a woman cry."

Clementine let out a shaky sigh once she was sure she wouldn't cry. "It's not that, obviously. It is only the realisation that I might not ever learn about these details, myself. You might know my father better than me, and I adore him. I always wanted to become just like him."

William looked at her thoughtfully. "You're right, you might never know him as I did. But perhaps that is best when you have clearly idolised him for your entire life."

"What do you mean?"

"Only that when you idolise people and then get to really know them, well, sometimes we are disappointed when we find out our heroes are merely human, with human flaws..."

"You could never burst my bubble, "Clementine smiled. "If you can share anything about Papa, I would love to hear it." She dabbed her eyes with a napkin.

William sighed. "Well, that is understandable, I suppose. Let's see. Did he tell you about how we came to find out where to start our excavation site?"

Clementine's eyes brightened, sparkling in the candlelight.

"Well, we had just arrived at Alexandria and had to find our way about. We did not know anyone, had no clues of how to best reach the Temple of Hathor . It was late, we were tired, and had no plans for where to stay overnight."

"That must have been exciting,." Clementine could not wait to hear more.

"Your father was a much more seasoned adventurer than I." William avoided saying treasure hunter. "He said he knew one place guaranteed to give us a good start. He had used the same logic in different countries, different cities, and different cultures."

"My father seemed to always know best," Clementine sighed.

"Quite. So he gestured for me and his valet to follow him. We were in the Alexandria harbour. Your father fixed his eyes on the captain of our vessel and we followed the chap across the harbour to an establishment down one of the many alleyways. It was one of those dark and shady alleys with scents you could not quite recognise but made you grimace. But a warm light shone through the windows of the building we were about to enter; a most welcoming sight for worn out travelers."

"And did you find the clues you were looking for?" Clementine asked with excitement.

"Turns out your father was right. We did discover the information, through some bribing. Eventually." William grinned, and his smile made Clementine's waver.

"What–" she started.

"Your father took us to a well-known brothel. The madam was lovely, and with a not-so-small bribe, she was able to tell us who to go to for more information on recent dig sites, and which of her girls knew which English lords had been to which parts of the country before they left."

"Oh," Clementine said, not knowing what else to say.

"And you know what your old man said?" William smiled drily and looked at Clementine. "Business is business, but let's have some fun first."

Clementine gasped and her hand rose to her mouth.

"So, dearest, your father had many sides to him. He was– is a brilliant adventurer and knew to have a good time, even when dead tired." William shook his head. "So how about that for a story about your father?" He leant his chin on his hand.

"You really are a bastard," Clementine hissed.

"I can assure you, I am my father's son, even if I wish I wasn't," William said. "You asked me to tell you of your dear papa and I am telling you how I knew him."

"Fine," Clementine snapped, "In the future, keep the brothel stories to yourself, if you would be so kind."

"As my bride wishes. But the lesson is this: you might not know all there is to your father. And also, brothels can be great for information if you are ever in a pickle."

Luckily the waiter arrived just then with their late dinner: poulet au vin blanc and seasonal greens, steamed lightly.

"Let's just eat, shall we?" Clementine said and dug in without waiting for William's reply.

"Bon appetit, darling."

They ate in silence for a while, as the rest of the restaurant compartment chattered and clinked their glasses and cutlery. Soon, Clementine started to relax, feeling more like herself instead of a hungry swamp monster.

"So, let us talk while there is still loud enough noise around us," William noted after the waiter had cleared their plates and they waited for dessert.

"What do you mean?" Clementine asked, sipping a very good red wine. The wine pairing had been as excellent as the food, and she was feeling content and slightly lightheaded.

"I assume you wish to know more about our plan to get to the tomb."

"Well, what's the plan then?" Clementine asked.

William waited until the waiter had finished pouring their coffee and port wine, and had set the lemon custard tart in front of them.

"So, the plan is this," William said while Clementine took her time enjoying the first mouthful. "Are you listening?" he asked.

"Yes, of course" Clementine said, setting her fork down.

"The plan is to switch to The Neva steamer in Marseilles. We should be well in time to make the change from train to steamer ship, which will take us to Alexandria."

"Yes, the steamer will take us to Alexandria in four days and we will have time to enjoy the port before changing to a Lloyd Express which will take us to Cairo, where we will board a cruise boat which will take us up the Nile," Clementine added .

"Indeed, and we will have to disembark in Dendera to reach the tombs around the Temple of Hathor," William said, "I've sent a telegram to my contact, who had been helping your father and I in the excavation. We should have modest accommodation, in tents, near the temple grounds where most excavation groups gather before heading out to the desert and the different dig sites of that area. From there, we will get a guide and some men to take us to the site of the tomb of Hathor's priestesses. Dozens of them have been found so far, all identical, and we do not yet know which is the tomb of the first high priestess."

"Oh," Clementine said, "I did not realise we still need to find the right tomb. If you know where the dig site is, why do we need a guide? Why not just go alone and minimise the risks?" she asked, and poured them both some more coffee from an ornate silver pot.

"The desert can be difficult to navigate, which is why we will need help. I could perhaps find the tombs on my own, eventually, but we don't want to lose time in case someone else has also found them. Depending on the sandstorms in the area, we will need help digging them out from the sand."

"What, you didn't leave someone — that contact of yours — to guard the area?"

Shaking his head, William looked out the window into the darkness. "No, Clementine. It goes back to trust. Never trust anyone in this business. If you tell someone about a possible untouched tomb, they will rob the treasures as soon as you turn your back. I'm sure my contact has tried to go back and find the tomb, and it may be that he has done so. Besides, I'm trusting that the recent findings in Luxor have drawn most tomb raiders from this side of the Nile. Hathor's temple doesn't have anything to rob, to my knowledge, so this isn't as busy a location, or at least it wasn't when I left."

"I see. So there is a chance that someone has found the right tomb and taken the Tears of Hathor already?"

"That is always a possibility," William nodded. "But it is not a well-known myth, or at least I did not hear anyone talk about it aside from myself and your father at camp. So, if we are lucky, it could be that the Tears are still there."

Clementine nodded. "Along with any clues about my father," she added. "And then we'll head back to England for a new task, if we are successful?"

"Let's hope we are. Her Majesty does not like her adventurers returning empty-handed. Even if we don't find the exact items she requests, it is still better to return with something if you want to keep your job."

"William, do you ever feel bad about the items you take?" Clementine asked suddenly. It was the only thing she had doubts about whenever she dreamed of becoming an adventurer like her father. She wanted to explore and discover, but not necessarily steal.

William looked at her in silence for a moment. "I try to think of it that I am merely a tool for Her Majesty to use. If it's not me it would be someone else," he said quietly. "Her Majesty, other rulers, and influential people will get what they want, and there will always be people lending them the necessary skills and knowledge to achieve their goals. Besides, it pays for food and bills. As a second son with no other prospects, unless my dear brother dies, this is as good a job as some other profession."

"Well, you could have become a priest." Clementine smiled at the idea. "Second sons become priests or military officers, don't they?"

"I confess to having too little faith for both vocations," William said with a shrug. "No, I am happy where I am, and when I can, I try to show kindness to the locals I encounter or employ. Fair money for fair work or help. But not trusting anyone," William reminded.

"It must be hard to gain your trust," Clementine remarked as the waiter came to take their plates away.

"Very few people have my trust, even less if you count the ones who live. In fact, you can count them with one hand," William said.

"And do you trust me yet?" Clementine cocked her head, her dark curls pouring over her left shoulder.

"No, I do not," William said. "It's nothing personal. Well, actually, it is personal, since I don't like you having slithered your way into this mission, which has stuck us to each other till death do us part."

"That was the queen's idea, not mine," Clementine kept her voice low with effort, "I only wanted to find my father and gain my independence with my inheritance, or through work. And just like you, I didn't exactly have many options. You didn't want to become a priest or an officer; I didn't want to become a wife to some man I do not care for."

"And yet here you are, engaged to a stranger," William said, with no little resentment in his eyes. "For all you know I could be a wife-beating, raving lunatic. By the end of this journey, you might wish you had married an old, rich lord who would die soon enough. In fact, I am counting on you quitting once we find some evidence of your father."

They sipped their coffee in silence, Clementine seething in her annoyance and William quietly observing her.

"What?" she finally asked.

"Well, if you want to make people think we are an old bickering couple, you're making a success of it," William said with amusement.

She smiled back at him, despite herself. It was annoying that he could disarm her from being irritated in the first place. She thought a change of subject might be helpful. Outside, it was well past the twilight hour and very dark. Clementine saw her flushed cheeks in the window's reflection. She let her shoulders relax and turned back to William. Perhaps she was being too easily annoyed.

"You remembered the flowers," Clementine said. "I thought it was sweet that you remembered, since it's not something I ever said to you."

William smiled a crooked smile and his green eyes seemed to spark. "When I saw you hanging from that apple tree branch, I swear I could smell the scent of your lilac perfume long before I reached you. It was not difficult to guess. And in that lavender dress, you looked like a lilac blossom anyway."

Clementine snorted a very unladylike laugh. "And pray tell, how does a human look like a lilac blossom? Plump and ready to drop from the branch?"

"Delicate and exquisite," William said, looking at her with amusement.

"Oh," Clementine said and sipped her water. "Thank you, that is kind of you to say."

"It is the truth. I see no reason to not say it."

"Which means you trust me a little then? If you can trust me to not swoon when you say nice things like that?" Clementine smiled.

"Why is trust such a big issue for you?" William asked, his long fingers playing with a coffee spoon.

"Why wouldn't it be? I am about to pledge my life to this mission, and as you said, we are stuck together. I have to trust you to help me find my father, and it would help me trust you if I knew you gave me the same benefit of the doubt."

"So, if I show trust in you, you will trust me more?" William asked.

Clementine looked at his handsome features. His dinner jacket was immaculate and face clean shaven. She briefly wondered if he knew that he too had a scent that lingered about him — like a mix of soap and coffee. It was not an unpleasant smell.

"Yes, that is what I mean," Clementine said.

"But I have told you not to trust anyone. The same goes for me. You should not trust me either, Clementine."

She dismissed his words with a frown. " We can learn to trust each other. We can have what you and my father surely shared; some level of trust in knowing you could rely on the other person to pull their weight. Just give me a chance to be worthy of your trust. After all, I am giving that chance to you."

William's expression was a mystery to Clementine. His green eyes seemed darker and intense. So intense that Clementine felt herself dropping her gaze to his lips. She quickly averted her eyes and sipped her coffee. The champagne and wines were swimming in her head, and she hoped the coffee would help.

"I can see your point, Clementine. But trust is built over time, with actions, not with words, so it cannot happen simply from us speaking of it. Still, I am willing to open myself up a little to see if you can be trustworthy."

Clementine clapped and raised her glass to him. "To a little bit of trust!"

William clinked his glass to hers. "Don't say I didn't warn you," he said, and sipped his glass of port.

"Oh pish," Clementine said.

The waiter came to ask if they wanted something more. Clementine declined and they rose to leave.

William placed his hand gently behind her lower back to guide her away. She stiffened, but did not want to cause a scene. He was so close to her, and she could feel the warmth of his hand on her back, spreading lower and lower. She could feel her annoyance melting away and a blush creeping up her cheeks, a very relaxed feeling accompanying it. She blinked, thinking perhaps that last glass of port had been too much. She turned and they left the table, his hand still resting on the nook of her back, burning through the fabric of her dress.

"Lilacs," William murmured behind her, and she wasn't sure if she had heard right.

Before Clementine could say anything to the surprising remark, they passed Bob and JoJo's table. "See, Bob, that is how it should be between people in love. Him so close to her, and her as pink as peonies in the summer," JoJo cooed to them.

"Excuse us," William said with a grin, and led the still blushing, lightheaded Clementine away as they slowly made their way back to their compartment.

William opened the door to her carriage for her, and when she turned to say goodbye to him, he gently kissed her hand, his lips lightly touching her gloved hand. "You know, I much preferred it when you had no gloves. These silk gloves give no credit to the softness of my lady's hands," he smiled and looked up at her.

She had to laugh at this remark. "You mean my rough hands from punching, hitting and grappling? Oh, and from wielding a fan at anyone with unwanted advances?" She challenged him with her eyes .

The train rocked, and the sudden motion sent Clementine staggering against William's chest.

"Careful now," William said as he gently steadied her. His hands lingered on her sides, and even through her corset, Clementine could feel his fingertips as if they were touching her skin. She shivered and cast a curious glance at him from beneath her lowered lashes. She felt a sudden pang of yearning for something she couldn't quite describe.

"That, my dear, is a very dangerous look on your lovely face," he murmured. "Remember what I said in that orchard." His face was so close to hers she could see the speckles of golden brown in his green eyes. It was so very easy to just forget herself and keep gazing into them.

"What was that?" she whispered, as if this moment might break if she spoke too loudly. Her lips parted softly as she continued to match his gaze.

"I will only do to my lady as she asks." William smiled and kissed her hand again. "Good night, Clemmie." With that, he disappeared into his cabin, his long, lean frame moving quickly and without a sound.

Clementine blinked at his quick disappearance and had a sudden, violent urge to scream in frustration. She stood in the corridor for a moment, unsure of what had just happened. William seemed to want to keep her on her toes for his own devilish reasons. It was most annoying. She ignored the small voice in her head that had been urging her to kiss him; to rise on her tiptoes just a little and invite him to lean in until their lips met.

Shaking her head, Clementine went into her compartment and shut the door behind her. She looked out at the dark night passing by her window and went to close the curtains before the inevitable task of undressing. She vaguely heard steps in the corridor; likely people moving between their sleeping cabins and the bathrooms before going to bed. The door of William's compartment opened and closed next door. Clementine shook away any thoughts of William bathing. Those images were most dangerous and indecent! Shaking her head, she started to take off her jewellery.

* * *

SHE HAD JUST REMOVED MOST of the pins from her hair when there was a knock on her door. She blushed, as she immediately guessed it to be William, wishing to woo her for something more. This would simply not do. They had to focus on the mission. She would tell him just that, and tell him to go to bed, alone.

Clementine opened the door.

"Look, William–" she began, and then two things happened at once.

One: it was not William behind the door, but three masked men.

Two: she had the instinct to try and close the door very quickly.

Clementine's reflex was the only thing that saved her from being on the receiving end of the first man's kick, which hit the door instead and slammed Clementine painfully against the wall of her cabin. She managed not to hit her head too badly, instinctively crouching in defense.

The first man came through the smashed doorway and Clementine had no time to see if she was injured or not. It wouldn't have mattered anyway — she moved on instinct, slamming her elbow into the man's head before he had time to grab for her. The man went down with a grunt but Clementine was now stuck in the small corner.

"William!" she screamed, hoping that he or anyone else would soon come to intervene as the two companions of the first man proceeded inside. She gaped at the size of the larger of the two. He barely fit through the door! It all happened so quickly, but she noted they had no visible guns in their hands. Or knives. *Something positive*, she tried to tell herself. *Must not be intimidated by being outnumbered, or by facing anyone bigger than you are!* She ignored the tight feeling of fear in her stomach and gave in to her instincts and her training.

The first man threw a punch at Clementine with his massive fists. She blocked as best she could, noting how different it felt to block a heavy hitter. With effort, she landed a kick on his shin. Somewhere in her brain she could hear Mrs Edith's firm voice. *The main thing is to keep them from hitting any critical areas: head, joints, chest or crotch.*

The smaller man swung a piece of the door at her and she ducked. The strike hit his huge companion instead.

"Idiot," the big man bellowed, and Clementine used the distraction to duck under the broken doorframe to get out into the corridor, but her dress kept getting stuck and the splintered wood ripped at her skin. She felt hands trying to grab her, but she kicked them away, managing to poke her head out of the opening.

"Help!" she screamed. Some of the sleeping cabins opened, but people hesitated in the doorways. *Why won't they help?*

Strong hands around her waist yanked her backwards. Her feet kicked in vain as she was lifted upright, the hands squeezing all the air out of her. She couldn't scream. Her fists hit the man's hands to no avail. She tried prying herself free like a kitten in a bear's hug, but she wasn't strong enough to twist the man's thick fingers or cause any real pain to him.

It was no use, and she felt like crying from the frustration. She could feel herself tire at the struggle, realising it was very unlikely that she could squirm herself out from the grapple. She stopped struggling and panted for air. Her hair was drenched in sweat, and blood dripped from her forehead into her eye. She glared at the man approaching her, not allowing herself to feel the full weight of fear. Not yet. She saw that the first man was still on the floor, and it gave her comfort and a surge of confidence. She could take these ruffians down. She mustn't give up! What did Edith used to say when they practised? *Use any advantage, any item as weapons, to win.*

"Where are your father's notes? Where is the tomb?" The smaller man came to stand before her while the other kept her in a tight embrace.

Clementine waited, gasping shallowly for air. She needed to buy some time.

"In that reticule… papers from Papa," she said hoarsely, and nodded towards the fallen pouch. The man came closer, picked it up and rummaged through it, dropping most of the items to the floor. He read the letter then ripped it to pieces. Clementine winced at the sight of Papa's last letter being destroyed, but ignored her sorrow for now. She needed the idiot to come closer.

"Not what we are looking for. Where are the rest of his notes? Tell us, girlie," the man snarled and leaned in, his stinking breath much too close to her face.

That's close enough! Clementine managed to quickly heave her legs up and kick him in the face with enough force to send him staggering out of the cabin.

"Bitch," the man yelled as he slammed against the corridor wall, holding his nose, "I'll kill you for that!"

"Let go of me," she growled, gasping for air as the man holding her tightened his grip.

"Clementine!"

"William," she croaked, and watched William swiftly attack the man she had kicked into the corridor. William's fists were fast as a boxer's, and Clementine was relieved to see him hold his own. The two men disappeared in a flurry of punches, out of sight. Clementine squirmed, wanting desperately to help William.

"You're not going anywhere. If your pal tries anything, he'll stop soon enough when I squeeze you just a teeny bit more," the man holding her said with a disgusting laugh. His arms were like two tree trunks, and they held her without trouble.

Clementine fumed. She couldn't let herself be stuck in a deadly squeeze with this goon. When William returned, she would be used against him to make him surrender. *Think, Clementine! Use anything, anything as a weapon.* She glanced at her iron fan, which she had foolishly set down on the dressing table when she had been removing her hair ornaments. *Hair! That's it!*

Clementine let out a fake cry of desperation, squirming furiously, and made an effort to claw at the man's face. He was too tall for her to reach properly, and he merely squeezed her tighter.

"Steady on, girlie, we'll wait for your boyfriend to be brought in, and then this will all be over," he laughed.

She groaned with pain and thought she could feel the bruises forming around her ribcage. Clearly, he did not want her killed, nor unconscious yet — he had plans to bargain with her or question her.

Good for me. Clementine palmed the two last hair pins she

had managed to snatch from her hair while pretending to scratch his face.

Outside in the corridor, William was winning. The other man had fallen down, and Clementine needed William to distract her captor for just a moment.

"Clementine!" William ran to the room — shirtless, his face and hands bloodied, looking like a glorious gladiator from the past. "Let go of her this instant," he bellowed.

Clementine tried to twist herself free, but the ruffian kept her tightly against him. Her feet dangled helplessly and her hands did little to soften the iron embrace.

"I think not," the man laughed, "Tell me where the tomb of Hathor's priestess is, and I might give her to you alive." He squeezed in demonstration and Clementine's lungs burned. This was worse than any corset she'd ever worn. She needed to act soon.

"You utter bastard, who sent you?" William spat, but did not come closer. The man squeezed again, and Clementine fought to stay conscious and ready. She panted for air while her vision filled with spots. She pretended to faint and hung like a ragdoll in his arms.

"Stop it," William said, "I'll tell you what you want!"

The man chuckled and relaxed his grip on Clementine just a little, but it was enough. *Now!* She quickly stabbed a hair pin into the man's arm. The sharp pin went deep into the man's flesh and he screamed in agony, staggering forward with Clementine still in his grip. She twisted as much as she could and swung her other hand up to hit the man in the neck. The second hair pin went in with a disgusting crunch and the man finally went limp, releasing her.

She fell, coughing, and would have hit the ground without any strength to soften her fall if William had not lunged to catch her.

"Saved you," William said softly. His gentle hands cradled her head in his lap.

"Rubbish, I saved myself. You just helped," she croaked, but managed a small smile.

"My god, what happened here?" JoJo's voice came from the doorway.

"Fetch the train doctor, if there is one! Bob, get the train manager here!" William barked.

Clementine looked up at him with sudden confusion. Had she just killed a man? She wasn't sure what to feel about that. After all, they had attacked her and had no good intentions.

"Well done, Clementine, you did well, very well." William wiped the worst of the blood from her face with his handkerchief. She realised he was holding her very gently against his bare, warm chest. It felt nice in all the absurdity.

"You are putting me in an indecent position," she muttered and tried to sit up.

"No, no, hey, stay there until the doctor comes," he said.

She glanced at the first thug she had knocked out. He was still laying on the ground. "Are they all dead?" she asked.

"The one you skewered definitely is," William said drily. "I see you handled two, almost three of them while I had one follow me to the men's bathing area. That's why it took me so long to get to you. I heard the sounds of fighting, heard you calling for me. I was sure–" He shook his head, his hair stiff with sweat and blood, and concern in his green eyes.

"You came, and that's all that matters," Clementine smiled weakly. "Help me up."

He hesitated but did as she asked. "Are you feeling nauseous? It is normal after such excitement. It is quite alright to feel shock." He looked at her with genuine worry.

"That can wait. I want to address this train compartment." She nodded her loosened hair towards the corridor where the other passengers had finally gathered to gawk at the sight of blood, bodies, and splintered wood.

"If you really want to," William said with hesitation, and very gently supported her small frame out to the corridor where people gave her space with soft gasps. One of the train attendants lay unconscious on the floor with blood on his face. Old and young aristocratic faces showed disapproval and fear, clutching their shawls and huffing disapprovingly into their mustaches. Clementine felt some of her spirit come back when she looked at these people, her alleged peers. No one had stepped up to help her fight against three grown men. No one!

She staggered and leaned heavily against William. Her black and gold dress was ruined beyond repair, only parts of it left intact, showing her ankles, and her bloodied bare feet. She had no idea when she had lost her brocade slippers but it mattered little. Let them see her like this.

"Dear fellow passengers, thank you for standing by like idiots and letting me almost die," she said in her mother's native language.

She saw the faces grow stiff and stoic around her with confusion, as if she was talking gibberish. She switched back to her native, upper-class English, hatred seeping into her voice. "Had I been a traditionally English-looking girl in this luxurious carriage, I wager many of you gentlemen would have come to my rescue without hesitation." She wiped blood from her forehead, which dripped from the still open head wound. "But I think you took one look at me and saw a foreigner. An Oriental. And so you clutched your belongings closer to yourself and thought: this does not concern me. A foreign girl like that, perhaps she is not even an aristocrat like us. Perhaps she is an entertainer or a paid woman who is getting her due? No, better not get involved, you thought. None of you helped when I screamed, when those thugs kicked down my door and attacked my fiancé and me. You heard me, I know you saw me. And you did nothing!"

Clementine spat blood on the ground next to the thug who had been knocked out by William. "Shame on you! You let a peer, Lady Clementine Whitham, be beaten for your own comfort, or discomfort," she sneered her own title. "I shudder to think what you would let happen to a commoner. No one should be left alone in a time of need, no-one!. You are a shame to our class," she said, her voice straining. The spots were back in her vision.

"I took down two of these thugs. How many of you could have done the same? You fucking cowards," she hissed, shocking herself at her cussing. They flinched too. "And now, William," she turned to his astonished face. "I think I will rest a little." And she let him carry her into his cabin, exhaustion washing over her muscles and mind.

TO EGYPT

Clementine startled up from the bed she had been tucked into. The window did not offer any additional light, so she assumed it must still be night.

"It's alright, Clementine," William's voice came from nearby. She looked around her, not understanding where she was and why her body hurt all over. Even her most brutal exercises with Edith hadn't been this bad in the days after.

Then she remembered. The dinner, the fight with the thugs, giving a speech about race and privilege to the people in the wagon. Killing the man with her hair pins. Her head hurt.

"Did it all really happen?" she asked hoarsely.

William climbed down from the upper bed and turned on one of the lamps. Clementine closed her eyes at the sudden light. She slowly opened them to see William pouring a glass of water which he gave to her. She gulped it down her dry throat.

"It did," William said. "The train's doctor examined you and found nothing wrong aside from cuts and bruises. He did warn that hysteria might follow if you cannot process what happened." He looked at Clementine questioningly and sat down next to her on the bed, "Are you alright?"

Clementine gave a small laugh. "Am I alright? I don't know. It's too soon to tell. I know I'm sore and that I seem to be in your sleeping cabin. Oh," she exclaimed, and made an effort to throw off the covers and get up. Noting that she only had her chemise on, she quickly covered herself again. "I seem to be in less clothing than before," she said.

"Yes, the doctor took off your ruined dress and corset to make you more comfortable after you collapsed. Quite the speech you gave to those people," he smiled.

"They deserved it. Rotten, the lot of them."

"Well, if it makes you feel better, some of them came to ask if they could help, to which I obviously said no, so they'd feel even worse. The train manager looked like he wished the earth would swallow him. He and the attendants were in a meeting about the shift schedule, which is why there was no immediate response to the ruckus. Bad luck, or well-planned by the thugs. I suspect some of the attendants might have been bribed not to hear anything happening. Anyway, the manager has already offered us a complimentary ticket back, whenever we wish to use it. I'd say he should have given us free travel for life, but with all expenses covered it matters little."

"True enough," Clementine huffed. "My things — are they still in the ruined cabin?"

"No, I fetched all of your things once we put you to bed. Here, I'm sure you missed this," he handed her the iron fan, which she took with relief.

William gently reached over to examine the bandages on Clementine's arm. She didn't have time to protest as he removed the bloodied gauze.

"What are you doing?" A stupid question, but she felt almost dumbfounded. William, who disliked her, was tending to her injuries? She must have hit her head after all.

"Cleaning your wound, of course. It likely came from the splintered wood of your cabin's door."

He reached for a small pouch and took out a clean napkin. He dipped the napkin into a vial and Clementine winced as the carbolic acid left a burning sensation on her cut. "But– but you hate having to deal with me," she blurted.

He didn't say anything as he finished wrapping her arm in fresh bandages, taking such care as if he thought she might break. "I do not hate you, Clementine. When I realised you were at the mercy of those men, I thought I was too late. I couldn't stand the thought of having failed you. You are mine to keep safe, Clemmie and I'm sorry I wasn't there faster." He kissed her hand. "Seeing you hold your own doesn't remove my duty to protect you."

Clementine opened her mouth but couldn't think of anything to say other than, "Thank you, this was very kind. " The look on his face baffled her. She'd expected him to sneer at her for getting caught so easily by that giant man.

"Would you mind passing me my dressing gown?" she said, thinking it might be best to just move on from whatever this strange moment was.

William rummaged through her luggage to find a cream dressing gown with embroidered lilacs and carnations, and a matching shawl.

"Do you mind?" Clementine said pointedly as she took them.

He cocked his eyebrow. "I've already seen you in your chemise, and trust me, there is nothing to be embarrassed about."

"Still," she said, and gestured for him to turn, which he did.

Clementine slipped on her dressing gown, the shawl, and her day shoes. "Come on," she said, and tried not to wince from her bruises.

"What?" William blinked. He had on his dinner trousers and a loose white shirt.

"You're well-enough dressed." Clementine opened the door.

"We need to take a look at the thugs, see what we can learn of them. Are they all still unconscious?"

"Ah, well, one of them escaped and the rest are dead."

"Escaped?" Clementine exclaimed, waving her hands in frustration. "From a moving train? How?"

"Apparently he jumped out the window when the train slowed down before a scheduled stop. They were all either dead or unconscious when they were locked in one of the unused cabins."

"We'll need to go in there right now and search for clues to see who hired them. One of them asked me to tell everything about the tomb. They knew why we are here."

William cursed. "We will have to be even more careful for the rest of this journey."

"Are you coming?"

An attendant and the train manager rushed to Clementine as soon as she stepped out into the dim corridor. Dawn was colouring the outside world.

"My lady, you have awoken." The train manager introduced himself as Mr Blanche — a short and stocky fellow with an efficient manner. "My sincerest apologies for everything you went through last night. On behalf of the train line, I would like to offer–"

"Quite so, Mr Blanche," Clementine interrupted him in French, adopting a manner of speech she had learned from her aunt, the Duchess. It was a commanding voice that allowed no arguments. "You will offer me and my fiancé access to the bodies of the thugs that attacked us. We wish to see if there are any clues to this vulgar act, as well as check if they stole anything that we might not have noticed." Her accent was not native, but it was good enough, along with her tone, to make the efficient Mr Blanche sputter.

"But, my lady, the investigation should be left to the police in Marseilles. We will arrive in a few hours, I assure you–"

Clementine continued in the same tone and turned her cold eyes on the man. "I understand you have already managed to let one of the surviving thugs escape. I do not trust you to handle this matter, especially since none of the attendants came to my aid when I was left alone to fight these men myself. Let us examine the bodies and I promise I will not tell the police of your incompetence. I might even not mention the horrible experience of La Train Bleu to my aunt, the Duchess of Clearwater. I assure you, the news would be most distressing to her and her peers."

The poor Mr Blanche stuttered and huffed, but eventually gave in and let them into the cabin where the bodies were kept.

"I must warn you, it is a gruesome sight, my lady. Three bodies, it is not pretty."

"I killed two of them, I'm sure I can manage to look at them now," she said grimly.

The man blinked and bowed before he left them alone.

William let out a small laugh. "I'm starting to see a new side to you."

"Not just pretty words, right?" Clementine said, "Still, it's not nice to look at them."

She had been to funerals, of course, and seen bodies in open caskets, but this was something different. These men had attacked her, and she had killed some of them in self-defense. The hair pins were still stuck in the thug who had squeezed the air and almost life out of her.

"It's alright, we won't have to stay long. They are gruesome to look at, but Clementine," William turned her to him, "I doubt these will be the last bodies you will see if you continue this line of work. Treasure hunting is a cruel game and people do die. So take this lesson: there is nothing to fear from dead men. It is the living you need to be concerned about."

She nodded, took a deep breath, and turned to look through the thugs' pockets.

"I also wanted to say that the use of your hair pins was quite inspired," William said.

"I was lucky I hadn't taken them out of my hair yet. But anyway, the suffragettes are instructed to use hair pins and keep them long and sharp."

William smiled. "Ah, it does not surprise me that you are involved with the suffragette movement."

"I support them absolutely." She narrowed her eyes at him. "Is that a problem?"

"Of course not. I merely meant that it fits. I believe them to be very bold in the way they take their cause forward. Quick, efficient action, and ruthless measures if needed. It matches you, and I mean that as a compliment."

"Careful, or you will run out of compliments if you keep this up," Clementine said. "Aha, what's this?" She dug a note from one of their pockets.

"Look," she said, and opened the crumpled paper. "*Test them. Find Lord Whitham's notebook*," Clementine read out loud. "That is strange. The handwriting is curt and impersonal, likely on purpose to avoid handwriting comparison," Clementine mused. "But my father's notebook is a strange addition, since I don't have it. They clearly thought I did, or knew of it, anyway. And if they had rummaged through my things before, without finding it, perhaps that's why they tried to torture the answers from me."

William nodded. "Sounds plausible to me. There was nothing on the other thugs. And neither of us recognise these men."

Clementine frowned. "Why would someone need these men to test us? It makes little sense, unless another attack is planned."

"There is nothing more we can do here. We have confirmation that they were looking for us specifically, by the orders of a person or persons unknown. We will have to wait to see if they try again to find out their identity. Come, let's get you back to rest for a bit before we arrive." William turned to open the door.

* * *

WHEN THEY RETURNED to their cabin, they saw JoJo at the door, fumbling with it.

"JoJo," Clementine said, "What are you doing?"

The woman turned in her dressing gown. "Ah, there you are, I was just knocking on your door. What a horrible ordeal, dear, you must be exhausted!"

"Yes, thank you, I am alright," Clementine said, her manners kicking in. "It's early, JoJo, what did you want with me?"

"Well, you know, I couldn't sleep. Who could, after a night like this? I didn't feel safe!" JoJo babbled, her eyes wide in terror. "What if the murderers came back for the rest of us? Bob could not sleep because of me fretting next to him, so he urged me to order a cup of tea. And when I received it, I heard the two of you talking with the manager, so I thought perhaps poor Clementine couldn't sleep either after such an experience. I thought: I shall take her a cup as well." She gestured to the cup and saucer in her hand. "I did not realise you had left your cabin when I came knocking."

Clementine took the cup, grateful for the kind thought.

"What is that in your other hand?" William asked sharply.

"Oh, this?" JoJo smiled. "My brains tonight, I will forget my own name, too. Bob found this dinner jacket and notebook in the men's bathing area after the mayhem of the fight. He realised they must be yours, William, since the notebook says 'Lord Whitham' on the cover."

Clementine drew a sharp breath. "My father's notebook? You had it all this time?" she blurted with an anger that made her wounds throb. She glared at William.

"Oh dear," JoJo started, but William snatched the jacket and notebook from her.

"Thank you, Lady Blake, and please forward my thanks to Bob as well for retrieving these. I had no time to fetch them in the midst of all the fighting and taking care of Clementine. Now, if you'll excuse us…"

William pushed Clementine inside, despite her fuming, and slammed the door behind them.

The teacup made a loud clatter, and it was a wonder it did not break as Clementine slammed it roughly onto the small table. She turned to William with her hands on her hips.

"You had my father's notebook all this time?" she said in a menacingly low voice. "How dare you not tell me? How dare you not give it to me the instant you returned to England and came to us with the news?"

William calmly took in the angry pose of her petite frame. "You know, you could just sit down and calm yourself. You've had a rough night, and your tea is getting colder by the minute."

"William!" Clementine exclaimed.

William lifted his hands in a gesture of peace and sat down on the sofa opposite the beds. He was now almost eye level with Clementine, making it easier for her not to crane her neck at him as she glared daggers with her eyes.

"Perhaps I should have mentioned I had your father's notebook," he said slowly, checking the book for any tears or other evidence of tampering, but found nothing out of the ordinary. "But truthfully, Clementine, I did not know if I should trust you with this. I did not know if you would lose it or let it be stolen. I did not know what kind of a person you would turn out to be on this unexpected journey. So I thought it best to keep it to myself while I took a measure of you."

He ran a hand through his hair and rubbed his eyes. "Besides, there could be vital information about the tomb, or the treasure hunters that I have not yet deciphered. Most of it is generic notes about our journeys, descriptions of Hathor's temple, musings on some of the findings, and rough sketches of the tomb. There is no map, nor any coordinates to the tomb itself. It seems your father didn't trust anyone, either."

"You knew how much my father means to me, and you did not think I should be trusted with his belongings? Hand it over right now, William. It is my father's, and by right it should now be mine, at least until we find Papa."

She reached for the book, but William did not let go.

"William, I am serious. This book might be the last keepsake of my father's thoughts I'll ever have."

Sighing, William let go. "Fine. Keep good care of the book. We might yet need the notes, and who knows if there is anything else in there that we might not realise. Will you promise to keep it safe and let me know if you find anything crucial to this excursion? We still do not know the exact location of the tomb."

"Why should I tell you anything?" she hissed, cradling the book carefully in her lap as she finally sat down. "You didn't trust me enough to even tell me you had this in your possession. This doesn't work one way, William. Either we both trust each other, or neither of us does. Did I not prove anything today by defending myself as well as I could, without any hysterics? I deserve more credit than you are giving me, William," she said coldly.

William stayed silent for a moment, his green eyes looking at her with intensity that made her wonder what he might be considering now. Would he try to steal the notebook back? Or abandon her and continue on his own?

"Yes," William said suddenly, "You have proved yourself tonight, on that we can agree. I will trust you to keep the notebook in a safe place and I will trust that we will share any information we might get by our own means from now on. But Clementine, proving yourself once will never be enough in this job. You will be asked to prove yourself over and over again, both physically and mentally, and sometimes it might prove too much to ask. Be prepared for that. Do not lower your guard."

"Fine." Clementine breathed deep and exhaled. She could get over this mistake for the sake of their mission. "Trust and openness between partners."

She extended a hand for William to shake. He took it with a hint of a smile.

"And may I point out," Clementine said, in a slightly less angry voice, "that you already lost the book once."

"Technically, I did not lose it. I knew where it was, but I was fighting a goon and trying to dash to your aid as quickly as possible, and I ran into that poor devil whose nose you broke. One gets busy and might not remember to retrieve everything when saving damsels in distress," William said.

Clementine laughed. "It is debatable whether you saved me, Will. I'd rather say that you provided good timing for me to save myself."

"And it was very well done," William admitted.

Clementine lay down and tucked herself into bed with the book and her iron fan.

"And now, if you don't mind, I will rest for a moment before we arrive to Marseilles," she muttered, sounding sleepy already.

"Right, that is a good idea." William checked his watch. "We will be awoken by the attendant in two hours or so. That will be enough time to pack our things, have breakfast and make our way to the docks."

He took off his shoes, climbed to the upper bed, and turned off the lamp.

"And William?"

"Yes?"

"You and Her Majesty owe me a pair of proper hair pins, an evening gown, corset, and matching slippers. Write it down."

"I shall," came William's amused answer, but Clementine was already slipping into dreamworld.

* * *

AFTER THEIR THINGS were packed and breakfast served, Clementine felt a little better, though she was still very sore . The train manager had insisted they breakfasted with him, and did everything he could to persuade them to give a favourable account of the train company once they were asked for testimonies by the French police.

The other first-class passengers either avoided Clementine's gaze or were back to their ignorant selves. Only JoJo and Bob were civil enough to ask how Clementine was. Nothing could be done about ungracious rich people, but Clementine hoped her little speech had given them something to think about if ever there was another time they could offer help to someone who might not be 'one of them'.

Clementine had flicked through her father's notebook in between breakfast and supervising the packing of their belongings. An attendant carefully packed everything else, but the notebook Clementine tucked away into one of the hidden pockets of her travel dress. Truthfully, she was waiting for the chance to change into a lighter outfit when they got to Egypt. Even now, at Marseille, Clementine could feel the air growing hotter, and her travel dress would definitely be too hot for desert conditions.

She had found nothing of huge importance in the notebook, unfortunately. It was what William had described and little more. Some jotted thoughts, drawings and musings, all in the very familiar handwriting of her dear papa. She noted that there was a description of the tomb of Hathor's high priestess but no location. There was a note that described the interior of the tomb, however. It mentioned three main chambers, corridors and some traps to be aware of, but the descriptions were only for the early parts of the tomb. *Perhaps Father never made it far enough to the final chamber before he disappeared?* Something else seemed strange too...

"William," Clementine said, frowning at the book.

"Yes?" William peered out the window. The train had stopped, and the passengers of the sleeping cabins had been asked to wait until the police could take their statements regarding the attack.

"How do you not know the location of the tomb when clearly my father has descriptions of its chambers in the book?"

William sighed. "We were working on a few different sites and the one your father worked on most was, in the end, the likely tomb of the High Priestess. The thing is, your father, well, he wanted to explore the sites on his own and he had sneaked out alone to find the tomb. When we discovered he was missing, we followed his tracks to a tomb, but found no trace of him and had to retreat from the storm. So, technically, we know the whereabouts of the ruins where the tomb is located, but not how to get inside the right one. We can only assume your father knew."

"Hmm." Clementine tried to think. "I find it odd that he would wander to the dig site without you or the notebook. He seems to have used it very actively — why would he go in there on his own, without it?"

"Hard to say," William said. "Maybe he did not trust me in the end. Or it may be that he had a eureka moment and wanted to check something quickly, so left the camp without a word to me, since it was in the very early hours of the morning. He did take his valet with him, though."

"And you found this book among the belongings in his tent?" She fingered the book's rough edges and slightly scuffed cover.

"Yes," William nodded, his mouth forming a grim line. "It is not a morning I remember fondly. The sandstorm was savage."

"I can only imagine," Clementine said, her voice lost in thought, "But it does give hope that he is alive somewhere."

"Ah, the gendarmes are here," William said. "Let's get through this quickly."

Clementine nodded and tucked the notebook away in a pocket inside her skirts. "Ready."

*　*　*

THE POLICE OFFICERS let them leave among the first passengers after they had given their account and described their itinerary to Egypt in case they needed to be contacted for further questions. But so far it seemed like a robbery. The officers said it had unfortunately become more common for thieves to try their luck with luxury trains and their first-class passengers. All in all, a very unlucky coincidence, they concluded, to which William and Clementine of course agreed.

William hailed them a carriage and they made their way through Marseille to the docks where Steamer Neva was waiting to take them to Egypt. Clementine peered curiously out of the carriage windows as the carriage moved through the paved streets of the town. People looked no different here than in England, she thought. Everyone minding their own business, dashing to the baker's, running after unruly children, hurrying with deliveries, or taking slow promenades in chic day dresses. Perhaps she had thought to see something very different in France, but so far it was as if people weren't that dissimilar on a surface level. And maybe deep down, too. Maybe people had one and the same thought, no matter where they were from: to get through the day to the best of their abilities.

"Have you been to Marseille before?" she asked William, who sat opposite her.

"Many times," he said, turning his head to look out the same window. His top hat almost touched the carriage's roof — in fact, Clementine was sure she saw it hit the roof a few times when the road was bumpier.

"And do you find it much different to our own towns of similar size?"

William gave a laugh. "With time, Clementine, many places will lose their newness. The novelty of travel wears off quicker than you would think, and you find yourself wanting to go ever further to more secluded, unexplored places to feel the same awe you did when you first travelled outside of your hometown or country."

"And what happens when you have explored every corner of this world, and no place gives you that rush of excitement anymore?" Clementine asked.

"I don't know," William said with a smile. "I don't suppose that will happen anytime soon. But perhaps then it will be time to settle back in dear England, grow old and remember fondly the old times, while also despising the new times."

Clementine laughed. "I have a hard time imagining you as a grumpy old man longing for the good old times."

"Me too," William agreed.

* * *

THE SEA AIR filled the carriage: a mix of salt, rotten seaweed, and fish. The docks were buzzing with people and Clementine was glad of William taking charge with their luggage. There were many ships ready to sail, the noise of their horns deafening at times. People were boarding different ships, luggage was carried here and there, and a crowd had gathered to say goodbye to passengers. Sellers haggled at market stalls, newspaper boys yelled the latest news, and dock guards were barking orders at one person or another. All in all, it was a lot of noise after the relative quietness of the train. Clementine kept close to William as they joined the line of first-class passengers boarding the steamer to Alexandria.

"She is magnificent," Clementine commented on their vessel.

"Yes, I suppose so," William said. "They sail weekly between Alexandria and Marseilles. Safe ships, good company, for both people and post."

Clementine nodded as they slowly moved forward on the long stone pier leading to the boarding stairs of the Neva. Steam rose from its huge cylinders and seagulls sat screaming on the ship's railings. It shone in white and black, like keys of a piano against the sunny, blue skies, and even bluer sea.

"Have you been on a ship before?" William asked, noticing how Clementine looked keenly on all the details.

"Yes," she said, and avoided his gaze.

"When?"

"Well, when we left England," she said, as if he was silly for asking.

William sighed. "That was only a ferry to cross the channel. Let me rephrase: is this your first sea voyage?"

"Yes," she said sheepishly, "That I know of."

"Right. Do you have any seasickness or fear of drowning? Anything I should know? Do you know how to swim?"

"Of course I know how to swim. Though…" she hesitated and glanced down at her dress.

"What is it?" William urged.

"Well, even though I can swim, these heavy dresses are likely to work against my odds of surviving. The fabrics will pull me deeper into the water and make swimming tiring very quickly. So that's something to consider, should we ever get into water."

"That is good to keep in mind," William said, surprised. "I did not guess that you would be aware of how silly it is to dress yourself in clothing that makes it so much more difficult to run or swim when needed."

Clementine shrugged. "We are all victims of the fashion

expectations of our times and rank. But I do look forward to changing into my secondary travel outfit in Egypt. A split skirt dress was my mother's favoured outfit when she travelled. Being a foreigner, she accepted that she would never truly belong in society, so she gave up trying to blend in by dressing accordingly." She smiled fondly. "It's an outfit with very wide pants, which are cut scandalously just above my ankles. It will be easier for me to move, less hot, and hopefully I won't drown in the Nile due to my dress.

"I hope so too, and," he leaned closer, "it will be most interesting to see your legs in such an outfit. I shall have to keep an eye on possible suitors who might swoon at the sight of such well-formed and delicate legs." Clementine elbowed his side and he laughed. "I jest Clemmie, I obviously cannot yet say if your legs are well-formed or not."

Clementine rolled her eyes. She had given up on him not calling her Clemmie.

They finally boarded the steamer and were led by a steward to their cabin.

"A junior suite for the lovely couple," the steward said. "I hope it pleases my lord, my lady."

William did not bother to correct the man that he was no lord. He swiftly looked through the rooms. There was one sitting room, two bedrooms and a luxurious private bathing room. Clementine looked around the plushness of the accommodation. It was as if someone had attempted to make a room from whipped cream and strawberry jam. Everywhere she looked there were plush textiles of cream and red. Chandeliers sparkled in each room and dark red carpets covered the floor like soft and soundless clouds. There was a scent of strong cleaning perfume. Roses perhaps. It was a good sign, since it meant the room had been cleaned recently. The windows were to the right side of the ship's highest cabin deck, with a promenade reserved for first-class passengers only. The ornate tapestries on the walls portrayed mermaids and ships on a golden map. This would be their home for the next few days.

"It will do," William said. "Please make sure my fiancée gets fresh flowers in her bedroom every day, there's a good man." He slipped a hefty tip to the steward who nodded eagerly.

"So," Clementine said, taking off her red gloves, "Who gets the bigger bedroom?"

William raised an eyebrow. "The older and bigger person gets to pick first, which happens to be me." He pointed to the room with a double bed, "This one is mine."

"Fine," Clementine said. "Your giant frame wouldn't fit into this bed anyways," she commented on the other bedroom.

"But your petite frame would fit into this double bed," William grinned with a flash of that mischievous, emerald-green light in his eyes.

"You wish," Clementine said, earning a chuckle from him.

* * *

THE JOURNEY WAS PLEASINGLY UNEVENTFUL. The steamer made good time through the Mediterranean Sea and they were not troubled by storms. Clementine found her sea feet easily and avoided the seasickness that seemed to trouble some of their fellow first-class passengers.

Bob and JoJo Blake had also boarded the Neva, and this made Clementine happy. She and William had found a delicate balance between themselves, for now, but Clementine still welcomed the company of her own sex.

On one sunny afternoon, the men went to a shooting competition and Clementine and JoJo enjoyed cocktails on deckchairs under their parasols, safe from the blazing sun.

"So, JoJo, how are you enjoying your honeymoon so far?" Clementine mused as they observed the men take turns shooting clay discs. It seemed to bring out some natural jovial competitiveness in them. Some women followed the competition more closely, while others had taken seats on the deckchairs, and some stayed indoors during the hottest hours of the day.

JoJo had on a light muslin dress with shades of cornflower blue and leaf green. Clementine wore a white dress of silk and muslin, with white embroidery around the lace of her low neckline. Their cotton chemises were drenched in sweat but at least they helped make it appear as if they were fresh and unbothered by the heat. The sea breeze helped too, thankfully.

"Oh, it has been lovely so far," JoJo smiled, fanning herself. Her fan was much more traditional than Clementine's, but luckily Clementine's fan hardly caught anyone's attention at a glance.

"What in particular?" Clementine prompted.

"Are you looking for tips for your eventual honeymoon?" JoJo laughed and winked. "It has been wonderful to be alone with him so much. I can have him all to myself every evening, and at night as much as I want," she whispered with an air of scandal.

Clementine blushed. "Yes, I see," she managed to say, and hid her face in her cocktail of lemonade, gin and ice.

"Oh Clementine, don't be such a prude," JoJo grinned. "You are marrying an absolutely gorgeous man. I mean look at him," she gestured.

"JoJo!" Clementine was afraid someone would notice them ogling at William.

"Oh, don't worry, they only have eyes for their guns and those silly discs now," JoJo waved her hand. "But seriously, you are a lucky woman. My Bob, I love him dearly, but I can still appreciate male beauty. And darling, your man has it. Be careful of women who would do more than just admire from afar."

"I'll keep that in mind," Clementine muttered, feeling her cheeks burn.

"You really aren't married yet." JoJo looked at Clementine and narrowed her eyes. "Please tell me that you have at least kissed him, since you clearly haven't done more."

Clementine shushed JoJo, who now seemed to be dying of laughter.

"Seriously, if you haven't even kissed him, how will you know what to do on your wedding night?"

"I know what happens between a man and a woman," Clementine blurted. "At least the basics of it. My mother, you see, was not shy to tell how babies are made when I asked out of curiosity. But she did not elaborate on the aspects of, um, romance or," she faltered, searching for the right word.

"Seduction? Desire?" JoJo's grin reminded Clementine of the Cheshire Cat. "I would be happy to tell you more, dear. Help you prepare yourself, so to say — like a less prudent big sister would. After all, I've had my fair share of fun before I married, and I regret none of it. The art of seducing a man to his knees can be very useful, and you'd be surprised how natural it can feel when you have the power to make them whimper and beg for you to release them of the torment."

Clementine sputtered and coughed as she almost choked on her drink. She certainly did not expect JoJo to speak of seduction as if it was a weapon to harness. It reminded her too much of William talking about using brothels for fun and information when needed. She did not wish for that image in her head and yet — another image flashed, of him naked, on his knees before her… She squeezed her eyes shut, as if trying to banish such an image forever from her mind. But deep down she knew it would not leave her any time soon, and she did not fail to notice the way the image had prompted a flutter of butterflies low in her belly.

JoJo rose and patted Clementine's back until the coughing stopped.

"I apologise, dear Clementine!" JoJo had a look of genuine concern, "Are you alright?"

Clementine nodded and fanned herself. "I was simply caught off guard." She paused and looked around to see if anyone else had heard JoJo's remarks. "But thank you, JoJo. After my mother left, I don't think anyone else has ever offered to speak so plainly about, well, romance." She did not know how else to describe it.

JoJo sat down. "Perhaps I was being too forward. Honestly, the sun and the drink are making me much too eager to tease you. I truly like you, Clementine, and I admire you the fact you have been able to hold him off before your wedding day." She cast another admiring glance at William, who shot his clay discs with ease. "I certainly would've lacked your resolve," JoJo grinned. "As did many others, or so the rumors say of the rakish Mr Hunt. With so many conquests, he should be an excellent lover, so you can trust him to guide you through any shyness from your own inexperience."

Clementine's face burned, and she tried to change the subject with some desperation. "So, about the honeymoon. Was Egypt always your first choice or were you considering some other destination?"

JoJo chuckled at this sudden change and took a long sip from her drink. "Hmm, we did have other options. I would have enjoyed staying in the French Riviera, and to be honest I will suggest staying there once we are on our way back from Egypt. Bob likes these historical things so much that I simply had to indulge him, even if I would have preferred cooler surroundings, and more parties."

"It sounds lovely," Clementine said, despite being of the same opinion as Bob, preferring historical sites to society events. "Whereabouts will you go in Egypt?"

"Oh, here and there," JoJo shrugged, "Bob planned our itinerary and all I remember is Alexandria, then down — or is it up

— the river Nile to Lake Victoria. And in the middle there's a pile of stones here, a pile of stones there, rubble and more rubble."

Clementine smiled. "Perhaps you will have a good enough guide to bring some of those piles and rubbles to life. They were once even more magnificent and fascinating than they are now. It is a wonder how we are able to visit something that spans thousands of years and has not been destroyed by time or people."

"My dear, it sounds like you should be going with Bob to those rubble piles," JoJo smiled. "So, where are you planning to go to look for your father after we arrive to Alexandria?"

Clementine shrugged. "It might be too early to tell. We will ask around for any possible sightings and will try to trace his travel up the Nile. I don't know if we'll find out anything, but I have to try. William is kind to offer his help; he understands how important this is to me," she added.

"Of course, my dear. I suppose it might also be the fact that he too lost his father a few years ago. Though there were some rumors, unpleasant ones, that circulated," JoJo said with a lowered voice.

"What rumors?" Clementine was well aware that she did not pay enough attention to society gossip compared to her peers.

"It was about their mother, the late Lady Knightwood. Her death was said to be caused by William's father. By accident of course, or so one assumes. A tragedy for the young boys at the time."

"Oh, how horrible to have those rumors in the midst of grieving," Clementine said. William had not been eager to talk about his family and she couldn't help feeling curious.

JoJo whispered, "It is said that William will leave a woman before she can. He'll never let anyone near him, poor thing. Such trust issues." She shook her head, her red curls bouncing. "Look at me, dampening our mood with such old and nasty rumors when you have already proven me wrong by being engaged to William."

She waved at the waiter for another drink. Clementine declined, already feeling the gin heavy in her shoulders. "So, Clementine, since you know about the rubble in Egypt, what are you most looking forward to see?"

"Oh, all of it. I wish we had time to see the pyramids, of course, and wander around Thebes and Abu Simbel and Karnak. The Temple of Hathor is less known, so–" Clementine had gotten overexcited but paused, not wanting to say anything too much. "We likely won't spend too much time there. There is just so much to see." She changed the course of her enthusiasm. "We might have to come back to Egypt for our honeymoon to be able to see it all! It'll be like a second honeymoon."

JoJo laughed and raised her second glass. "To many honeymoons and all the rubble."

"To rubble!" Clementine joined the laughter.

"Seriously though, Clementine. If you wish to, hmm, explore things with the gorgeous Mr Hunt without consequences before the wedding day, you do know what to do?" JoJo whispered, as if they were discussing treason.

"What? Clementine gasped.

"I can provide you a list of trusted sellers in London. You need only ask. There are certain devices to prevent you getting with child. Skins you can buy for the man, internal devices for the woman. And if nothing is available, then at least do not let him finish while–" She looked pointedly at Clementine's lower belly.

Clementine merely nodded, unsure how to continue the discussion without it ending in her being swallowed up by the sea from pure embarrassment.

"Oh dear, did I go too far? I should know not to tease a bride so much, even though this is information that is spoken much too rarely." JoJo's snickering had Clementine smile a little. "So, back to this Temple of Hathor then. Tell me more of that, and the blotches of your décolletage will soon vanish!" JoJo said, sipping her drink some more.

Clementine laughed with relief and happily told JoJo about the myth of the goddess Hathor, her highly esteemed priestesses, and the myth of the Tears. It felt good to laugh and talk with a female companion, especially one who was as confident and joyful as JoJo. Clementine hadn't realised how much she had needed a friend to talk to during this upheaval of her life. And if talking about the Temple of Hathor would provide distraction from talking about marital matters, well, Clementine was happy to change the subject. No harm could come from such a generic discussion amongst friends.

"You know so much about these old things!" JoJo said, astonished. "And do you think it's true, the legend of the Tears and their healing properties?"

"Oh, I did not realise the myth of the tears was so well-known." Clementine was impressed by JoJo's knowledge. "I thought people knew only that Papa was searching for the tomb of a high priestess of Hathor. Anyway, I have no idea, but we will find out, I'm sure. Once we get to the temple, it is only a matter of finding the tomb's entrance. William will be able to navigate us there and hopefully..." Clementine sighed, "Hopefully, we will find my papa, or clues about what happened to him at the tomb. It has been so long already, but I have to know if there is anything to be found."

"You poor dear." JoJo squeezed Clementine's hand. "It has been such an ordeal to you. If you need help with finding your father, you need only ask, since we'll be thereabouts in one or another pile of ancient rubble. And should we hear anything about your papa, how should we find you or send you message?" JoJo asked with a frown. "I haven't the faintest idea how to send a letter to you if you are..." she shifted her hands in a vague way, "out there somewhere."

"Oh, thank you, JoJo. Yes, thank you, if you hear anything about Papa, anything at all, do contact me or William. We will be staying at the campsite north of the Temple of Hathor. It should not be too long from there to the dig site of the tomb. A messenger from the camp should be able to find us, I'm sure."

JoJo took out a notebook from her purse. "Right, I will write this down. North of Temple of Hathor, campsite. How far did you say the tomb was?"

"Oh, I don't know exactly. William has that information, but as I said, if you can get a message to me at the camp, a messenger should find us without trouble. And in any case, we will get the message once we return."

"Quite so," JoJo nodded and put away the notebook. "Now, how about we cheer our men as they continue to shoot those clay discs? I find that men always love to be cheered on, whatever the contest might be."

They rose and joined the small crowd of spectators.

* * *

LATER THAT EVENING, Clementine told William how lovely JoJo had been to offer help.

"She is such a lovely one," Clementine said as she took out her evening gloves before dinner. "They will keep their eyes and ears open in case they hear anything about Papa while they are honeymooning around Egypt, so I told her where we will be camping before finding our way to the dig site."

"What?" William stiffened. "You told her exactly where we are going?"

"Really, William." Clementine resisted the urge to roll her eyes. "She told me about their travel plans and I shared ours, since it is common knowledge that we are searching for Papa. She just wants to help."

William pinched the bridge of his nose with a deep frown.

"Clementine, what have I told you about caution and trust? Remind me?"

"Never trust anyone, ever, even if you would die," Clementine said, mocking his low voice. "What's so wrong about accepting help? You cannot possibly understand how lonely I've been in the middle of this. I felt lighter from speaking to a friend, and it has been months since I've felt light, William." She could hear her voice crack just a little from the emotion and saw the sharpness of his eyes soften just a little.

He let out a deep breath. "Yes, well. Nevertheless, it will be difficult to get a message to us once we disembark. Damned difficult to get a messenger who will actually track you down in a tricky location. I will let the team at the campsite know that they can ask for any letters addressed to us in the shore village."

Clementine's thoughts had drifted, and the feeling of desperate uncertainty threatened to surface, no matter how much she tried to push it away.

"William," she said and turned to him, her dark green silk dress swishing around her. It had been her mother's, and she had brought it with her for some additional luck. Good thing too, since her other evening gown had been ruined. The green silk made her dark brown eyes pop, and she wore her dark hair like a crown: high and intricately braided.

"Do you think we really will find any clues to my father's disappearance after all this time?"

"I cannot promise anything." William rose from the sofa of their sitting area. "But we will try our best, that's for sure."

He came closer and kissed Clementine's hand. She shivered and could feel him grin against her knuckles. The soft breath of a smile tickled her and made the room feel hot.

"You should be used to me kissing your bare hand by now," William smiled as he met her eyes. "You've certainly made me prefer gloveless hands."

Clementine shook her head but felt her lips twitch . "You

really are impossible," she said, and put on her gloves. "How do I look?"

"Like a flower inside a giant leaf, ready to be plucked and enjoyed with tenderness."

Clementine laughed, feeling a blush creeping up her neck.

"Ah, a flower that changes colour, too. Even more delicate and special!" William exclaimed as he offered her his arm.

"Perhaps you should have become an explorer of horticulture instead," she remarked, "since you seem to be full of sweet words for flowers."

She clasped her hand into his and they left the cabin, making their way to dinner. Live music would be played tonight, and Clementine wondered if William would ask her to dance.

"Have you noticed that you have been less annoyed by my presence ever since the thugs attacked us on that train?"

"Oh, have I?" William said, "I must try not to get too soft with you. A little bit of blood is no excuse for fraternising after all."

Clementine was happy to be rid of the bandage on her arm. The cuts had healed faster than she expected.

"Or perhaps you simply trust me more after seeing me in action? Could it be that I managed to persuade you, not with words, but with deeds?" They descended a beautiful staircase to join the others in the dining area.

"I suppose you did better than an average woman of your rank and esteem. I did not expect it," he admitted.

Clementine cast a winning glance at him, which he ignored.

"I am glad you are accepting me as something other than an average woman. I would be more offended if you said I was like everyone else."

"Don't get too cocky, Clemmie. Being too sure of yourself is a sure way to failure."

"Oh, do cheer up, Will. It's alright to admit you made an error of judgment when it comes to my character."

*　*　*

THEY HAD JOINED the other first-class passengers and were led to a table with a large ensemble of flowers. Southern flowers, Clementine observed: lilies, orchids, palm tree leaves, all arranged into a beautiful display. Even though she had grown up in houses with plenty of decorations of gold and glass and wood, she still felt it was somehow more impressive at sea. After all, there was a great vastness around them, and it was a marvel that they were surrounded by such opulence and the best food money could buy while floating in the middle of nowhere. It was almost a horrifying thought when she let her mind wonder too far.

"A penny for your thoughts?" William said. The waiter had brought them champagne and hors d'oeuvres.

"Oh, nothing much," Clementine said, selecting one of the scallops, which burst with a delightful buttery taste in her mouth. "These are good," she urged William to try his share. "I was only considering how funny reality can be. Here we are eating scallops, under gilded crystal chandeliers, surrounded by rich and powerful people, and all the while we are floating on a bauble when you consider the scale of the sea compared to this ship. There are only bits of metal and wood between us and the dark sea, and yet," she raised her glass to him, "here we are, having a wonderful evening, without a thought to the monsters that might lurk beneath us right at this very moment."

"What an odd thought," William commented, and chewed his scallop. "Do you know, I don't think I've ever heard another lady make such remarks as you sometimes do. Why do you think that is?"

Clementine laughed. "Because I do not care about making an impression to please a man I am having a conversation with, while sacrificing my own thoughts."

"Interesting. So, all the times I have had normal discussions with your peers, they have not been themselves," William noted. His bright smile made his white shirt and bow tie pale in comparison. "I must have been fooled to have such excellent topics of conversation."

"Oh yes," Clementine nodded and sipped her drink, "You cannot imagine how much we are taught to keep up interesting conversations about topics we know nothing of, nor care of. A conversation is a possibility leading to a proposal, as my governess used to say," she huffed.

"And you disapprove of this?"

Clementine rolled her eyes. "You try it. Do not talk about what you want to talk about for the full evening. Only follow my conversation starters and follow them up with interesting, unique questions, and see how your opponent — apologies — *conversation partner* shines when you make them feel as if everything they say is very, very interesting indeed. Believe me, no one wants to do that day after day, from one social situation to another."

"I think I will pass," William chuckled.

"Point proved," said Clementine.

"So, you pick a conversation theme, and I will try to keep it up?"

Clementine smirked. "I could go for something very boring like embroidery and make you wish you could jump off this ship."

William laughed. "Spare me, I beg you, my lady."

"Fine. Let us talk of fighting. How do you prefer to fight and why?"

"Again, I do not think I have ever heard a lady ask me this. Reading, yes, sport preferences, yes, and kissing, yes. But fighting? No, I do not believe anyone has asked me."

Clementine ignored his comment on kissing, even though her treacherous mind instantly wondered who had asked him about the subject, what indeed was a preferable way to kiss, and were there many ways to do it? JoJo would likely know.

"I favour plain old boxing," William said, after a moment's thought. "I believe in the simplicity of fighting. Knock them down as soon as possible, however you can. Boxing works most of the time, but if needed I am quite good with a sword as well. And, of course, if push comes to shove, I can always use my gun. But it is a rare occasion when I would need to. "

"Interesting. And were boxing and fencing the preferred ways for you to learn to defend yourself, or were they simply part of your upbringing and you were naturally good with both?"

William smiled a grim smile. "It was not voluntary. It is expected for us gentlemen to learn to fight with a sword and our bare hands. But I enjoyed it well enough, and have been glad of those skills many times."

"And have you encountered such a situation often in your present line of work?"

The waiter brought to them a soup of clear broth with fresh bread and William waited until the waiter had left before he replied. Clementine tried the soup and the simplicity of it surprised her, since the taste was so very good: the earthy tones of a good bone marrow base complimented with fresh herbs was a delicious combination.

"There is almost always someone wanting to try you out. Sometimes other treasure hunters from other countries, even rogue ones, and sometimes one of our own will try their luck with you. They will try to beat you to the treasure and, if encountered there, they will try to beat you for it. One of the reasons why we don't work alone, but in pairs."

"And are they always easy fights?"

William grimaced. "No, they are not always easy fights. Each fight is a risk of injury and death. And believe me, you do not want to be left injured and alone in some tomb to bleed to death, because no one will find you, or even know you're there."

Clementine paled. She could not help but imagine her father trapped in the priestess' tomb, unable to get help and slowly bleeding to death.

"I apologise," William said, noticing her silence. "It was perhaps not the best example to give."

"It's alright. I have to be prepared for all possibilities," Clementine said, shaking her head slightly, as if trying to rid herself of those thoughts. She now felt uncomfortable and sad, and wondered, not for the first time, if this was all a mistake.

"Well, how about a dance to take your mind off it?" William said, getting up from the table.

People these days danced between different courses, so there was no need to wait until afterwards and have to dance on a full stomach. Clementine disliked dancing after a long and heavy dinner. But now, before they had finished eating, she thought it might be a good idea.

She gave her hand to William and he led her to the dance floor where other couples were already taking their turn. A swish of skirts, a flap of coat tails, and round and round they went. Clementine waved to JoJo and Bob as they passed them. JoJo, in her dark blue evening dress gleamed like a gem, and it seemed that she was the one leading their dance.

The band changed into a Viennese waltz, which Clementine adored. "Now this one I know," she smiled to William, and he gave her a bow, to which she responded with a perfectly learned curtsy. He took her arm and pulled her closer with one hand on the side of her waist. With sure steps he led her into a gliding, dreamy waltz, where everything felt like a fairytale. The slow, swinging movement was delightful, and she felt herself relax. She smiled at William, whose height had her craning her neck. He gazed down at her, and without missing a beat sent her twirling several times. With a gentle pull, he brought her back into a deep bend which made her heart leap with excitement. No one had ever dipped her so low without making her fear they would drop her, but William had no problem lifting her back up and continuing the waltz without missing a step. *One must appreciate a good dance partner*, Clementine thought. They were rare to come by. This dance had been so very enjoyable, and she found herself longing to dance with him through the night.

"You dance well," she said, when the song ended and they returned to their table.

"Another useful skill we men need to learn," he smiled.

"Yes, but not everyone makes the effort to actually dance like it was an act of–" she fumbled for the word.

"A mating game?" William raised his eyebrow as he helped her sit down.

"No! Well, yes, I suppose it is part of a mating game within our society's rituals," Clementine laughed.

"Dancing has its uses, too," William said. His eyes seemed to shine a shade darker.

"And what uses are those when adventuring for treasures?" Clementine asked. The room was full of music, laughter and talking, so she had no fear of someone listening in to their discussion.

"A dance, like a mating game, is a ritual of seduction, and there is a great deal to be won." He swirled his wine glass, watching the red liquid go round and round. "Sometimes you dance for fun, sometimes you snatch a dance with someone who has what you need, and use seduction to get it."

"What?" Clementine lowered her voice this time, "You mean you have seduced women to gain the upper hand in treasure hunting?" Clementine could hardly believe it. Her cheeks flushed and her breathing became shallow against her corset.

She opened her fan to hide her rising bosom. Something dark and ugly settled heavily in her chest, and shame prickled her skin when it occurred to her that it might just be the feeling of jealousy. *Don't be a fool, Clementine! You cannot be jealous of something that isn't there!* This relationship was not real, and she could not confuse her silly feelings with the acting. And yet, she couldn't shake the feeling of wanting to smack him with her fan or claim his lips with her own. Possibly both. She did not know how long she could stay immune to his charms, or if indeed she ever had a chance in the first place. It annoyed her to no end that he was able to affect her so easily.

"Clemmie, I have told you not to trust anyone in this work. People do anything to get the upper hand and take your loot. I am the same, and if you want to do this work you will learn to be like that too."

"And what if I do not want to be a ruthless villain?"

William downed his wine. "Then you are not suited for this profession. I find it most amusing that you had no problem discussing how fighting might prove helpful to get to the treasure you are after, but seduction? Is that so much worse? In fighting you might die; in love and passion you are left only with a broken heart."

Clementine closed her fan with a snap, annoyed at the confirmation of William's rakish reputation.

"A broken heart might be far worse than death," she said curtly.

"Perhaps," William inclined his head, "But the choice between the two is easy for me." His eyes gazed deep into Clementine's. She turned her gaze to watch the dancing partners and the flashing colours of their twirling clothes. It was not a thought she wanted to entertain, but if she and William were to marry in order to work together, would he continue to seduce other women? And what did that mean for Clementine?

It would be a public humiliation, Clementine decided, and felt better after realising that it was only worry for her reputation that made her so upset. Not jealousy. She could not bring herself to talk more of the matter, so they ate in relative silence while enjoying the music of the band.

AT ALEXANDRIA

The week went by fast, and soon enough they arrived in the port of Alexandria. Clementine was eagerly gazing at the shores of Egypt up on the deck. "How beautiful it looks. Familiar and different at the same time!" she exclaimed.

"How so?" William asked next to her. He had changed into a light, casual suit and an equally light top hat. White became him well, Clementine thought, but did not stare too long.

"I grew up listening to my papa's tales of Egypt. I believe he spent most of his adventures here, though he did visit other places too. He brought his drawings and photographs from his visits to Egypt home, and it's as if those pictures, along with his stories, became living memories to me, which is why I feel an odd mix of strangeness and familiarity upon seeing Alexandria ahead of us."

In the distance, mosques could be seen in colours of terracotta and sand and gold. Even the air smelled different: a mixed scent of spices from the docks, the markets and the sea air. Clementine breathed in deep and thought of her father, who had once had the same experience of a new and wonderful beginning. If only her adventure wasn't to find out if he was dead or not.

The ship docked, and in due time they were disembarking the ship. The ground seemed to tilt as they made their way to the carriage William had ordered. Men carried their trunks and secured them to the back of the carriage. Clementine frowned and took hold of her parasol, leaning it against the ground. She felt a swaying, swelling movement beneath her. It was not a welcome feeling, and for a moment she feared she might be sick from the nausea of her balance being off.

"Clemmie," William said, worriedly, "You look pale, what's the matter?"

"I don't know, William!" She did not care to correct his use of the nickname. She tried to focus her eyes on him and squeezed them shut again. "It's as if the ground is shifting and I am bobbing on waves. A most unwelcome feeling. I hope I'm not getting sick with something."

William offered his hand, and for once she took it, hoisting herself up the step to the carriage where she slumped on the bench. William sat across from her, as he always did, and knocked on the roof to let the driver know they were ready. The horses jerked into movement.

"Worry not," William said as the carriage moved through the crowds of people, "It is a common ailment after spending so many days at sea. There is a name for it: mal de debarquement syndrome. It is not known why some people suffer from it after a sea journey, but they almost always recover within a few days, once they find their land legs again. Try not to think about it too much."

Clementine's eyes widened. "What do you mean 'almost always'? Are you saying some people don't recover from this horrible feeling?"

William nodded. "It does not happen often, if that is a comfort."

"Goodness." Clementine rubbed her temples and focused on breathing.

"It should help once the carriage gets faster. The even movement of the carriage will cover the feeling of the swaying, you'll see."

"I really hope you are right. If I am sick, you will be an unfortunate victim, since you sit opposite of me."

William grinned. "Worry not, if you start to look green, I will use my fast reflexes to open the door and throw you out of this carriage sooner than you can blink."

"I am so glad to hear that," Clementine rolled her eyes, which was a mistake. She quickly turned her gaze outward and let it rest on the surroundings. They were still slowly trying to make their way through Alexandria and there were many people selling all sorts of things to the passing carriages. She leaned closer to the window to see what was being sold.

"Bread!"

"Flatbread!"

A grandmother had a basket full of dates. "Sweetest dates you've ever had!" She was missing one or more teeth, but she smiled widely at the tourists who stopped to buy small pouches of her wares.

"Jewels! Genuine turquoise from P haraoh's tombs!" A woman had come to the window to sell the trinkets. "Beautiful lady, an ancient charm for luck and love!" she shouted through the window and showed Clementine a pendant of an ankh.

"I don't think that's for luck and love — it's a symbol of eternal life and protection!" Clementine tried to shout back, but the carriage had already moved forward.

"Clementine," William sighed, "Please don't buy anything from sellers who come to the carriage. You will end up paying twice as much as anywhere else and soon it won't just be one seller, once they see that someone is open for business."

"How did that woman not know what an ankh stands for?

The symbol is well-known for its connection to death and eternity," Clementine wondered.

"It is because she and the rest of the sellers, here and everywhere, assume that a tourist won't know anything. Not the meaning of the items, not the prices, nor the authenticity. They only seek to sell to tourists who wish to have an exotic souvenir."

"But it is so silly," Clementine said, "Do people know so little when they travel all the way here? Are they not at all curious to learn anything about the country they come to as guests?"

"We are not technically guests so much as occupiers, if you ask a native Egyptian," William corrected.

"Right, I'm sorry, guests was the wrong word," Clementine admitted, "But still, one would think that people wouldn't travel blindly, without any knowledge of new places."

"It happens all the time," William said, "Besides, did you learn anything about how the people are living now, instead of thousands of years ago?"

Clementine realised she didn't really know that much about the current situation in Egypt. "No, I didn't," she said, and felt shame turn her cheeks pink. "I know of the history, I can read a little of the hieroglyphs, but I confess I know not of current affairs. England and France have occupied parts of Egypt, and for now that is how things are?" She phrased this as a question, for she was not sure. She would do differently next time, when she had more time to prepare.

"Yes, that is so. We and the French have secured areas for now, but there is always a question mark over how long we have a hold on the places we march into." He peered outside. "If it were up to me, we would focus on how things are back home instead of seeking to widen the empire even more."

"William," Clementine gasped, "Isn't it borderline treason to doubt how our queen leads her empire?"

"This isn't the Middle Ages," William smiled, "I won't be

hanged, drawn and quartered simply for disagreeing with Her Majesty on imperial strategy." He shrugged. "Or at least she hasn't hanged, drawn and quartered me yet."

Clementine shuddered at the thought. But she also noticed that the steadier sway of the carriage was helping her feel less nauseous.

"You have more colour in your cheeks," William noted, "Did the carriage movement help?"

"Yes, I think so. How extraordinary." She touched her cheeks, which still felt warm.

"Any particular reason why your cheeks are a lovely shade of rose?"

"Oh, shush," Clementine said, but after a moment she did tell William how embarrassed she was, realising that she knew very little of how people lived in the current day compared to how much she knew of the ancient past.

"That is not uncommon for people who travel without a genuine interest in the places they travel to," William said. "Not many of our peers are ready to actually get to know the cultures we've settled in."

They slowly moved through the city towards the railway station, where they intended to board a train for Cairo and its port. Clementine felt glued to the window as she tried to take in everything: the colour of the sand on the road, the shapes of the houses and what the air smelled like. Among the palm trees she could see smaller bushes that she did not recognise, and on the sides of the road people carried goods on donkeys and camels. She had never seen a camel. Or had she? Clementine's last visit to London Zoo had been some time ago, and she couldn't remember each and every animal she had seen, but now a camel felt like a fascinating creature.

"What makes you smile so?" William asked.

"Stop observing me and look outside," Clementine said, but

her smile did not fade. "I am looking at the camels. They are quite funny-looking, aren't they?"

"Have you ever ridden one," William asked.

"Of course not! Are they good for riding?"

"It is different to horses, but they are quite steady and can withstand the desert conditions much better than an average horse back home. They do have a temperament, though. Like you," William added.

"Ha ha," Clementine said. "I hope I'll get to try riding one while we are here."

"That I can guarantee," William said.

"Really?" Clementine's voice held a child-like enthusiasm. "I would love that!" She was quite a good horse rider, which made her confident she would get used to a camel too.

"How else did you think we would move around the desert and get to the tomb? These kinds of carriages won't work there, Clemmie."

"I– I hadn't really thought of it," Clementine admitted.

"Always think of transportation, mainly to have an exit plan." William took off his gloves and Clementine looked at his long bare fingers. They seemed delicate, as if he was meant to be playing the pianoforte. "Trust me, in a pinch, an exit plan can save your life."

"It is not often that I have needed to think of such matters, but I will keep it in mind," Clementine said drily.

"Ah, so you have had to think about an exit plan?"

Clementine dug herself deeper into the bench, watching cows and a shepherd pass their carriage. The cows looked like the ones they had in England, but smaller.

"When you are trying to avoid certain gentlemen, you learn to keep in mind where an exit can be found," she explained.

William leaned forward, his mouth a grim line. "Did someone try to force you into anything inappropriate?"

"Oh no, well, not usually." She noticed him squeezing his

cane. "It's not anything unusual. Sometimes men are too eager, and you might not wish to entertain the idea of having to marry them, so you seek an open door or window or a fellow guest to help you get out."

"Seriously, Clemmie, you will let me know if there is anyone troubling you?"

"It's hardly your concern, William. Besides, I am perfectly capable of defending myself if needed," Clementine said, and fumbled her fan. "I simply do not wish to create a bloody mess if I can avoid it."

"We are engaged. It is my duty to keep you safe and defend your honour. And believe me: I will gladly beat a man for touching you against your will ," William said, without a trace of humor.

"I really don't have any expectation of that, since this relationship is just an act." But even as she said it, she couldn't help but feel a warmth spread in her chest from his words. Clementine didn't know why, but she believed he would do exactly that — perhaps more — and it made her feel safe. But then, surely any woman would swoon over such words from a handsome man.

William straightened in his seat. "It is part of playing the part believably. Besides, I promised Dickie I'd keep you safe."

"Oh, Dickie! I forgot to send a letter while we were still in Alexandria. I suppose we will have time for that in Cairo?"

"Yes, you will have time in Cairo. We should arrive there in another three hours, once we board the train," William nodded and tucked his pocket watch away. "I need not remind you to keep the letter very vague, without many details?"

Clementine laughed. "I don't think Dickie would mind me telling him about what happened on the train, but my aunt might see it as yet another way of losing suitors. Not ladylike to be fighting thugs."

"You are engaged now, why would they think of other suitors?" William asked, playing with his gloves.

"Until a lady is married, there is still a chance to choose a better suitor. Trust me, mothers and aunts will not stop looking for son-in-law candidates just because there is an engagement. Engagement means nothing yet, just like in our situation."

"Well, let me know if you switch me for a viscount."

"I don't even know many viscounts," Clementine smiled. "Oh, except one. Terribly handsome, and a king at playing pall-mall games. Dancing with him was a highlight of any event we attended together. Even though every lady wanted to dance with him, he always made himself available for me as well. We had a terribly good time talking about history," Clementine smiled. She did not fail to notice a muscle feathering in William's jaw as he crossed his arms in front of him, and was glad to have caused a reaction in him for once!

* * *

THE TRAIN JOURNEY was quite different to what Clementine was used to. The people-filled environment of Alexandria was loud, and Clementine released a sigh of relief once they reached the relative quietness of their train compartment. They soon arrived at Cairo and made their way to the docks where ships cruising up the Nile were waiting for passengers. Palm trees swayed here and there and the soft breeze from the river was a relief in the hot weather. Clementine couldn't wait to change into her lighter attire once they were boarded.

Their river boat, a steamer called the Karnak, looked like it had seen better days, but it seemed to be a popular enough selection for tourists. After making sure their trunks were transferred to their cabins, William excused himself and said he had some business to take care of before they embarked.

"Oh, then I will find a post office, once the ship's maid has finished unpacking."

Their cabins were separated by only a door, which meant Clementine was able to supervise both sides at once.

"Right, if memory serves, there is a post office just across the dock. Look left after stepping off the ship. Don't get lost, we have two hours before the ship leaves and I will not send a search party if you are nowhere to be seen," he said, donning his top hat. "Until we meet again, lady Clemmie." He bowed and disappeared out the door.

"I really need to give him a lesson on names," Clementine muttered.

"My lady?" the maid asked.

"Oh nothing, please continue," Clementine said. But inside her mind, she was trying to make up a silly name for William. Willy? Liam? Limmy? None of those worked. Besides, she liked his name, it suited him and, well, it was a beautiful name for a handsome man, which he very well knew himself to be.

"Clementine!" a voice came from the open door, and the familiar frame of JoJo appeared from the deck outside. "How lovely to see you here too." JoJo kissed Clementine's cheek. She wore a beige linen dress with black embroidery and looked like she belonged in this climate with those colours. The dress had only small sleeves and Clementine longed to change into more suitable attire too. Her riding pants and half dress were waiting for when they disembarked to the Temple of Hathor, and it would still be another four days before they would reach it.

"I did wonder if you two lovebirds would be on the same ship or not, since there are so many here just waiting to go."

"Yes, what a lovely coincidence! Is Bob already in your cabin?"

"Oh yes, he is very particular in the way they unpack his suits — fusses over them terribly," JoJo laughed. "I hardly care," she added.

"And yet you always look so nice, and perfect for the occasion," Clementine said sincerely. Even JoJo's hair did not seem to mind the humidity, whereas Clementine's had curled into dark waves that were impossible to keep in place for a neat hairdo.

"Oh pish," JoJo waved her hand. "But it is perhaps better for me to go and see that he isn't too strict with the maid. We wouldn't want there to be any motivation for revenge. Burned shirts from ironing, that sort of thing."

Clementine laughed. "Does that happen often?"

"More so than you would realise," JoJo said, grimacing, and disappeared with a wave.

* * *

Clementine opened her parasol of cream silk and stepped off the pier. In the hidden pockets of her travel dress she had tucked away her father's notebook and most of her money, along with her ticket for the Karnak. In her hands, she held only her parasol, the iron fan, and a small purse with a little bit of change.

She took a deep breath, looked left, and tried to make her way through the crowds to the post office. She had asked the maid to confirm the directions and had been told it was the smallest building beside the dock, painted in light blue and white. It was supposedly impossible to miss, but Clementine had some trouble finding it. As she moved through the crowd, she was constantly blocked by others. Locals in their tunics and scarfs, and tall tourists in their top hats and parasols, making it impossible for her to see. Not necessarily tourists, Clementine corrected herself — British or French who might live here.

Eventually, she made it to the far side of the square and spotted the white and blue building. A doorbell jingled as she stepped inside the post office. Clementine was surprised to see an older fair man behind the desk.

"Good day, may I help you?" he said, putting away his glasses, which he had been using to read the newspaper. He spoke as if they were in the middle of London.

"I, yes, I would like to send a letter or a postcard to my family before our ship leaves."

"Certainly. We don't often get young women travelling alone here, so your family must be happy to hear from you, miss–" he looked pointedly at her and the 's' at the end of word sounded sharp and accusing.

Annoyed, Clementine straightened to her full height, which of course was not much, even with her heels. "It's Lady Clementine Whitham, actually."

The man's face was only a little less disapproving.

"Show me your postcard collection," Clementine said.

She chose a postcard for Dickie, and one to send home to her maid, Mary. The postcards depicted beautiful shots from different sites in Egypt. One was of the great pyramids and the Sphinx, and the other showed the Temple of Karnak. All places where Clementine could finally go, in theory, and yet couldn't in practice. How very frustrating this work could be, she mused with a sigh. All those majestic sights, almost within reach!

She sat down at a small table to write her greetings, telling everyone how happy they were, and that by chance they had run into Lord and Lady Blake on their honeymoon.

"Two stamps to England," she said, leaving out the please on purpose, and gave him the payment. "May I ask why it is that you run this post office and not someone local? I was expecting to be in trouble for my lack of Arabic."

The man looked at her as if she were an idiot. "We couldn't rely on the locals to handle the Royal Post. That simply would not do, no. Nothing would be sent in time or to the correct places. Once Egypt became England's protectorate, we made sure to put things right."

Clementine squeezed her fan, annoyance creeping up her spine. "Oh my," she said coldly, "And yet, before we came here, the locals somehow managed the post without our help, I would assume."

With that, she left, fuming. She was irritated that she had been gathering up her courage to finally speak to a local, despite the language barrier. And now that man had taken the experience away from her. She registered that it was of course all because of her discussion with William, and how she had not taken enough effort to get to know this country in its current state. She looked around, trying to find someone else she could talk to, but it felt odd to stop someone hurrying to an appointment just so she could have a chat. No, it would be rude of her to assume people wanted to speak to her just because she was on a mission to better herself.

Suddenly, out of the corner of her eye, she saw William. Was it him? It certainly looked exactly like him. He hurried from one of the buildings towards the busy alleyways with a brown bag in his arms.

Clementine did not pause to consider if she should follow him or not. She did not exactly feel that he was doing something untrustworthy, but she was curious, as always. Besides, what if he was getting himself into some trouble? Surely it would be better that she was there to help if needed. Backup was always good, she nodded to herself. She could be his surprise exit plan. After all, he had not said that she shouldn't wander around. Perhaps she would just happen to be in the same area if he should need her.

And so, Clementine gathered her skirts and hurried after William to an alleyway, trying to keep him in sight as they weaved through the crowd of people. The loud sounds of bartering, people shuffling in and out of shop fronts, and a call for prayer all mixed in Clementine's ears. Above her, colourful fabrics hung on clothing lines, casting a soft shade of reds and yellows when the sunlight filtered through them. She passed mouthwatering stalls filled with sweet pastries and fruit. Other shops brought the scent of so many spices she could not recognise them all. Once or twice, she felt small fingers trying to get at her purse, though she was quick to give them a light but determined snap with her fan, which made them run away laughing. It was the same everywhere, she thought. In London you could not walk far before a child was trying to beg or rob you in one way or another.

William and his distinctive top hat took a sharp turn to the right into a smaller alley between two stalls selling fabrics and shoes.

"Excuse me," she said as she squeezed past women haggling very animatedly with a shopkeeper. They did not hear her, so Clementine simply pushed herself through them. She could just see William's coat tails vanish around yet another corner. She hurried after him, her heels clacking on the stones. She was at least gaining on him, since there were fewer people here compared to the street.

She turned the corner and came to a very narrow alley. There was no sign of William. The alleyway had several doors and entryways to inner courtyards. A few people leaned against the walls, idling and looking at her.

A beggar tugged at her skirts with rough knuckled hands. The woman's eyes were a beautiful hazel shade, but sunk too deep in her thin face. Clementine pulled her skirts back, not sure what to do. She could give some money, but she had been warned against it. It would not be enough, and the beggars would not leave her alone until she had given every last penny she had. At worst, there were criminals behind the beggars who would leave them with very little. And yet, she turned and glanced at the beggar woman. She could not help it. She took a coin from her purse and asked, "Do you speak English?"

The woman shook her head. The dress and scarves she had around her had once been of good quality, but they had been worn into colourless rags. A small cup of water beside her looked as dusty as the ground. Clementine switched to French and the woman nodded eagerly.

"Did you see a man, a tall English man in a light suit and a top hat pass by? Which way?" Clementine asked.

"He went behind that door, the dark one at the end of this alley," the woman said in a husky voice, pointing vaguely towards it. Her accent was strong, but both of them spoke as best they could in a language which was not their native.

"Thank you," Clementine said, giving the woman the money. Probably too much, but she couldn't help herself.

"May God bless you, lady," the woman said and tucked away the coin. "Beautiful lady, you do not look like the English ladies, more beautiful, like the moon, not proud and rude," she said.

Clementine smiled. Even here she did not pass as an English woman, but at least she did not look as proud and rude as some of her peers apparently did.

She went swiftly to the dark door. The paint was flaky and barely resembled any colour anymore. Should she just wait in case William needed her? Would she hear sounds of fighting or cries for help? Clementine suddenly considered another option, remembering William's tale of the brothels he and her father used to visit for information. She did not want to find William in a place like that. *Not because of jealousy!* Only because she did not need to see that. And, as his fiancée, she shouldn't suffer him going to other women at all. Unbearable images appeared behind her eyes, and her discomfort turned to annoyance. *How dare he embarrass her like this, if he truly was in the arms of another woman?* It was not good for their credibility. She tried to listen outside the door and heard a woman laughing, which made her stomach tighten.

Before Clementine could think twice, she had opened the door with a bang. "Will–" she started, and then stopped.

Inside was a small room with worn but beautiful ornamental tiles of blue on the floor. The walls were coarsely plastered with light sand. She saw no furniture, but an older woman was pouring what looked like coffee for William as they sat on the floor, surrounded by three children of various ages, propped up by pillows.

Clementine did not know what to say. "Ah, there you are–" she blushed and saw William raise his brow.

The woman asked William if he knew Clementine, and he replied in French, "I'm afraid so. This is my fiancée, Clementine." He shook his head, "Apparently she got lost trying to find the post office."

The woman scrambled to her feet and the children giggled and gazed at Clementine, openly whispering to each other. The woman looked a hundred years old to Clementine, but the hands that grabbed hers were strong, and she let the woman guide her to one of the pillows on the floor. Clementine sat down, carefully arranging her skirts around her and trying to get comfortable in her corset, which was not meant for sitting on the floor at all.

"The bride of Mr William, enchanté," the woman exclaimed in a surprisingly young-sounding voice. She offered Clementine a cup of coffee. "Very beautiful," the woman said clearly in French.

Clementine remembered her manners and took the cup, careful not to spill any. "Merci, Madame," Clementine replied, also in French, "You have a lovely home."

She glanced at William who said nothing. Clearly he was waiting to see what Clementine would say to squirm her way through this intrusion.

"I do apologise for my very rude interruption. You see, I was looking for William — we are about to embark on the Nile cruise, and I was afraid he would be late, so I searched for him in a dreadful panic that something had happened. How glad I am to find him here, and with friends who are keeping him safe." She grinned at the children who giggled, despite clearly not understanding her.

The old woman laughed and patted Clementine's arm. "It is right to look after your husband," she nodded at William. "He is charming, too kind sometimes, and gets into trouble."

"Oh yes," Clementine agreed and sipped her coffee. It was wonderfully strong and aromatic.

William cleared his throat, "Madame Layla here helped me when I was in a pinch, back when I was trying to find your father, Clementine. I had gotten into some trouble with the local authorities for asking too many questions and felt like vanishing might be best before trying to make my way to Cairo. I searched for a place to hide and Layla here…" William flashed the most dashing smile at the old woman, who laughed, and Clementine could swear there was blushing in those wrinkled cheeks, "She tugged at my sleeve and took me in here. She had a fortune teller stall out the front and she hid me first under her table and then for the night in her house. I promised to come back to thank her if I was able to return. I am in her debt," William said, "and I came to pay for that." He gestured at the generous amount of money he had laid out, along with loaves of bread, and boxes of fruit and candy he must have brought in his bag.

The grandmother waved her hand. "No one likes the guards, they are corrupt," she said, and tucked the money into her skirts. Clementine smiled and felt a sigh of relief as she looked at William.

"Thank you for helping my darling," she said to the woman, who took Clementine's hand in hers.

"It is your father who is missing?" she asked.

"Yes, I am very afraid for him. We came to look for answers," Clementine nodded and finished her coffee.

"May I tell your stars?" The woman turned Clementine's hand over and peered at her palm. "I do it for free," she said with a grin to William, who laughed.

"Please," Clementine said, trying to be polite. She did not believe in fortune telling but she did not mind. Perhaps she would meet a tall- Clementine glanced at William. Well, perhaps another tall and handsome stranger would come into her life.

"Such beautiful skin, clear lines, pale like porcelain," the woman muttered and bent close to Clementine's palm. "It is clear that you have a strong destiny. Once you decide what to do, you will follow it to the end, even if the end is not happy. You are determined, but it might bring you grief." The woman rubbed at Clementine's palm, as if trying to make it clearer. "But sometimes the greatest happiness comes from much unhappiness."

It was as strange of a wisdom as Clementine had heard her mother mutter.

"Thank you," Clementine said, "You are kind to say that, even though I do not fully understand the meaning."

"Oh, lady, you will find out." The woman let go of her hand and patted Clementine's cheek. "It will not be unclear to you in the end."

"Well," William said, "Clementine dear, will you go ahead and return to the ship while I finish my business here? I won't be long." He helped Clementine up from the floor. "You do know your way back?"

Clementine nodded and turned to the hostess. "Thank you, Madame Layla, for the coffee." The children gathered around the woman and one of them, a young boy of perhaps six years, whispered something to his grandmother. They looked at Clementine and the woman laughed.

"What?" Clementine smiled, unsure.

"Oh, he says he did not meet a princess before this day. But now he will marry you and become the prince of your kingdom."

Clementine laughed and blew a kiss, to the boy's great joy.

"My prince," she curtsied to him, which made the children giggle and cheer.

William walked her out and kissed her hand before returning inside and closing the door behind him.

Clementine smiled and took a few steps forward but then she stopped with a frown. A gut feeling was telling her that something was fishy, and it wasn't the smells from the harbour. Why wouldn't William want her to wait for him, instead of making her walk alone back in a city that was new to her? She very quietly crouched beneath the side window of the house. The alley was empty for now, and even the beggar had changed places, so there was no one out here to frown at her eavesdropping. The space between the houses was very narrow and Clementine pressed herself against the wall to hear better. At first, she could only hear low talk between the woman and William. Perhaps she was unfair not to trust him, Clementine thought with a pang of guilt. They had just agreed to trust each other, after all. She was just about to tiptoe away when she clearly heard another man's voice. Freezing in place, she kept listening.

"What was she doing here?"

Clementine thought the man's voice sounded familiar.

"She followed me, apparently," William said, as if it was the most natural thing. "She is quite resourceful, I've learned."

The other man groaned. "You need to be careful, William. This could all blow to pieces if you're not careful with her and your libido."

William chuckled. "Don't worry, old boy. She isn't my usual type."

Clementine's fists clenched.

A loud sigh came from the other man. "No, if she has a brain, I don't suppose she is. But heed my warning, William. If our mission is compromised, she will need to be taken care of. And we need that notebook back as soon as possible! We still haven't deciphered the location of the tomb. The old man must've written it down in that notebook. Why you haven't taken it back, I cannot understand!"

"Because, Asem," William said sternly, "she made a fair point. She deserves to see her father's thoughts. You know as well as I do that those might indeed be his last words."

Another loud sigh. "What a mess. Just take care of it, William, the sooner the better. Deal with her."

Clementine's heart was racing as she realised that the conversation inside might well be coming to an end and she needed to scramble. As quietly as possible, she snuck away on her tiptoes to avoid her heels clicking against the ground.

She quickened her pace and retraced her steps through the alleys, her thoughts running wild. Asem was here talking to William about her and her father's notes. *Why on earth?* A chill ran through Clementine's skin. What did he mean that she needed to be taken care of? She felt a familiar feeling of distrust in her gut. She wanted to trust William, but how could she, after everything she heard? He had not agreed with Asem about everything, it seemed, but still — he had sent her away on purpose. There was something he was hiding with Asem, and whatever it was, she wasn't supposed to know about it.

She stopped by some stalls to buy sweet meats, fresh dates and oranges, and didn't even haggle. Her brain was racing fast and she needed to physically stop and think. *Deep breaths and think it through, Clementine!*

It seemed that the best course of action would be to play

innocent. To try and find out what she could from her father's notebooks on her own and see if William might come clean about whatever it was he had going on with Asem. If he kept lying to her, she would uncover his lies at an opportune moment. She needed to keep her eyes and ears open for now, and try and learn more from William without revealing too much.

"Here you are. Hungry already?" William's voice came so suddenly behind her that Clementine jumped and dropped an orange. William laughed and bent to one knee to retrieve it from under the stall table. He held it up to her, and Clementine thought the scene looked like a ridiculous proposal. Him on one knee and her flushed. This would probably be the closest she would ever get to a real proposal. She snatched the orange back and stiffly took William's offered arm.

"A girl has got to eat," she said quickly, trying to sound light-hearted as they walked slowly towards the harbor. "I couldn't resist these food stalls, so colourful and new!"

"So, do you want to tell me why exactly you followed me, alone, in a foreign city, where it could have been dangerous?" William asked as they passed the stalls on the market street.

"Oh, I simply wanted to make sure you were not getting into trouble. You know, be a backup, since I happened to see you go into the alley," Clementine said nonchalantly.

"Ah," William said, "And here I thought you followed me in case I stole a visit to the brothels I told you about. I am touched by your concern."

"And why did you not take me with you from the start for an innocent visit like this?" Clementine said.

"Why, I wanted to see what you would do left alone for a while. I have nothing to hide," William grinned and Clementine wanted to smack him with her parasol for many reasons.

Her smile did not reach her eyes.

ON THE NILE

*I*n the past years, cruises had been taking tourists up and down the Nile, and it had become the fashionable thing for everyone who was anyone to take one. The Karnak seemed to be full, and passengers flocked on the deck as they departed. Clementine leaned against the wooden railing of the white ship and watched as the docks were left behind and the beautiful green gem of the Nile spread out before them. She sighed and tried to clear her head of William and what she had overheard. Clementine welcomed the soft, hot breeze on her face and felt a jolt in her stomach. Not fear, not worry, but excitement. A part of her wished she hadn't heard him, but surely not knowing would have been worse.

"Magnificent, isn't it?" William commented.

Clementine tried not to jump. The man moved with silent steps and seemed to enjoy catching her off guard.

"Yes," she gave him a small smile. "It feels as if I am slowly gliding to my destiny. I cannot wait to get to the tomb." She lifted her face to the sun's afternoon rays and did not care that her complexion might suffer from it. She got freckles from the sun, but she never cared. They would fade as soon as it was winter, and the sun might not brush her cheeks as gently as it did right now for months.

"Let's hope things go smoothly. I had hoped that your father's journal would have told us more about the actual inside of the tomb."

Clementine glanced at him, trying to ignore the irritation that still rose up when she remembered how he had not told her about the journal right away. And the discussion with Asem Smith .

"Tell me again, why didn't my father share that information with you before he disappeared?" Clementine asked with some sharpness in her voice.

William thought for a moment. "Your father had," he paused to consider, "some peculiar ways to deal with his findings. He did not trust anyone, so he even kept some information from me until he was absolutely sure. He always wanted to be the first to find the location or the items," he sighed. "He went out on his own some nights, after we had agreed to stop for the day. He would say he was going to bed with a whisky, a glass of milk, and that book he always carried with him. What was it now? *Around the World in Eighty Days*. And then I'd hear later from some of the crew members that they saw him sneak out of camp all on his own to visit the dig sites." William shook his head. "Dangerous, foolish, and yet he still wanted to do it alone like that. And as I said, we were exploring other tombs with our crew, so I was dividing my attention between them. It seems your father wanted to explore the right tomb on his own before telling me or the rest of our crew, and then it was too late."

"Hmm," Clementine said, "I realise I cannot say much about this, but the Papa I knew, or thought I knew, does not sound like the one you describe. At home, he was always eager to share stories of his findings, at least once they had been found and secured."

"We cannot really know another person, no matter how close we are to them. I'm sure what happened with your mother must have been a shock, even though you and your father knew her so well."

Clementine felt her throat tighten at the mention of her mother in this context. "I do not know what my mother did, really, but perhaps she had her reasons."

William looked like he wanted to say something, but Clementine turned on her heels, claiming a headache, and went back to her cabin after requesting a passing steward bring her some tea.

* * *

It was stuffy in her cabin, and she opened every one of the small windows to let in some air. It didn't help much. Soon there was a knock at her door, and she received a small pot of hot mint tea. The scent of the fresh tea leaves was divine. She quickly poured herself a cup and sat down on a wicker chair with a heavy sigh. The cabin was comfortable and had been designed for the upper classes, who were used to having such luxuries. The gilded frame of the bed shone as if it had been recently polished. The white linen curtains around the bed posts would help both with mosquitoes and to dim the light. There was even a small palm tree in the corner next to a beautiful lacquered vanity with an ornate mirror. Clementine's dresses hung in the wide closet next to it. There was also her own bathroom, which was the true luxury, where her toiletries had already been organised by her attendant.

The small set of rattan furniture was embellished with plush pillows, and on the floor there were several carpets with red and blue embellishments, bringing some colour to an otherwise plain cabin. She sipped the hot tea and enjoyed the soothing taste of the mint. She felt something pressing at her thigh, and, shifting a little, she realised it was her father's notebook. Clementine put down her cup and took the book out of her skirt pockets. She remembered that she might as well change into her lighter dress . It was still hours before dinner and she was already too hot in her usual red travel dress with its drapings and layers of petticoats.

She put the book down next to her tea and undressed. She rinsed herself quickly in her bathroom with the water that had been brought to her and felt a little better. Cold water for washing, that was the thing, she decided. Applying her lilac lotion, she then put on silk drawers, chemise, silk stockings and her corset, which was of a peach colour, with yellow and pink violets embroidered on it, as well as the matching skirt. The skirt had no bustle, nor any drapings, and was divided in the middle into very wide trousers. Clementine felt light as a feather wearing it. The outfit had not been altered much, which meant her mother had also enjoyed dresses which freed a lady's legs for running, or other activities as needed. Her leather boots would wait until they were off this ship; for now, she slipped on her slippers with a slight heel. Looking at herself in the mirror, she was startled to see how much she resembled her mother as she remembered her.

Clementine closed her eyes and summoned memories of them as a family. Papa often joked how he had been a victim of the fae folk, since clearly Lan's beauty could not be of this world. Clementine loved that memory. The two of them laughing together at the thought of Mama having appeared from nowhere. Mama had rolled her eyes and said Papa's head was clearly filled with sand and dust from his travels, before kissing him gently. As a child, Clementine had thought her mother to be the most beautiful woman she had ever seen. She had been darker than Clementine, and while the porcelain shade of her skin and slightly lighter shade of hair were a mixed heritage from her father, Clementine's facial structure resembled her mother as she grew older. Her high cheekbones and narrow chin brought to mind the shape of a heart, she thought. A heart-shaped face with coal dark eyes.

She felt her heart ache for her family, but took comfort in knowing that even if she might never see her parents again, she could see them in herself. She touched her braid and went to retrieve her remaining hair pins to lift it into an updo of sorts. It was better than having the braid stick to her sweaty neck.

Satisfied and feeling refreshed, Clementine sat down to finish her hot tea, and opened her father's notebook. She had read through the pages many times, though some of the scribblings were barely even readable. She flipped through the yellowed pages. Some were stained — with tea, perhaps — and other pages were smudged with ink. Papa clearly was not very neat in the way he took notes. And yet, Clementine thought of the letters she had gotten from him over the years, and the tales he had told her on the rare occasions he had been home. Had he not always recorded his findings in as much detail as he could, adding not only written descriptions but drawings, too?

Clementine looked at the last pages of the book. Only outer descriptions of the tombs. No map, no descriptions of what lay inside or which one he thought was the right tomb. Clementine looked at the rest of the empty pages. She held them up to the light, trying to see if perhaps there had been something written and removed, and a pressure mark remained. But she could not see anything, even though she peered very close to the paper. Then she halted.

Clementine smelled the paper, and true enough there was a scent, very faint among the smell of the leather cover and of the paper itself, but recognisable: milk. Papa had often drunk a glass of milk at night, which now made sense, given the gastric problems William had described. And milk could be used like lemon juice as invisible ink!

Clementine laughed at this. She had played with milk and

lemon juice secret messages as a child. Surely William would have noticed such an easy and childish way of hiding writings? She sniffed the paper again and caught very lightest scent of milk. What did she have to lose?

She closed the windows that looked out on the deck, while keeping the waterside windows open, and lit a candle on her bedstand. She then proceeded to very carefully spread the first empty page open, close enough to the candle that heat reached the paper but would not burn it. Her eyes widened as the invisible ink appeared in front of her. *Unbelievable*, she thought, and quickly gave the next pages the same treatment until no more text became visible. There wasn't much of it, only a handful of pages, but they revealed something very peculiar. There were no coordinates, but a string of numbers, followed by descriptions of the first two chambers of the tomb of the priestess. The last entry from her father was a brief mention that he believed there was a third chamber, and perhaps even more.

Clementine sat down on her bed and blew out the candle, amazed at the simplicity of this little trick. Why had her father gone through the trouble of hiding this? Who was he hiding it from? William had said Father did not trust anyone, but that sounded so strange. And yet, Clementine had to admit that she perhaps did not know Papa so well anymore. Still, how funny that she should try this children's magic on the book, and that it worked!

She read again the entries about the chambers. There were several mentions of traps and a drawing of some lethal looking spikes poking up from the ground. Clementine shivered. She knew from her father's stories that traps and surprises were to be expected, but seeing it described in the very location they were headed left her with an uncomfortable feeling. Father had described rather well the spikes of the first chamber, and something about pressure plates for the next chamber, so at least they would have a warning.

She then flipped back to the first page, where there was a series of numbers, separated by commas. She took out a pen and tried matching the numbers to alphabets. It made no sense. She tried to see if there was some pattern but there was none she could see. Besides, numbers were never her strong suit. She tried the numbers and alphabets backwards without result. Getting quickly frustrated, she put the notebook aside and rose to put her pen back in her bag. Her fingers brushed the book she had taken with her to keep her company. It was Papa's favourite, *Around the World in Eighty Days*.

She smiled as she took out the much-read copy and remembered how Papa had come home one day, years ago, with two copies of the book. One for himself and one for Clementine. That way, he said, before his next departure, it was almost as if they were on the same journey. What a coincidence that William had mentioned Papa retiring with a glass of milk and this novel before sneaking off!

The light turned golden, and Clementine was deep in reading the adventurous story when memories of her and Papa playing with coded letters started to surface in her mind. What had he shown her? She had been so very little, but the lesson had been a fun one since it included the use of invisible ink. Papa had told her that even royalty was known to use such a simple method to send sensitive correspondence to their allies. He had proceeded to demonstrate it with milk and lemon juice and then... Clementine frowned, trying to remember the details from so long ago. She had asked how else she could send secret messages to Papa if she didn't have milk or lemon juice, since her governess was very strict on when one should be eating and drinking, even though Clementine felt she should have milk whenever she wanted. Papa had ruffled her hair and proceeded to show her other ways of sending letters with a simple code. And then they had gone together to the kitchen to ask for more biscuits and milk. Clementine stiffened as the memory poked her mind. He had shown her how to use a book as a cipher!

She quickly took out the pen again and sat back down, *Around the World in Eighty Days* in one hand, and her papa's notebook in the other. *Could it be?* If her book and her father's copy were of the same edition, the page numbers and words would match identically. The numbers could represent first the page number and then a word counted from the upper side of the page! Clementine felt herself tremble as she searched for the pages and the words and wrote them down.

From/ the/first/
   towards/home/
   take/80
   water/in/sun

CLEMENTINE STARED at her writings and wanted to squeal in delight. It wasn't the best of sentences, but it definitely sounded like directions to the location of the tomb! This would save them so much time if they didn't have to go through a hundred tombs to find the right one. Maybe there was a tomb that represented 'the first'? Yes, it was likely. Perhaps the oldest, or the first tomb within the area? 'Towards home' meant England, surely, so one should look north-west. Clementine frowned. She did not understand what the last part meant meant. Taking eighty might mean eighty steps, or perhaps feet? There would be time to think it through, especially once she could see the landscape.

She rose to take her findings to William immediately — how surprised he would be to hear she had it almost figured out! — but then she stopped mid-step and sank back down on the chair. She shook her head, trying to think this through. She closed the notebook and looked at her deciphered text. Could it be that her father hadn't in fact trusted William for some reason, and that is why he had hidden the details of his last moments at the tomb, hastily writing them down in invisible ink?

She bit her lip, frowning at the thought. She trusted easily by nature, and she and William had come to an agreement to try and build trust between them. But hadn't William himself always said not to trust anyone, right from the start? And if she thought about it, she could well imagine William wanting to do this treasure hunt without her. Then there was the ominous discussion with Asem, where he had said to William that Clementine needed to be 'dealt with'.

She swallowed a lump in her throat. If William believed he had all the information on the tomb's location and the chambers, he might decide to jilt Clementine and go without her. Or worse. Surely they didn't mean to deal with her in a more sinister way? She did not want to believe it, but everything she had learned about treasure hunters made them sound as if they would do anything to secure their loot. In the back of her mind, a small voice insisted that William could never harm her. Clementine wanted to believe that there was something more than just a cold-hearted business deal between them. A blooming friendship perhaps, with mutual respect. And something else too. Clementine quickly shoved that small voice back to the back of her mind.

She looked at the notebook, as if an answer might pop out of it. Could William do that? Abandon her here? He'd made it clear he did not wish to be stuck with her, even though she had handled herself well on the train. Was it enough to convince him it was worth keeping her with him? She hated to admit that she was not sure at all.

She flicked her fan open in irritation and fanned the air to cool her flushed cheeks. She could not risk William leaving her on this ship and hopping off into the night. No, she would keep this information with her for just a little while longer. Just long enough to be certain she could trust him not to leave her stranded. They needed to get to the temple, and then she would appear to have found by accident the hidden text, right then and there. Yes, that was it! It wouldn't be exactly lying — simply a delay in giving out the information she already possessed. Just in case, she tucked the deciphered paper in between her corset and her chemise. Then she tucked the book into her dress pocket and finished the rest of the soothing tea.

The complete journey up the Nile and back would take weeks, but for Clementine and William the journey would be over on the fourth day, when they reached the Temple of Hathor. In a way, Clementine thought it was a shame. She would have loved to be here as any other traveller, stopping to go ashore and marvel at the history in front of her. Perhaps there would be another chance to take a cruise like this, once they were not engaged in such an urgent task.

Clementine surprised herself by thinking of them as a 'we', even though she was not yet at all clear if she wanted to go through this scheme with William. Why, why must they pretend to be a couple? If only the rules were different for women, or she was born a man.

Clementine sighed and stroked the cool fabric of her light silk dress. It had been the perfect idea to take mother's modified dress with her . The hem reached her mid-calves, which was perfect to help her cool off in these temperatures, as were the silk stockings underneath.. Clementine and her jiujitsu teacher Edith had tested a linen version of the skirt to see if it allowed Clementine a greater range of movement if needed, and it definitely helped her kick and run much more easily than a traditional skirt. She might cause some eyebrows to rise with this attire, and the other one she had packed with her, but Clementine tried not to care about the stares, as always. These skirts had slowly become more and more common for ladies to use when they rode horses, played tennis or did anything other than sit still at a tea party. Times were changing, and she was glad her mother had been ahead of the times with her outfits. Besides, Clementine would get unwelcome ogling even when she was dressed as a true English lady, right down to the last piece of jewellery, and still the staring would make it feel as if she did not belong. She rolled her shoulders back and decided to go and test the dress' effect right away.

* * *

THE SUN GREETED her as she left her cabin and set off to promenade from one end of the deck to the other. Her slanted hat had a slightly more orange tinge to it today, along with two soft white feathers. She nodded to a passing couple and received a slight stare at her ankles, which were revealed by the outfit. She walked with her head high, but responded to each stare with a sweet smile. She would likely never meet these people again, so it did not matter if she made a bad impression. She paused at the rear deck where people were gathered in small groups. JoJo waved her to come over to their table. She and Bob were playing bridge against another, older couple.

"Here, Clementine, darling. What is that you're wearing? It is simply audacious! I like it," she said with an enthusiastic glint in her eye.

"Thank you, JoJo. This skirt was my mother's, and now, with a few alterations, it is mine, and it truly helps to stay cool in this weather." She nodded to Bob and greeted the two strangers, "How do you do?"

The older couple looked her up and down.

"Do we know you?" the older woman said with an air of disapproval.

"Apologies, Mrs York, where are my manners?" JoJo said,

and introduced the couple — wealthy shopkeepers from London — to Clementine.

"Lady Clementine Whitham," Clementine introduced herself.

The couple exchanged glances.

"Ah, my lady," said the man, "I believe I have read about you." He spoke loudly, either out of habit or because he could not hear properly. "You speak English, do you?"

"Indeed, I believe I have just now spoken English in this very company," Clementine said with slightly less warmth in her voice. "You might have read about my father, the Earl of Whitham, disappearing in Egypt on one of his journeys."

"Quite so," Mr York said, "But such things happen, eh? You have to make peace with the risks of being here in the middle of nowhere. I would never have come here if my wife," he glared at Mrs York, "if she hadn't insisted that this is what all the nobles did these days. That we might get new and important clients for our business. And what has happened? We have met only the two of you. The rest don't seem to be aristocrats, even," he barked, and his mustache quivered .

"Dear, remember that you mustn't excite yourself so much in this hot weather," the woman said. "My husband of course appreciates all potential customers. You simply must visit our cheese and chocolate boutique one day." She glanced at Clementine. "If that is something people like you enjoy, that is. I wouldn't know. We do not eat rice or curry or any such odd foods. Horrible, some of them, not human food at all," she said, letting out a small laugh from behind her cards.

Clementine felt her blood boil. She glanced at JoJo, who raised an eyebrow. Clementine turned to the Yorks. "Yes, well. I will be sure to mention your open and gracious attitude to my people. I will be especially detailed in my exchange with my dear aunt and uncle. You might have heard of them, The Duke and Duchess of Clearwater? And, based on my experience with the two of you, I'm sure my aunt will do all she can tell her friends at court, perhaps even to Her Majesty, of how kind and welcoming you were to me here. Now, if you'll excuse me."

Clementine left the table and went to the railing where she sat down beneath a large parasol and ordered sandwiches and another pot of mint tea from an attendant. Clementine felt peckish when she was annoyed.

Soon after, JoJo and Bob joined her.

"I hope you don't mind," JoJo sat down with her husband. Her white muslin dress fluttered slightly in the gentle breeze. Her amber hair had been left half down, and Clementine wondered how JoJo did not sweat beneath her long hair, but she looked absolutely beautiful and cool in this weather. "We had to finish the round," JoJo said apologetically. "What a horrible couple." She huffed and ordered a pink gin for her and Bob from the attendant. It seemed the couple could hold their liquor no matter what the conditions were. Clementine feared she would fall asleep if she had anything stronger than tea or coffee.

"It is not good for me to stay long when people are so deep in their prejudices. I fear I get terribly angry very easily when they question me or my mother and the way we look and live," Clementine said, feeling her jaw muscles clench.

"As you should," JoJo nodded, "I would be damned upset too. I will also see to it once we return that none of my friends order anything from their nasty little shop."

"Actually," Clementine said, "it's rather sad. I know we have previously ordered chocolates from York Delicacies, and they were rather good. But not anymore."

"Hear, hear," JoJo nodded. "So where is William? I hope he hasn't caught anything to make him less, hmm, vigorous," she grinned, and Bob cleared his throat.

Clementine's sandwiches and tea arrived, as did the pink gins for the Blakes. Bob glanced at the assortment of sandwiches.

"Those look rather good," he remarked.

"Oh, please, help yourself. There's too much for just me anyway," Clementine said. Bob smiled and took two ham and pickle sandwiches with gusto.

Clementine helped herself to a cucumber sandwich and a rather different sandwich which seemed to be filled with a paste of pistachios and honey, sprinkled with a little bit of salt — a divine combination which Clementine described to the Blakes.

"I would love to, but I have to start looking after my figure," JoJo said.

Clementine tried not to roll her eyes too much but failed. JoJo smiled and sipped her drink.

"You look gorgeous, JoJo, as well you know. I really wish you would try a pistachio piece of heaven. I promise it will be worth it and that you'll forget the nonsense of figures and weight once you taste it," Clementine said.

She always thought her peers spent too much time worrying about their weight; whether they were small enough or round enough in the right places as the fashions changed. Clementine had no desire to participate in such worries. She enjoyed eating and had a healthy appetite, especially on days when she had been exercising. Which was most days.

"Well, I suppose I might try one," JoJo said, biting into the soft bread, and her eyes widened with surprise. "It is a delight!"

"See?" Clementine leaned back happily with her teacup. "Ah, here is William."

William greeted the Blakes with surprise and kissed Clementine gently on the hand, which Clementine tried to take as if it was the most natural thing to happen between her and her imposter fiancé.

"Darling, you do look beautiful," William said, his gaze lingering on her outfit as he joined them.

He wore a light suit to help with the warm weather and it looked like his face had some colour from the sun. Clementine thought he had one of those faces that would look good no matter what season it was, or whether or not he was smiling. *Very annoying*, Clementine huffed to herself.

"I wondered where you were," he said, and without anyone offering, he took his share of the sandwiches and tea.

"What's mine is yours," Clementine noted as William ate.

"I figured," William said. "I have to say, I love these pistachio sandwiches every time I visit here, but I never remember to try and have these made at home." He glanced at the Blakes and Clementine saw just the slightest frown appear and disappear. "It is once again a surprise to see the two of you. How are you enjoying the Nile? First time you're here?"

"Oh yes, quite the coincidence, isn't it?" JoJo said. "As mentioned, we are doing the fashionable thing by coming here. Bob is enjoying himself so much with all these rubble piles we plan to visit."

"I don't believe in coincidences," William noted, to Clementine's surprise. He sounded polite but she could sense something was off. "But then, Egypt is the place to be these days," he continued in his usual relaxed tone.

"Yes, quite. Very much waiting for Luxor, but that's still a few days away. Plenty of stops before that we can go to. So, William, where are you planning to disembark?" Bob said.

William smiled, shrugged, and sipped his tea. "That's still a bit of an open plan, old boy. We'll likely need to stop at different locations."

Clementine kept a straight face and did not say anything but focused on filling their cups.

"Yes, can't be sure around here," Bob agreed. "One might disappear anywhere," he said as a final note and took the last cucumber sandwich from the tray. It was hardly the most tactful thing to say but Clementine let it be.

For a while they sat there in comfort, and made William laugh with their tale of the Yorks and their attitudes. William also promised to spread the word of the merchant couple's unfortunate attitude. Clementine was happy that they agreed the couple had been arrogant and rude, but she was still sad to encounter these comments. No matter how much she tried to look, act, and sound the part, society would never truly see her as one of them. She would forever be someone who was just a bit too different. She'd had enough of trying to meet their expectations. It was a mission she was doomed to fail, and was not a battle she wanted to fight for the rest of her life. Which was why she needed her independence, whether through the means of her inheritance or by supporting herself. She did not want to make a living of begging and pleading to belong with her peers. She simply wouldn't.

THE REST of the afternoon passed, and they admired the sunset's colours from the ship's deck. Their first stop would be at Beni Suef which was scheduled for tomorrow, late in the night. After that, the next stop was at the Abydos, which might be the right place for Clementine and William to leave the ship. It was close enough to the Temple of Hathor but did not make their destination so obvious, or so William thought.

William and Clementine walked slowly back to their shared cabin . The evening had become dark quickly. In these parts of the world, darkness was much more regular compared to the far north. Clementine remembered meeting once a woman from Finland — or was it Sweden? — who claimed that during summer they had sunlight throughout the night. It sounded fascinating, and Clementine had mentally added the northern parts of Europe to her list of places she wished to explore.

"So, did you enjoy your first day on the Nile?" William asked, to Clementine's surprise.

"I, well, yes, it has been very beautiful. Aside from the rudeness of Mr and Mrs York, everything has been just as I had imagined."

"Did they really upset you so much that you still talk of it?" William asked.

Clementine felt irritated again. "Why shouldn't I remember and talk about what they said? It is nothing new, but believe me, it does not hurt any less the more you hear it."

"They are ignorant fools, why must you let them affect you so?" William wondered, leaning against her cabin door. "You will be filled with anger and resentment if you take in every snide remark you'll hear."

"I am filled with years-worth of anger and resentment, just so you know," she said sharply. "But I wouldn't expect you to understand. A full-bred British aristocrat with your looks and your exciting job — what suffering have you had when your peers are only happy to accept you with open arms?"

William fell silent and his eyes were shadowed in the darkness. Clementine thought his silence an answer.

"See? You have not suffered because of who you are. I have and will suffer because *your* people," she huffed, "will never truly allow me to belong as I am. Never. And I am tired of it, William."

William said nothing at first, and Clementine let out an annoyed sound, digging out her cabin key.

"There are many ways to suffer, and to be ignorant. Do not presume to know what suffering has occurred in another person's life, or people will soon say that you are the rude and ignorant one. Not everyone is as open as you about their experiences," he said in a quiet voice, and turned to open his door.

Clementine stood there, stunned, staring at him with her dark eyes, struck by the truth of his words.

She did not like his insinuation at all. "Yes, well, you would know all about keeping secrets! How on earth would I know what you have experienced when you do not share them with me? You're withholding information as we speak!"

William's eyes narrowed. "And what information is that?"

"How about you not telling me about your family, since there clearly is some reason you withdraw from the discussion whenever I ask about your parents."

She breathed heavily and looked at William who said nothing.

"Silence? Is that all? Then how about this for secrets? I heard you in Alexandria talking to Asem! I heard how you planned to get rid of me. And let me tell you right now, that won't happen. Because I solved the location of the tomb. That's right! I have the information and you cannot leave me or kill me unless you want to figure it out without my father's clues," she hissed.

William's eyes burned with green fire but she was not afraid of him. If anything, she wanted to get a reaction out of him. She wanted to hear him say he wouldn't ever leave her, that the whole conversation had been a misunderstanding.

"So you do have a hysterical side, it seems," William said in a low voice which sounded somewhat strained. She could see his jaw muscles twitch and his hands clenching into fists, until he visibly forced them to relax. "See you at dinner at eight, Clementine. I trust you will have something more suitable to wear for the occasion?"

Without waiting for an answer, he abruptly disappeared, and Clementine was left to fumble at the tricky lock on her own.

She hated that he had been able to hold his ground despite her outburst, and her knowledge that he and Asem were plotting something sinister. She did not mean to reveal what she had overheard but he had a way of making her feel everything in his presence. And even worse, although s he was still convinced William could know nothing of her suffering, in her heart she felt a pang of guilt at his words. It was true: she did not know him, and she immensely disliked the fact that he was right because he wouldn't let her know him. Not truly. And that, to her horror, made her both furious and endlessly sad. She wanted to know him in all the ways one person could know another, damn it all. That small voice of her subconsciousness made her even more annoyed, and she quite forcibly opened her door and slammed it shut before stripping off her garments.

A STRANGER IN THE NIGHT

Clementine and William had a subdued dinner with the Blakes. Clementine felt ignored by William, and in turn did not feel she should be the one to break their silence. It was a busy evening in the ship's restaurant. The musicians were playing in the corner and people enjoyed an opulent spread of refreshments after the long, hot day of travelling.

William chatted politely with JoJo and Bob, and Clementine did the best she could to follow, but she was still bothered by their argument earlier. William should have admitted that he knew nothing of what Clementine had to endure, and he should tell her what that meeting with Asem was about, without any more lies.

And she, well, she should apologise to him at some point for losing her temper when he had been at least partly right about her. She frowned at the thought of apologising first, but perhaps that could help him do the same and tell her why Asem was here. And why on earth he would be concerned about her.

But this did not feel like the right setting, so Clementine picked at a loose thread of the white tablecloth and looked around the dining room. She saw many who looked like they could be French, British, and perhaps even American. But she also saw more variety in the people around her. Different shades of skin, different shades of hair. On occasion, she heard many different languages being spoken too. In addition to the obvious English and French, there was also German, Spanish and Russian. If she strained her ears, she could hear Hindi as well, but it was difficult to tell over the music and chatter of people. Add the clink of dishes and glasses into the mix, and Clementine could barely hear what JoJo said from across the table.

"How do you like the music," JoJo asked Clementine.

"It's lovely. Truly wonderful." Clementine raised her voice and used her fan to make the air flow a little bit around her. It was very hot, and the air heavy.

"What?" JoJo laughed, unable to hear Clementine.

"Wonderful," Clementine almost yelled over her fan. "I especially like the waltzes."

"Yes, me too!" JoJo nodded, and she too fanned herself.

JoJo's sea-blue dress was one of the most beautiful this evening. The delicate drapings mixed the blue brocade with cream silks, and her corset had a lavish pearl embroidery which made sure to capture the attention of everyone.

Clementine's surviving evening dress was dark purple, the colour of a tulip, with sprinkles of gold embroidery which created flame-like patterns on her chest and hips. Her train had a ruffle of purple and gold which flowed down over her bustle in purple waves. Since she had ruined her brocade slippers in the train fight, she had put on her black leather boots and hoped no one would notice. Then again, if they did, it mattered little. William did not seem to want to dance today, so the shoes would not be an issue.

The band finished a song and were again greeted with plentiful applause from the dining guests. The food had been excellent, Clementine thought. Lovely selection of dishes. Some too heavy for her taste in this weather, but she especially enjoyed one that resembled a meat stew, with many spices familiar to Clementine. It reminded her of the foods her mother had sometimes asked their cook to make. Star anise, cinnamon and cardamom. The flavours had been delightful. She almost turned to William to tell him about her memories but stopped, as he was very much not looking at her direction.

She felt a pang of annoyance. If only it wasn't so hot in this blasted room, then perhaps Clementine could've asked William to dance so they could get back to some natural conversation instead of this tiresome avoidance. She had barely even touched her wine, knowing well that she would wake with a headache after mixing these temperatures with alcohol. She fanned herself and tried to focus on JoJo's gossip about one of the gentlemen on board. Dessert would be served soon, and Clementine hoped it might be something as precious as shaved ice. Unlikely though, on a vessel.

The band started the first notes of *The Blue Danube*, Clementine's favourite waltz, and she couldn't help but glance at William again. She was reminded of the last time they had danced, on the ship to Alexandria, and how good it had felt to be in his arms. Despite everything, she longed to feel it again. Her hand reached out and barely touched his, but his green eyes turned to her with a cold stare and she moved her hand to her glass instead. William's gaze then moved past her as he extended a hand to JoJo.

"This is my favourite waltz," William said, and Clementine stared at him with surprise. "Would you like to dance, JoJo? My dear Clementine is having some shoe issues and I would not want to put her in an awkward position. I feel it would be wasteful not to have this dance." He smiled his dashing smile at JoJo, who agreed.

"You don't mind, do you, Clementine?" she called, but William was already leading her away.

Clementine squeezed her fan, which was luckily sturdy enough to take it without bending. She glanced at Bob, but he was already concerned with waving the waiter closer for more drinks. He did not even notice when Clementine took a deep breath, excused herself, and left for some fresh air on the deck. William clearly wished only to vex her today, so she might as well leave him to it.

* * *

CLEMENTINE WALKED along the deck where a few lanterns lit her way. She saw an attendant hurry past her, but otherwise it was nice and calm in the darkness of the evening. The Nile glistened in the darkness, and she saw lights here and there on both sides of the riverbanks. The night air felt cooler, and it was a welcome change from the stuffiness of the dining room. Clementine breathed in deep and decided to take a stroll around the back of the ship. It would be a while before dessert and coffee were served, so she had time for herself.

In the hazy dimness she could not see the water, only hear it ripple, and sense the darkness of the river gliding around the vessel. Her heels clicked against the wooden deck, and she could still hear the laughter and music from the restaurant. They must have opened the windows to let some air in. Clementine reached the back of the deck and leaned over the railing, looking at the lights on the riverbanks. She wondered if the people there could hear the laughter and the waltz tunes too, and if it made them smile, or if they simply did not care after seeing and hearing them so many times. She wondered if her father had looked at the same lights of the villages and towns. Clementine sighed and felt a cool breeze raise goosebumps on her arms. She wrapped her silk shawl around her neck in case it became even more breezy. It would not do to catch a cold, not now, when she was so close to the tomb.

Her father had been a mystery, she had to admit that. He had told her and taught her so much, but the man himself was a mystery. If Clementine had to guess her father's thoughts on this same spot, she thought perhaps he would have been more interested to see the famous river crocodiles than pay attention to the people.

She dug the notebook from her pocket and flicked through the pages in the dim light. *Who were you, Papa?* The book contained very few personal thoughts; her father had mostly only observed and ruminated on possibilities. The book did not offer Clementine a better view of her father's mind, but she somehow felt that even holding the book brought her closer to him. She gazed again into the distance, listening to the splashes of water and the faraway sounds from the dining area. She sighed and tucked away the notebook. She idly wondered if William liked dancing with JoJo, and it even mattered to her if he did.

Her next thought was that of shock.

Clementine gasped as someone pulled at her shawl so hard and tight that she choked and coughed. Someone was strangling her with her own silk, pushing her against the ship's railing. Trapped, she immediately struggled to free herself. She could not see who was behind her — the scarf was too tight for her to turn — and all she could do was keep her fingers between the fabric and the skin of her neck.

"Give me the notebook, Clementine," hissed a voice behind her ear. The voice had an accent, but mostly it seemed to be seething with hatred. Clementine struggled again, trying to aim a sharp blow from her elbow behind her, but the stranger deflected it easily and laughed.

Clementine still had some breath in her, and she gulped to fill the air with a scream. But before she could, the shawl tightened to an even more painful pressure around her throat.

"Do not scream. One peep from you and my man will cut the

throat of your companion. I'd hate to see his handsome face disfigured. I suggest that you stop struggling and hand over the notebook. Do not force me to search for it," her attacker said with disgust.

Hearing his threat about William, Clementine forced her muscles to relax and raised her hands in a gesture of surrender. The scarf loosened just enough for her to gasp for air and cough.

"Good," the stranger whispered. "Where is the notebook?" he asked in that loathing tone, keeping a steady pressure around her neck.

"In one of my pockets," Clementine croaked, her voice almost gone. She wouldn't be able to scream much, even if she wanted to.

"Take it out, slowly."

Clementine did as she was ordered, cursing herself for coming here alone. She slowly reached into the folds of her skirts, and as she tugged to free the notebook from the narrow pocket, she managed to flick her fan to reveal its spikes. She had no time to thank any gods for the fact that the fan still hung from her wrist. She took out the notebook and lifted it up.

"This is the notebook," she said in a raspy voice.

"I'll take that," the stranger said.

Clementine felt the pressure on her neck ease just slightly as the man reached for the notebook. He shifted to put it away, letting go of her scarf with one hand. Clementine knew this was her moment.

She flipped the fan into her right palm, using it as a knife, and heaved to the left, stabbing at the man's ribs. The man grunted with pain and let go of the scarf in surprise. Clementine wasted no time. She turned, slashing the man in the face with the iron fan's spikes and lunging away from him.

"Fuck!"

Clementine saw the man's face was bloodied, as was the

right side of his abdomen, where the fabric of his dark tunic had been ripped. The man's features were difficult to place, but they were angry.

"Like mother, like daughter, eh?" He smiled a joyless smile and wiped his dark and bloodied hair from his face.

Clementine did not need to hear more, she needed to get away quickly. She turned and tried to run back to where the people were gathered, but her dress was heavy and it made her movements clumsy. She tripped on her own train and the man soon grabbed her and threw her to the ground. Clementine lost the air in her lungs, but she was not unused to such throws and was left unhurt. She scrambled up faster than the man clearly expected. His well-aimed kick would have hit her in the face had she still been on the ground. But he blocked her from getting past him. And what of William?

"What do you want from us?" she croaked. Her throat hurt like hell.

The man smiled and attacked her with cool confidence. She parried with her fan, deflecting his punch aside, and flicked it back to slash diagonally at him. But this time he had no problem disarming her. Surprised, she did not have enough time to react and dodge a kick to her abdomen. She fell backwards against the railing with a soft cry.

"Let's not do tessenjutsu today, since I did not think to bring my fan with me. Come, Clementine, try me fist-to-fist, let's see how you do," he grinned and came for her.

Clementine glanced to where her fan had fallen and realised it was too far away.

"I think I won already, don't you? Or is that merely a tickle on your ribs?" she hissed.

He laughed without humour. "Funny, very funny," he said, and relentlessly attacked her with a series of blows and kicks.

She parried, blocked, and had to work harder than she ever had with Edith to keep her mind calm, to anticipate what the next move might be. He came at her like a viper, too quick to try and stop him with any counterattack. He matched her every blow with a strong block. She considered trying a throw, but it was impossible to get close enough. Unless she could somehow take him down and lock him.

"Getting tired yet?" the man sneered, and his next blow hit her on her shoulder.

She *was* getting tired. She lowered her guard only slightly, inviting the man to come closer, which he did. She blocked another incoming blow and managed a light hit to his face which stunned him for a few crucial seconds. Clementine used the momentum to kick as high as her dress would allow and heard her boot's sturdy heel hit the man's groin. He cursed and backed away, which was Clementine's chance. She dropped and twisted with one leg extended in a flurry of skirts and petticoats, kicking the man's legs from under him. He fell to the ground and Clementine leapt on him, trying to quickly lock him into a choking position.

"What do you want?" she spat at him, her arms locking around his neck.

"Everything," he laughed, and easily heaved her off him. He crashed himself on top of her and began choking her, sitting on her chest.

Clementine gasped for air again, trying to kick or shove him to the side, but he was too heavy, and she was quickly running out of air.

"Back at square one, it seems," the man said, leaning close to her face while he choked her slowly but steadily. "You know, I was supposed to only take your notebook, but since we are here, I might just say my goodbyes."

His fingers dug deeper into the skin of her neck. Clementine could see herself reflected in his dark eyes. She could see herself dying, and this stranger hating her with everything he had. Sparks and darkness filled her sight.

"Will—" she rasped, but it was no use. She was going to die, and she would never find out what happened to her father. William would never forgive her for being so stupid to put herself in this position. Darkness spread from the edges of her vision until she saw only the stranger's sneer. *This cannot be the last thing I see*, she thought to herself.

Suddenly, there was a loud whack and the pressure eased. The man was thrown to the side with a grunt and Clementine's consciousness came back with a painful rush. Her lungs filled with air and her throat felt like it was on fire. She held onto her burning throat and coughed. She heard cursing, and finally her blurry vision cleared to see William coming over to her with an oar in his hand.

"Clementine!" He leaned over her with worry painted all over his face.

"I should've thought of using the oars from the lifeboats," she muttered through the pain in her throat and felt her eyes flutter closed. "Stupid of me."

Fighting to keep conscious was so difficult. She could feel herself trembling from cold, despite the warm evening. Her teeth clattered against each other and she had no control over her jaw muscles.

"God, Clemmie, stay with me." William looked frantically around, cupping her head gently in his hands and tugging the discarded shawl underneath her head. Clementine would have smiled if she wasn't so exhausted. Darkness loomed over her like a blanket. She felt him gently but firmly pat her cheek and was again ripped from the edge of consciousness, back to the dim deck, only to throw up, very painfully, to her side.

"Help," he yelled, and soon enough there were footsteps.

Clementine heard a loud splash and turned her head carefully. The stranger had apparently jumped into the water.

William followed her eyes and frowned. "He's gone," he said, "Good riddance, too, I hope he goes straight to hell." He turned back to bark orders to a frightened looking attendant. More running footsteps.

Clementine tried to croak something.

"What is it, Clemmie? Darling?" William brought his face so close to her that she could again see herself in the reflection of a pair of eyes. But these eyes were kind and full of worry, not hatred. She did not see her death in those green pools.

"My fan," she whispered, pointing in the general direction of where it had fallen, "Take it, before…" She coughed and could not finish her sentence. William understood though. He retrieved the fan and Clementine felt relief wash over her. .

"The fan is safe, and you will be too. A doctor is on the way." He gently stroked her hair away from her face with a trembling touch.

"Good," she whispered, "And then dessert?" With that, she finally lost herself to darkness, and it was as if she had been submerged into soothing water where she finally felt nothing at all.

RECOVERY

Almost two days had passed when Clementine woke up with a start. A soft light seeped through the windows of the cabin; it looked like afternoon light. She tried to sit up, confused, and winced when the movement hurt. It felt as if she had been driven over by a carriage.

A muffled voice came from next to her and a strong arm gently wrapped around her waist, tugging her softly back to bed. She froze. She turned to see William sleeping, fully dressed, next to her, in the same bed, as if they were a married couple. Her eyes widened, and as she looked down at herself, she was relieved to see that she had her nightgown on, at least.

She let out a sigh of relief, although this was another line crossed between them. Not to mention both of his arms gently around her, pulling her closer to him in his sleep. The feeling of shyness she should have felt melted away when she felt the warmth of his body, and she found herself settling against his chest and finding soothing comfort in the closeness to him.

She looked around and saw that they were in her cabin. On a chair, she saw her evening dress; the one with dark purple silk and gold embroidery. It was in a crumpled heap. She remembered suddenly. That's what she had been wearing that night, When the man attacked.

Memories came back, making Clementine's head hurt. The man choking her. She had been fighting him all over the ship's deck. Clementine relived the many punches and kicks she'd received, and her futile attempts to get a grip on the man. She had been thrown aside as if she were a ragdoll, and it had almost cost her life. She carefully moved each of her limbs. Nothing seemed broken. Her hands went up to her neck and she could feel the skin was tender. She likely had ugly bruises. Clementine slowly turned her head to the right and to the left, feeling stiff but thankfully unbroken. Another sigh of relief. She would be able to continue this journey and find her father–

Oh no! Clementine gasped. Her father's notebook had been stolen! That stranger had it. Her hand flew up to her mouth. There was nothing she could do now, unless someone had apprehended her attacker.

"Are you going to vomit again?" William's voice came from beside her.

She shook her head carefully and turned to look at him. His eyes still had that dreamy look of one who has just woken up. He looked at her with a frown and suddenly she felt like they really were a married couple; her waking up next to him, her dark eyes being the first thing his green eyes saw, each and every day.

"Did you stay with me when I was sick?" she whispered with a blush. At least her voice was coming back. "I'm sorry you had to see that."

William rolled his eyes and carefully turned to face her. It seemed very intimate, and Clementine's face still felt hot. She did not say anything about him continuing to embrace her

"I never left your side, Clemmie. In this profession, we see everything about each other. In many ways it is like a marriage, 'til death do us part and all that. Which luckily didn't happen to you quite yet, but I have to say when I saw you being strangled like that, I really did fear the worst." He gently touched her hand. "How are you feeling?"

"I, well, I don't know really. I think I feel alright, under the circumstances. It seems nothing is broken," she said with an air of questioning.

"No, nothing should be broken," William confirmed, "The doctor examined you thoroughly while you were unconscious and she checked on you every few hours. Are you nauseous or very sore?"

Clementine shook her head. "My throat hurts and it seems there are bruises here and there. I feel as if I could drink a pitcher of water." She gently touched her neck. "How long have I slept?"

"On and off for almost two days. You've awoken for a few sips of water and once to be sick, but otherwise you have been dead to the world, so to say." William carefully released her, reaching over to the bedside table to pour a glass of water. She held out her hand for it but instead William settled next to her and lifted the glass to her dry lips, very gently helping her drink. "Slowly, the doctor said," he cautioned.

She sipped, and it was as if a dam had broken into a rocky, dry valley. Her throat felt dry as the desert, but with William's help she resisted the urge to take greedy gulps and sipped cautiously. Once William saw she could control her thirst, he gave her the glass.

"What about my attacker? Did he survive after that blow?"

William's mouth tightened to a grim line. "It is difficult say. He jumped into the water after I hit him, but if he survived the swim..." He shook his head and Clementine noticed his sand-coloured curls were a sleepy mess. He ran his hand through his hair, which did nothing to help the wild curls. "Damn it, Clementine, I wish I could say I'm sure he is dead, but I can't," he sighed.

"You did not see a body in the water?" Clementine squeezed her glass.

"No. I gave him a decent blow once I saw he was strangling you. Imagine my shock, seeing you there, underneath him. At first, I thought he had attacked you, well, for other reasons." William frowned. "I saw the lifeboat oars and decided it was best to deal with him as brutally as I could."

"Good," Clementine said. Trying to avoid the flashbacks of the man's hateful face, and of his fingers around her neck.

"He simply dropped off the ship, and I cared more about looking after you than going after him. After the doctor arrived, I rushed to look over the railing, but we had moved forward and in the darkness I could not see anything floating or swimming."

"Perhaps the crocodiles got to him," Clementine said, but her small smile did not quite reach her eyes.

"What happened, Clementine? Why didn't you scream for help? Did you recognise the man?" William sat up and faced her. His face was a mix of worry and frustration which made Clementine feel ashamed.

"I simply went outside before dessert," Clementine explained, sitting up too, "While you were dancing." She did not want to mention her being upset with him. "I wanted some fresh air — the dining area was so hot and stuffy, so I walked to the back of the ship where it was calm and quiet to enjoy the breeze and the company of my own thoughts."

"Ah, you did wake up from your slumber once to tell me how *The Blue Danube* was your favourite too," William smiled, and his frown almost vanished.

"Oh," Clementine felt mortified, "I do hope I did not say anything awkward."

William grinned and she ignored him.

"And then someone was choking me with my silk shawl, pinning me to the railing. He was too strong, but I tried to struggle myself free. I obviously never surrender just because the opponent is bigger or stronger," Clementine gestured at herself, "Otherwise I wouldn't be able to fight anyone. He wanted my father's notebook and kept me pinned and choking, despite my struggles."

"But I don't understand why you didn't call for help," William said.

"I wanted to, but he said his companion would kill you if I made a scene. I had no way of knowing if he was telling the truth," Clementine exclaimed, frustrated. "I did not feel like risking it."

"Assume that I am fine, Clementine. Next time, fight for yourself, first and foremost." He grabbed her hand and squeezed it for emphasis, "Do you understand? Never trust anyone. Always fight and save yourself first."

Clementine looked down. "I don't think I can do that. But I can try," she gulped, "Next time."

"Not that I'm not touched by your concern, old thing," William said, and squeezed her hand again. "Can you remember anything more?" He took away his hand from hers and she felt cold without his warmth.

"Yes," Clementine said, shivering. After he asked me to give him the notebook, I fought him, stabbed at his side with my fan, but he disarmed me much too quickly. Even recognised tessenjutsu, which few do," she said, and William gave a low whistle of surprise.

"I fought him, and he was good, William. It's like he matched what I did, but did it quicker and stronger. I could barely keep up. The spikes of my fan did not scrape him deep enough, even though they did hit their mark. I was running out of ideas fast, so I decided to take the fight to the ground. I did manage a good sweep under his feet, but I shouldn't have tried to apprehend him. I went with instinct, and the instinct should've been to run. But I didn't know what he might do to you, or that alleged man of his, and I just... I saw red, William. He had such hatred in his eyes, his voice, I couldn't understand it." She shook her head. "I'm sorry, it was a mistake."

William's eyes softened. "You will remember it next time."

"Let's not keep saying next time," Clementine said.

"So, he fought you, and you fought back, and he seemed to hold a grudge. And you did not recognise him?"

Clementine shook her head and finished her water. "No." She licked her dry lips. "I have not met him. His voice had an accent of some sort but I could not place it. Based on his face only, I would guess he is from somewhere eastern, but as with me, he could be from anywhere, despite how he looks."

William nodded but the frown was back on his face. "With the Suez Canal open for business and leisure, we are in a place where people pour in from all sides of the world."

Clementine passed over her empty glass to be filled again and sipped some more. "I really thought I would die," she said quietly.

"You'll get used to it," William said with a dry laugh. "Next time it won't be so burdening to your thoughts."

"Stop saying next time," Clementine said.

William ignored her, turning to look at her with narrowed eyes. "Wait, he told you to give him the notebook? How did he know you had it with you?"

"I, well," Clementine struggled to find some excuse but failed, "I had it open just minutes before the attack happened. I read it because I missed my father. You can hardly blame me for that." She pursed her lips together.

William sighed and rubbed his forehead. "No, I cannot blame you for missing your father, but for God's sake, Clementine, we agreed that you should keep it safe and not flaunt it around as if it were a poetry book."

"I didn't flaunt it around! I thought I was alone on that deck and decided to flick through it for just a moment. Again, you cannot blame me for actions someone else made. I did not attack myself," she insisted.

William pinched the bridge of his nose. "Dare I ask if you still have it?"

"I do not," Clementine said, and it felt as if she shrunk from saying it. "He got it from me by saying he would hurt you."

"Clementine," William started, but Clementine interrupted him.

"And I bloody well wish that you would do the same for me, Mr Hunt, if someone threatened my life! I'm not so cold as to trade your life for an item. Besides, he did not get everything." She gestured to her dress, "Give me my corset, will you."

William rose and did as she asked.

"Now don't get angry, I was going to tell you eventually," Clementine warned him. She really didn't want to do this now, but she saw little reason to delay it under the circumstances. If he was going to leave her, to abandon her, and continue without her, he would do so anyway, with or without the knowledge of the traps she had discovered. The escape from near death, thanks to William, dismissed the fear of him hurting her. Clearly his discussion with Asem had not been about getting rid of her by killing her, otherwise he could have just let the stranger do what he wanted with her. Clementine knew she had seen real worry and fear in William's eyes when he had found her. It felt real, and just now when she woke up with him next to her, holding her, she had felt safe. He could leave her, but she chose to trust that he wouldn't. His actions spoke louder than words, and truthfully, it would not have been difficult for him to go through her clothes and find the pages she had managed to decipher. Besides, if he did leave her to go and explore the tomb on his own, well, she had to admit that she did not want him to go there without any knowledge of the traps that would be waiting for him. She could not stand the idea of him being hurt. Clementine took a deep, shaky breath and met his gaze.

William cocked his eyebrow. "Do I want to know?"

"I think you do," she said, and pulled out the deciphered pages from a hidden pocket. "Here. I think it's directions to finding the right tomb. The code was based on numbers and words from a book my father gave me." She passed it to William.

"What is this riddle?" he said, surprised, "Where did you find it? I looked over and over again, and could've sworn in court that there were no details about the tomb's location."

"Ah, but you did not think to turn to childish tricks as I did," Clementine smiled. She nodded at the paper, "Or doesn't the ink seem a bit different to you?"

He frowned and looked again. "What the devil? Did your father actually use fruit ink?"

Clementine grinned. "Milk. He taught me when I was little, so we could send secret correspondence while he was away for long periods. You said he suffered from gastric problems, so having milk was part of his evening routine. I was astonished he had actually taken the trouble to hide this. It is strange — his lack of trust in you, for example," she said pointedly and crossed her arms.

"Ah, I see that you are starting to learn. Are you implying that your father did not trust me, his assistant, and hence you were also reluctant to trust me once you found this information?"

Clementine nodded, hardly able to breathe. William might leave just now if he decided she could not be trusted.

He studied her with those green eyes and Clementine felt naked under his searching gaze. A slight frown played on his face, and the way his jaw clenched indicated to Clementine that he was upset about something. She waited in silence for him to say something, to decide if they could continue onwards together. The thought of him leaving felt like a dull pain in her chest. She wanted to beg him to let her stay with him, but her pride prevented her from voicing a plea out loud.

Just as she had feared, William left the room, slamming the door behind him, and Clementine jumped at the sound of it.

So he left. Clementine let out a trembling sigh. *Well, it was always a possibility*, she thought sadly and rose slowly from the bed. She hardly noticed the tears falling from her eyes. Stifling a sob, she grew angry at her own reaction. Crying after that man, of all things! On an impulse, she hurled a pillow at the door and immediately regretted it as her body protested with a jolt of pain. Rubbing her fists across her eyes, she took a moment to let her anger subside, but it was no use. She wanted to punch and kick and scream all at once. And what's worse, more than anything she wanted him to hold her again, to feel his strong arms around her, to hear his breathing and the steady beat of his heart… To feel safe with him, despite everything. Clementine shook her head, carefully, to rid herself of these foolish, idiotic sentiments. Clearly he was done with her. And on top of it all, she now needed to make a plan for herself if she could not travel with William anymore.

Minutes passed and Clementine decided she might as well get up and get dressed. Her tired muscles shook as she rummaged for her clothes, but try as she might, her aching heart did not calm down.

Just as she was taking off her nightgown to put on her day dress, William barged back in without knocking.

"You devil," she hissed and covered herself with the half-removed gown. "Not only do you decide to leave me for one tiny mistake — after you yourself had hidden the notebook from me, if I may add — then you barge in here as if you have a right! You are rude, Mr Hunt!" Her cheeks flamed warm and red, and William stared at her for a quiet moment, his eyebrows raised in surprise. In his hands there was a tray of breakfast.

"Say something or leave me be forever," Clementine said, flustered.

William slowly put down the tray on the table next to Clementine and she was very aware of how close he was to her naked skin. The soft curves of her body were barely covered by the nightgown, and as she felt William's eyes on her she could swear she felt the touch of his gaze.

"I hardly know what to say. Such loveliness has disarmed me from any irritation I might have felt just now." His voice was low and she looked up at him, standing her ground and refusing to be intimidated by his tall frame looming above her.

He stroked a loose hair behind her ear and she shivered. Her breathing was shallow and she felt an odd sensation cover any pain from her bruises; a warmth in her belly which seemed to seep throughout her body.

"Will," she said, her lips parted, not sure what to say.

He leaned very close, reaching behind her, and she instinctively leaned nearer to him. It was as if their bodies were drawn to each other, and she could not stop herself from wanting to be closer, much closer to him.

He chuckled, and suddenly she felt a light blanket wrapping around her.

"There, now you can stop blushing so fiercely." He shook his head. "If only you could see yourself now, or when you sleep. I swear, Clementine–" he huffed, "A weaker man would have chosen to drown himself in the Nile already."

Clementine did not know what to say, which happened more often with this man than anyone else. *How vexing.*

"Now, go and dress in your bathroom, and then we'll see if you can manage some breakfast. Or late lunch, actually."

"So, you're not leaving me?" she blurted.

"No, though I won't deny having had moments when I considered it. But no, not now when that lunatic might still be out there, trying to kill you. Besides, your brain might yet be very useful once we get to the tomb."

"But I thought, when you left so suddenly, that–" Clementine continued, but William waved his hand.

"I remembered the attendant had brought a tray of food in case you woke up, and it was in my cabin. The doctor did say that you should try to eat, if water did not make you nauseous. That is all. Oh, and here," he gave her the iron fan.

Her eyes brightened and she reached out to take her beloved possession from him. "You remembered," she said gratefully, not noticing how one side of the blanket slipped to reveal an ample part of her bosom.

"Damn it all, Clementine. I might be a strong man, but have some mercy." William grinned that crooked smile of his, but his eyes seemed to be lit with a fire and he did not look away.

Clementine realised her mistake with a small cry and scrambled to cover her cleavage. Thank goodness not everything had showed, but it was not far off. William laughed and she straightened her posture, wrapped the blanket tightly around herself, and disappeared into the bathroom with a flourish and a growling stomach.

* * *

ONCE SHE HAD CHANGED into her peach-coloured dress, she sat down to eat with the appetite of someone who had been starved.

"Remember to breathe too," William commented, pouring them another cup of tea.

"I'm sure you would be ravenous after sleeping and not eating for two days," she said, between mouthfuls of date porridge and toast.

"True," William said, "I am perhaps used to young women eating like birds in my presence. To be honest, I often wondered how they could accomplish anything with so little food."

Clementine rolled her eyes and buttered another piece of toast.

"So," William said, "Back to the invisible ink and the pages that the mystery man now has. It was clever of you to remove the deciphered page. That might at least slow him down a little, if he's still alive, that is. Were there other pages written with the milk ink?"

Clementine hesitated a moment.

"Are you sure you will not leave me once you have all the information I can give you?" she asked once more.

"I am sure," William said and pressed his hand to his heart, "Upon my honour."

"Fine," Clementine said, "I will trust you — against your own advice." She took a bite of toast and chewed for a moment. "I think it has been proven enough times that nothing good comes from not trusting one another. Anyway, there were descriptions and a few drawings of the first two chambers. Not much, but some useful information on what to expect."

She explained as best she could the descriptions of the traps and how one might work around them or go through them. William listened and nodded.

"Sounds familiar, or something that I would have expected. We will just have to be careful. Traps can usually be solved or avoided," he said.

"How can you be so sure?"

"Because I'm still alive and in one piece after encountering many interesting contraptions while treasure hunting," he smiled.

"Oh," Clementine bit her lip.

"Is there something else?"

"Yes, perhaps. One page had a list of places and very crude sketches of some objects. Outside of Egypt. I think Papa had planned to visit all of them. Unless you already did," Clementine took out the last deciphered page from a separate hidden pocket in the ruined corset and gave it to William. This was it. He now had all the information she had withheld.

William's eyes widened. "No, these are not places we've been to. The drawings aren't the clearest, but I think some of these are recognisable. I never discussed this list with your father, but it seems that this might have been his travel plan."

"It could be a clue for where to look next, if we don't find him here. Or if we find him dead, we could continue his planned work, if the queen allows," Clementine said in a quiet voice. She still refused to think her papa dead.

"Hmm, it's certainly an option to keep in mind." William handed her the paper back. "And is that everything you haven't told me? You haven't forgotten any other clues in your undergarments, for example? I'd be happy to look." His lips twitched.

"Yes, William. I am now an open book when it comes to you," Clementine said, and resisted rolling her eyes again. There were still some things unsaid, but those she would keep close to her heart for now. That same heart that seemed to skip a beat when he smiled at her.

"I am glad you wanted to share vital information with me and make this journey slightly less complicated," William said.

"As long as we are on the subject of sharing vital information, don't you think I deserve to know why Mr Asem Smith is here, and why you and he were talking about getting rid of me?"

William sighed. "I had hoped you would let that tiny little detail be."

"Tell me, William."

"Some details are not for me to tell. But Asem is a good person, and he is invested in the safekeeping of the extraordinary treasures. His father runs the British Museum, but he is his bastard son, and let's just say the two of them don't exactly see eye to eye. Asem is a man of honour; his father not so much."

"Oh," Clementine said. "And by extraordinary items you mean magical items. So, he is one of the queen's treasure hunters then?"

"Not exactly," William said. "You should really ask him these questions directly if you get a chance. I do not feel comfortable in sharing the personal details of my friend."

"Fine. Then tell me, why is he against me being here?"

"He, well, to be honest he does not trust you, and he felt that you being attached to me complicates the work we do."

Clementine was about to say something unkind but William stopped her. "Honestly Clemmie, I did tell him that he simply didn't know you. That you had proved to be a skillful fighter with a sharp mind. I'm on your side."

"Prove it. Tell me something I don't know about you. Something real that will help me know more about you and trust you." Clementine crossed her arms. She knew this could be a risky thing to ask, but after everything she had been through, she felt it was his turn to reveal something meaningful to her.

William's emerald eyes regarded her for a moment, and she almost thought he would deny her request.

"You asked about my family and I do not wish to speak about them much. The truth is that both my brother and I suffered at the hands of our father. Boys get punished, yes, but what he did was much more than just discipline us. He had trouble controlling his anger and he took it out on weaker members of the household. Sometimes it was the servants, sometimes it was my brother and me. But most often it was…"

William's voice faded and his eyes darkened with a mixture of hate and sorrow that made Clementine's chest tighten as she realised the rumors JoJo had mentioned about Lady Knightwood were true.

"Your mother?" Clementine's voice was full of emotion.

William nodded, and his hand resting on the table clenched into a tight fist. "He beat her. Often. Once the bruises started to appear on her face, she stopped socialising with her friends. She stopped going to dinners, to balls. She withdrew from life and was a little more than a prisoner at our house. And still she loved him, as he still loved her." William shook his head. "He killed her, eventually. Strangled her too long, or so he says. Claimed it to be an accident, and had the audacity of being devastated by her death." He let out a shaky breath.

"William, I–" Clementine swallowed hard. She had not meant to dig out such painful memories. "I'm sorry to have asked. And I'm so sorry about your mother. You and your brother must have been so young." Tears dropped from her eyes to her lap.

"We were too young to stop him. We tried, but he would only beat us first, before getting to her." William let out a hapless laugh. "You know what he said to me, years later? That his father had been the same, and one day my brother and I would understand too, because we would become the same. Monsters, unable to control ourselves, no matter how much we loved the people we hurt."

William closed his eyes and set his mouth in a grim line. "Love can be worse than death."

Something in the way he said it broke Clementine's heart. The words had such heaviness in them that it made her reach out for his hand. She gently coaxed his fist open and took his fingers into hers. "It doesn't have to be," she whispered.

She felt just the tiniest squeeze from his hand before he met her gaze. "Aren't you afraid of me?"

"No," Clementine said, without a second of hesitation.

"Perhaps you should be," he said with a grim expression. "When I saw that man strangle you, saw your life slowly slipping away, I was overcome by red. That's the only way I can describe it. Everything was red, and when I struck that man with the oar, I wished it was a sword, so his head would roll off his shoulders for what he had done to you." He looked away from her.

"Hey," Clementine said, reaching out to touch his jaw and turn his face back to her. His stubble felt rough against her fingertips, and she fought the urge to softly glide them against his cheek. "Look at me with those beautiful eyes of yours." That coaxed a flash of amusement in William's expression as he turned to meet her gaze. It was enough to encourage Clementine to keep going. "I would've reacted in the same way if someone I cared about was brutally attacked. You did the right thing, and these hands–" she lowered her hand on top of his, "These hands could never hurt me. I do not believe it is possible."

He regarded her with such a tender expression that colour rose in her cheeks. Then he kissed her hand and Clementine felt the warmth from his lips spread through her arm and up to her heart. He looked up, his lips still almost touching her skin. The intimacy of it took her breath away.

"Well, well," he said, that crooked smile slowly coming back to his face, "Not only does she describe my eyes as beautiful, but she also admits to care for this handsome rake. I wonder what she might be persuaded to do, given these new feelings she has for her dashing knight in shining armor."

Clementine blushed and yanked her hand away. "Remind me not to try and make you feel better next time."

William chuckled, and to Clementine's relief, he seemed more like his usual self again. "Seriously though, Clemmie, thank you for your words. I do not like to talk about my past, but perhaps I will reveal the rest of it to you someday. For now, I hope this was sufficiently real enough for you?"

"Yes William. I promise not to tell anyone, and not to pester you with questions about your family." She meant it.

For a moment, they stayed in comfortable silence. Clementine felt the air somehow cleared between them, and together with the breakfast, she felt rejuvenated and content with where they stood.

"What's next then?" Clementine asked as she finally finished her late breakfast, feeling satisfied.

"Next, I suggest that you take some time to rest and pack before we disembark at Abydos. We will arrive in the early evening, so there is time."

Clementine nodded and rang the bell for the attendant to clear away the dishes.

When the attendant came, William also sent her to fetch the doctor to give Clementine one final check.

"I'll go to my cabin to finish packing," William said. "Oh, and Clementine. Don't be too alarmed — this might have to do with the attacker, or perhaps it was some other opportunist, but our cabins were searched. Or at least mine was, so I can only assume that yours was too — either while you were under attack or beforehand, when we were at dinner. Check your belongings."

Clementine nodded. After the attack, it seemed that nothing surprised her anymore. "Do you think the two instances are connected? The train attack and this?"

William shrugged. "Impossible to say, but I would not rule it out. Too many coincidences are suspicious."

"Trust nothing," Clementine smiled.

William nodded and turned to leave. Impulsively, Clementine grabbed his hand. He turned to her with a question written on his face.

"William," she said, and her throat felt dry again. She wondered if her hand felt hot in his. To think she had to say this aloud. "I haven't thanked you yet. You saved me. Fair and square this time, so there. Thank you."

He grinned, and she felt that tingling feeling in her stomach again. That smile, and the light in his green eyes...

"Why, thank you, Clementine. I must say I did not expect

you to bring this up, but it does seem that I did clearly save you. You are most welcome," he teased, and kissed her hand with a lingering touch of his lips. He did not release her hand when his gaze met hers, nor did she pull away.

Clementine felt the unbearable magnetism of two people standing so close to one another without touching. Who would have thought there might be such a distance between two people in the same room? It made her want to scream in frustration. She looked down, embarrassed by her thoughts, and felt her chin gently lifted by William's feather-light touch.

"That expression. What lies behind those eyes, hmm? Do tell," he smiled as she looked up at him.

"I–" she whispered, her eyes fixed on his lips.

He moved slightly closer, leaning in as if to hear her words better.

"Yes, Clementine…? You need only ask," he said, so close that Clementine could feel his warm breath on her skin.

She swallowed. Her heartbeat felt as if a hummingbird was trapped in her chest.

At that moment, the door opened rather brusquely and an efficient-looking woman came in, making Clementine jump several steps away from William.

"Ah, the patient lives," the woman said, nodding to them both and walking past as if nothing outrageous had just happened. She had a rather thick Scottish accent. "I trust you haven't excited your bride too much, Mr Hunt, after such an ordeal?" The woman raised her eyebrow with a slightly bored look.

"No, indeed, Dr Todd ." William smiled his most dashing smile. "You know I would never, unless the lady in question asked me," he winked to Clementine before leaving the room.

Clementine was left quite breathless with the doctor. She was surprised to find a female doctor on board, which she expressed aloud.

"You wouldn't be the only one who finds me to be an oddity," Dr Todd said.

"Oh no, I did not mean an oddity! I'm just glad to see a female doctor for the first time."

"Yes, well times are slowly changing. Not fast enough, if you ask me. But I'm sure you hear the same all the time as a female archaeologist. Your man told me about your travels to find your father and rummage around the ancient sites. Good looking chap, by the way, and he knows it," Dr Todd said, brushing a strand of graying hair behind her ear. "I congratulate you on getting one of the good ones." She gestured for Clementine to lie down and started by taking her pulse.

"Good ones?" Clementine asked.

"Yes," the doctor said, gently testing Clementine's limbs for movement and soreness. "He is a rake — that, anyone can see — but he has a heart somewhere in there that is warm and beating," she chuckled.

"Oh really?" Clementine gave a weak laugh.

The doctor turned her head from side to side, touching lightly over the bruises, which made Clementine flinch a little.

"Yes. You know he never left your side after he carried you in here? Insisted on sleeping right next to you and watching over you in case you woke. I think you might be in some danger from that young man where your heart is considered. He really can take your breath away with those looks. And, apparently, by his kindness, too."

"And that is a bad thing?" Clementine asked, as the doctor listened to her heart and lungs with a stethoscope.

"Yes, because you will stand no chance against his charm, that's for sure," the doctor laughed. "Any nausea? You keeping food and water in?"

"No nausea and I finished breakfast without any incidents," Clementine said, "I feel as if I have been run over by a train, but that's all."

The doctor nodded and closed her bag. "You were lucky to get away with just bruises and some scrapes. The neck certainly looks worse than it is, but the bruises are already fading, don't you worry. You seem to heal remarkably fast. Strange, really, but don't look a gift horse in the mouth. Your recovery is nothing short of miraculous."

"Thank you, Doctor. What do I owe you?" Clementine asked before the other woman could disappear through the door.

"Don't you worry about that. Your beloved took care of it. You stay out of trouble now, young lady. Meanwhile, I shall continue with my holiday." With that, she left with a whoosh of grey skirts.

Clementine had only a moment to open her cupboard to start taking her dresses out before there was another knock on her door.

"Come in," Clementine called, and tried not to flinch so much at just a knock. *I'm safe*, she assured herself.

"There you are." JoJo sailed in with her day dress of light blue and white, and a matching parasol in her hand. "We have been worried sick."

"Thank you," Clementine said, "It has been quite a journey."

"You poor dear, look at your neck!" JoJo flopped onto Clementine's bed. "Does it hurt very much?"

"No, thankfully," Clementine said, and laid down her dresses next to JoJo to wait for the maid to arrive and help her pack. The purple evening dress was ripped in several places after her attack. William and the queen now owed her two evening gowns.

"You seem to have the most terrible luck. First the train and now this!" She shook her head and her red curls bounced along with the movement. "However did you survive? You must have some secret powers to call upon!"

Clementine laughed drily. "I wish I had. But sadly I only have my own physical body to help me stand my ground."

"You keep doing that," JoJo said eagerly. "I wish I had your energy, to be honest! Oh, but are you packing?" She gestured to the pile of dresses.

"Yes," Clementine said, "We disembark this evening to look for my father."

"At Abydos?" JoJo asked.

"Yes, it's a start at least," Clementine nodded.

"I wonder how far you'll have to search," JoJo said.

"As far as we have to. It probably won't be easy, but I'm prepared to do whatever it takes," Clementine said with determination.

"You know I believe you," JoJo said. "If anyone can find what they are looking for, it has to be you." She rose from the bed. "Well, I guess this is goodbye then." She kissed Clementine's cheeks. "Don't be a stranger, and I wish you every success in your hunt!"

Clementine smiled. "Thank you, and enjoy the rest of the honeymoon. I think the Temple of Abydos will be fascinating for you to explore. I'm sad we will miss it," Clementine sighed, "I so would have liked to see the place dedicated to the cult of Osiris and the Great Temple of Seti the Second."

"Seti the First, darling," JoJo said, and Clementine raised her brows in surprise at the correction. "It shall be absolutely fabulous. What horrible tales we'll hear! Bob is so excited."

With that, JoJo left, and Clementine refocused on packing. And trying to ignore what had almost happened, twice, with William. She wanted to think about the almost-kiss very much — every second, in fact — but she could not afford distractions now that the hardest part of their journey was about to start.

She touched her neck gingerly. Not that the first part had been easy.

THE TEMPLE OF HATHOR

*I*t was dark when the Karnak moored by the ruins of Abydos. The rest of the guests would stay on the ship overnight and explore the ruins in the morning before it got too hot.

Clementine and William left behind a trail of anxious attendants, as well as the captain and general manager, who were all very worried that Clementine was on her feet already. But after many assurances of her recovery from Dr Todd, they headed off into the night.

They were greeted by a local man, Abayomi, who William said had been with him and Clementine's father when they had been looking for the tomb of Hathor's priestess the first time.

The man bowed to her and spoke in accented but clear English, "My lady, you are the lord's daughter? Very sad, very sad indeed. I hope you and he will find peace after this journey. I will help you." He smiled, and Clementine thanked him.

Abayomi had with him three camels and Clementine thought they looked much funnier than in paintings or drawings. Chewing with their big lips, spitting occasionally, and looking around from behind those thick eyelashes as if humans were the most boring thing in the world.

William helped her climb onto one of the camels. No, a dromedary, Clementine corrected, as the creature had only one hump. Once she settled herself on the structure balanced on top of the hump, she realised it wasn't that different from riding side saddle. On a horse, she would have preferred to ride with a normal saddle, but here she did not complain. At least she was holding on, and her split skirt was perfect to keep her modest and not too restricted.

"Ready?" William asked, and Clementine nodded. "Lean back," he instructed.

The camel stood up, lifting its rear first, and Clementine leaned back with a gasp. Then the front of the camel straightened, and she could feel the sway of the animal. *It's just a different kind of horse*, she told herself.

"Alright?" William called up, handing her the reins.

"Yes, of course." Now it definitely did not feel similar to a horse, but she tried to cover the uncertainty in her voice.

"Of course," William laughed and climbed into his saddle.

Finally, the three of them were on their way in the darkness of the evening. Clementine knew the temperatures would drop soon after sunset and had thought to bring with her the thickest, widest, wool shawl she owned. She was glad for it now as they passed Abydos and turned west towards the Temple of Hathor.

* * *

It was some two hours later when they finally arrived at the campsite. Night had come and there were very few people up and about.

Clementine vaguely wondered how many women there were here. So far, she had seen none.

"A tent for lord and lady, here," Abayomi said, once they had dismounted. The camels sniffed, and seemed insulted to have been used in such a manner, based on their sour expressions.

William talked through the schedule for tomorrow morning, but Clementine could not concentrate just now. Grasping her shawl tighter, she let her gaze wander around the edge of the desert. Compared to the greenness of the riverbank, it seemed as if they had been transported to a completely different location. Dry sand covered her boots, and she was glad she had packed the ones with very little heel for riding.

Two dozen tents stood in a group, and behind them, in the darkness, Clementine could just see the outlines of the Temple of Hathor. Her heart fluttered at the thought of standing here, finally, where her father had been. The square-shaped shadow silently loomed against the starry sky, and it was amazing to think how many people had stood here, century after century, just like Clementine, and gazed upon the temple. She could just make out the columns in front, reflecting the lights of their fires. It felt haunted, and yet also exhilarating. Clementine did not believe in ghosts, but whenever she thought about ancient locations she got goosebumps.

"Clementine," William said, after Abayomi had left them.

"Yes, I was just admiring what little I can see," she smiled.

"Let's hope we have time to visit the temple after we examine the tomb." He lowered his voice and Clementine leaned closer. "We are a married couple, so it looks better if we do some tourist activities after the search. And keep in mind there might be grave robbers here in the camp or just outside of it," he warned her.

Clementine looked at him for a beat. "Isn't that what we do?" she whispered back to him, shrugging to emphasise the silliness of the comment.

"No, well, yes," William said, "But what I meant was that

there might be people here who murder and rob others to get to the people who actually find the ancient treasures."

"Hmm, take the treasures and kill some people..." Clementine pretended to think about this, "I repeat, isn't that what we do?"

William sighed. "Just be careful not to be left alone. Trust–"

Clementine interrupted him, "Yes, yes, trust no one. I promise not to leave the tent without telling you first. Is that to your satisfaction?"

"Not nearly enough," William muttered. Then he took their remaining luggage and led Clementine into their shared tent through a piece of fabric acting as a door. He lowered the fabric back down to seal them in.

The tent was as simple as to be expected under the circumstances. The sand-coloured canvas of the tent thankfully covered the floor, which meant less sand and fewer insects. Clementine shivered and tried not to think about scorpions. In one corner stood a worn wooden crate which served as a table of sorts as it balanced a metallic water pitcher and two crude but efficient-looking mugs. Several old rugs covered the floor and two bedrolls were spread out for them.

"The beds are quite close," she commented.

William laughed. "You have just slept two nights next to me. I think we'll manage."

"I wasn't conscious back then," Clementine muttered. "Bath?"

William laughed again. "A rare luxury. Water and a basin are provided, but I'm not sure you want to go and have a bath outside with the men. I suggest a washcloth and a pitcher of water in here."

Clementine nodded. She had known this would be very ascetic — it was nothing she hadn't been prepared for — but she really did miss the warmth of a hot bath. The tent was just as cold as the outdoor air.

"I think I'll just sleep in my clothes, since there isn't that much time for it anyway. We leave at dawn, correct?" Clementine sat on one of the bedrolls, feeling the coolness of the sand underneath, despite the layers.

"Yes, Abayomi and his men will accompany us. They worked for us the first time, so they know the general location of the different tombs we explored. But, as I said, only your father knew which tomb was the high priestess', and we did not get to explore it together. When I left, I paid Abayomi good money to keep an eye on the tombs, but I don't for a minute believe that he hasn't already searched them with his men."

"And do you think they found something?"

William nodded. "It is possible. Then again, I don't think he would have agreed to take us if the tombs were robbed empty. He was eager to get paid, so they must not have got rich if they did find something. Besides…" William hesitated.

"What?" Clementine asked.

"Your father did let it slip that he had found a pressure plate that opened a doorway to the tomb. I did not get details from him, but based on his excitement it was well-hidden…"

"Oh," Clementine said, yawning. It was getting late, and her thoughts were getting muddier. Her injuries hurt, too. "How odd that he would confide that to you but keep the drawings hidden. Perhaps he was simply too excited to explain it all."

William nodded. "Ready for bed?"

"Yes, I'm starting to feel my bruises again."

William nodded. "Quite. You are still in recovery. Will you need help undressing?"

Clementine glared at him, and he raised his hands in defense.

"I am merely offering assistance."

"I have slept in corsets throughout my childhood, like any other of my peers. How else would we ever be able to nap?" She rolled her eyes.

"Right," William smiled. He took off only his hat and gloves and went to bed fully clothed, too.

"So," Clementine said, turning her head to face William.

"So," he said, turning on his side to smile back at her.

"How safe are we here, what do you think?"

"From the grave robbers, and the men who help them for money? I'd give it a half a chance that we can sleep in peace, and another half a chance that we'll be mugged in the night."

"That's not very assuring," Clementine said.

"Are you sleeping with your fan?"

"Yes," Clementine smiled, her eyes closed now. "And you with your pistol?"

"Yes," William confirmed.

"Wake me up if there is trouble," Clementine said, half-asleep.

She did not hear William murmur goodnight before she gave into her dreams. She couldn't exactly say if she dreamed of green eyes, or if that simply meant the last thing she saw was William.

* * *

DAWN CAME QUICKER than Clementine would have thought, but no one had tried to attack them in the night at least. She was still stiff, but not as sore as she had been the day before. Her tender throat seemed better, and the small mirror next to the water basin confirmed that some of the bruises had started to take on a lighter shade of brown and yellow. People would stare, but Clementine shrugged. *What else was new?*

They ate a humble breakfast of flatbread, eggs, and some strong tea, and were ready to go in a surprising orderly manner. Some of the tents were still closed, but Clementine could see that they were not the only ones here waiting to get started with all the digging, crawling and exploring. There was an air of haste in all of the adventurers, for daylight was limited compared to their more northern homelands, where summer evenings were long, and darkness fell like a soft blanket instead of the true darkness that covered the desert once evening came.

"The men are ready," William said.

Clementine had once again been staring at the Temple of Hathor. The sun peeked over the horizon and coloured the sky into pinks and yellows, mixing with the velvet darkness of the stars. It was light enough that she could see the details of the temple's exterior; the statues and columns that dominated the front. It was more beautiful than she ever could have guessed, and the sight brought her such joy. *To still be able to see these ancient beauties!* She longed to see inside and try to read the hieroglyphs. It called to her with an intensity she had rarely known. She felt as if it was almost enough to just see and admire this ancient construction, a place of worship, as it had been for thousands of years.

Once again, she felt a pang of guilt. Why should they take anything from these beautiful places when they so clearly belonged here, where they were built, next to the Nile and the desert? Not in a museum somewhere far away. But then, if the items were left here, how could people around the world learn about these ancient civilisations? She bit her lip and tried to shake her thoughts, which were not helpful for a treasure hunter at the start of her career.

She nodded to William.

"Anything you would like to share?" He came to stand next to her. He had taken off his jacket and stood there in his boots and grey trousers, the white of his shirt bright against the rising sun.

"Oh, nothing really. Only..." she sighed and lowered her voice. Not that anyone was standing close to them. "I'm starting to feel worse and worse about stealing items from other countries." She gestured at the temple, "Look at it. This is where it belongs, along with anything inside it. What right do we have to rip everything apart and take anything that's movable back home?"

"I don't disagree. But the reality is that Egypt is our protectorate, so I suppose that gives the people much above us the right to demand its riches and curiosities are handed over. Besides, the British Museum would be alarmingly empty without people like us working ourselves to the very end to keep it filled," he winked, and Clementine laughed.

"Yes, imagine that. A museum containing only things found on our own soil."

William nodded and put on a hat to shield him from sun. "That's the joke, Clementine. We would have plenty, but the question is what we consider to be our own soil."

Clementine put on her gloves, also peach-coloured, to match her dress.

"I got the joke, William."

"Oh good, I just had to make sure."

She glared at him.

"And anyway, think of it this way, if it brings you comfort: we are not doing it for fame and fortune. We do it only for the money. A man's got to eat, and a woman too," he added. "We are merely tools for Her Majesty as we take on our jobs as thieves."

"I– Ugh, I suppose you're right. Doesn't make me feel much better, but that's what we are. Glorified thieves." She shook her head and smoothed her peach-coloured skirt. She was sure the beautiful colour would not last for long in the sand and the sun, but she also felt strongly that she should do this in her mother's old dress. Besides, if this one got ruined too, she could always order a similar one to be made.

William gently put his hand on her back and led her to the camels. A handful of men greeted her with grunts, and Abayomi with more flourish.

"Ah, lady, good morning. Did you sleep well?"

"Like a baby, Mr Abayomi," she assured him, settling herself on the side saddle and adjusting her hat. "Now then, I think this is a beautiful day to go and find my father. Shall we?"

* * *

As they got the camels moving, they watched the sun climb above the sands and felt the temperature rise swiftly. Clementine was relieved that her dress was of such a thin material. The undershirt had long sleeves, but that too was of the finest linen, which meant it was very light and yet protected her a little from the burning sun. She had her parasol with her and soon opened it. Even with her hat, the sun here was very different from the sun they had back at home. Luckily, she did not burn easily, but poor William had started to look red already.

"William, perhaps you should have taken a parasol with you," she called.

"I will keep that in mind next time," he called back, and she saw that he had a scarf in his hand, which was of a colourful cotton. He wrapped it over his head, his hat, and around to cover half of his face. "The locals taught me this the last time I was here."

"Very good of them not to let you fry like an egg from the heat," she noted.

Abayomi laughed. "Young lord not as bad as old lord. He was red like crab. Very unhealthy it looked," he tutted.

Clementine nodded politely, even though she felt a pang in her heart. Had this been too much for Papa? Perhaps he had suffered a seizure or heart failure when the sandstorm surprised them. "Yes," she said, "Papa always was sensitive to the sun. That and his stomach issues, I wonder how he was able to travel as much as he did."

"Passion, lady," Abayomi said, "He had passion for what he did. Sly as a fox and very strong-minded about what he wanted.

Always so sure he would find this priestess of Hathor's tomb and take everything he could find, if something was still left."

"And do you think there is still something left, Mr Abayomi?"

His eyes smiled, even though his scarf covered his mouth. "Yes, lady. I do."

The sands grew drier, if one could say such a thing. They left the riverbank far behind them as they turned north-west of the Temple of Hathor, and there were fewer and fewer plants visible. Gone was the green lushness of the riverbank with its palm trees and flowers. Here, Clementine thought, one could truly die by accident and be simply forgotten.

"So, tell me about the area, William. What should we expect?"

William guided his camel next to hers. The tassels and bells on the dromedary let out a bright jingle with the sway of their steady walk.

"We are not far away really. It simply seems that way because the tombs are located behind a dune that we'll cross in just over two hours. The tombs are barely visible because of the sand and the collapse of the outer buildings over time. There once were beautiful columns, filled with colour and writings — that much we could see from the rubble that still stood — and the hieroglyphs confirmed to us that this was indeed the burial area for Hathor's priestesses. We counted at least thirty mounds in different conditions. Some were still buried, some were still accessible. And one of the tombs was the High Priestess', the holiest of them all," William said.

"They were bound to a life of servitude, were they not?" Clementine said, "Princesses and other noble ladies who became tattooed priestesses for the goddess, until their names were wiped from history for some unknown reason."

"Who knows?" William shrugged, "Much is yet unknown, but we do know that these were high-ranking women. Appreciated and respected by the people. The High Priestess herself was seen as a symbol, or even reincarnation as Hathor herself, and she was known to bless women with fertility difficulties, and those who were sick beyond redemption."

"And were they healed?" Clementine asked.

"The remaining legend certainly spins the tale as miracles," William smiled, and wiped his face with his head scarf.

Clementine flicked out her iron fan to bring some air to her face. She could tell her chemise would be drenched in sweat by the end of this.

"Perhaps there were miracles back then," Clementine said with some melancholy. "I can only hope one will be granted to us to help find out what happened to Father."

"Cheer up, old girl. Don't let the sun and the heat take the fight out of you." He offered her a flask of water. Even though the river was only half a day away from the tomb, there was still plenty of water for both themselves and the animals.

"William," she said.

"Yes, Clemmie?" He raised an eyebrow.

"If we find my father dead, what shall we do then?"

"Well, that would be sad, of course, but perhaps there is some silver lining in the matter. You would get to bury him, and it would be proof for you to get your hands on your inheritance."

"How can you speak so... so matter-of-fact?" Clementine blurted.

"Because that is how it would be. Perhaps the better question is: what if you *don't* find him? What then? His body might not be there, and the trail might have gone cold. In addition to that, what if there is no treasure to be found? What will you do then?"

"I would beg for Her Majesty to let me prove myself with another assignment. I would beg for her forgiveness, and for her to take pity on me." Clementine squeezed the parasol tightly at the thought.

"Sounds like a lot of groveling, to be honest," William noted.

"She is the queen."

"And only human, just like most of us," he said so quietly that Clementine wasn't sure she had heard right.

They rode on in silence and Clementine let her mind wander from ancient times to past weeks. Was this really something she wanted to do for the rest of her life? Could she? Without William, she had to admit, she would be dead or severely injured. Then again, she had been able to stand her ground when needed, so there was that. She still wasn't sure what she thought of working with William. And what if she had to return with empty hands? What then? Get married off to someone who would be willing to take a woman previously engaged? Could she even consider marriage with someone else?

A long while later, based on how numb and sore Clementine started to feel, they arrived at a valley between the dunes. There had once been some kind of shrubbery, but it had long since dried. Otherwise, it was sand and stone and brightness everywhere she looked.

"I wonder if there used to be water around here." Clementine pointed to the dead-looking plants. A snake slithered near her camel and she shivered. Perhaps it wasn't poisonous. Not like the asps that Cleopatra had allegedly used on herself.

"That's what we thought when we were here with your father," William said. "It might be an underground source of the Nile."

In front, Abayomi and his men had stopped. Clementine could see small mounds of sand and rubble stretching out in front of them a long way. The mounds had not been set closely beside each other — rather, there was ample distance between them. Enough space for an old building to have stood on each spot. There were at least forty mounds that she could see at a quick glance, but she knew the number could be hundreds.

"Which one, lord?" Abayomi called to William.

"Clementine?" William said.

Clementine took out the deciphered page from her pocket, shading her eyes from the blazing brightness of the midday sun to read the burnt words once more.

FROM/ the/First/
  towards/home/
  take/80
  water/in/sun

SHE LOOKED AROUND. The dunes blocked the way into the valley from any other direction, so this had to be the starting point, and the closest mound of a tomb had to be the 'first'. She walked over to it.

"We dig here?" Abayomi asked.

Clementine shook her head. "Wait, Mr Abayomi. We are trying to find out which tomb is the right one. Does anyone have a compass?" she asked, not trusting herself to navigate with the sun so high.

William gave her a small compass from his pocket.

Clementine took it and her hands shook slightly from the excitement. Balancing a parasol and compass in one hand, and the piece of paper in the other, she started walking towards north-west. Towards home.

"One, two, three," she counted her steps.

"I'll just march along, since my steps are probably closer to your father's, compared to your small feet," William grinned.

She ignored him and kept counting. By eighty, she was in

between two tombs, but William was standing in front of a pile of stone and sand.

They gathered around the tomb. Standing closer, Clementine could see the mound was more than it seemed. The rubble contained pieces of ancient stone and a half-standing wall with faded markings on it. She crouched down to look closer.

"There are hieroglyphs here. Very faded, but I can see Hathor's symbol clearly, as well as her servants'. Beautiful." She gently brushed sand from the surface and revealed more faded hieroglyphs in her shadow. "The next tricky part is to find a way in, as I'm not sure what the rest of the hint means."

William frowned and removed the scarf from his head. "I think there was an entrance here, before the sandstorm hit us. The rubble just needs to be cleared away." William gestured to Abayomi and his men, then he rolled his own sleeves and started to shift the first pieces of stone.

Clementine offered her help but the men ignored her, so she shrugged and kept herself under her parasol's shade. The collapse had been made worse by the sandstorm which had ravaged the area for three days. Any clearing that had been done before, by Clementine's father and his men, had to be done again, at least on the surface level. It was likely that beneath the sand and rubble, the entrance would be fairly clear.

She felt her chest tighten at the thought of her father underneath the sand and stone. Trapped with no water, no food and no light. How long could a man survive there? Some days, at most? Unless he had run out of air to breathe... *No, stop it.* Clementine blinked away the tears that threatened to surface and pushed the unhelpful thoughts away with some difficulty.

The men moved the stones by hand and with shovels, and in the heat it could not have been an easy task. Clementine felt sorry for them, and she made sure to make rounds with the water flasks. She even put some water in a small bucket for the dromedaries to drink. No different than the horses, she reminded herself. The dromedaries looked at her, unimpressed, and she was afraid they would spit at her, but eventually they drank from the container in her hands. She even patted one or two of them fondly on their necks. They did not object, but maintained their air of boredom and superiority.

After an hour or so, William eventually removed his shirt, which was already moist with sweat, and Clementine tried not to stare. She obviously had not seen many men without clothes, but she was quite sure that his body, with its toned muscles, was among the finest she could imagine. Not that she did imagine his body but–

"Clementine," William called, and she snapped out of her thoughts with a guilty blush. It was just from the heat, surely — though that did not sound very convincing, even to herself.

"Yes?" she said, and approached him.

He gestured to the ground. "Look, we are almost through the sand. Not long now until we can clear this opening. It looked worse than it was."

"I can't wait to see how it looks inside," she admitted.

William smiled and took a long gulp from her flask. "It's dust and sand and history."

"Yes," Clementine nodded. Those words summed it up nicely. Buried history and lost knowledge. She wished she could stay to simply read and decipher the hieroglyphs. If only she could read them faster, but alas, it had not been the main part of her studies. Being able to read hieroglyphs rarely helped a lady land a husband.

When the men finally stopped the digging, in front of them lay an entrance, barely visible in the sand but still clearly an entryway. The remaining stone walls stood there silently, indifferent to the changed world. Faded hieroglyphs covered the door and walls in the form of the goddess of Hathor.

"Wonderful," Clementine said to Abayomi, "Thanks to you

and your men. We'll continue from here with William and see if there are any signs of my father."

William nodded and pulled his shirt back on. Before he had time to button it, Abayomi and two of his men moved to block the entrance.

"I'm afraid not yet, lady," Abayomi said very politely. "You see, we have been waiting here for a long time for the old lord or the young lord to return. We have not received enough payment."

"Ridiculous," William huffed, buttoning his shirt and pulling his suspenders up over his shoulders. "I paid you personally before I left, to keep guard of this general area, and I paid much more than average for such an easy task."

"It is not enough." Abayomi spread his dusty hands again, as if he were very apologetic.

Clementine's eyes darted between Abayomi, William, and the other four men who seemed to have made a circle around them. She took a deep breath and casually opened her fan, as if to cool herself. She needed to take on at least two of them, should this come to a fight.

That's not so bad, now, is it?

They might go easy on her at first, since they didn't think she was able to even carry the rubble. She tensed a little, while keeping her stance neutral, and slowly fanned herself. *Bouncy knees, weight slightly on the balls of your feet.* In her left hand she still held the empty bucket of water for the animals. *Solid enough to land a hit. You can do it, Clementine.*

She pulled out her most radiant smile. "Oh, but Mr Abayomi, please be reasonable. Surely you have a good Samaritan in you, who has taken joy and grace in helping us as we search for my poor Papa." She kept her voice at a pleading pitch — a noble woman in distress — while she kept the other men in the edges of her vision.

Abayomi chuckled. "You are too lovely, lady. Truly, your face is as pale and beautiful as the moon, surrounded by a shroud as dark as the stormiest night. But I am afraid I must insist. You will show us how to access to the lower chambers and we will take any treasure there might be, as well as your money and jewellery."

"Now look here, we are not here to negotiate such unreasonable conditions," William started, but his stance changed subtly, and Clementine could see the pompous aristocrat act was only a ruse to get ready.

"Abayomi is never unreasonable," the man in question said, as if offended by such accusations. He put his hand on his heart. "I would never make a bad deal. If we find the old lord, we will let you have him without question, yes?" He smiled, and Clementine had had enough.

"Respectfully," she said, "we do not accept."

"Get them!" Abayomi bellowed.

From the corner of her eye, she saw the man on her right take steps towards her. She did not wait for him to grab her. She stepped to the side and turned with enough force to swing the bucket against the man's head. She barely registered him attempting to block the blow. Seeing him go down on his knees, holding his head, was enough for her. She leapt over him and flicked out the claws of her fan. Clementine had but a moment to see William using his shovel to keep Abayomi and two other men at bay.

The man in front of her widened his eyes in surprise when he saw her coming at him with her iron fan spread out. She slashed with the open fan and the man blocked without realising there were sharp claws at the tips of the iron slats, leaving his hand bleeding from multiple gashes. Clementine snapped the fan shut and swept it up to his chin. The strike sent him backwards, but he did not go down. He whipped out a knife and advanced towards her, stabbing fiercely. She dodged it without effort by bending backwards. Using the momentum, she continued the move into a backflip, kicking up into the man's face with force. The man dropped his knife and Clementine moved in fast with a forward kick to his chest and another jumping kick to his already bruised face. He finally went down like a rock.

Clementine made her way towards William, but someone grabbed her into an unfriendly bear hug. She cursed. She had not hit the first man hard enough with her bucket. She struggled, but he did not let go of her. Why must men always be bigger than her? She really needed to address this with Edith in their next training session.

The man yelled to Abayomi and William froze at the familiar scene. Clementine guessed they were using her being captured to make him surrender. *To hell with this again.* At least her feet weren't dangling off the ground this time, so she used her hard-gained flexibility to kick upwards as high as she could manage. She felt the tip of her boot smash against the man's jaw. She heard William bark a laugh and continue his fight.

The man behind Clementine was thrown off balance and fell to the ground. She scrambled to grab the bucket and smashed it on his head. This time he stayed on the ground, his face bloodied.

She wiped snot from her nose and hurried forward to William, who had lost his shovel and was locked in a fight with the two men while Abayomi stayed to one side. She wanted to finish him off, but she had to help William first. Clementine spread her fan and attacked one of the men from behind, slashing a deep flesh wound on his back. He screamed and turned on her with a clumsy hook. She dodged it easily, flapping the open fan against his face for distraction before landing a sharp kick on his ribs, and another to his knee. It popped with a disgusting sound and he fell screaming.

Done, Clementine thought, and turned with a whirl of her split skirt, like a dusty cloud surrounding her. Her eyes were furious and her chest heaved against her corset with her heavy breathing.

"Let's stop this already," she said.

William was winning his boxing match against the biggest of the men, landing a sharp jab right on the man's nose, followed by a crushing elbow to his temple.

Just as Clementine turned to Abayomi, there was a harsh yell.

"Hey!" A dark rider approached the dig site with some other men on horses. To Clementine's horror, she saw Abayomi turn towards the figure with a small pistol in his hands.

She moved in a blur and lunged at him. Her petite frame was not much of a mass for knocking anyone down, but when used fast enough she was like a small, peach-coloured arrow.

"No!" she yelled, thinking only of not letting Abayomi shoot at outsiders; at possible rescuers. She slammed into him, and a second later, or perhaps simultaneously, her ears rang with the sound of a gunshot. She had a firm grip of his pistol hand as they fell to the ground, sending up a cloud of dust around them. Blinded momentarily by the sand, she slammed Abayomi hand repeatedly into the ground until she felt the pistol falling from his grasp.

"You traitor," she shrieked, bringing her elbow down on his face. Abayomi whimpered and brought a hand to his nose. Clementine rose and kicked the pistol further away.

"Clementine!" William came to her. He had finally knocked down his opponent. His brow was bleeding and a bruise was forming, but other than that and a rip in his shirt he seemed fine. He grabbed her face with a smile, "You were incredible, as if Athena herself had taken control of you!"

"Well, I am no goddess, but I suppose I did handle most of them," she said, panting, a feeling of pride and warmth inside her chest from his words.

The sound of hooves and men dismounting their horses

snapped their attention back to the strangers. Their leader, the man who had yelled at them, stepped forward. His head was a mess of dark hair and his face was covered with a scarf — the skin around his eyes matching the brown tunic he wore. He was of average height with a sturdy, muscular body, which was evident from his wide shoulders. His stride had confidence in it.

"She fights well. Curious for a lady who has never set foot anywhere dangerous in her life," the man said as he stopped in front of them. Clementine flushed and saw William shift and tense, his shoulder angled slightly in front of Clementine.

This annoyed her. She didn't want to be hidden behind the towering frame of William, so she took a step forward and extended her hand.

"Lady Clementine Whitham and my, f- husband, Mr William Hunt," she introduced them, ignoring the tense atmosphere.

"Indeed, a husband and a wife," said the man with a hint of a smile in his voice, but did not take her hand. Clementine shrugged. Perhaps it was a cultural matter. Then the man took off the scarf covering his face and Clementine realised with surprise that it was none other than Mr Asem Smith.

"Mr Smith! What on earth are you doing here?" she blurted.

He nodded his head. "We meet again, despite my wishes." He glanced at William. "I am apparently helping my dear friend William and his fiancée out of a tight spot. You seem to be a magnet for trouble, my lady." He gestured towards the thugs around them who were being apprehended by his group of men.

"We were searching for this tomb," Clementine said, still breathless from the fight, and waved at the entrance behind her.

"And you have found it." The man smiled, and his voice was polite, but there was an undertone of something darker. "So now you may leave."

"Now listen, Asem. Friend," William said, keeping his voice

light, "We are yet to search the tomb. The lady's missing father might be there. You know this."

Asem straightened slightly. "You know what we are, William. Do you want her involved?" He nodded at Clementine as if she wasn't there.

"The lady has proven her worth in tricky situations where some men would have faltered in her place. She stays," he said, matter of fact, and Clementine felt a warmth spread in her chest.

Asem raised a dark eyebrow. "I could have her removed by force. You know we do not reveal our purpose to outsiders." He put his hand on his cutlass — slowly, but with intention.

Clementine saw the same move echoed by the dozen men behind him. She did the maths: the odds were bad. They were already tired from one fight, and they were losing daylight. She looked at William and he shook his head with a warning look. So she went for plan B.

"Please, Mr Smith," she said, and tucked a loose strand of hair behind her ear. Where her hat was, she did not know. "Have some mercy. We came here, trusting these treacherous men, to find evidence of my father who disappeared while exploring this tomb. There was a sandstorm and he got separated from William here — right here! I cannot bear being so close, not knowing what lies in that tomb, if there is any sign of him or even…" she gulped, "his body."

The man looked at her and then William with a steady gaze.

"I see," Asem said, and his eyes searched hers for something. "And are you your father's daughter? Why should I let you in there when I warned your father against taking anything with him? Your father was keen on finding something here for his own purposes. He proved himself untrustworthy, and so may you." Asem's eyes were cold. Clementine's dark eyes matched his with anger.

"Asem, you forget yourself. There is no need–"

"You, sir, have no right of accusing me of such a thing," Clementine cut William off and took a step closer to Asem. She felt William grabbing her hand but she shook it off with annoyance.

"As of yet I have not taken anything from anyone. My need, first and foremost, is to see for myself if my father died in that tomb, or if he left any evidence that he was alive after the sandstorm. That is my main goal. And as for my father, we have yet to find him, so how do you know if he even took anything from the tomb — assuming he went there at all?" She had no idea what her father had done, but it would have to wait.

Asem narrowed his dark eyes and Clementine did not flinch from the piercing stare.

"She speaks the truth, Asem. She has proven herself to be trustworthy if somewhat reckless and naive," William said. "She could be of help inside the tomb, since her father's notebook was violently stolen from her. She fought to almost certain death had I not interfered. Whatever information was in that notebook about the traps inside that tomb, it's now in her head. Give her a chance with my word that she will prove her worth."

"That is touching, but you will excuse me if I do not trust you to be completely clear-headed in this matter." Asem turned back to Clementine. " I know you are looking for the Tears, but what you will do with them is the real question here. Why should I grant you access when I could simply extract the information about the inner chambers from you by force?"

Clementine crossed her arms, her fan hanging on a loop around her wrist. She was grasping at straws, but she was running out of ideas. "You will grant me this because honour demands it," she said, using the only thing she could think of.

Asem raised an eyebrow but did not argue, so she hurried to continue, "I very likely saved your life when Abayomi was about to shoot you. I stopped him, and as such, you owe me a boon, upon your honour. Are you a gentleman or not?"

Asem stared at her intensely. From the corner of her eye, she saw William hide a smile behind his hand. Men were strange, she thought. Then Asem let out a loud laugh, joined by his crew. Clementine thought they were all making fun of her. Her cheeks flushed and she flicked her fan open, baring its claws.

"Put away your fan," Asem waved a hand at her. "I cannot believe it, William, of all people you have chosen a wife who could be an incarnation of Sekhmet. A wild warrior goddess. She who mauls and—"

Clementine snarled. "Yes, I know who Sekhmet is, I'm not completely ignorant, having come all the way here. This is my dream, despite the circumstances!"

"You wouldn't guess how many explorers are ignorant to anything but the value of the items the find," William noted, and Asem nodded in agreement. "And she isn't really my wife," he said to Asem.

"Ha, I did not think so. Why would such a talented young woman want to bind herself to you?" Asem smirked. William did not return the smile but looked rather annoyed.

"I heard the two of you speak at that house in Alexandria," she glared at Asem, "So excuse my rudeness, but how exactly are you involved in all of this?" She did not know how to ask if Asem was also one of the queen's treasure hunters.

The two men exchanged glances.

"We have met occasionally, and worked together," William said. Asem said nothing but nodded slightly.

"Ah, so I guessed right," Clementine flicked back the spikes of her fan. "William, you and I need to have another talk about secrets, don't we?"

Asem's eyebrows raised again and he glared at William, who shrugged.

Clementine turned back to Asem. "So, will you let us pass as a boon for saving your life? One way or another I will get into that tomb, and you will be rid of me sooner if you grant us access."

To her surprise, Asem bowed slightly. "You hit a rare target, Lady Clementine. Not many of your peers would see honour in me, a bastard, but you have invoked it, and I cannot deny your request. However, there are conditions."

William laughed a small laugh and shook his head. "There always are with you, Asem. You never let things be easy and straightforward, do you?"

"I promise that my conditions are simple," Asem replied drily, "Unlike you, a silver-tongued thief, your lady here seems to appreciate bluntness. She has stated her intention and request; so shall I."

Clementine gestured impatiently for him to continue, "Come on then, we are losing daylight."

Asem nodded. "One: I will accompany you at all times inside the tomb. Two: you will take nothing out of the tomb, unless it is your father's body or evidence of him having been there. Do you accept these conditions?"

"I do," Clementine said without a thought. Asem had not said that *William* couldn't take anything from the tomb, so there was still that loophole to explore if they found the Tears of Hathor. Otherwise, she would need to have a very good explanation, or lie, for the queen. She did not want to think of that now.

This time, Asem put out his hand and Clementine reached out to shake it, but he raised her hand to his lips instead, barely touching her bloodied knuckles. "At your service, Lady Whitham."

THE TOMB OF THE HIGH PRIESTESS

*I*t was agreed that some of the crew would wait outside and guard the entrance in case any other looters or explorers got too curious about it. Clementine had found her hat, which she returned to the baggage on her dromedary. The creature had not flinched during the fight, it seemed, but looked as bored as ever. They stopped to eat some flatbread, dates and nuts, and filled their flasks from the bigger containers. Each of them took a torch and matches to carry, and they were ready to get into the tomb.

The worn outer wall still showed the outline of the goddess Hathor, the colours long-faded but traces of the engravings still visible somehow after all this time. The goddess' head was still visible, her one eye seeming to stare at Clementine.

The rubble-filled entrance was, in essence, a small room, with no doors or pathways to the next chamber. Only a crushed altar remained, along with some crumbling statues and pieces of clay amphorae.

"How do we move forward?" Clementine asked, admiring the remaining hieroglyphs on the walls. The prayers were about the goddess and her priestesses. Clementine felt her skin shiver at the thought of how much time had passed since this wall was engraved.

"Perhaps the last line of the riddle you found is the key?"

"What riddle?" Asem asked.

"Oh." Clementine dug out the piece of paper with the hints her papa had written.

"*From/the/First/towards/home/take/80/Water/in/sun,*" Asem read out loud. "Water in the sun is a vague hint, if it even is the way to open a pathway to the tomb's inner chambers."

"So perhaps we search for any water or sun symbols?" Clementine suggested.

"It's something," William nodded. "I'll start clearing the rubble in this corner and will keep an eye out for anything that might look like a pressure plate. Clementine, you see if any of the hieroglyphs on this wall containing sun or water symbols look different. Asem, you take the hieroglyphs on the opposite wall."

William crawled on his knees to the ruined altar and pushed some rubble around. They worked in silence, but nothing seemed to stand out.

"This might take us nowhere," Clementine murmured. "Do you have anything, Mr Smith"

Asem shook his head. "Nothing. There are plenty of sun symbols but none of them move or twist to reveal anything hidden."

"Neither do I," Clementine admitted.

"The rubble had neither sun nor water," William grunted as he lifted a brick. "The floor so far has not revealed anything out of the ordinary. No pressure plates, no odd cracks or different materials either."

Asem ran his hand along the wall. "The sun is a common enough symbol, but it has no connection to water that I can see. I wonder if the hint is about combining a sun symbol and a water symbol. But again, I cannot feel any that could be manipulated in such a way."

"Hmm," Clementine said, frowning. The day was getting hotter and she was feeling stiff after the fight, so she decided she might as well take a break. "I'll just take a moment to stretch my legs," she called over her shoulder as she headed back outside, but neither of the men paid her attention.

She went to her dromedary and gave it a tentative pat. She turned to look over the area while carefully stretching her arms and legs. Asem's crew had left a few men to guard the entrance, but most had returned to wherever their main camp was.

Clementine did not know what to make of Asem. Why was he here to guard the treasures? She tried to remember what she knew of him but could only recall that he was the bastard son of Sir Edmund Thomason, director of British Museum. Could that be why he was here guarding the dig sites, to make sure the items went to the museum?

She frowned, but there was little else she could deduct with so little information. Clearly William knew more, but for some reason couldn't tell her what it was. Her eyes wandered to the faded engraving of the goddess on the tomb's wall with its horns and sun disc symbol. Clementine cocked her head. *A sun symbol?* She walked towards it and peered up at the image on her tiptoes. The engraving was faded but deep enough for her to still have a spark of hope. With excitement sending shivers up her spine, she started dragging over some broken stones to make a pile to stand on.

"What are you doing?" William asked. He'd clearly heard her rummaging around and came over to her, wiping sweat from his brow.

"Oh, just having afternoon tea," Clementine scoffed, "I'm investigating, obviously!"

"A spot of tea would've been nice, I have to say," William grinned. "Did you find something?"

"I'm not sure. I'm too short to see it properly."

"Wouldn't it be easier if you simply let me take a look, with your guidance?"

Clementine scowled at this suggestion. "Fine. But remember that it was my idea if this hunch turns out to be correct!"

William chuckled and mock-bowed, "Now then, my love, what would you have me do?"

A dozen images flashed before Clementine's eyes regarding what she wanted him to do. And she need only ask... *Focus, Clementine!*

"Uhm, well, I only now realised that the engraving of Hathor on this wall has a sun disc, obviously. It was rather stupid of us not to take note of it earlier! The engraving looks deep enough that it might hold a secret to opening up a passageway, don't you think?"

William peered up, shading his eyes from the blasting sun. "It does look that way."

Asem came to observe as well. "Indeed, it looks different from the rest of the engraving on this wall. Well-spotted, my lady," he nodded to Clementine and she felt a surge of pride. Now she could only hope she was right.

"I'll look closer." William casually moved away the few pieces of rubble she had gathered to stand on. With his height, there was no need for a stool, ever. He turned to trace his fingers around the shape of the sun disc set atop of the goddess's head.

Clementine looked at his broad back, the muscles visible through his white shirt, which clung to him with sweat. She swallowed and turned her gaze to his hands. Her wandering eyes and thoughts really weren't helpful. But ever since they had almost shared a kiss on the ship, she seemed to think more and more of this man.

"Anything there, Will?" Asem asked.

"It doesn't move, and I cannot see a mechanism of any sort. There is a small hole at the bottom, though. It seems to be slanted, and not big enough to push a finger into. Perhaps a pen might go in, if there is something to push?"

With excitement, Clementine quickly checked her bag for a fountain pen and handed it to William.

"Try this," she said.

"How prepared you are, my dear," he smiled, and she felt herself smiling back at him.

"Just try it," Asem said.

William did, but nothing happened. Clementine took back the pen with disappointment. She had been so sure this was the solution.

"Wait, William, did you say the hole is slanted? Which way?" Asem said, his hazel eyes lighting up.

"Yes, from the little I can see, it seems to be slanted downwards, disappearing inside the stone. Why?"

"The clue in your paper, Lady Clementine," Asem said, reaching for his water flask and shaking it. "Water in sun?"

Clementine's grin felt like it spread from ear to ear. "Of course! Do you think your flask is enough?"

"We shall see," Asem said, and handed the flask to William.

The anticipation was almost too much for Clementine. William slowly poured the water into the small hole. "It seems to be going in," he remarked. They stood in silence, waiting for any signs. The flask soon emptied but nothing happened. Clementine let out a breath she'd been holding, together with her hopes. *What now? If–*

Suddenly, there was a rumble somewhere, deep beneath them, and the slow screeching noise of dragging stone within the tomb.

"Now that sounds promising!" William grinned and hurried back inside, with Clementine and Asem close behind. Behind the half-collapsed altar, one of the large floor tiles moved. The water had triggered some ancient mechanism, revealing a steep staircase heading down into the tomb.

"We did it!" Clementine gasped, "You figured it out, Asem!" She almost hugged the man with joy.

"We were lucky," Asem said, "And fortunate to have you notice the engravings." He gave her a hint of a smile.

"See, I told you she could be useful," William noted.

"Hmm, perhaps," Asem said.

Every ten steps or so, mirrors framed the walls and reflected the light from above. Asem called one of his crew and shortly explained to him the importance of the engraving in case the doorway closed. It was agreed that only the three of them would enter the tomb. Collapses and weak structures were not uncommon, and the fewer people there were, the simpler it was to deal with possible traps.

"What a beautiful way of lighting the way," Clementine admired, touching her fingertips to the worn surface of one of the mirrors. "I think my father's notebook highlighted the importance of the lighting mechanism, by turning these mirrors," she called to William and Asem, who followed her in.

"Tell me again how it is that you lost this notebook with such valuable information?" Asem asked, glaring at William, who shrugged.

"No, it wasn't William," Clementine glanced back at him. "We — that is, I — lost it on the SS Karnak."

"How did that happen?" Asem asked, directing the question with some accusation to William.

"I gave the notebook to her, Asem," he sighed, "It was her right as his daughter."

"Yes, but you did not part with it until you had been discovered hiding it from me. He lied and then he was sorry that he had lied," Clementine noted.

A dry laugh escaped Asem. "What did I say about this one having a silver tongue?" He gestured at William.

Clementine nodded. "He gave it to me, and unfortunately I lost it in a fight on our way here."

"You mentioned that before. What exactly happened on your journey here?" Asem sounded concerned.

Clementine and William told him about the attack on the train, and later, on the steamer ship. Clementine stopped to turn one of the misaligned mirrors to a right angle and they once again had light ahead of them as they continued to descend the stairs.

"That is not good, William," Asem murmured. "It might be other treasure hunters?"

"Possibly. Both instances mentioned Hathor's tomb or Clementine's father and his notebook. Even for me, two attacks on the same journey is more than usual," William said as he kicked aside a loose stone from the last of the stairs. And finally, they saw the way forward in the dim light of the mirrors.

A wide, open doorframe stood before them. Clementine read: *first chamber*. Her skin prickled from excitement and fear of what they might discover. Her nerves must have been on edge, because she could feel a strange sensation — as if something was very faintly tugging her forward. *Ignore it. There's no time for imaginary sensations!*

"Do we know what the High Priestess' name was?" she asked.

"Nefertehepes," Asem said, and showed Clementine the hieroglyphs where her name was engraved still, after all these years, above the door. "She is said to be the first priestess of Hathor, hence the title of High Priestess."

"Nefertehepes," Clementine whispered, letting the name roll out of her mouth softly, as if a wind was blowing life to these corridors. "We greet you," she said quietly.

"I'm not sure she hears you," William said.

"I'm trying to show some respect! This is her last resting place we are entering," Clementine defended herself, and William raised his hands in a motion for peace.

***

THEY MOVED FORWARD to the first chamber, which seemed to be a square room. Some old bones lay scattered here and there, which made Clementine alert. She did not want to step on ancient human remains. Then she remembered another reason to be alert.

"Wait," Clementine said, "I think the notebook had a mention of traps in here. Pressure plates and spikes. The bones tell us that someone died here long ago."

They peered cautiously ahead of them, looking at the floor and walls for signs of danger. The walls had several mirrors angled for light, but one mirror lay on the ground in a heap of sand, which was somewhat odd. Asem picked it up and blew off some dust.

"Do the mirrors have something to do with the solution of getting through this room?" Asem asked.

"I think so," Clementine said, "Perhaps they will help us find a way forward that is safe." The tiles in front of them had ominous holes in them, likely for the spikes. But it seemed every tile had holes, so they could not pick safe-looking ones to step on.

"Here, let me try," William said, and carefully took the mirror from Asem. It had a worn surface, but it still reflected the light from the previous mirror. William caught the light at the right angle and carefully turned to point to the first mirror opposite of them. He tried to reflect the light to as many mirrors as he could, but none gave any hint as to what they should be looking for.

"Oh, there is one more mirror right next to us," Clementine said, noticing it had been half hidden behind her, "Try that one."

William tried to twist himself around without stepping onto the tiles, but he could not bend the light to reach the mirror next to them; the angle was too steep.

"Can't do it, the physics are against us," William said, "But perhaps if we go forward, the angle might just be right."

"Wait, how do you know which tiles are safe?" Clementine cried and grabbed his sleeve as if to pull him back to her.

"Relax, Clemmie," he grinned, "I'm not skewered yet. See the faint footmarks on the tiles?" He reflected the light on the ground.

"Ah, yes," Asem nodded, "Some tiles have slightly less dust on them, or the dust has been shifted relatively recently."

"If we are lucky, we won't need to solve the puzzle. We can just follow the footsteps of, well, your father, most likely," he said to Clementine.

"I'd rather not place my life on 'if we get lucky'," Clementine said.

"There is no blood on the tiles with the footprints. No one has been injured here recently. Not talking about those poor bastards..." He illuminated the skulls with the light. One of them had holes through it and Clementine shivered.

"I will go first and the two of you will follow exactly where I step. Got it?"

Clementine lifted her split skirt to reveal her riding boots and silk stockings. She did not want to risk the hem tripping her into a horrible death.

"Don't distract me with those lovely legs of yours. Though I wouldn't mind if they were the last thing I saw," William joked, looking at her with appreciation glinting in his green eyes.

"Oh, just shut up and go already, before I push you," Clementine blurted, and Asem laughed. "I apologise if my outfit offends, but it is necessary for practicality and comfort," she added to Asem. She did not want to cause any ill will between them.

"Of course, Lady Clementine. The few women in my crew ride in loose pants and do not use a side saddle. I do not care for the show of your legs, even if they are indeed finely shaped."

"Oh," she blushed slightly. She was not used to men commenting on her legs. Why would she, when most of her youth she had been trained to keep them hidden for the sake of modesty?

"Now then," William said, shooting Asem with a pointed look, "If you two are quite finished, we need to hurry before the sun sets and we lose the mirrors. Trust me, you do not want to sleep in an old tomb filled with traps and ghosts," he said with some amusement, and stepped onto the tile that was two steps forward.

Clementine held her breath and then sighed in relief when nothing happened. William was not reduced to a pool of skewered meat and blood. He turned carefully on the spot and caught the light on his mirror, turning it towards the mirror he could not reach before. The light split to land on various tiles across the room. The mirror's surface had likely been either smudged or otherwise altered to allow multiple rays of light to reflect upon selected tiles — presumably the safe ones.

"There, you see? The light touches the same tiles where there are footprints," William said, and stepped to the next one with confidence. Nothing happened. Clementine looked at Asem who gestured to her to go first. She took a deep breath and followed William through the chamber, Asem trailing behind her, and they soon made to the other side without harm.

"If the chambers are this easy, we should have no problem reaching the burial chamber before the light fades." Asem said. "The stairs continue down."

William turned and tossed the mirror smoothly to the heap of sand where it landed, unbroken.

"Why did you do that?" Clementine said.

"Well, isn't it obvious?" William said, dusting off his hands. "There was a pile of sand where the mirror lay for some reason. The next person who enters needs to have the use of the mirror, so it must be returned to the entry point. And this one," he turned to a stone column with a mirror that caught the light from the previous staircase, "has the light we need to go forward." He turned it slightly and the next staircase was illuminated by several mirrors, angled with precision.

"Let us move forward and keep our wits about us," Asem said.

"Not much to loot, it seems," William noted as they descended. "Then again, usually the main treasures would be in the main burial chamber."

"You would know," grunted Asem.

Clementine made a note to herself to get to the bottom of the history between these men.

"I think I see the next door," she said. The closer they got, the more horribly the place started to smell. Clementine covered her nose with one of the handkerchiefs her aunt had given her, not that it helped much. Something was rotting and Clementine feared the worst.

"Prepare yourselves," William said quietly.

Soon enough, they arrived at the next chamber, which was bigger than the last one. Clementine fought back her nausea. The smell was strong, and they discovered the reason for it. It was a body — the decaying body of a man. He was a much smaller man than Clementine's father, which was the only reason why she took a hard look at the horror in front of her. Killing those thugs earlier had not been something to take lightly, but it was kill or be killed. But this... A rotting body in a tomb seemed wrong in some way, along with the knowledge that it could easily have been her father. She tried her hardest not to be sick.

"That isn't him," Asem said, carefully breathing through his mouth.

Clementine shook her head and tried to look elsewhere, at anything.

"No," William confirmed, "It is not Lord Whitham. The

clothes are wrong, and the size of him as well. Though based on his clothing I think he might have been one of your father's men."

Clementine shook her head. "I wouldn't know. Let us please move on quickly. Let me think..." She tried to remember the details from her father's notebook but her mind kept replacing them with the image of the rotting body and she couldn't remember any notes about this room. She turned a mirror near the door and searched for the next one.

"Wait," William called, "Look beyond the body, on the ground."

Clementine turned the creaking mirror and they soon saw that the floor had collapsed. The drop was deep and there was a heap of rubble at the bottom. *How far below did this tomb reach?*

"What now?" Clementine said, "We can't jump that far."

"We use the narrow ledge on the side," William pointed. On the left side of the collapsed chamber there was a strip of flooring which had not been destroyed. It looked dangerously narrow and parts of it had crumbled.

"That?" she said with disbelief. "It doesn't look like it can hold us."

William helped her aim the mirror at the next one across the chamber and moved to the ledge. "There are faint footsteps here, which means it has been used before."

"True enough," Asem said, "We go." He gestured to Clementine to go in front of him.

"You two are so sure of this, and yet you call *me* irresponsible," she muttered.

William leaned his back against the wall and began to slowly edge his way across. "Keep an eye on the ledge. There are holes, but not too big ones."

Clementine sighed and positioned herself with her feet wide on the narrow ledge. It was not unlike a ballet stance, she thought to herself, but did not try a plié. She tried not to look down, keeping her eyes on the ledge to her left as she crept behind William.

"Keep close to William, within grabbing distance," Asem said from her other side. He was also staying close to her in case she stumbled.

The ledge felt like it continued on forever because they had to move so slowly and with such care. It started to feel almost easy when William shouted in surprise. A piece of the ledge had crumbled beneath his left foot, causing him to lose his balance. Clementine reacted with instinct, slamming her left hand against his chest, and felt Asem holding her in place by her shoulder.

"Oof." William steadied himself against the wall, out of breath. "That was close. It was sturdy enough before... it wasn't." He took a deep breath. "You know, you didn't have to hit my chest quite so hard," he said to Clementine, and put his hand on hers. Despite the ridiculous position they were in, Clementine felt her stomach flutter at his touch.

"Right," she cleared her throat, "Next time I'll let you fall then." She took back her hand.

"You can let go," she said to Asem, who still held her steady by the shoulder.

"Of course," he said.

They continued on, and William helped Clementine to cross the parts where the ledge had crumbled. In turn, she offered her hand to Asem, which he refused. She shrugged and kept going.

Finally, they reached the other side, where William adjusted the mirror to the next corridor. The walls were filled with well-preserved hieroglyphs. The turquoise colour of the paint was still visible, though it wasn't as vibrant as it had once been. It did not cease to amaze Clementine how things could be preserved for thousands of years.

"Looks like we are approaching the third chamber. It says here something about a leap of faith. My father's notes did not describe the third chamber, nor the final one . It ends with the leap, whatever that means." She read further. "After the third chamber we will be admitted to the High Priestess' burial chamber — if we are deemed worthy."

"We shall see," Asem said, "Many are not worthy."

"You are a man of few words and even those few words are discouraging," she said drily as they continued to descend the corridor.

"Not much else to say," Asem said. "For my part at least," he added after a pause.

Clementine wondered what he meant.

"I see the door," William called.

They passed through it to the next room. Asem turned the mirror toward the next one, which in turn dramatically lit a hole in the ground that took up most of the room's floor. They carefully approached the edge. This one had not collapsed; it was a neatly constructed round hole with a metallic trim that had rusted over time, but was still intact. The engravings circling it had lasted the test of time and the hole itself was large enough to fit a grand dining table. Darkness loomed through it like an abyss.

"I'm guessing this is the leap of faith," Clementine shivered.

Asem took a pebble from the ground and dropped it into the hole. After a few long seconds, a splash could be heard. It sent an eerie echo around the room below.

"Water," he said, "to soften the landing."

"Right. No other way than to jump," he said , after peering around the chamber. It was a dead end, apart from the hole.

"Take a leap of faith, trust the goddess," Clementine read slowly as she crawled around the hole to look at the faded markings. "Those who are worthy shall shine their inner light to the source of the goddess's tears and enter the most sacred. Join hands in prayer and take a deep breath to inhale the holy air."

She noticed something glinting on the ground.

"Look," she exclaimed, "It's a bullet shell. A silver one." She looked at William. "Same as the treasure hunters use?"

William took the bullet in his hand and nodded. "Same as we use," he said grimly and put the bullet in his pocket.

"Why would someone want to hurt my father?" Clementine said.

"Perhaps your father made enemies," William said curtly.

Asem said nothing, which was not unusual.

"Well, no use wallowing here," Clementine finally said, sensing this wasn't the best place or time for longer conversations. She settled for trying to push away the thought of someone shooting at her papa. "We need to go in."

"She is right, we have to go through before the sun sets and the mirrors offer no more light," Asem said, and offered his hands to both Clementine and William. They clasped hands and peered into the deep drop.

"Ready?" William asked Clementine.

"Are you?" she shot back with a raised eyebrow. "On the count of three," she said, feeling her heartbeat quicken.

"One." She squeezed William and Asem's hands.

"Two." Deep breaths. Clementine felt William squeeze her hand back.

"Three!" They took a step forward and dropped down into the darkness. Clementine couldn't help yelping as they fell for what felt like a lifetime. In reality, they were in the cold water soon enough. Kicking up, Clementine could only thank herself for not wearing a dress. They emerged at the surface, spluttering.

* * *

CLEMENTINE WIPED her face and kept herself floating with slow kicks. It was a vast chamber, consisting mostly of the pool of deep water they were in. The chamber was still big enough to host a royal ball, and judging by the height of the enormous statue of the goddess Hathor, the chamber was easily the height of a grand house. The statue's stone legs were as wide as the biggest trunks of ancient trees. Clementine looked around but couldn't see any other dry floor than the pedestal the statue was on. They would be stuck in the water until they could figure out a way forward.

"Someone really built a pool here," her voice sounded a little out of breath. "A bit cold, though."

"I think it is the water from the Nile. Has to be," Asem said, wiping his dark hair away from his eyes.

"Agreed," William said. "There has to be an underground source they used to build this. I can't understand why. Fancy statue though," he pointed in front of them. At least fifteen feet high, the figure of the goddess Hathor loomed, as if judging their worthiness.

"I wonder what we are supposed to do next," William said. They looked around and saw nothing in the darkness except the small ray of light from the mirror above them, which pointed at the statue's feet.

"There doesn't seem to be another mirror," Asem noted. "Wait, can you feel that?" he said, a sharpness in his otherwise calm voice.

"What?" Clementine began, but she suddenly realised what he meant and felt a pang of fear. The water was rising. The statue's feet were now beneath the surface .

"It's rising, and fast!" William's voice rang around the chamber. "Look up!"

The hole above them was slowly narrowing as they floated upwards with the rising water.

"Oh God, it's closing isn't it!" Clementine tried not to panic, but it was difficult as she could feel the mass of water pushing them higher. The statue's thighs were already covered. Clementine forced herself to slow her quickened breath. *Slow kicks, slow breaths.*

"Certainly looks that way. Better find a solution to this chamber, quickly!" William said.

"Do we have anything to jam the hole to stop it closing?" Asem asked.

"The lanterns and water flasks would likely break if jammed in there," William said, "And with the pace it's going, it looks like it will close before any of us can reach it. Once it closes, we will lose the light and–" he did not finish the sentence.

"We'll drown," Clementine said with a shaky voice. "Think," she said, more to herself than to her companions. "We need to reflect the mirror light somewhere, that has to be the point of this chamber. We took the leap of faith. What else…?" She closed her eyes, trying to visualise the hieroglyphs she had just read. Suddenly, she remembered. "The Tears — we need to find the source of tears! *Inner light... Shine a light...* I think we need to reflect the mirror's light on the goddess." She pointed to the huge statue.

"Sure, that seems logical, but with what? Did you bring a compact mirror with you?" William asked.

"I wish I had," Clementine said. "Asem, do you have anything reflective?" Her teeth clattered from the coldness of the water and the looming fear of drowning.

Asem rummaged through his pockets with effort. "A pocket watch is the only thing I have, but I doubt it is bright enough to reflect."

"Try it!" Clementine urged, "Point it at the source of tears, the goddess's eyes!"

Asem took out his pocket watch and caught the light of the mirror from above, but as he suspected, it was not bright enough to reflect far enough. The goddess's painted eyes looked down on them, unimpressed.

Clementine felt the hope in her slither away with each

exhale. *This can't be happening. I cannot die in my first mission. I only just had the chance to start my life.*

"It's no use, I cannot reflect the light!"

"Hurry, there must be something else that reflects," William said between clenched teeth. He pulled out his pocketknife, but it was too dim to reflect the light enough. Same result from his pistol. "Damn it all! I'll dive and see if the bottom of this thing has anything we could use! Asem, come with me!"

They resurfaced after a while.

"Nothing," Asem panted.

"Too dark to see and be sure," William spat water. "We should try again. Keep trying until the very end!"

They were now level with the statue's navel. The water kept rising fast and the hole above them was becoming narrower by the minute. Clementine desperately went through her pockets. It was hard while treading water and shaking from the coldness. Her fingers felt numb, water was in her nose and mouth, and she spluttered as she turned her pockets inside out. She found nothing of use in there. But then she remembered her iron fan. Its sides were of polished iron, brighter and larger than the pocket watch or knife!

"Wait," Clementine said, and carefully took her fan out from her sleeve, where it had been tucked away. "This might be bright enough."

She raised her hand to catch the light, and sure enough, a ray reflected onto the goddess. She let out an excited, hopeful sound, but struggled to move the ray of light in the sloshing water.

"William, help me stay still!"

He swam to her side and lay his warm hands on her waist, steadying her. "Try it, Clementine!" She leaned against his chest and angled the fan to shine a light into the eyes of the goddess, but nothing happened.

"It's not working!" Asem said, "The riddle must mean something else. *Source of the Tears...* what else could it be than the eyes?"

Clementine looked up and saw that the hole had almost closed. If they did not solve this soon, they would die once the water rose up to the ceiling. Her throat felt tight at the thought of gasping for last mouthfuls of air before one final exhale. She felt her eyes prickle and her own hot tears mixing with the cold water. It wasn't fair to die here, before she had truly had a chance to live her life! Before she had even told William that she– She felt exhausted and looked up to William for just a second. His eyes were shadowed with worry, but she could see a softness in his expression when he met her tearful gaze.

"Not time to give up yet, Clemmie." His thumb brushed away her tears with the gentlest touch and lingered for a fleeting moment on her trembling bottom lip. "Try again."

Clementine turned and saw that the water was creeping up to the statue's chest level. *The chest. Could it be?* Clementine raised her fan again to catch the light. "Hold me tighter, William!"

"I thought you'd never ask," he said with a ghost of a smile as he gently pulled her tighter against him. Instinctively, she wrapped her legs around his waist to steady herself against the moving water. This was a ridiculous time to blush, and yet she still felt herself flushing, especially when his hands came to rest on top of her buttocks.

"I might just die a happy man," William murmured in her ear, and despite everything a giggle escaped her lips. She must be going mad, which wasn't completely unlikely in the context of their current situation. William flashed a devilish grin at her, and she could have sworn his hands gave a gentle squeeze.

"Got an idea?" Asem asked with a no little impatience in his voice. "Now would be a good time to see if it works!"

Clementine nodded, raised her iron fan, and guided the light to reflect at the heart of the goddess. Immediately, something reflected the light back into the water below them. Relief washed over her. They still had a chance! She let out half a stifled cry.

"Yes, Clemmie! Asem, quick, there's something in the water where the light is pointing. Dive down there!"

Asem did not wait another second to do just that. After a few moments he emerged from the water again. "It's a stone plate with a handle! But I need another pair of hands to pull it. William, let's go!"

Clementine looked at William with fear in her eyes. Fear of being left alone. Of waiting to see if they could stop water from rising, or waiting for the water to kill them. He met her fearful gaze with surprising calmness. Her heart ached as she thought of them dying here without ever finding out if there could have been more between them than a pretend marriage and endless vexing of one another. He still held her in that intimate way, and she refused to let go first.

"Kiss me," she blurted. It made no sense, and it certainly was not the right timing, but if they were to die, she would rather do so having experienced a kiss from a man she had fallen in love with. "For good luck," she added breathlessly.

William's green eyes lit with that mischievous fire. She felt his warmth and his gentle hand tilting her face to meet his lips. The kiss was soft but strong, like the current around them. Clementine melted against him, cupping both her hands to his cheeks and kissing him back fiercely, all her instincts on fire. She tasted his desire as their kiss deepened, and responded with her own, letting out a small whimper, wishing the kiss would never end, desperate at the prospect of not being able to experience this ever again. She felt everything, all at once and it was almost too much: his warmth, his lips smiling against hers, his hand tangled in her wet hair, his other hand squeezing her behind, and she couldn't help a moan escaping her. Nothing had felt as right as she felt right now in his arms, at the threshold of death.

"Could you please find another time for marital bliss?" Asem's voice broke the spell of their kiss and they parted, out of breath. "William, will you come and help?" Asem said drily. "Preferably before we drown, if you can find the time in your busy schedule?"

William grinned at Clementine and kissed her quickly once more before letting her go. She felt an immense emptiness where his body had been pressed tightly against hers. "There will be more, I promise," he said, and disappeared into the water with Asem.

Clementine held back tears and struggled to hold her hand steady to keep the light reflecting for a few more moments. She looked up. The light would soon be cut off. A handful of seconds and they would be left in darkness. She braced herself to accept either bliss or the abyss. *At least you kissed him.* Clementine closed her eyes as darkness filled the room and the hole above her closed with a thud. In a moment, she would feel the roof against her raised hand, and she waited with the sound of rushing water and her heartbeat loud in her ears.

Then she heard a low thump below her in the water and a click of the mechanism above. The hole in the roof was widening! Clementine had never been so happy to see the light pouring in once more, and she let out a relieved laugh, mixed with a sob. She could feel the water levels lowering steadily, and soon William and Asem emerged from the water, spluttering and coughing.

"Damned tight, that plate was," William panted, and Clementine reached out to hug him from sheer relief.

"Are the two of you alright? I feared the worst," she said.

"You? Afraid? I will not believe it," William said gently, wiping her wet hair from her face. He kissed her cold fingers, which still clasped the fan.

"We are fine," Asem said, "Some blisters on our hands from pulling, but otherwise no harm."

"I am glad, "Clementine said, her eyes still on William. His green eyes looked at her with that mischievous glint and a touch of gentleness. Her heart ached.

"How did you know where to point the light?" Asem asked.

She broke William's gaze with some difficulty. "Oh, the water was almost up to the statue's chest level and that's when I had a thought: the source of tears aren't the eyes — not really. They come from the heart."

"Clever girl." William kissed her forehead. "You saved our lives, you know."

"We did it together," she said, blushing at his words.

"Without you, we would have drowned," Asem nodded. "You did well, Clementine. My thanks to you, again," he said, keeping his gaze firmly on her eyes, as if he was avoiding looking anywhere else.

Clementine instinctively glanced down to discover her wet chemise was clinging to the curves of her chest. She felt heat creep up her cheeks but shrugged it off. What could she do about it? At least she still had her corset on to cover her breasts, thank goodness.

The water lowered, and soon they were standing on their feet, catching their breath. Clementine shivered as her wet clothes clung to her in the underground coolness. The pool of water had drained to reveal a staircase and a door, and the ray of light from above was pointing right at it. There was an eerie silence. No more sloshing of water or echoes from their words. A sigh of relief came from the whirring of the mechanisms behind the ancient walls as they finally stopped and continued their slumber.

THE TEARS OF HATHOR

"Let us see what kind of a lock this door has," William said, leading the way down to the small staircase. He held Clementine's hand as if they had always done so. She felt almost dizzy just thinking of the kiss they had shared, and as much as she wanted to talk to William about it, now just wasn't the right time. Poor Asem had already been subjected to their intimate moment. Clementine reasoned that on the brink of almost certain death, the usual social rules about modesty could be broken.

The heavy-looking stone door had no handle that they could see, only a symbol of Hathor the Goddess. The sun sigil was lit by the light from the opening above. William touched the symbol and a mechanism allowed it to be slightly pushed inwards. The door started to move aside, but they were soon disappointed by another door that lay just behind the first. This one was dry, made of equally sturdy stone, and had on it rows and rows of hieroglyphs. Some of them were very faded and some were still visible, with coloured details.

"There must be a riddle of some kind," Clementine said.

"Welcome, worthy stranger, to the last resting place of the High Priestess of Hathor. Worship the goddess. All of her," Asem read the larger hieroglyphs above the many rows of smaller ones.

"It seems they are to be pushed, just like the symbol on the first door. See here, they are not only carved into the stone but there are small edges around them, meaning they can be moved, I think." William ran his finger lightly across the hieroglyphs, and his still-wet hands left dark stains on the surface.

"I think you're right," Asem nodded, "We will need to find the right ones to push. Who knows what trap we might find from a wrong choice."

As he said the words, they heard something that made all of them look up. Distant sounds like steps. And muffled voices, perhaps?

"We're not alone," William said grimly. "Asem, any chance they might be your crew?"

"Unlikely. They knew to keep guard outside and wait for us to emerge by sunset. If someone has gotten past them, I fear we will soon be facing more danger."

"Clementine? Any ideas?" William asked.

"Me? As if I'm some sort of expert about ancient riddles and traps?" she scoffed, but already her mind was fixed on the hieroglyphs. She looked over them, read some of them, but failed to see anything coherent forming. She did feel that pulling sensation again, stronger now, but it did nothing to help with the lock, so she pushed the feeling away.

"There is no sentence that I can recognise," she said, "They are just symbols that are not supposed to make sense."

"Should we find if there are some that are similar and push those, perhaps?" William suggested.

"We need to be sure before we start pushing anything, or it could end badly. You know this, William," Asem said, and earned a smirk from William.

"Ah, you're thinking of that time in India."

"My eyebrows were burnt off because you turned the wheel of the mechanism before thinking it through!"

"Your eyebrows grew back. And besides, I got it right on our third try," William countered.

"Wait," Clementine interrupted them. Her eyes had stopped on the symbol of a cow, and something tickled her memory. "In my father's notebook there were doodles that I did not pay much attention to. But later, on the page with the invisible ink, there was another drawing."

She closed her eyes as she tried to remember it all. It was just before she had been attacked on the deck of the ship. *Come on.* Her mind slowly filled the gaps of the doodle and her memory of the goddess.

"The Seven Hathors! The goddess is often depicted in the form of a cow or a set of seven cows, as it was mentioned in one of the spells of the Book of Death! And it makes perfect sense!" She opened her eyes and gestured at the wall. William and Asem raised their eyebrows.

"My father doodled cows in his notebook, and there was a random number written in invisible ink which appeared on the secret page, so it had to be important. It was the number seven. I don't know if he made it this far, since the notes ended before the flooding chamber, but he must have noticed certain symbols being repeated all over the tomb and made a note."

"And the clever fox he was, he left one doodle invisible, just in case it turned out to be critically important," William smiled. "Sounds like Lord Whitham. Never one to give up all of his knowledge."

The sounds were getting louder. Definitely steps and muffled voices.

"Go ahead, Clementine," Asem said, glancing up. For now, they were still alone.

Clementine nodded and quickly counted the symbols with

cows. Her hands still dripping with water, she pressed the first one. They held their breath, but nothing happened — nothing bad, that is. The symbol stayed pushed.

"That has to be a good sign," Clementine muttered and pushed the six other symbols that included cows. All of them stayed pushed, and as she pressed the last one, they could hear a familiar mechanism whirring as the door began to slide open.

"Well done!" William exclaimed and they stepped inside. "Now then, why don't we finish our mission?" he said with a strained voice.

Clementine glanced at him but could not read his expression. Whatever it was, they would have to talk about it later. As well as that kiss. And their future, and– *Later!*

The light from the mirror above hit a mirror on the floor of the tomb and reflected the light to a mirror in the ceiling, which in turn reflected the light to four other mirrors. A dim light illuminated the ancient room. The long, rectangular chamber stood still in the silence, and Clementine's sensation of pulling came stronger than before. Something was calling to her in this room.

A massive sarcophagus dominated the chamber. The final resting place of the priestess was guarded by a statue of the goddess Hathor, which had been engraved into the wall behind the sarcophagus. Smaller, life-sized statues decorated the other walls, and Clementine could only guess they were other priestesses, here to oversee their mistress. Richly painted scenes showed moments from the priestess' life, accompanied by rows and rows of hieroglyphs. The room must have been gloriously colourful back then, as the colors were still in many parts very vivid.

Before Clementine could fully take in the sight in front of her, she screamed, "Footprints!"

William and Asem crouched to look closer.

"Relatively fresh ones, if you think about the timeline,"

William muttered. "From a modern shoe." His eyes glanced to Asem, who nodded.

"Dripping with blood," Asem said, almost too quietly for Clementine to hear. Rust-coloured drops of dried blood followed the footsteps in alarmingly close proximity.

She frantically searched around the large sarcophagus, not pausing to admire anything, only looking to see if she might find the body of her father, but the footprints disappeared next to one of the walls. "Papa isn't here," she said in a hollow voice. A larger stain of blood remained, but the rest of the sand and dust seemed too disturbed to reveal anything else.

"He isn't?" William said, and he and Asem came to stand beside her with matching frowns.

"That's good news, surely?" Clementine hurried to say, "Though I'm worried about the pool of blood here. If this was Papa, why was he bleeding so much? Perhaps his leg was caught in one of the previous traps."

"Perhaps," Asem said slowly, looking further into the chamber. The sarcophagus filled most of the space, and beside it were rows of canopic jars and boxes of valuables — for the dead to enjoy in the afterlife. There was also a beautiful bed, but the wooden frame had collapsed and shattered among the statues of servants.

"The footprints continue beyond this wall," Asem noted from a low crouch, and carefully cleared most of the bed frame from the ground beside the wall. "It must have been an exit for the builders while they built the chamber. There should be a switch somewhere to open it."

"Papa must have gone that way!" Clementine cried, and immediately looked around for the switch. She could not see, hear or think properly. Only her papa mattered, and the fact that he might still be alive.

"The prints are quite messy, but it does seem he made it out, if it was him." William lay a hand on her shoulder. "But there is a lot of blood, Clementine. I don't want you to get your hopes up too much."

Clementine turned to him, batting his hand away. "Too much? This is the first time I have had any hope since that damned letter of yours arrived, telling us that Papa had gone missing. Allow me to feel just the slightest bit of hope, even for a moment!"

"Found it," Asem interrupted her raised voice. He reached into a small nook behind the servant statues and pushed one of the stones.

"A smear of blood revealed it," he explained.

The door slowly slid open to reveal an opening in the wall. Clementine peeked through it. Daylight poured through from another set of mirrors. Blinking in the light, she looked around. *No body*, she sighed in relief. The footprints were more faded here, as there was more sand and a rush of wind from outside. That could only mean this steep corridor would lead them up to ground level, which must have been the way Papa had left. Bits of limestone rubble littered the way, but it wasn't too difficult to get through, unless you were injured and bleeding... She was halfway through the door when William took hold of her hand.

"What?" she said impatiently.

"The Tears of Hathor," William reminded her gently. There was firmness in his voice. "We have to look for them and complete the assignment before we leave. We're too close to abandon them now."

Clementine was astonished. "You go ahead, then. You stay here and rummage through the dead. I am more concerned about the living now that I have a slim hope my father might be counted among them!"

"Clemmie," William did not let go of her, "I know it's important for you to find your father. But we are this close to finding the Tears of Hathor, or at least knowing if they are real. We will need to bring Her Majesty evidence either way if we are to be paid."

"Right now, I don't care about the money," Clementine hissed and tried to yank her hand free, but his grip was firm. "Asem, tell him to let me go before I do something I might regret." She slid her iron fan out of her sleeve. Their kiss was now a distant memory, and she wouldn't hesitate to fight him if it came to that.

Asem glanced at William with a raised eyebrow and William sighed, his grip softening a little on Clementine's arm. "We could use your help. Not just for the payment but also to make sure the treasure won't fall into the wrong hands if we leave without searching for it. We have to protect the Tears."

"I don't even know what you're saying, Asem, since you're the one who told us not to take anything from here, but I'm going."

Clementine shook her arm free and turned to leave when a bright voice laughed from the entrance. Clementine heard a click: the sound of a gun's safety being unlocked.

"I do hope you'll stay, Clementine, for your own sake."

Clementine turned in surprise at the familiar voice and saw both JoJo and Bob at the entrance, JoJo's revolver pointed at them. The honeymoon was over, it seemed.

"Hands up, where I can see them," JoJo said.

They raised their hands.

"So, not friends after all," Clementine said. Next to her, William cursed under his breath.

"Oh, we were friends, dear Clementine. But business wins over friendship. Hand over the Tears of Hathor."

"You came too early then. We have not found them yet," Clementine said. Her eyes shifted to the huge sarcophagus with its heavy lid. "Mind helping us move the lid?" She was buying time, trying to think of a way to disarm JoJo from this far away. Squeezing her fan, she wondered if she could throw it at the gun, but the distance might be too much for a precise hit. If only they would come closer, then she might have a chance to get the upper hand.

"How about you do the heavy labour while we oversee it?" JoJo's hand did not waver.

"And if we refuse?" William asked.

"Then you'll have fewer hands to help. Like this," JoJo said with a cold smile. She turned the gun to point at Asem and pulled the trigger.

"No!" Clementine could do nothing but extend her hand in a reflex, as if it could stop the bullet. But then there was a high-pitched clink as the bullet bounced off the side of Clementine's fan. "Are you alright?!" Clementine looked at Asem with fear. She turned to see if he was bleeding, but his chest seemed unwounded when she patted her hands against it. Disbelief filled her. Surely her reflexes couldn't match a bullet, but perhaps today she was blessed with some luck! Clementine prayed it would last.

"It seems you saved me yet again, Lady Clementine," Asem said, without a trace of a shock. He too patted his chest and took out his dagger, which he concealed while Clementine still stood in front of him, blocking the view.

"That was quite astonishing, wasn't it, JoJo?" Bob said, "Well done, Clementine. Though it matters little."

"What's wrong with you?" Clementine turned to JoJo, "Are you treasure hunters for the crown? Is it serving Her Majesty to kill people on a whim?"

JoJo inclined her head. "It was too easy to eavesdrop on your discussion with the queen at the palace. They should look into the security of the servant's passages, honestly. Funny how far a simple maid's outfit will get you, since no-one really looks at a maid. I had to hurry to the restaurant where we knew William liked to enjoy a spot of lunch. You would think the noise of a restaurant hides discussions but that's not strictly true. You didn't even notice me walk past your table several times!"

Clementine realised she had bumped into JoJo when she left the queen. And she had not even noticed. And at the restaurant JoJo hadn't been crying, but wiping sweat from hurrying to spy on them!

"We serve the crown with the assumption that we'll get the job done, no matter what. Sometimes that takes getting rid of fellow treasure hunters, as I'm sure William here knows well. And other times there are casualties. Witnesses, for example. I do not enjoy killing, but my motto is not to leave anything to chance," JoJo shrugged.

"Besides," Bob chimed in, "He is just a local." He nodded at Asem. "Do you know how many locals the Brits have killed? He is one in a pool of thousands and thousands, so who cares if there is one more, eh?"

"Enough, Bob. No-one needs to hear your rude opinions," JoJo snapped. She turned back to Clementine. "I really hoped it wouldn't have to come to this. If only you had given me the information of the tomb on the train. We could have avoided this and remained friends."

Clementine felt helpless and angry. She glanced at William and saw in his hand one of the small amphorae from the pile next to the sarcophagus.

"Here," he called, and quickly tossed the delicate amphora to JoJo, "The Tears of Hathor."

His gamble paid off and JoJo reflexively lowered the gun to catch the amphora. Asem waited not one second before he threw his dagger. She screamed, dropping the gun to cradle her arm where the blade had sunk in.

Clementine had already started to move forward when she stopped in shock. She watched Bob's widened eyes go from surprised to glassy as a sword emerged from his chest.

"Bob?" JoJo shrieked, still holding her wounded arm. As JoJo turned towards Bob, Clementine watched the blade rip through her side. JoJo fell with a cry and Clementine gasped in horror as the man wielding the sword was revealed.

Clementine met his brown eyes and recognised him as the man who had almost killed her on the Nile cruise. The one who had matched her every move, despite her skills.

"You," she said.

"Do we know this man?" William asked.

"Yes, he is the stranger who tried to kill me on the ship," Clementine said, her voice tight.

"So, a foe," Asem noted, and Clementine nodded.

"What do you want?" she asked the man, who still stood in the doorway, sword in hand. It looked like a scimitar. *Quick and deadly, but lightweight enough for my fan to block it.*

He grinned, and Clementine was eerily reminded of someone.

"What I want, my dear sister, is everything you have. And the Tears of Hathor."

Clementine felt her heart skip a beat. "Who are you?"

"Clementine," William said, with a warning in his voice, but Clementine was too focused to hear or think of anything else but the stranger's words.

My dear sister, he had called her. In the language of her mother.

"Surprised to see your brother again? I must say I was also surprised to see you on this journey. I did not believe for one second they would let a lady like you venture out of your golden cage."

"Brother..." Clementine muttered, her eyes widening. "Can't be. I was the only child my parents had." But that grin of his was as if she were looking at a mirror. Her lips had the same curve. It was their mother's smile.

"When mother was forced to leave your country in shame, she was pregnant with me," the man said. "I was born at sea, on our long voyage back to Indochina. It was not the happy start to life you had, dear sister. Hence my name, Hải Hoang, the wild sea. A fitting name for someone who became an adventurer and treasure hunter in our parents' footsteps."

"So, you have been stalking Clementine, is that it? Trying to find ways to dispose of her and her father?" William asked, his anger unmasked.

Hải nodded to William. "You are the one who knocked me out on the ship, I assume. That blow almost drowned me when I swam away," he said, with an odd sort of respect. "I am rarely surprised, but I was momentarily too caught up with my sister. I was only supposed to steal our father's notebook, but killing her seemed like a good idea. Believe it or not, I originally came here for the Tears of Hathor, just like you and our father. It was sheer coincidence that I heard my sister was searching for her lost father. I couldn't miss the opportunity for a family reunion."

He walked slowly towards Clementine, who backed up in the limited space.

"Let's finish what we started on the ship, shall we? Sword against fan, hmm?" A smile spread on his face and Clementine saw no mercy in it.

Before Clementine could answer, Asem jumped on Hải, throwing them both to the ground with a scuffle. Asem struggled to pin him down but Hải was too skilled for it. William tried to seize the sword from Hải's hand, but he escaped Asem's grasp too quickly. A kick to Asem's chest sent him back to the ground and William had to back up, evading the slashes of the sword in the small space. Amphorae and boxes clattered and shattered around them. William found a large silver plate to use as a shield of sorts as he deflected Hải's blows.

"Get the gun," William yelled. Asem and Clementine scrambled to retrieve the pistol that had dropped from JoJo's grasp. Again, Hải was too fast. He picked up one of the larger amphorae and threw it at Asem, hitting him in the head. Asem dropped and lay unmoving on the ground.

"Asem!" Clementine screamed, and turned to see if he was dead. It was a mistake. Hải swept William's legs from underneath him and in seconds was attacking her. Clementine had only a second to see William holding his head, struggling to get up. The glinting blade swung close to her head and she parried with her fan as best she could.

"William! The gun," she cried out, blocking a slash while landing a kick on Hải's side. He grunted but did not slow.

It wasn't the most practised scenario she and Edith had gone through in her training, but she knew how to manoeuvre the iron fan in her hands to deflect and counter strikes from swords. She twisted and turned her body in rhythm with Hải, opening and closing the fan. Sparks flew from the impact, but she held her own. It might have looked like an elaborate dance if it hadn't been a question of life and death.

"You don't really even care about the Tears, do you?" she asked, panting as she pivoted to avoid a diagonal slash. She landed a quick elbow-strike to his jaw with a satisfying thump. He spat blood and shoved her forcefully aside. He needed distance for his sword, and she needed to keep close to land efficient blows.

"Not really," Hải said, with much less breathlessness, Clementine noticed. His stamina seemed never-ending.

"But right now, they are not the priority," he grinned, and went for a deep thrust with his sword. Clementine danced to the side, landing a backhanded hit on Hải's stomach with her fan, and a hard knee to his ribs. He grunted, and she realised his ribs were not yet fully healed from the last time she had stabbed them. A smile came to her lips.

"How are your ribs then, brother?" she asked.

"Not bad, sister. You should really learn to hit harder. Like this," Hải said. He lunged with a horizontal slice, but it turned out to be a feint. As she moved to parry and dodge, he was ready, hitting her with a straight kick to her side. She felt the blow in her ribcage, likely breaking some of them, despite her reinforced corset. Stupid of her to leave her side open like that. It hurt like hell now. And the next slash would have cut through her stomach if not for the steel in her corset, preventing her flesh from being ripped open. The peach fabric ripped, revealed the boning inside. She gasped, startled by the near fatal impact. Hài immediately aimed to cut her again and her clumsy parry was almost too late. The blade sliced the tips of her fingers on her right hand. Clementine cursed through her gritted teeth. Hài looked amused as he slowly circled her.

"You really are prepared for anything. Is that one of mother's corsets? To this day she is as prepared as you are, you know."

Clementine's focus dropped as she registered the mention of their mother. It was just what Hài had expected, and his next kick to her stomach sent her flying.

Clementine felt her ears ring and saw stars in her vision. Her back had slammed against the heavy sarcophagus and she lay there in pain, holding her ribs. She tried to refocus her eyes and move, pushing through the pain. *Get up, Clementine!*

A gunshot rang out in the chamber. Hài roared as his arm turned crimson red just below his shoulder. William pulled the trigger again, but the gun jammed at that critical moment, and Hài launched himself at William. Clementine tried to get up, but she was slow, her muscles like lead. She knew William could not withstand Hài's attacks for long, even with a bullet wound in one arm. Hài was too good a fighter. She staggered forward, fighting the overwhelming pain in her side. Desperately, she advanced towards the men, but she couldn't make it in time. She saw Hài bring his sword down with a force strong enough for beheading, despite the wound on his sword-wielding hand. It came within inches of William's throat as he dodged away, narrowly escaping death. Clementine let out a sob of relief.

To her surprise, William advanced immediately, before Hải had managed to stop his movement. He fought viciously with his fists, getting through some of Hải's blocks with a quick series of jabs to the ribs, which slowed Hải down just enough for William to land a heavy hook on his bullet wound.

The sword clattered to the ground. But William failed to notice a dagger in Hải's other hand. Clementine saw the glint of the blade and scrambled forward, flicking out her fan's claws.

"Dagger!" She stumbled the last steps toward them, stabbing the claws of her fan deep into Hải's left thigh.

She had almost reached them in time. Hải yelled in pain, but not before sinking the dagger deep into William's stomach.

Clementine felt blood drain from her face as quickly as it was now draining from William's wound. He met her eyes and collapsed on the floor, next to the bodies of Bob and JoJo, holding the hilt, which still stuck out from his stomach. A pool of red quickly spread around his white shirt. His green eyes had sorrow in them as he mouthed, "I'm sorry."

"No!" she shrieked, wildly stabbing her fan's claws into Hải's back and launching herself at him in a rage. She heard him yell in pain as she pulled the fan out, slashing his face with the claws and attempting to stab his throat, but he blocked and quickly disarmed her of the fan. Her focus had been shattered and Hải knew it.

"What's the matter, sister? Was he more to you than just a travel partner? I am sorry, but I did tell you: I'm here to take everything you have. Everything that should have been mine," he laughed. He was on top of her now, reminiscent of their fight on the ship. She barely blocked his blows, feeling blood burst from her lips. And soon his hands were again squeezing her throat. She tried to throw him off, but he was too heavy, straddled on top of her aching ribs. She tried to lock his fingers into a painful twist, but her hands were slippery with her own blood. She growled, coughed, and gasped for air, desperately clawing at his face, which already bled from the slashes of her fan. But nothing helped.

"You will die now, Clementine. You will fail William, you will fail your queen, and you will never get our father's fortune. I will. And I will finally get to enjoy the life that was taken from me." His grin was bloody, and Clementine did not want it to be the last things she saw in this life.

She started to feel her strength leave her. Her hand fell to the side, into a deep pile of dust. One of the jars of organs from the mummified priestess. Irrationally, she felt sorry the remains were now bloodied by her hands, and hoped the priestess would forgive her.

Clementine felt her mind slipping away from the present: the pain in her throat, the burning sensation in her lungs, the sorrow she had for not being strong enough to save William. She would have to speak to Edith about this scenario, she thought idly, as the last seconds of her life stretched out for what seemed forever.

Edith would be so disappointed Clementine had lost to strangling again! So stupid. She could hear Edith, even now, as she lay dying: *Use any unholy measure to win! You think they will treat you fairly? Fight!* Edith screamed in her darkening consciousness.

From behind her fluttering eyelids, Clementine could just make out the shadow of JoJo, bloodied but alive, and crawling closer to them. Clementine thought she must be dreaming as she saw the determination on JoJo's face. With a grunt of agony, JoJo stabbed Hải in the thigh with the dagger that had been embedded on her arm. A sudden burst of foul words left Hải's lips, and his hold momentarily slackened around Clementine's throat. He turned to backhand JoJo and she slumped to the floor. Her stab had been a weak one, but it was just enough for Clementine to fill her lungs and delay her death one crucial moment. Hải's attention returned to her neck.

Clementine did not have long. Just one chance. She apologised again to the priestess, grabbed a good handful of the mummified dust, and held her already lacking breath. She threw the dust into Hải's eyes and he instantly let go of her throat with one hand, coughing and trying to clear his vision. Her throat hurt like hell but she summoned the strength to headbutt Hải as hard as she could, extracting her last hair pin from her hair and stabbing into the hand still around her neck. It went right through his palm and the tip hit her in the collarbone. She screamed, but he screamed more.

Clementine felt her blood pumping again and the rage gave her strength to yank her hairpin out of his hand and slam it into his chest. It didn't go very deep, but the pain was enough for him to recoil, and Clementine used the momentum to throw him off her. She crawled to the gun and another shot rang out in the tomb, hitting Hải in the right shoulder. Seeing her with the gun, Hải did not hesitate to limp through the very same door Clementine had wanted to use before all of this started. The same door her father had used to escape this place. But Hải's escape did not matter now. She dropped the gun and crawled to William.

"Will," she cried, cradling his head, "Darling, what can I do? What can I do?" she asked frantically. His white shirt was soaked red. He opened his eyes and immediately Clementine felt tears filling her eyes. The mischievous glint was gone but the warmth in his gaze hurt in her heart. He was still alive, although the pool of blood meant it would not be for long.

"Clemmie," he whispered, losing consciousness.

"Will!" she screamed, too afraid to shake him.

"Clementine," she heard Asem call hoarsely. He slowly sat up, holding his head, which was covered in clotted blood. One of his eyes was swollen shut.

"Asem," she all but sobbed, "Thank God you're alive. Help me," she gestured at the dagger in William's stomach.

Carefully, Asem shook his head. "No, only the Tears might help him now. Find the Tears of Hathor and try to heal him."

Her eyes widened. *Could it really be true?* Clementine didn't waste time thinking about it and rummaged around the tomb. The remaining boxes and amphorae contained nothing but relics and dust. Some still had jewels in them, but Clementine tossed them to the side, ignoring the throbbing pain in her bleeding fingers.

"I cannot find it, Asem! "

Asem had crawled over to William. "He is soon gone, Clementine. Keep looking. Perhaps inside the sarcophagus..." His voice trailed away. They both knew they would have no hope of moving the heavy lid with just the two of them and no tools. Clementine had no choice but to try. She pushed the lid as much as her tired, injured body could, but it would not budge. Tears started to run from her eyes.

"The tears come from the heart," she muttered between sobs. She forced herself to quiet her whirling thoughts and think. "It has to be in the priestess' wrapping linens where her heart... No, that's not right. The ancient Egyptians did not preserve the heart at all–" she paused her ramblings suddenly. She felt again that pull, that odd tugging sensation she'd had earlier when they entered the last chamber. It felt stronger now, and she closed her eyes, gliding her hands along the sarcophagus, guided by her instincts as she followed the pull. She couldn't explain it, but she knew where to stop. She looked through tear-soaked eyes to where her hands were leaning against the sarcophagus. There was a tiny carving of Hathor and the symbol of a tear, almost faded away. Clementine's hand trembled as she pushed it, her blood smearing the lines of the symbol. A second or two passed and nothing happened, but then the blood from her fingers seemed to suddenly soak into the symbol, making it look as good as new for a fleeting moment. Clementine blinked. She must have imagined it. A click as soft as a sigh followed, and near the head of the sarcophagus a small locker opened slowly. Inside, an ornate little vial filled with liquid gleamed.

"Oh!" Clementine cried, and carefully took out the vial. "Asem, I found something." The tugging sensation turned into tingling as she held the vial in her hands.

Clementine scrambled back to William. His breathing was so slow it was barely there.

"Pour it on the wound," Asem said hoarsely. "What harm can it do to try?" he added grimly. He gently tapped William's cheek. "William, brother, wake up. Your love is about to try a miracle on you, and you don't want to miss it."

William slowly opened his eyes and locked them with hers. Clementine's heart leapt with hope.

"This might hurt," she said. She took out the handkerchiefs her aunt had given her, swiftly pulled the dagger from his stomach, and used the cloth to staunch some of the bleeding. Blood pumped even faster than before and William cried weakly from the pain. His skin was sickly pale and grey. There was not a moment to lose. She lifted the blood-soaked handkerchiefs and quickly opened the vial, pouring the liquid on the open wound. A familiar scent filled her nose.

"It's honey," she said to Asem in a panic, "It's just honey, Asem! How will that help? Nothing's happening!"

She looked at the wound. At William's face. Her hands trailed his cheeks, the curve of his lips. His eyes were barely open, and Clementine could not stand the thought of losing him. She wanted to bicker with him one more time. *Please, let me have one more argument with him, one more teasing smile just for me, one more moment in the warmth of his arms!* They had just found each other. Her heart felt like it might burst out of her chest from the pain. Her eyes hurt from crying, and yet she could not imagine ever stopping if he died now. The pain from her injuries was nothing compared to seeing the man she had fallen in love with dying in her arms.

"I failed you," she whispered, covering her face as she sobbed.

"Mix your blood into it," Asem whispered, "On the wound. It sounds ridiculous but try, Clementine. Try."

Clementine didn't understand, but she gently swiped her bloody fingers over the honey smeared on William's wound. Clementine vaguely wondered if her blood had the power to heal him or if this was simply unhygienic. She could feel her mind wanting to wander to other things — anything else to spare her from what was happening in front of her, to the man she loved. She watched with astonishment as the honey absorbed her blood with a swirl and started to bubble.

"Clemmie..."

She startled, barely hearing his voice.

"Yes, darling, just a little longer, hang on just a little longer." Clementine leaned close to him, clasping his hand in hers and kissing it with her bloody and tear-soaked lips. "I'll never forgive you if you leave me now," she said with a weak smile.

"Listen, I have to..." he gasped for air, but his eyes refused to leave her face, "tell you. I shot your father, just before the leap. It was me. He wanted to steal Hathor's Tears." A painful spasm made William grit his teeth. "I shot him and lost him," he whispered finally.

Clementine couldn't understand, couldn't comprehend these words.

William squeezed her hand. "I love you and I'm sor–" His eyes rolled as he lost consciousness and his chest stopped rising.

"What?" Clementine said, "I don't understand. You can't be serious. Will!" She felt a cold sweat on her skin as her overloaded mind tried to make sense of what he had said. A panic rose in her and she tried to fight the thoughts of betrayal, anger, confusion, love, fear and hurt, all at once. It was too much for her mind and body right now. Her heart was beating too fast, her head and wounds pulsing.

"Look," Asem gasped, and Clementine brought herself back to the moment.

In front of their eyes, they watched the wound close as the honey seeped into it with a soft glimmer of golden light. Clementine saw the colour come back to William's face, and his chest started to rise again. He now looked like a man who was merely sleeping. Bloody smears around his stomach and his shirt were the only proof of the fatal wound.

A soft glow shone from the wound for just a moment after the last of it closed — a miracle that could not be explained.

Clementine leaned back against the wall next to Asem and wiped tears and snot from her face, feeling relief and shock and a sense of betrayal. She let the coolness of the stone seep through her wet clothes and soothe her aching wounds.

William would live. Somehow her worst fear had not come to pass, and yet also it had. *William had shot Papa, and all this time he had lied. And you're the ultimate fool for trusting him with your heart. Foolish, stupid, naive Clementine.* She closed her eyes and wondered if it was bad manners to just disappear without a word to anyone ever again.

"Look, Clementine–" Asem started.

She raised her hand. "This is too much. We'll talk, but not now. We need to get out of here and alert your crew, if they aren't already looking for us. Promise me you will tell me what you know, once we get out."

"You deserve the truth and more, Clementine," Asem said, and offered her his hand to help her get up.

Clementine retrieved her battered fan, and together they carried the still-unconscious William out into the desert where Asem's crew members had been waiting. The crew helped not only with William, but they also took care of Bob's body, and very carefully carried JoJo to be treated by a local doctor. Clementine was grateful enough for JoJo's help that she offered to pay for the doctor from her own funds. She might not want to see JoJo ever again, but she wanted to pay her dues. A life for a life.

The setting desert sun was blood red and beautiful, but for once Clementine didn't want to admire it. She had seen enough of that colour to last her a lifetime.

The sun set and Clementine welcomed the darkness, both outside and in her heart, as they headed back to the campsite.

EPILOGUE

Clementine walked briskly to see Mrs Edith in London. Her ribs seemed to have healed nicely, faster than expected, but the journey home had been exhausting. At least there had been time to think and process everything they had gone through.

William had stayed behind with Asem's crew to recover, and Clementine had not seen nor spoken to him before she left. They had offered her sanctuary to heal her wounds, too, but there wasn't much they could do about broken ribs and bruises, so she had said her thanks to Asem and left Egypt. For now.

Asem had accompanied her to the steamer ship that would take her back to Europe. Initially, Clementine had been too hurt and upset to talk, and only listened when Asem revealed that William worked for him — an association of treasure hunters who tried to stop governments and illegal entities from taking mythical treasures for their own gain. The organisation was simply called: The Relic Protectors.

Clementine didn't know what to feel about all this new information, let alone the fact that something magical had happened with the Tears of Hathor. Magical items, legends of old, all true? Apparently not, Asem had said. But some of them were real and unexplainable — and dangerous in the wrong hands.

William had been working for Queen Victoria as a double agent: taking assignments, trying to intercept the relics before they were stolen away to England, and replacing the originals with well-crafted replicas. The association was spread thinly across different countries, and agents were incorporated into various governments — sometimes even criminal underworld groups. Clementine's father had also been a member of The Relic Protectors, but he had started to sell his services to other, higher-bidding entities. Lord Whitham was not only a traitor to the crown, but also to Asem's association.

When William had discovered Lord Whitham's betrayal, he had followed him into the inner chambers. He had argued with Papa, and they had gotten into a fight. William had shot at Clementine's father, who had fallen into the leap of faith chamber and was presumed dead. William had been forced to retreat due to the sandstorm and lost his way. When he returned, the storm had wiped away any traces of the correct tomb, and even if William could have found it, he did not know how to open the first door.

Asem had known about all of this, but had not said anything to Clementine when they first met. He had been sorry, but he also said he wanted to keep their organisation as safe as possible, and Clementine, at the time, had been an unknown risk to him. William had been sent by Asem to see if Clementine knew anything more about Lord Whitham or his findings in Egypt. The Tears of Hathor were much too valuable to be taken by some individual or empire. It was better that they never leave the tomb, which was now the end result, in a way.

Asem had offered Clementine a place amongst The Relic Protectors, and she had promised to think about it, since she was in no state to make such an enormous decision. After all, as

Asem had promised, their resources could help find clues of Clementine's father and her brother Hải. That was something to consider.

One of Asem's crew members had found a sheep herder who remembered seeing someone matching Lord Whitham's description leave the temple area, aided by a woman, sometime after he had vanished, but they could not be certain if it really had been Lord Whitham or not. After all, Egypt's historical sites were full of older white Englishmen, and one might look the same as the other from afar. Nevertheless, it could be a lead worth pursuing with Asem's organisation.

She would follow a lead of her own for now. The list of places and items that had been concealed in her father's notebook. If he was still alive, Clementine trusted he would follow his own plans, and perhaps she could catch up to him eventually.

Clementine had met with the queen, alone, soon after she had returned to England. She had been very nervous when she had explained the circumstances of Bob and JoJo ambushing them, and the stranger who had wounded William.

She left out Asem, the fact that the stranger was her brother, and the miraculous healing of William. Instead, she gave Her Majesty the small, delicate glass vial, which had since been refilled with ordinary honey, and explained how she had found it in a secret compartment on the side of the sarcophagus. The queen had been pleased to accept it, even if the legend of the Tears' powers were proven untrue, and had offered Clementine a permanent position in the Extraordinary Treasure Hunters. Clementine had gladly accepted.

The queen did not seem to care much of Bob's death, nor the fact that he and JoJo had tried to take the treasure by force. Her Majesty had been curious to hear that JoJo had helped Clementine to survive and had made a full recovery, despite the sword wound to her side. "That girl always had the heart of a man," the queen had chuckled. "I do think she will make an excellent travel companion for you until you are re-united with your future husband. She might teach you a thing or two William cannot." Clementine had wanted to protest, but the queen's amusement was laced with such finality that was not to be questioned. Apparently, it was of little importance that JoJo had tried to attack them.

Clementine now had a letter of passage from the queen, funds for her travels and living costs, as well as her own gun with silver bullets. The same bullets that had William had shot her father with. Asem said that William had also shot her papa's manservant in self-defense.

She shook her head at the thought of the killing. Clementine had found one of the bullets in the leap of faith chamber and William had said it was from a similar gun to his. Just as he had said in the collapsed chamber that the footing had held *before*. Just as he had been so sure about using the mirrors in the tomb. She had been a fool not to be suspicious of him when he himself had told her not to trust him!

Clementine's heart hurt when she thought of William. They were still officially engaged, and she had told her family a much more censored version of their journey, simply saying that William had to recover for an unknown time, and in the meantime the queen wished her to take over some of Papa's planned travels.

Her aunt had hardly been happy about it, but she was now in mourning after her husband, the duke, had passed, some weeks before Clementine had returned. Cousin Dickie had taken on his new title with a heavy heart, but still found time to spend with Clementine and seemed truly happy for her new career. Clementine mourned for her uncle, but in a way it was better for him to be freed of his pains. Everything she had experienced made her almost numb to death, which scared her, as she wanted to feel more devastated about her uncle's passing. But then she thought he would have wanted her to continue on with the opportunity she had been given, and not linger because of him.

As for William… Clementine felt she could not trust him, and she did not know how to heal after such a betrayal. She already felt betrayed by her father and mother, but William was an added blow to the already horrible turmoil of emotions.

She hadn't had enough time to know what to feel about her brother and his threat to claim his inheritance, nor what to do with the knowledge of her papa and William having betrayed the crown. Wasn't that high treason? She shuddered to think of the punishment. At least her mother had been able to leave with her life. Clementine had tried not to think about her brother's remarks about their mother. If she was still alive, why hadn't she contacted Clementine? These were not thoughts she needed right now.

She was supposed to meet William in Greece, at the ruins of the Temple of Poseidon, in a month's time, so she couldn't avoid him forever. It was the next location on Papa's list and it had taken surprisingly little to convince the queen to let Clementine go there next. Clementine felt nervous about the upcoming encounter. She would have to keep it strictly business only, and guard her heart from the spell of his green eyes. She would heed his advice and never trust him ever again. She had promised to let Asem know where she was going, to keep William up to date as well, but she had refused to share details of the assignment for now. She wasn't ready to make that decision yet. How many young ladies had to decide whether to follow in the traitorous footsteps of their parents and fiancé?

She closed her eyes and shook her head to rid herself of the image of his face; that glint in his eyes and the dimples from his crooked smile. *No*, she said to herself. *Never again.*

She stepped into Mrs Edith's house and was immediately greeted by the teacher herself.

"Before we begin, I have a request," Clementine said, after they had exchanged pleasantries and Clementine had changed into her training dress.

"I need to learn techniques to help me when being strangled by far stronger and bigger opponents."

Mrs Edith raised her eyebrow and asked only one question, "Did you win the last time?"

Clementine nodded. "It was a close call, but yes, I won eventually."

Mrs Edith nodded with approval. "Good, show me how you did it and we'll start to work on it."

Clementine nodded and led the way to the dojo where she could forget all about William for a moment.

"Oh, and if you know a seamstress who would be willing to make corsets with steel reinforcements, do tell me," Clementine added, and took up her fighting stance opposite Mrs Edith.

* * *

THIS IS the end of Lady Clementine and the Tears of Hathor. If you enjoyed the book, I would sincerely appreciate it if you could take the time to leave a review. It would mean so much to me!

Can't wait for Clementine's next adventure? Receive a bonus epilogue for Lady Clementine and the Tears of Hathor and stay up to date on Camilla Taipalvesi's next releases by joining her mailing list now! Scan the QR code to subscribe:

ACKNOWLEDGMENTS

I'm not exaggerating when I say I'm tearing up and grinning when I'm writing this last part of this book. Clementine popped up in my mind in spring 2022 and wouldn't go away (you know how stubborn she can be), so I wrote the first draft and enjoyed myself immensely in Clementine's company. I've written other full novels before, but Lady Clementine and The Tears of Hathor is the first one to be published. This is a dream come true and some special thanks are in order.

My lovely editor Jo Gatford, thank you so much for showing so much excitement from the very first outline I sent you! You immediately got the vibe I was going for (The Mummy, Uncharted games, Indiana Jones) and kept pushing me gently forward with much encouragement. I can't wait to get to editing the next book with you! Thank you also to the awesome team at Miblart for making my gorgeous cover. I remember seeing the first version of my book cover and getting goosebumps already then.

Author Sarra Cannon and her Publish and Thrive course and writing community. During the pandemic years, I really focused more on my writing hobby and Sarra has been an absolutely crucial part of getting me through every step of novel writing and publishing. Thank you for helping me and so many others conquer our fears and making us believe in the importance of writing our stories and sharing them with the rest of the world!

A special thank you to my friend and colleague Brooke, who

understands the joys and hardships of writing. Thank you for listening to me ramble over so many cups of coffee and tea!

My deepest gratitude goes to my darling husband Tuukka. He may not always get why I cry over fictional characters, but he's always there, pushing me to chase my writing dreams. He believed in me when I wouldn't, so here we are: he will actually have to read my published book, haha! I love you so much, and I truly wouldn't be where I am without you. You help me be the best version of myself.

Thank you to the bookish community of Bookstagram. My joy for reading brought me together with so many other like-minded readers and writers and the past years with you have been a blast. Thank you for all the excitement you've shown me when you heard of my writing project!

And finally, a big thanks to you dear readers! I'm so grateful that you decided to support an independent author. I hope you had fun with Clementine and look forward to her next adventure as much as I am!

ABOUT THE AUTHOR

Camilla Taipalvesi, a Finnish-Vietnamese fantasy author, weaves tales of wanderlust, romance, and magic that feature heroines who are strong, capable, and unafraid to save themselves.

When she's not writing or working, Camilla indulges in swooning over fictional characters, embarking on adventures with her husband, and sharing her love for books on her very active Bookstagram account. Don't hesitate to say hello!

Her debut novel, "Lady Clementine and the Tears of Hathor," kicks off an enchanting journey into a world of mystery and magic as the first instalment in a planned series.

Follow her socials for updates on her next book or check out her website:

https://www.camillataipalvesi.com

www.ingramcontent.com/pod-product-compliance
Lightning Source LLC
LaVergne TN
LVHW091704070526
838199LV00050B/2271